Miss New India

Books by Bharati Mukherjee

The Tiger's Daughter

Wife

Days and Nights in Calcutta (with Clark Blaise)

Darkness

The Sorrow and the Terror (with Clark Blaise)

The Middleman and Other Stories

Jasmine

The Holder of the World

Leave It to Me

Desirable Daughters

The Tree Bride

Miss New India

Miss New India

BHARATI MUKHERJEE

MARINER BOOKS
HOUGHTON MIFFLIN HARCOURT
BOSTON · NEW YORK

First Mariner Books edition 2012

www.hmhbooks.com

Library of Congress Cataloging-in-Publication Data
Mukherjee, Bharati.
Miss new India / Bharati Mukherjee.
p. cm.
ISBN 978-0-618-64653-1 ISBN 978-0-547-75037-8 (pbk.)
1. Young women—India—Fiction. 2. Arranged marriage—Fiction.
3. Self-actualization (Psychology) in women—Fiction.
4. Bangalore (India)—Fiction. I. Title.
PR9499.3.M77M56 2011
813'.54—dc22 2010025569

Book design by Victoria Hartman

Printed in the United States of America

DOC 10 9 8 7 6 5 4 3 2 1

For Priya Xue Agnes Blaise

Which of us is happy in this world?
Which of us has his desire?

—WILLIAM MAKEPEACE THACKERAY, *Vanity Fair*

Prologue

In the second half of the past century, young Americans — the disillusioned, the reckless, and the hopeful—began streaming into India. They came overland in painted vans, on dust-choked, diesel-spouting buses, and on the hard benches of third-class railroad cars, wearing Indian clothes, eating Indian street food and drinking the people's water. The disaffected children of American affluence: college dropouts, draft dodgers, romantics, druggies, and common criminals; musicians, hedonists and starry-eyed self-discoverers. These weren't the aloof and scornful British administrators or the roustabout traders of earlier centuries. You could see them at dawn or dusk, pounding out their kurtas on flat stones along the riverbank like any dhobi or housemaid. These rich Westerners—the Aussies, the Canadians, the Germans, the Finns, but especially the Americans—the ones who stayed a few months, then years—lived like poor villagers; these rich Western kids sometimes resorted to begging and got sick, and others died from beggars' diseases.

Among them, one in a hundred, a thousand, ten thousand, became reborn, with no interest in returning home. They settled down in towns and villages, learned the languages, and lived Indian lives. They took modest jobs with foundations and charities. They taught English and took to the countryside to collect music and folktales, arts and crafts. They married local girls or stayed celibate, and identified themselves with Indian needs and aspirations. Until connecting with India, their lives had seemed without purpose. Their real lives began in India—for all its bribery, assassinations, race riots and corruption. America had been wiped from their memory at precisely the time that young Indians were fantasizing about the West, wanting schools and jobs that promised money and freedom. We were hungry for America, but they were sated with it. They professed no interest in American wars, but when India stumbled, they mourned. They loved us more than we loved ourselves.

We thought Peter Champion was strange. In our tradition, professors carry their lectures typed on foolscap tucked inside dossiers tied with silk cord, and dictate them to students in a monotone, without looking up. Generations of students learned to rank their teachers by levels of flatulence: "elephant farts" for our Goan and South Indian priests, down to "mouse farts," a little gas that left a pellet of knowledge behind, even some wisdom. The two lay senior professors boasted of medals they'd won in college and alluded to grants that had taken them on epic mental journeys, in their relative youth, to universities in England or Scotland, where they had sat at the feet of Sir Somebody-or-other. They never let us forget that a chasm separated their legendary achievements from our wan potential.

But Mr. Champion joked about his average grades and his aimless journeys, fumbling for a profession. He'd studied archaeology, astronomy and geology, linguistics, mathematics and religion—anything that teased out infinity. It wasn't until we started planning a festschrift last winter that we discovered he had double-majored in political economy and folklore at a satellite campus of a Midwestern university, and that his grades had been very, very good. While we were his students, the only fact about him we knew with certainty was that he came to class without lecture notes. And yet his influence hangs over some of us like the vault of heaven.

America was at war when he'd opted for the Peace Corps. He was assigned to a village in Bihar. After two years, forty pounds lighter, immune to diseases that would flatten most villagers, fluent in dialects no white man had ever mastered, instead of going back to America he'd embarked on a countrywide study of Raj-era houses and public buildings. Of course we didn't know this during the years we were his students; we were an incurious lot. Everything he learned in those years he'd gathered by tramping through villages and the long-ignored small towns in the mofussils, where children who'd never seen a white man would jab their fingers into his pale, dusty arms. He was always alone and traveled like a poor villager by bus and on foot, carrying his few belongings in a cloth bundle. The energy! The love! In those first three years in India he completed the work of a lifetime.

When we knew him, he was living monklike on a teacher's modest salary, funding his forays into the hinterland by moonlighting as a private English-language tutor, American or British. By the time our lives intersected his, he had acquired a scooter and taping equipment. He went to villages and recorded long litanies of anecdotal history, family memories verging on fantasy, and, especially, local songs. He scoured ancient, abandoned temples. He discovered and catalogued shards of terra-cotta sculptures. He tried, and failed, to interest us in his eccentric history of modern India.

Of course, not all the houses he investigated were crumbling shells, and not all their inhabitants were humble village folk. Some of the houses, and their owners, were survivors of another era, shuttered off from modern India. A few of the houses—dilapidated these days—had been glorious mansions, bearing Raj-era names taken from British literature. Some of their contents were of museum quality.

Classic Indian Architecture: Public and Private (photos and sketches by the author) is a guided tour of those great public buildings and stately colonial residences from Calcutta through the Punjab, down the coast to Bombay, through Goa, and then to the South. Only a newcomer to India could have the eyes, the energy, and the devotion to swallow our country whole and regurgitate its remains with all the love of a mother penguin feeding her chick. Thirty-odd years ago, our teacher, then twenty-three years old, had presented himself at the front door of an 1840s mansion with a rolled-up scroll — the original floor plans — and asked the owner, then a fiftyish widow, if he could date the various additions to the mansion and catalogue its contents. In its 1840s configuration, before the piling on of late-Victorian turrets and towers, the widow's home had set a standard for Anglo-Indian architecture.

The widow had been flattered by the attention from a dashing young foreigner. The eventual beneficiary of that flattery would be one of Mr. Champion's students.

What did we give him? What do we owe him? Every developing country has its subsociety of resident aliens — refugees from affluence, freelance idealists, autodidacts collecting odd bits of "exotic" knowledge. Ours was trapped by beauty, love, spirituality, guilt, the prison of his own self-righteousness — and couldn't leave. He thrived on hardship while we pursued professional success and material comfort.

For whatever sinister or innocent reason, every now and then he conferred special attention on a young man or woman. "You will carry on," he would say. "You have the spark — don't crash and burn. India is starting to wake up. India is a giant still in its bed, but beginning to stir. It's too late for me, but India is catching fire."

One such woman is named Anjali Bose.

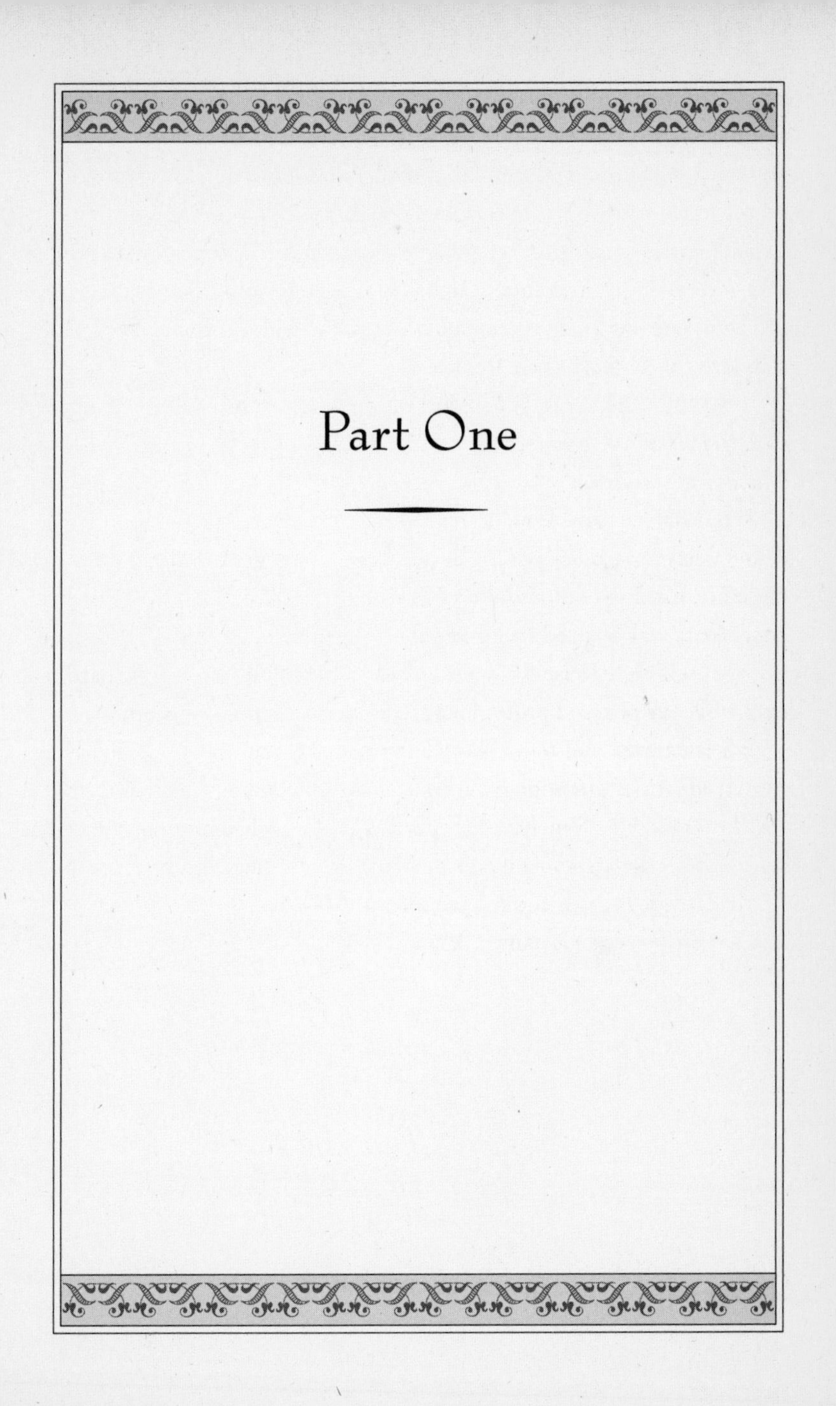

Part One

1

Through the car horns and jangle of an Indian street at market hour came the cry "Anjali!" but Anjali was not the name she answered to. Over blaring music from open-front shops she heard it again, sharper for its foreign edge: "Anjali!"

At nineteen, Anjali Bose was a tall girl, one hundred and seventy-three centimeters—five foot eight—taller than most boys in her college. She was on the girls' field hockey team. She smiled readily and when she did, she could light up a room like a halogen lamp. The conventional form of Indian femininity projects itself through long-lashed, kohl-rimmed, startled black eyes. Modest women know to glance upward from a slightly bowed head. Anjali did not take in the world with saucer-eyed passivity. Her light, greenish eyes were set off by high cheekbones and prominent brows. Her face resolved itself along a long jaw and generous mouth, with full lips and prominent teeth. Her parents, looking to the day they would have to marry her off, worried openly about her overly assertive features. But the rare foreigners who passed through town, health workers or financial aid consultants for international agencies, found her looks striking and her boldness charming. Speaking to them, she sometimes claimed a touch of Burmese or Nepali ancestry. She told many stories, all of them plausible, some of them perhaps even true. She always made an outstanding first impression.

On any street at market hour in the provincial town of Gauripur, in the state of Bihar, there could be a dozen Anjalis—"offerings to god"—but no man not a relative would dare call them by name. Most of those other Anjalis would be married, hobbled by saris, carrying infants or clutching the hands of toddlers while their husbands haggled for fish and vegetables. To be hailed from the street by a man on a scooter would be scandalous. The call had to be for her, the strider in jeans and a T-shirt advertising the maiden tour (Hamburg, Stuttgart, Köln, Basel, Zürich, Wien, Bratislava—she loved the umlauts) of Panzer Delight, a German punk-rock band, some few years back—the young woman who could wait to be called by the name she preferred, Angela, or better yet, Angie. A rusty old Lambretta scooter, the kind that had been popular with Gauripur's office workers way back in the 1960s, braked to a wheezing stop; its driver waved and nudged it toward her through the blue diesel smoke from buses and trucks, the dense clutter of handcarts and bicycles: swollen, restless India on the move.

She was standing outside Gauripur Bazaar, known locally as Pinky Mahal, the town's three-story monument to urban progress. When Pinky Mahal was being built, bricks had been carried, one by one, by dozens of child laborers hired by the day. Rows of women workers had threaded their way along single planks, balancing bowls of cement on their heads and then dumping the contents into plastic buckets. During the construction a corporate billboard had stood on Lal Bahadur Shastri (LBS) Road, an epic portrait to feed a credulous public: a magnificent, five-story office tower behind a small landscaped forest of shade and flowering trees, lawns, fountains, and sundials. On the billboard turbaned doormen greeted the gleaming row of imported cars pulling up at the building's entrance. And above the turbaned heads floated two legends: YOUR NEW CORPORATE HDQS IN BEAUTIFUL, EXCITING GAURIPUR! and ACT NOW! COMMERCIAL SPACE GOING FAST!

Fanciful renderings of a future that would never come.

The office tower, with three stories instead of the advertised five, was completed in a year, but within six months of its ceremonial opening the pink outer plaster had begun to crumble, leaving long veins of exposed brick. The contractor claimed that the pink paint was sour and had reacted to the sweet plaster. Acid and alkaline, the developer explained to the press, then absconded to the Persian Gulf. And so Pinky Mahal, its two top floors unoccupied, its ground floor leased and subleased by owners of small shops who put up with fluctuating electrical service and no air conditioning because of the low rent, had become an eyesore rather than a proud monument in the center of town.

When Pinky Mahal failed, the spirit of Gauripur was crushed.

Then the call came again, slightly revised: "Angie!"

Mr. Champion pulled his scooter into the safety of the gutter, and Anjali towered above him, standing on the high edge of the cracked sidewalk. She hadn't seen much of her former teacher in the twelve months since she'd graduated from Vasco da Gama High School and enrolled in Vasco da Gama College's B. Comm. program. During that time he'd grown a reddish beard speckled with gray. A patched book bag was slung over his shoulder, and he still wore his trademark handloom cotton kurta over blue jeans. From her elevated vantage point, she saw that his hair was thinning. Mosquitoes buzzed over the bald spot. They landed, but he appeared not to notice.

He had to be over fifty, considering that he'd been in Bihar for nearly thirty years, but was still so slim and energetic that he seemed boyish. All American men—within the tiny compass of her experience—seemed boyish. Her father, a railway clerk, was younger than Mr. Champion but looked older. It was impossible to think of her stout father, with his peremptory voice and officious manners, in anything but the role of upholstered patriarch. He would never wear a wrinkled shirt in public or shirtsleeves to the office, and he had never owned blue jeans.

“I thought you were leaving,” the American said. Then, with more emphasis, “In fact, I thought you *told* me you were leaving, and that was months ago.”

When in doubt, smile. She smiled. “I like your beard, Mr. Champion.”

“I’m not your teacher anymore, Anjali. You can call me Peter.”

“Only if you call me Angie.”

She’d had a secret crush on her teacher her last three years at Vasco da Gama High School, though, like all other da Gama students speaking to teachers, she’d addressed him as sir and Mr. Champion to his face, and as “the American” behind his back. He was the only layman under sixty and the only white man in the school run by Goan and South Indian priests.

“Angie, why are you still here?”

It was a question she often asked herself. She could more easily visualize herself in a fancy Mumbai café overlooking the Gateway of India, stirring a foamy pink falooda with a long spoon in a frosty glass, than nibbling spicy savories from a street vendor in Gauripur, something she had been about to do when Mr. Champion startled her.

“I might ask the same of you, sir—I mean, Peter,” she retorted, grateful that her lips and chin weren’t greasy from eating deep-fried pakoras.

“Same as you, Angie. Studying.”

It was their special joke: although he earned his living as a teacher, one in fact openly admired for having introduced a popular course on U.S. business models and advertising strategies with supplementary units on American culture and idiom, he considered himself “a perennial student.” But not like typical Indian students, those driven rote learners with one obsessive goal: admission to an Indian Institute of Technology. A lifetime of prosperity and professional success or poverty and shame depended on how relentlessly they crammed for national entrance examinations.

“I thought you said you *had* to get out if you wanted to stay sane.”

"There were weddings," she lied. "My sister got married. I couldn't just pick up and leave." A spontaneous untruth; it just slipped out.

He frowned and she felt a liar's momentary panic. Maybe she'd already used the wedding excuse, and forgotten. Family weddings and funerals are the incontestable duties and rituals of Indian life. There's always a sister or cousin being married off, an ailing uncle being nursed, a great-uncle being mourned.

Truthfully, Angie had a sister. Her name was Sonali, and she had been married five years before to a bridegroom whose ad and picture in the matrimonial column of a Bangla-language local newspaper had met Sonali's, and their father's, approval. Now Sonali was a divorced single mother, living with her four-year-old daughter in a one-room flat in Patna, the nearest large city, and working as steno-typist-bookkeeper for the stingy owner of a truck-rental company. The bridegroom was discovered, too late, to be a heavy drinker and philanderer. But when Sonali had finally got up her nerve to institute divorce proceedings, their father had turned against her for wreaking on the Bose family the public shame of divorce.

How could she explain to Mr. Champion how difficult—how impossible—it was for a daughter in a family like hers to just up and leave town except as the bride of a man her father had hand-picked? Why did family honor and fatherly duty involve *his* shackling *her* to a stranger when he had already proved himself so fallible? It was *her* life he was threatening to ruin next. Her father had a simple explanation: "It is not a question of happiness, yours or ours. It's about our name, our family reputation." Even at nineteen, Anjali was determined not to yield her right to happiness.

Mr. Champion, oblivious to what she had to contend with at home, was back to smiling. Maybe all Americans were inscrutable in that way. You couldn't tell what they really thought. Maybe he hadn't noticed her little lie; maybe he'd noticed but forgiven her. She sailed through life with a blithe assumption that she would be forgiven.

"Remember what I told you. India's leaving towns like this in the dust. You've got prospects." He shifted a heavy jute shopping sack strapped to the back seat of his scooter and patted the empty space. An overripe orange tumbled out of the bag into the gutter. Two crows and a pariah dog zeroed in on the smashed fruit. "Hop on, Angie."

If Gauripur was that doomed, why hadn't *he* left?

"I'll give you a ride to your house if you don't mind stopping off at my place while I put this stuff away." He retightened the strap around the jute sack. "There's fish at the bottom."

She liked the idea of not having to go right back home to her father's bullying and her mother's tearful silence. They were obsessed with finding a respectable son-in-law who would overlook negatives such as green eyes, a stubborn personality, and a nominal dowry. Her father blamed her for his lack of matchmaking success. Usually he pointed to her T-shirts and jeans: "What you wear, how you talk, no wonder! What good boy is going to look twice?"

Plenty, Baba, she could have retorted but didn't. She was not lacking for admirers. Boys were attracted to her, though she did little enough to encourage them. She knew what her father meant, though: prospective bridegrooms—"good boys" from good families—would back off.

With her sandaled toe, Angie traced a deep dent on Mr. Champion's scooter. The strappy sandal was the same shade of lilac as her painted toenails. She knew she had pretty feet, small, high-arched, narrow. He had to have noticed. "Looks like you need a new set of wheels, Mr. Champion," she teased.

The American wiped the passenger seat with the sleeve of his kurta. "Don't wait until it's too late."

He didn't understand her struggles; how could any aging, balding American with tufts of nose hair do so? She had one, and only one, legitimate escape route out of Gauripur: arranged marriage to a big-city-based bridegroom. That B. Comm. degree would increase her stock in the marriage market.

"Okey-dokey, Mr. Champion." She laughed, easing herself in place beside the jute sack on the passenger seat. Let the sidewalk throngs stare;

let the crowds part for the young unmarried woman on the back of the bachelor American's scooter. When the word got out, as it inevitably would, that Anjali Bose, daughter of "Railways Bose" of Indian Railways, sister of a working-woman divorcee, was riding off in plain sight, with her arms around the stomach of a foreigner, her parents would find it harder to make a proper-caste Bengali matrimonial match for her. So be it.

"And I've got someone I'd like you to meet," he said.

"You are inviting me to go to your flat, Mr. Champion?" She tried not to sound shocked.

It would not be her first visit to her teacher's home. Mr. Champion offered an English conversation course on Saturday mornings, and an advanced English conversational skills course on Sunday afternoons, at his apartment. Anjali had completed both courses twice, as had a dozen ambitious male da Gama students hoping to improve their chances of getting into professional schools in engineering or medicine or business management. A few of Mr. Champion's students were now doctors in their early thirties, waiting for immigrant visas to Canada or Australia.

The very first time Anjali showed up for Mr. Champion's Saturday conversation class, she had been severely disappointed with how little he owned in the way of furniture and appliances. No refrigerator, no television, no air conditioner, no crates of carbonated soft drinks. He owned a music system, professional-looking tape-recording equipment, and a bulky laptop and printer. Wooden office chairs and a pile of overstuffed cushions served as extra seating. Dozens of Indian books in every language were stacked on a brick-and-plank bookcase. A divan that surely doubled as his bed was pushed alongside a wall. Anjali had expected a professor's home to be shabby, but a shabby portal of learning, crammed with leather-bound books by world-renowned authors.

Anjali had been the only girl in those classes. She had been brought up to revere her elders and teachers, but whenever she visited Mr. Champion's place, she'd imagined his shame: the rooms were so barren, so like a servant's quarters. Some Saturday afternoons the sheets on the divan still looked mussed. She was embarrassed to be in a room with a man's bed, with his clothes hanging from pegs on a wall as though he had undressed in front of her. His apparent loneliness depressed her; his exposure agitated her. The silence of Mr. Champion's room made the beehive drone of an Indian family seem less insane. She was not much of a homebody—according to her mother's complaints—but if it hadn't seemed too forward a gesture by the only girl student, she would have brought her teacher small house gifts, a flower vase or just a wall calendar, to make the room look cozier.

Now terra-cotta pots of blooming flowers lined the narrow walkway to Mr. Champion's back staircase. Vines hung over the stairwell, and the stairs themselves were fragrant with flowers she couldn't name in any language. Could it be the same place?

"Mr. Champion! Have you gotten married?" She laughed, and from the top of the stairs he turned to her with a smile.

"Some difference, wouldn't you say?"

The door was painted bright blue. It opened inward before he could even insert the key. By then, Anjali had gained the top step, and there she faced a young man wrapped in a lungi, bare-chested, rubbing his eyes. "Jaanu," he said in a low voice, and Mr. Champion said a few words in what sounded like Urdu. Angie made out the universal "tea" and "biscuits" and maybe a version of her name.

There were cut flowers on a round table, a colorful tablecloth, and paintings nailed to the walls. There were two comfortable-looking cane chairs and a floor lamp. An old wooden almirah now held the clothes that had been hung on pegs, and bookcases ran along every wall, right up to the sleeping alcove. The bed was not made, almost as though the boy had been sleeping in it. She didn't see his sleeping mat. "Angie, this is Ali," said Mr. Champion. Then he added, "He is my friend."

Americans can do that, she thought: make friends of village Muslims. Young Ali, Mr. Champion's jaanu, his life (if the Hindi and Urdu words were congruent in meaning), a handsome enough boy if nearly black, with long hair and flaring cheekbones, had painted his fingernails bright red. He opened the almirah to find a shirt for his half-naked body. Either the shirt had been donated by Mr. Champion but still hung in the master's closet, which was cheeky enough—or else the two men shared closet space, which to her was unthinkable.

Mindful of parental wrath if she was to return home on the back of a man's bike, Anjali insisted that she would stay only a few minutes and then take a bus back. If Baba or the nosy neighbors saw her get off the bus at the stop close to home, they would suspect nothing. She wasn't ready for a screaming match with Baba. But she stayed an hour, speaking more freely of her longings than she did with her girlfriends. She didn't want marriage. Her classes were dull. She wanted something exciting, life-changing, to save her from the tedium of Gauripur. "I understand," Mr. Champion said. Ali was sent off to buy sweets. Angie had been Peter Champion's fondest project, someone very much like him, he said, who couldn't live in the small town of her birth. What a pain it is, to know that one is somehow fated to set sail for the farthest shore. "What a calling it is for someone like me," he joked, "to fill that ark with passengers."

Mr. Champion was in high teaching mode, in full confessional self-display. He was, he said, a man in love.

"So that explains the woman's touch," she said. "But where is she?"

"Angie, Angie." He tut-tutted.

She wondered for a moment if she herself was the woman he'd chosen and if the next words from his mouth would be "I love you, Angie, I always have, and I won't let you leave until you agree to go to America as my bride . . ." She had a romantic nature; she assumed any man could love her.

Bravely, she asked, "So who is this person you want me to meet?"

"You've met him, Angie."

She was left in the dark, still smiling. She hadn't seen anybody, and there was no place to hide.

"It's too late for me to leave," he said, "but for you I want the best." *Is this a proposal,* she wondered, and almost asked out loud, trying to help him. *I'll do it! I'll make you happy!* Then he said, "You must try a larger city." She'd always imagined herself in Bombay or maybe on the beaches of Goa, and so she mentioned those possibilities to him. *Eventually, even in America,* she thought, though she dared not say it for fear of inviting the evil eye.

"Bombay?" He laughed. "You've been seeing too many bad movies. Bombay is yesterday. It's a hustler's city. Bangalore's the place for a young woman like you."

She wondered, *Is that where he's taking me? Why not? I'll go.* Then: *What kind of girl am I?*

She knew nothing of Bangalore, a southern city as alien to her as the snows of Kashmir. Mr. Champion was back in teaching mode. He explained that for two hundred years Bangalore had been a British army base, a cantonment, and the Britishers had left a few scars—golf courses and racetracks and private gymkhanas—that moneyed Indians adopted a little too enthusiastically. But now it's a hopping place. And he had contacts in Bangalore, people who would listen to his recommendations. The call centers, luring thousands of young people from all over the country, people like her, the new people.

Ali returned with a box of sweets.

"In Bangalore," Mr. Champion said, "if you've got the talent, there's a market."

This time she asked the question that was always on her mind. "And what is my talent, Mr. Champion?"

"Peter, please. Don't you know what your talent is?"

"I haven't the p'oggiest."

"*Foggiest,* Angie. Initial *f*-sound, not *p.* Initial *w*-sound, not *v,* and vice versa. *Wedding,* not *vedding. Vagaries,* not *wagaries.* Not *wice wersa. Develop,* not *dewellup.* Keep practicing."

She could cry. They'll always find you out.

"Your talent, Angie? You have the passion. You're not satisfied. But you're still very innocent. Innocence is appealing in a young girl, but not blindness, not ignorance. Look at us." She smiled at his way of including her, but then he said, —"Look closely at *us,* Angie, take a long look at Ali and me."

At the mention of his name, Ali smiled and began to dance. The boy was a good dancer; he must have seen a hundred movies. And then Peter stood and put his arm over Ali's shoulder, and Ali nestled his head against Peter's cheek.

A clash of emotions met the dawn of consciousness: she could have screamed, but instead she whimpered, barely above a breath, "Oh."

Peter went on about places in Bangalore where she could stay. He knew old women from the British days who let out rooms in old mansions in the middle of the city, houses that could have been sold for crores of rupees (and leveled, their tangled gardens hacked down for parking lots and swimming pools), but where would the old women go? Old Anglo-Indian women whose children had fled to Australia or Canada, whose grandchildren would never see India, dotty old women whose sense of decorum reached back to pre-Independence days and who ("Believe me!" he laughed) would never be sympathetic to India's freedom fighters and Independence, but who nevertheless offered rooms and breakfasts of tea and toast and suppers of mutton stew at 1970s prices. Much was forgivable in such women. A place in Kew Gardens or Kent Town, that's what Angie needed. And he knew the women who ran the new money-spinning call centers were always looking for girls with good English and soothing voices who could fool American callers (*I can do that?* she was about to ask. *I'm good enough to fool Americans?*) into thinking they're talking to a girl in Boston or Chicago.

"Finally, a chance to use those regional accents I taught you," he said. "You're very good, Angie, you're the best student I ever had."

"That'll be five *dallars,*" she said, remembering.

Chicago *o*'s sound like *a*'s. So do Boston *r*'s.

"I told you at graduation you had to leave this place before you got trapped in a rotten marriage. I'm telling you again, let that happen and you're as good as dead."

Why do they say as *good* as dead? Why not as *bad*? But this was not the time to ask. He seemed about to put his hand on her arm and she felt excited. "I have dreams for you. You get married to some boy from here, and the dream dies. You'll never see the world." He studied her T-shirt. "No . . . Dortmund, no Bratislava. You'll have kids and a husband who's jealous of your intelligence and your English and won't let you out of the house, and that would break my heart." This time, he did put his hand on her arm — "You understand?"

Ali snapped up the plate of sweet crumbs as though it was crawling with ants and noisily dumped it into a bowl of soapy water. He was jealous of her! He was just a child. He lifted his dripping fingers to eye level and glared at a chip on a painted fingernail.

"All I've done is give you a start. The rest is up to you."

In the movies, there was a moment of accounting. She wouldn't be allowed to leave her benefactor's house, not without a favor, or worse. *The rest is up to me?* The door would be blocked. He'd reach for her hand, then close in on it, like a trap. But Peter was her teacher and a teacher's help had purity and noble intentions behind it. It came from his heart because she had earned it honorably. Peter was smiling and even Ali was smiling, and Peter held out his hand to her and said, "Good luck, Angie."

She took his hand. Ali thrust out his, which confused her: shake a servant's hand? Up close, she could see a fine line of kohl limning his eyes. In that moment of confusion she saw Peter's arm reach around Ali's waist and pull him close. "I hope you'll find happiness too," he said.

More words followed, in Urdu, and Ali laughed and said in English, "Good luck, Anjali."

Then he walked her to the bus stop.

2

If a girl is sufficiently motivated, she can distill ten years' worth of Western dating experience—though maybe not all the sex and heartbreak—from a few months of dedicated attention to the photos, backgrounds, and brief meetings with the "boys" her father selects. She can enjoy the illusion of popularity, glamour, and sophistication. She can fabricate "relationships" and fantasize about new cities, new families, and new worlds opening up, without the terror of leaving home and sneaking off to Bangalore. Even in the heavily chaperoned world of the arranged marriage market, a girl can fabricate passion and lose her innocence. Anjali was tuned in to her culture's consolations for the denial of autonomy.

She was nearly twenty, a few months into her bachelor of commerce studies. But why, her father wanted to know, delay groom-hunting for two more years until she received her B. Comm.? It was therefore decided that while he wore himself out in search of a worthy "boy," she was to resume attending the English conversation classes the American held in his apartment on weekends. Good English equals good match. He was willing to dig into his savings to pay the American's fees because if any misfortune was to befall her mythical husband, she could help out by tutoring school pupils. English-language skills would always be in demand.

"What husband, Baba?" Anjali protested, though she was pleased to have his blessing to attend the weekend classes. "You haven't even started looking, and you're worrying he'll be disabled or destitute!" This was as close as her father could come to admitting the horrible mistake he had made in hand-picking Sonali's husband. In the Bose family, a married woman forced by circumstances to hold a job to make ends meet was a tragedy. A divorced single mother supporting herself and her four-year-old daughter by working long days as an office typist was a catastrophe.

Mr. Bose went back to his nightly pegs of whiskey, ignoring her. Anjali toted up her assets and liabilities in the marriage market. Unlike Sonali, she was tall and slim, and under favorable light and clothing, pleasant looking—no, make that passably good looking. On the minus side, she lacked accomplishments such as singing, dancing, and sewing, traditionally expected of bridal candidates. She was also stubborn, headstrong, and impulsive, and by middle-class Gauripur standards, inappropriately outgoing. Those were correctible or at least concealable failures. The one flaw that couldn't be overcome was her eye color: greenish hazel. Her mother prayed for her pale eyes to turn black. Black hair, black eyes, fair complexion, sharp nose, and thin lips were unassailable proof of ethnic purity, whereas brownish hair and light eyes hinted at hanky-panky with a European in some long-ago time and place. Anjali reminded her mother that Sonali's long-lashed black eyes had fetched a lecherous cad who paid no child support and no alimony.

To marry her off was her father's Hindu duty: Anjali accepted that. Given her willful personality, he was eager to marry her off before she sullied her reputation and disgraced the whole family: she understood that too. She couldn't talk about her wants and fears with her parents, but she knew when to humor and when to defy them.

The matchmaking campaign began casually. Her father might come home from the office saying, "Took tea with Mr. Pradip Sen this afternoon. He's looking for someone for his son." Meaningful pause. "Anjali, you remember the Sens, no?" And she might drop what she was doing, which couldn't be much, since she was fairly useless in the kitchen, and say, "I trust you're not talking of Buck Tooth Sen. Good luck!" Little tests like that, easily deflected. And her father would shoot back, "Sen is good family. Everyone is remembering Mr. Pradip Sen's maternal grandmother's brother, just a boy, was hanged by damn Britishers on Andaman Islands." The formalities of matchmaking were conducted in English in the Bose household. Over breakfast Mr. Bose might linger on the page of marriage ads in the local Bangla paper, checking out the boys. "Promising lad, engineering, awaiting U.S. Green Card." The newspaper photo was reduced from a visa-size, visa-posed grainy black-and-white, rather insulting to her estimation of her prospects. She thought, *They actually think this clerk-in-waiting is worthy of me?* "Shall I drop this young chap a line?" her father would ask, and Anjali, feeling more like Angie, would reply, "You do that and I'm out the door, thank you very much." They sparred and chuckled. Their girl had self-respect, which the parents considered a good thing; she was also a little willful, which was not.

Angie wrote to Sonali that things at home were much as usual. Grumbling, threats, entreaties, criticism, and promises: the whole parent–unmarried daughter bag of tricks. Nothing she couldn't handle.

Sonali warned that matchmaking might start as a small cloud on the distant horizon, but before it was over, the marital monsoon would break, and no one in the world could hold the floodwaters back. Anjali secretly looked forward to its destructive fury.

THREE MONTHS LATER Anjali was still in Gauripur, making excuses to herself. The pre-monsoon summer was at its zenith. Nothing moved, all was heat and dust, but two thousand kilometers to the south, seasonal low pressure had been sighted. Low pressure meant monsoon. Monsoon meant mud, cooler weather, and a temporary reprieve from mosquitoes —and it meant that the next school year would soon be starting.

A sudden marriage, outside of her control, could certainly occur. Nonetheless, she felt it was only fair to her parents to let them test the marital waters. The possibility of going to Bangalore on her own would be a monumental life-destroying—or liberating—decision. She needed time to plan. She had saved the cash from occasional money orders Sonali had sent her over the years, but it probably wouldn't be enough for train fare. Hiding even the slim stack of bills from a family intolerant of privacy would be a challenge. Maybe she could stash it at the bottom of one of her mother's "just in case" metal drums in which was hoarded a six months' supply of rice, sugar, and lentils. "Just in case" was her mother's mantra. Disasters are waiting; they can't be avoided, and there's no one to trust. Everyone is corrupt, with twisted values. Even Anjali's father came in for scrutiny: "When bad times come again," she'd say as they chopped vegetables, "you think your father can save you? Hah! *My* father provided for my sisters and me. We never wanted, even in famine time. Five daughters all married, with decent dowry!"

"*Buzley?*" Did you understand?

"*Buzlum.*" Yes, I understood. This was Bose-family Bengali: an inside joke in an ancient dialect. But on this occasion it was meant to enforce. Do you understand what I am saying, and will you do as I say?

Buzley, buzlum.

The Boses were part of a remnant Bengali community inside a sea of Hindi-speaking Biharis. Angie's parents and three generations of once-prominent Boses had absorbed communal memories of riots and shop burnings, lootings, assassinations, and political scandal and had drawn a lesson from them. "These people . . ." her parents would complain, sometimes saying nothing more—"with these people, what to say?" *These people* could be anyone outside of their tight, dying, small-town "probasi" Bengali-Bihar community. Even other Bengalis—those exposed to the temptations of big-city Kolkata—were part of the plot against them. So was anyone not of their caste and general income level, or anyone with fewer than three generations of local roots, not to mention all minorities except maybe Parsis (not that any Parsi had ever stopped in Gauripur and stayed) and everyone from other regions.

"God, what I'd give for a little temptation!" Anjali used to say.

Even in Gauripur she had grown up on the modern side of a great national divide. From the backwater of Gauripur, she'd somehow caught the fever; she was part of the bold new India, an equal to anywhere, a land poised for takeoff. Her parents were irremediably alien, part of a suspicious, impoverished, humiliated India. How could they believe in the things they did and go through life hoarding food, denying themselves comforts, and delaying pleasure? How can you move ahead when all your energy is spent looking over your shoulder? They would never make progress; they were ill equipped for it. How cruel a fate, to be intelligent and ambitious and to crave her share of happiness—and to be denied the opportunity!

With her flawed Bangla language skills and no one to practice on except her parents, she'd always found herself attracted to Hindi movies, Hindi culture, and if it came down to it, Hindi-speaking boys. Bengali boys, like the ones in her ethnically isolated neighborhood, seemed too goody-goody, too cow-eyed. But given cultural patterns and long-nurtured prejudices, Mr. Bose would not consider non-Bengali applicants.

"No need to rush," Anjali would say. What if there was a perfect boy out there? Didn't she owe it to herself to give it a shot? She still had time to see if her father could find him, the Perfect Him, a Lord Ram with a trim mustache in modern dress. She doubted he could. His imagination was limited to boys who would grow into men like himself, boys in white shirts with secure prospects in a moribund bureaucracy. She'd be fair to her father. She'd give him another six months. If it looked hopeless, if he couldn't come through with a fancy catch, then she would definitely sneak out of the house, go to Peter, and wheedle a counter-dowry out of him, and send a postcard from Bangalore. Peter had made out Bangalore to be an asylum for bright, driven women from hellhole towns. Gauripur was a hellhole, but she didn't know if she met Peter's high standard for brightness, or desperation.

In the meantime, she could enjoy something new, the buzz of desirability, being the center of attention. Until the young Lord Ram was found, nothing that could enhance her beauty would be denied her. No new sari would be held back. There would be trips to the gold store, to Calendar Girl Hair-and-Nails Salon, even to the fancy hotel restaurant, just to be put on public display with her parents. She might even win the marriage raffle: get money and good-looking children from a sweet-tempered and handsome husband with loving in-laws. Then again, she'd never heard of such a marriage.

But a girl could dream, couldn't she? She could believe that she was still in control and that the orchestrated tsunami of marriage preparation could be reversed, that she had the power to call it off.

Now that it was time to marry her off, her parents reversed nineteen years of harsh assessments and suddenly expressed guarded approval. She could be advertised as modest and pliable, a flawless embodiment of Bengali virtue. Of course, she couldn't cook, dance, sing, or recite Tagore's poetry. But at least she wasn't a modern, citified, selfish materialist girl. Bihar was a sanitized bubble, far from the debilitating distractions of modern city life. Until the marital ax fell, severing her from all of life's promise, she would be the center of everyone's attention.

The monsoon was building, growing ever closer.

Her parents mandated that jeans and T-shirts could be worn only inside the house, early in the morning. After lunch and a beauty nap and bath, she was to appear decorous in a freshly starched sari, hair braided and decorated with flowers, eyes emphasized with eyeliner, face whitened with powder, in expectation of unannounced visits. After all—in the mutual ambush of marriage negotiation—a boy's parents might drop by, ostensibly to view the goods but also to assess the general character of the family, the quality of housekeeping, the mother's modesty, the father's authority, the spontaneous hospitality, the obsequiousness of the staff, the absence of ostentation. Certainly there was very little ostentation to worry about, and no staff to speak of, except a woman who came every morning to sweep the floors and scrub the cooking utensils used the night before and a boy who cleaned the toilet every afternoon. At dinner, Anjali's chapatis would be smeared with extra ghee to enhance her radiance, and sweetmeats (such as raabri, rasmalai, rajbhog, expensive treats the Boses would buy only when they had guests) heaped on her plate in the hope that she would add a little more weight in all the right places.

Most evenings, in the quiet hour when her father sat in the only comfortable rattan chair in the front room of their rented apartment, drinking his three pegs of local whiskey before dinner, and she and her mother sat on the floor, her mother darning frayed shirt collars and cuffs and Anjali tapping out hit Bollywood songs on the family's heavy harmonium, with its chipped keys and scuffed bellows, the dreams were almost enough.

"I shall find a good boy this time," Mr. Bose promised his wife regularly. "Your father wore out the soles of his sandals looking and looking before he found me. I am prepared to do the same."

He answered scores of matrimonial ads in the two Bangla-language papers. Angie didn't expect him to snare a single worthwhile candidate —he was a railway clerk, after all, not even a regional director—and the fact that he was still restricting his attention to a tiny fraction of available boys was just fine; her back-door escape plan was not in jeopardy. All the same, some siesta hours while her mother snored in bed next to her, she allowed herself to daydream that maybe a Bollywood hunk, a Shah Rukh Khan or Akshay Kumar, would find her irresistible during the marriage interview and would deposit her in Mumbai, Canada, or America. In daydreams, even Dubai seemed bearable.

Everything about the Bose flat, especially the front room, where any interview would have to take place, depressed her. This room, the larger of the two, was furnished with a mattress-covered wooden chowki, which served as seating for visitors and as a bed for her father, a glass-fronted bookcase, and two wooden office chairs with uneven legs. A grimy, rolled-up tent of mosquito netting was suspended above the chowki by its four loops from nails hammered into the plaster walls. The only wall hangings were two calendars, a current one with a flashy picture of Goddess Durga astride a lion, and a useless but auspicious one from ten years earlier, which had been current in the year her father had received his last promotion.

Her parents' continual squabbling made it hard for her to improvise bouncy Bollywood beats on the old harmonium. It was her lone feminine grace, hence, important.

"I'm not despairing yet of finding a decent jamai," Mr. Bose kept saying between sips of whiskey. "If your father could find someone like me, I can find someone equally good."

The silence was deafening.

"My father received many, many decent proposals," Mrs. Bose protested. "From day one. I could have married an actuary and lived in a big house in Patna."

"No actuaries," Anjali declared. "No dentists, no professors either."

"Who asked you?" Mrs. Bose shouted.

"And nobody from an armpit town like Patna!"

Mr. Bose made a menacing gesture, slipping the sandal off his left foot and holding it up as though he meant to strike her. "You think you can give ultimatums to your elders? Maybe I should marry you off to a village schoolteacher—would you approve of that? Iron his dhoti under a banyan tree every morning?"

"She's an obedient girl. She'll do what you tell her."

"You think my family and my salary are not good enough for an actuary or a tooth puller?"

"She is a Vasco graduate."

"Useless." Mr. Bose snorted.

"Drunk," said Mrs. Bose.

"Why only Bangla ads?" Angie demanded. "Why not English papers? I'm too good for any guy taking out ads in any Gauripur paper."

"You see what state you've reduced me to, woman, by not bearing sons? All my brothers are fathers of sons. But me? Two donkeys for daughters." He would never own a house, not with two daughters, two dowries, the larger one already wasted.

"Ill luck is ill luck." Mrs. Bose clutched at her throat. It was not the proper time for Anjali to bring up the known fact that sex determination is male-linked. "But this one isn't donkey-headed like . . ."

Mr. Bose was on a roll. "Donkey for wife, donkeys for daughters!"

"You're not wearing out your sandals, you're wearing out your tongue!"

She took hope from her father's proven incompetence. One failed marriage in the family, although her father took no blame for it, had weakened his authority.

For Anjali, he could no longer muster the pinnacle moment, the operatic ultimatum that he had risen to with her sister. She remembered the cold precision of that final night, after weeks of shouts and slammed doors: "I have told his father you will marry this boy. Astrologer has spoken, horoscopes are compatible. I am printing the invitations. There is no more to be said!" Her sister had run to her room to cry; her groans had filled the house.

"Give me a knife! Give me poison!" she'd screamed.

Then she emerged two hours later, pale, dry-eyed, and submissive.

"You are right, Father," she said. "I have been behaving badly." She'd dressed herself in a new brocade sari and raided the stash of dowry gold. Arms heavy with bangles, earrings brushing her bare shoulders, necklaces and chokers disappearing under the sari-fold into her bosom, she said, "Just as you see me now, so will you see me when I am dead."

Anjali remembered the chaos of the marriage ceremony itself. Invitations had been delivered to every Bengali family in Gauripur, but the presents were tawdry—outdated saris, cheap purses, re-gifted lemonade sets, an electric table fan, and nine flat envelopes, each containing 101 rupees in cash. Because Angie had a neat hand, her parents had assigned her the duty of keeping an accurate record of the wedding gifts. The food had run short, drawing churlish comments from the bridegroom's party. The priest had abbreviated the marriage rites and afterward complained about the poor quality of the silk dhoti-punjabi he had received from the bride's stingy family. A troop of hijras had shown up in their gaudy saris, with flower wreaths, plastic baubles, and bright lipstick on their leering male faces. They extorted money for their stumbling dances, frightening the children and even Anjali with their lewd sexual gestures, their deep voices, their braided hair and spreading bald spots. Her wedding, Anjali vowed, would have glamour and dignity.

And so it went, with variations, night after night in the Bose household. But during the day, with Mr. Bose away in the office, Mrs. Bose hatched new plans. "In six months," her mother practically chirped, "you will be a married woman." She reeled off common Kayastha-caste surnames: a Mrs. Das, Mrs. Ghosh, Mrs. Dasgupta, Mrs. Mitter, Mrs. De, Mrs. Sen, Mrs. Sinha, Mrs. Bhowmick. "You will have a new house in a new city with a new family of brothers, sisters, and parents. You'll become a whole different person." As appealing as a new family might sound in the abstract, it surely meant future entombment.

Mr. Bose didn't have access to a computer at work and did not know how to use the Internet. He asked around for help, for anyone's son or daughter who might have a computer to come to his rescue, but the computers were in the college and the college was on summer break until the monsoons started. Neighbors suggested names, everyone recommended Bengaliweddings.com as the most reliable website with the widest distribution. There was a boy in the neighborhood, Nirmal Gupta, called Sure-Bet-IIT Gupta, a classmate of Anjali's and a genius with computers. Go to Nirmal, the Boses were told. Truly, it takes a village to marry off a daughter. Mr. Bose sent the word to distant relatives in Kolkata and alerted managerial-level colleagues at work that he was on the lookout for a jamai for his number-two daughter.

All of the adult mysteries were about to unfold, her mother told Anjali. One's secret fate, hidden behind the stars, would suddenly burst forth like a seed in fertile soil, nurtured by sun and rain. The One True Mate whose destiny had been waiting for this glorious conjunction since the beginning of time would materialize in all his worshipful strength and beauty.

This was parent-talk from the other side of the great modern divide. Mrs. Bose was silent on what Sonali, in her first month as wife, saucily confided to Anjali about men's "animal nature." The sisters had giggled over Sonali's graphic descriptions of marriage-bed drama. Angie doubted that her father, even in his youth, had been endowed with animal nature. Her mother could not possibly have ever expected, let alone experienced, conjugal delirium with her father. Angie wished she could ask her mother what shape her dreams of married life had taken before Mr. Bose had become her bridegroom. Her mother had married at seventeen. The senior Mrs. Bose, her mother-in-law, did not want a vain, ambitious, educated woman in the family, so she had demanded that the girl drop out of school just a month before graduation. Anjali's mother had hoarded that grievance, polished and buffed it to radiance over the years, and brought it out to great effect during domestic squabbles. For her father, marriage was a sacred duty; for her mother it was an accumulation of insults and an avenging of hurts.

But for Sonali, as Sonali explained to Anjali on their rare secret reunions, successful marrying off of one's offspring was neither an art nor a science. Horoscopes might correctly calculate astral compatibility. But marital happiness? That was in the hands of fate.

The volume of response to the new ads was overwhelming. Along with thirty responses from India, three letters arrived from Dubai, two from Kenya, one from Canada, and one from Mauritius: a village of Bengali bachelors strung around the world, working their computers. The long list selected by Mr. Bose was so promising that Mrs. Bose, in high spirits, secreted a slim wad of rupees and instructed Anjali to go to Calendar Girl in Pinky Mahal. "Best to stay prepared for short-notice interviews," she explained. "They use bleaching creams and whatnot that last for weeks."

While her mother prayed to the household gods, Mr. Bose shifted into high gear, even reading English ads and reopening old school contacts. ("Remember the Dasguptas in Ranchi? They had a boy, I'm sure. Anil, isn't it? I will write Deepak Dasgupta and ask after Anil . . .") and so on it went, letters sent out, responses coming back . . . the promising, the disappointing. Deepak Dasgupta wrote back, "Our boy Anil is finishing MBA in Maryland-USA. I regret to say he intends to make his own match in the so-called modern manner."

Which means he's already living with an American girl, thought Angie.

"I will spread the word in Ranchi about your lovely daughter whose picture is very simple and pleasing . . ."

The mailman too began to take an interest as he left off envelopes thick with bios and photos. "Word is getting around, Big Sister," he would say with an ingratiating grin as he handed Mrs. Bose manila envelopes with foreign postage. "God willing, we'll be celebrating with sweetmeats soon."

"That man is just interested in getting his baksheesh for delivering the right application," Mr. Bose complained. "These people want something for nothing."

All of her life, Anjali had been made aware of the ways in which a prospective bride could lose her footing. In the Snakes and Ladders game of marital negotiation, a girl has a hundred ways of disappointing, then it's tumble, tumble down a hole or worse, like Alice in Wonderland. Leaving aside questions of incompatible horoscopes, rejected dowry proffers, ancestral scandals, and caste irregularities, a girl could lose points on the desirability scale for being too short or too tall, too dark or too fair, too buxom or too flatty-flatty, with eyes too small or too light, hair too frizzy, a personal manner too outspoken or too repressed, school grades too high (potentially showing too much personal ambition) or too low (indicating a potential hazard as breeding stock). Of course, a decent dowry can always smooth the edges. Needless to say, her father could not provide it.

Angie found 99 percent of boys simply unappealing. The idea of sleeping in their beds, bearing their children, cooking for them, sitting across from them and watching them eat and burp, and listening to their voices and opinions for a lifetime put the idea of marriage in a category with a life sentence on the Andaman Islands. Thirty boys rejected; none even progressed to the interview stage. "I will decide who is good," Mr. Bose now threatened. "I've left you too much in charge. You are abusing a privilege that was never yours to begin with."

She rejected the first batch of short-listed candidates on the basis of their photos alone. "Look at those shifty eyes!" she'd say. Or "He's fat as an elephant!" Or "Eeesh, what happened to his teeth? He's wearing dentures." Bald spots, double chins, hairy arms. She automatically rejected boys with fancy mustaches and sideburns, those striving for coolness in blue jeans and sunglasses, and those who appeared too goody-goody, too pretentious or too homespun. No pictures, please, with mommy/daddy or grandparents or household pets. No Man-of-the-People shots with servants. She detested foreign settings ("Here is a snap I have dug up from base of Eiffel Tower" . . . or "Buckingham Palace" . . . or "Statue of Liberty" . . . or "Gate of Forbidden City" . . .). Those were the easy ones. But if a boy with outstanding prospects or handsomeness actually turned up, she'd make a show of serious scrutiny before complaining, "He thinks too well of himself, he's posing like a fashion model." Or "A boy like that—if he's so perfect, why couldn't they find him a rich girl in Kolkata?"

"It's your fault." Mrs. Bose charged her husband with this failure, reminding him of all the trouble with "your other daughter," reminding him of all of *Sonali's* prideful rejections of acceptable boys from reasonably good families. Sonali had imagined their soft, round, *bhad-bhada* faces aging into double chins, their bristly eyebrows that could only grow untamed ("I'm sure he's already clipping his ear hair!" Sonali had complained). And look at what all her rejections finally got her—a man too handsome for his own good, a man with glorious prospects and no accomplishments, a man who stole her dowry gold and made a mockery of marriage.

"Two daughters!" Mrs. Bose wailed. "No jamais!"

After Anjali's final English conversation class—tuning up for interviews, she told her parents; prepping for Bangalore, she told herself—she informed Peter that this visit was to be her last class, her last public appearance in jeans and a T-shirt, her last day as a student. After all, she had a marriage-worthy English proficiency certificate, first class. Peter asked if she was perhaps having a bovine interlude.

"A *what?*" she asked, and he stared back.

"Cowlike," he said. But she'd turned down thirty-five potential suitors, a few of whom under different circumstances might have been worthy of a follow-up; that could hardly be considered cowlike. But Peter showed no interest. She assured him that Bangalore was in her plans; she was only testing the waters, placating her parents.

He said his offer of help—meaning money as well as contacts, she wondered—for Bangalore was waiting, but it had an expiration date.

"When?" she wondered aloud.

"Soon," he said. "All right," Peter said, "one bonus private English lesson before Bangalore. Do you like poetry?"

She didn't, but she knew the proper answer.

"I want you to read this, and then recite it."

Even the title confused her. "What is a rawen?" she asked. How could she read it if she didn't know what it was?

"A raven is a big black bird like a crow that can get an Indian student hired or fired," he said. "You just said 'ray-wen.' Try again."

She got it on the second try, and didn't mess up on "weak and weary."

"Good," Peter said. "You aren't too out of practice, Angie."

And then she was hopeless on "Quoth the raven, nevermore!" Two *th*'s in a row? Back-to-back middle *v*'s? She could cry. But Peter just kept tapping his pencil like a music teacher, muttering "Again, again" until, exhausted, she got it right.

Two days later, shopping with her mother for mangoes and oranges, she spotted Peter at the outdoor market. She was about to lift her arm and signal, but no, she couldn't, not in a sari, with jingling gold bracelets. Angie-in-sari was Anjali, a stranger to her student self.

And she thought, just like a hundred generations of potential brides had thought before her, why all this talk of new sisters and new brothers and a new house in a new city and not a warning about a new mother-in-law to ridicule her while her new husband sits back and criticizes her sloppiness and cooking? Her promised resurrection into the state of marriage would be little different from her mother's and grandmother's, except that she had education and ambition, Bangalore- and Bollywood-size expectations and a wealth of ready-made suspicion, thanks to her sister's fate.

In the months as a full-time bridal candidate, she finally grasped enough of the world to place Peter and Ali in a kind of murky marital matrix. And to think, not long ago, she'd imagined herself in Ali's role as Peter's beloved. It was all fascinating, and just a little sickening. And with the revelation of Peter and Ali came dozens more complications, as though they'd all been lined up, waiting for her to open the door and see with fresh eyes: new combinations, weird embraces, convoluted sexual dimensions with higher peaks of improbability and deeper, more complicated valleys, like the wrinkly march of the Himalayas across Nepal.

3

It took three hours of sitting in a crisp silk sari at Sengupta's Marriage Portrait Studio, WHERE DESIRABLE DAUGHTERS MEET THEIR MATES, Gauripur's center of marital entrapment for the dwindling community of Bengali girls. When old Shaky Sengupta had been a younger, steadier-handed roaming photographer without a back-alley studio, he'd taken Anjali's grandmother's photo, and then her mother's, and even the garlanded marriage photo of her parents that still sat in the middle of the bedroom dresser.

She was posed at a table in front of a Qantas poster of the Sydney Opera House, which could be replaced by All Nippon Airways pull-down screens of Mount Fuji and the Ginza district in Tokyo for additional shots; finally she was seated at a bistro table, with an unwashed espresso cup, in front of a Toulouse-Lautrec poster. The espresso cup had recently held sweet coffee. A fly struggled to escape the sticky residue. She kept her face a mysterious blank, saw that her silk sari remained uncreased, and allowed herself only five-minute breaks to dab the perspiration from her upper lip.

A British-era thermometer advertising Pond's cold cream read 121 degrees.

A tall young assistant lugged lights and reflectors. She tried to radiate allure from an imagined alpine café under a Martini & Rossi umbrella, with the Matterhorn in the background, while Shaky Sengupta, the palsied photographer, patted her face with tissues and tried to tease a dimple from a smile she could barely force.

"Never mind, I put in dimple when I take out frown," he said, in English. "Dimple very popular."

Shaky Sengupta and his diminishing breed of Indian marriage photographers shared a total disregard for truth, passion, or integrity. Which is to say they were ideal enablers in the inherent duplicity of the marriage arrangement. Every girl was fetchingly beautiful in a prescribed manner. The camera and its expressive potential worked more like a shovel. The art was in the touch-up: slimming down the dumplings, puffing up the ironing boards, inflating bosoms, enlarging eyes, straightening teeth, and moistening lips.

The young assistant caught Anjali's attention. He was extremely tall and thin, wearing blue jeans and a plain light-blue T-shirt. He moved with grace and competence, and his Bangla was even worse than hers. It was he who set up the shots, arranged the reflectors, and measured the focus, doing everything that Shaky in his earlier years might have been able to do by himself.

When he bent down to clean out her espresso cup, he said, "Studio sessions really suck, don't they?" His accent was pure American, without Peter Champion's decades in India to soften it. He had the longest, most delicate fingers she'd ever seen on a man.

"What did you say?"

A convincing American accent, easy enough to acquire these days in India though not in Gauripur, didn't give him the right to flirt with a paying customer. His major duty was to tell her how beautiful she looked. Instead, he was standing with his hands on his hips, insolently separating her from the pull-down screen of cherry blossoms on snowy Mount Fuji.

"What are you trying to prove?"

Now he'd insulted her in her zone of grace, fresh from the beauty parlor, in her uncreased silk. Indignantly, she answered, "I'm not trying to *prove* anything." She could feel the heat rising. "Just that I'm a worthy bridal candidate."

"No, you're not. Your heart isn't in it."

"My heart has nothing to do with it. It's just a marriage photo. You're not wearing a silk sari without a fan. It must be fifty degrees under the lights!"

She saw him glance at the thermometer. So, she figured, he needed a metric-system equivalence; he might really be American. He stepped behind Mount Fuji and returned with a metal cup of cool water. As she gulped it down, he confronted the mountain. "Everything's so fake, we ought to go with the joke." He tugged down on the screen and the mountain partially rolled up, exposing other rolls of tourist posters, ladders, and chairs behind them. "Voilà!" he said. "The Wizard of Oz." She decided on the spot that he was a very kind, very funny boy. Was he available?

"Everyone knows I'm in a hot little studio and the mountain is just a prop."

"*Exactly!* You're sitting like a corpse in a formal sari in front of a fake landscape. So if everyone knows they're fake, you should show you're in on it. A meta-marriage photo! You'd be the coolest, heat or not."

Shaky Sengupta called, "Restore mountain, please. No talking with subject."

"A godlike mission, restoring mountains. See you after," the boy said, pressing one long finger against his lips. "My name is Rabi Chatterjee." He squeezed the tips of her fingers. His hand was cold. "I'm a photographer too. Only different."

Chatterjee? A Brahmin, so marriage to a Bose was effectively out the window. She thought she knew all the Bengali families in Gauripur, especially those with interesting boys, even the Brahmins who these days couldn't always be choosy. She'd seen the ads, "Caste no bar," especially for the poor, less attractive, and less educated Brahmin boys or girls.

After she changed back to her jeans and T-shirt for the short walk home, Rabi was waiting. "Let the fun begin," he said. Before she could pose, there in the chaos of lights and reflectors and cables and half-rolled-up props, he took out a small silver digital camera and shot her, again and again. He promised her that the girl in his pictures was destined for a different fate than marriage, quite the opposite of Shaky Sengupta's girl with a dimple, in uncreased silk.

When they were walking along LBS Road past Pinky Mahal, he asked if she was really serious about finding a boy. He was the first boy her own age she'd ever walked with in public, alone, not in a student group. And probably the last. She answered hesitantly, wondering, as was her custom, if he was offering himself. He spoke so rapidly that his English sounded like a foreign language in a different cadence. She felt herself growing breathless, just trying to keep up.

"It's for my parents," she said.

He stopped, turned, and stared. "You're getting married for your parents? That's crazy."

"Other people have said the same thing." Of course, that one other person was American. She could get interested in a boy like Rabi, all energy and enthusiasm, with a quick mind, long fingers, and startling English. "You know how it works. I don't have a say in it." Then she wondered, *Did* he know how India worked? Despite his name and looks, he seemed more foreign than Peter Champion.

"India's on fire. If you get married now, you'll miss what's happening and you'll be sorry."

Gauripur, on fire? Peter used to say that, and it still seemed funny. "Bangalore and Mumbai might be on fire, but Gauripur is still in the deep freeze." Then, on a perkier note, "I thought I knew all the Bengali families in Gauripur. So where have you been?" *Where have you been hiding? Why haven't you come forward and answered any of the ads?* If she had to guess, he was one of those boys from boarding school, from Dehra Dun or Darjeeling, an Indian boy with international connections. Or maybe his parents were diplomats and he'd been raised overseas and gone to American schools.

"I've been in California all of my life."

She laughed. "Now *that's* crazy. Why would anyone from California come to a pokey little town like Gauripur? This is a prison!" She'd slipped into Bangla, just to slow things down. She was a little afraid of making a mistake in his rapid-fire American. His even-shakier Bangla fired her confidence. His long, skinny legs ate up the footpath; she had to run to keep up.

"You ask what I'm doing here? I'm having fun. When you're taking pictures, every place is interesting . . . every face is beautiful . . . every day's incredible and every night's an adventure . . . When you're looking through a camera, Gauripur's amazing. When I put my eye to the viewfinder, everything changes. I only see things, really see them, when I'm looking through the camera. They rave about painterly light in southern France . . . Ha! It's feeble compared to India. What is that thing called—Pinky Mahal? Just look at it! It's magnificent! Better than the Taj! It's your own Rouen cathedral. Monet would go crazy for it."

Normally she would have nodded and smiled, afraid to show her ignorance. But she trusted the boy; he wouldn't laugh at her. He was the first person, with the slight exception of Peter Champion, who after all was still a teacher and her superior, to understand, even blunder into, her nascent yearning to be respected. "Moray?" she asked. "That's a fish." A fish painted a ruined cathedral?

"Claude Mo-nay, M-O-N-E-T, the father of impressionism." His tone was offhand, conversational, as though Claude Monet and his weird cathedral in a town in France were the subject of everyone's lighthearted conversation. "I'd call him the father of photography too. He painted the Rouen cathedral at various times of the day, just to show the effect of different angles of light."

Angles of light! And he's only my age! she thought.

The pace of his speech was picking up. "Monet changed everything. He ended the tyranny of the subject. The medium became the subject, and the medium was light." Faster, faster.

Slow down, please, she thought. *I can't follow—you speak too fast. Tyranny of the subject? What does that mean? The medium becomes the subject; the medium is light? You walk too fast. You get too excited. You don't know how ignorant I am.* "He did the same thing with haystacks in different seasons. Usually I don't work in color, but I came out here yesterday at seven in the morning, then at noon, then at three, and finally at six, and each time the pink was different and the angle of light brought out different fractures and shadows . . . it was beautiful. Bihar is beautiful. Nothing in the world is as it seems—it's all a matter of light and angles. Anyway, even if it is a prison, there are lots of good pictures you can take from inside."

"Not if you're a prisoner," she said. Not if you don't have a camera and no one's ever taught you how to use one. "What were you doing at Shaky's?"

"Is that what he's called? Shaky? That's cruel. But funny." He had a broad smile, a lilting laugh. "I was learning studio technique, putting in the dimples and taking out the frowns. It's very retro, but there's an art to it: setups, lights and reflectors. And those pull-downs are so cool, I wouldn't mind having a few. I gotta be prepared for anything, right? Maybe I'll end up doing weddings and baby portraits—*not.* Anyway, I'll be moving on in three days."

She didn't understand a word, but the news of his leaving cut her like a slap. She was already imagining an inquiry to his parents, his visit to her house. "That's very disappointing"—a bold thing to say. "Why not stay? Why not keep the prisoners happy?"

"The rest of India's calling. There's Mumbai. There's Bangalore. I came to Gauripur because I heard there was an expat here. I met him, and I shot him—sorry, took his picture. I'm doing India's new expats—not the old Brits—and the gays, and the prostitutes and the druggies. And the villages. And the slums."

"My teacher is American."

"Yes, I know. We're everywhere, Anjali."

"Angie," she said.

They took a few more steps, Angie deep in consternation. What kind of boy was this? Why would an American want to be anywhere near the kind of awful people he shoots? Just thinking about them made her skin crawl.

"Let me show you something. Would you like to see a picture of the most beautiful woman in Gauripur?"

"Of course," she said.

What girl could refuse?

He guided her to Alps Palace Coffee and Ice Cream Shop for a cool-down. It was a college hangout, but school was not in session and the AC was broken. When Alps Palace had opened, it seemed like the Gauripur equivalent of all the Mumbai Barista and American Starbucks coffee shops she'd read about, something chic and air-conditioned, with uniformed girls behind the counter. Now she saw it for what it was, another sad failure, run down and a little unsanitary. Rabi asked for a moist rag, swabbed down a table, and dried it with a handkerchief. Then he reached into his backpack and took out a folder marked *Bihar* and set out a row of black-and-white prints, matted under clear plastic. She barely recognized the subjects. Their very familiarity—Nehru Park, the college, Pinky Mahal—was their best disguise. Now she understood about the light. He was truly, as he'd said, a different kind of photographer.

In Rabi's photos, Gauripur was eerie, exotic—even its most familiar monuments. The marble dhoti-folds of the iconic Gandhi statue in Nehru Park were pocked, streaked, and spray-painted. The market crowds looked furtive and haunted. Five kilometers south of town, under a small dark forest of untended mango trees, Rabi had found a MODREN APARTTMENT COMPLEX—according to its signboard—that had been abandoned early in construction with less than one floor completed. A rutted construction road and a row of workers' huts disappeared into a cryptlike darkness. She'd never imagined anything remotely like it so close to Gauripur. He'd focused on rows of rusted iron bars—rebars, he called them—like twisted sentinels bristling from the concrete half-wall, disappearing into the shadows. She imagined cold, dank air, even in the heat of a Bihar May, issuing from its depths.

Rebar: a word to avoid.

It was a relief to anticipate turning to "the most beautiful woman in Gauripur." She expected something cheeky from the boy, cheeky and American. Maybe he'd show her one of the digital photos he'd taken in the studio and come up with some flirtatious opening, like "You want to see beauty? Just look in the mirror." She was prepared to slap him for it, but not too hard. A tapping, gentle rapping, like in the poem. A playful tap, like in the movies.

"Here's the woman I was talking about."

Truly, he had not lied. Angie was staring at film-star beauty, goddess beauty, old-fashioned sari-jewelry-hairstyle beauty, deep, Aishwarya Rai beauty, twice the woman she could ever be. She *was* the most beautiful woman Anjali had ever seen.

"In Gauripur? I don't believe it."

"And you know her," Rabi said.

"That's a lie."

"Right! Only I think she pronounces it . . . 'Ah-lee.'" He seemed pleased with the wordplay. "I guess you could say that men make the best cooks, *and* they make the best-looking women."

"But you said 'she.'"

"Exactly," he said.

Over the weeks, with some difficulty, Angie had begun to accommodate to what it must be like, romantically, between Peter and Ali, but this revelation was something new, outside her ability to process. In her reconstruction, Ali had been the abused and grateful village boy, and Peter the all-powerful American who had saved him from a life of squalor. She'd seen it as a variant of a normal Indian marriage between economic unequals. Virtuous and beautiful village girl; spoiled, rich city boy won over by her goodness. She hadn't understood it as profoundly sexual, as it apparently was, because she'd always considered marriage a protection against sexuality—obligation, not adventure.

"That's Ali by night," Rabi was saying. "By day he's a pretty enterprising guy. He started out cutting ladies' hair in Lucknow and then he worked wardrobes and makeup in Bollywood. You watch—some day he'll open up his own beauty parlor."

"But those kind of men—they aren't—"

She started to speak, then paused, remembering swishy Bollywood characters who were in all the films—but they weren't to be taken seriously. You couldn't call them accomplished in any way. They were scared of their shadows. They dropped things; they were clumsy. They screamed when they saw a mouse, rolled their eyes and flapped their wrists and ran away from fights. They were put in the films in order to be laughed at.

Rabi stared back. "What about them?" he asked. "*What* aren't they?"

"They aren't servants," she said. Servants don't suddenly open their own business.

Rabi was fiddling with a larger camera. "And he's not a servant."

In the next few moments, the true education of Anjali Bose began. Many seconds elapsed. She thought she was going to be sick. Many questions couldn't quite form themselves and went unasked. She was reassessing probability, rewinding the spool of her experience and discovering that she knew nothing. Something treacherous had entered her life.

"Oh, my God," she said. "I know him."

"I know you do."

The next picture on the tabletop was of Peter Champion, Peter the expatriate scholar reading an Indian paper in his dingy little room, with a blurred Ali in his servant's attire of lungi and undershirt behind him, washing dishes. Peter, whatever else he was, was a serious man. He'd devoted his life to things in India that were disappearing. He couldn't be laughed at. But as she kept looking, Ali came into focus. It was as though he'd taken a step or two forward. He wasn't washing plates—he was staring at Peter.

"I got real lucky. I came to Gauripur to shoot an expat, *and* I get a gay and a tranny at the same time. Who'd have figured, in a town like this?"

She could accept it. It even restored Peter's mysterious edge. Being homosexual—did Rabi say "gay"?—was more exciting than being CIA, which is what the smart boys in her class assumed the American was. Tranny? She was afraid to ask. This tall, skinny Rabi with all his photos, the first boy she'd felt comfortable with, what was he? If all this intrigue was happening under her nose in a boring little town like Gauripur, where nothing was strange and nothing held surprises, among the people she thought she knew the best, then what was the rest of India like? Bangalore? Mumbai? She felt the terror of the unprepared, as though she'd been pushed onto a stage without a script.

What if, in the larger world, no one held true? What if everyone was two people at least, like Ali, like Peter?

What could she do but cry? It was involuntary. She wasn't sad or frightened. It was as if she'd missed a step in the dark and knew she was going to fall and hurt herself badly, but at that precise moment she was still suspended between here and there, between now and then, and Rabi snapped the picture. Years later, people would say that it made a beautiful composition, enigmatic, *Mona Lisa*–like.

When Rabi asked her why she was crying, she said, "I've seen more in the past two minutes than I have in nineteen years."

He said, "I'm eighteen. Photography teaches you everything."

She didn't have the foggiest idea of what he meant.

Nevertheless, that was the moment that sealed their friendship.

"When you look at great photos, you see the whole world in a context. The whole world may only be five by seven inches, and it might last only a five-hundredth of a second, but within that time and space it's all true, and it's the best we've got."

Angie Bose had lived nineteen years in Gauripur and was a year and a half from graduating with a degree from the best school in town, and no one had ever spoken to her about the nature of truth or art, or assumed she cared or knew anything about it. She knew there were plenty of pretty shots of the Taj Mahal—hard to mess that one up—and the Himalayas and animals and famous faces, but she'd never thought of them as plotted except in a Shaky Sengupta sort of way. Truth? Context? Composition? She'd never had a serious discussion about anything. She was the second daughter of a railway clerk; she was supposed to go to school, obey teachers and parents, graduate and get married, obey her husband, and have children. Truth was what the community, teachers, parents, and eventual husband said it was. Truths were handed down from the beginning of time and they held true forever, not for one five-hundredth of a second. The thought that things were not as they appeared to be, or that people were not what she thought they were, left her with a feeling akin to nausea.

She knew, vaguely, that worlds existed beyond the assigned books and lectures—Peter Champion would occasionally depart from scripted discussions in his corporate cultures class to sprinkle in asides on literature and history and politics, little moments no one paid attention to because they would not appear on examinations. She had learned a Russian word, *Chekhovian,* from something he'd said about the Indian social and political structure. But the idea that a mere child, someone even younger than she was, could show off such knowledge as well was unimaginable.

When she listened to her parents at dinner, she wanted to scream, "Life isn't like that! Nobody cares! It doesn't matter! Nothing matters!" Like any American teenager, she wanted to scream at her parents, "You don't know a thing!" But every day the same food was bought and every night it was cooked and served in the same way, and the same rumors and gossip were chewed over, the same questions asked, with the same answers given, and everything was meaningless.

"Did you have to fight your parents in order to come to India?"

From the way he laughed, she could tell she must have said something funny. "Why would they stop me? I've got an auntie in Bangalore, and I was with my mother's parents in Rishikesh until they died, *and* I've got my father's folks in Kolkata and cousins everywhere. The only hard part is finding a way of avoiding them. A billion people in this country, and it feels like half of them are relatives! Just imagine how helpful they'd be in tracking down gay bars and whorehouses! I went out with a bunch of hijras—a blast! Natural performers." What he referred to as a "gay bar" sounded like a happy place, but she wondered how a Brahmin boy from a good family would be admitted to a whorehouse, and when she thought of hijras and their leering made-up faces and men-in-women's-clothing and flowers in their oily hair, she felt sick. Performers? They were perversions!

They talked a bit about their parents, how hers were so loving and concerned, how supportive they were. Lies, lies! *Ask me, and I'll tell the truth,* but he didn't. He said he hadn't talked to his parents in weeks but sent them emails of some of his photos. She made her father into a bank manager, hoping that would impress; he said his father ran a kind of telephone company, but the man was housebound and partially crippled, and his mother wrote novels about India for American women. In their mutual inventions, they weren't so far apart.

"I was just thinking," he said, as he tore out a sheet from a pocket notebook. "My mother would *love* to sit down with you!" *Why?* she wondered. *I'm nothing special.* She was about to ask why when he announced, as if in explanation, "She is Tara Chatterjee." The name meant nothing to Angie except that Tara was a common enough first name and Chatterjee one of the few Bengali Brahmin surnames, all of which meant that there were probably a dozen Tara Chatterjees of varying ages even in Gauripur. He took in her blank look and laughed. "The Tara Chatterjee who writes, that's my mom. You mean you haven't read her stories? Anyway, here's my San Francisco phone number. And let me give you my auntie's Bangalore number. I stay with her when I am there." He scribbled a telephone number on the back of his San Francisco card. "You'll get there if you really want to," he said.

Bangalore? How did he guess?

• • •

THE GIRL IN Shaky Sengupta's formal glossies was definitely not Angie. Not even a version of Anjali. In fact, as Rabi had said, there was no one there, and that, of course, triggered a new wave of interest. The nature of Shaky's art was to drain personality from the frame and replace it with fantasy. She'd always seen herself as too tall and thin, made for T-shirts and jeans, her narrow dimensions lost inside a sari. But Shaky's magic had managed the impossible, implying cleavage and billowy wonders under the sari, along with the smudgy dimple. She was luminous and mysterious, a synthetic bonbon of indeterminate age. Shaky was a master of light and shadow.

While her parents were fretting over the caste purity and social standing of interested probasi Bengalis with twenty-something sons, vowing this time they'd wipe out the stigma of their other daughter's divorce, Anjali was imagining herself in the real world behind Shaky Sengupta's pull-down screens. The beaches of Australia were beckoning, the Ginza, the Great Wall, why not? Even in Gauripur a girl could dream, especially a reasonably attractive girl with good English, a dimple and cleavage, and an adventurous nature.

The girl/woman in the portrait had nothing to fear from an uncertain marriage market. She would definitely find a husband. She could imagine the crashing of teacups around the world as thousands of bachelor engineers, the loose network of longing that had thus far yielded nearly fifty interested inquiries from half a dozen countries, checked out the new photo on Bengaliweddings.com. She feared having to go through with the Bangalore alternative. When Peter first proposed it, Bangalore had seemed the answer to all her fears and all her anger. Bangalore was a great game, a way of profitably using her English, avenging Sonali, and becoming independent, while picking and choosing among thousands of boys with good English and the same ambition.

But that was an innocent Anjali and a different Peter. That was before she got swept up in the marriage current and before her vanity was engaged. The Bangalore commitment meant packing a bag and sneaking out and admitting she wasn't desirable enough to overcome the stigma of coming from nowhere, and her parents' poverty. Her parents could live with another failed marriage. They could tolerate her misery so long as they felt they'd done their duty. But they would not survive the shame of a second daughter's act of defiance and insubordination.

4

She wanted to—no, she *needed* to talk to Peter about the photograph of Ali that Rabi Chatterjee had shown her. But she didn't dare; so one day Shaky Sengupta's bridal portrait in hand, faking jauntiness, she showed up—as she now thought of it—at Peter and Ali's. This was a forbidden visit, according to her father's newest rules, but at least she was in a sari. She presented Shaky's marriage portrait and waited for the response. "Well . . . would you marry this girl?" she asked.

Peter frowned and then passed it on to Ali.

He checked it twice and gave it back.

"Who is she?" Ali asked in Hindi.

Peter said, "I think this picture is a monstrosity. So what kind of monster is it supposed to attract?"

He'd approved of everything she'd ever done. She was the model by which he judged all his students. She could only answer, "It was my mother's idea."

Peter stiffened. "Your mother, God help us. You're not a little girl anymore, Angie. If you get married—and I don't care how good he looks or what his prospects are—if you get married based on a picture like this, you'll get exactly the treatment you deserve."

She smiled, putting on that big halogen beam that always came to her rescue. "I met Rabi Chatterjee. He showed me pictures he'd taken of you. And Ali."

Peter frowned and looked away. He nodded at the mention of the photos but said nothing. No one was the person she thought she knew.

"Rabi Chatterjee is a serious young man. He has an indestructible ego—that's a good thing. I had one too. It means he's got the inner strength to stand up to convention. And he brings you along, into his wildest plans. He could be going to any college he wanted, so what is he doing? Walking to villages and taking buses and third-class trains. He reminds me of a younger me. He said, 'You can't take pictures of India through a limousine window.' His father happens to be Bish Chatterjee, and Bish Chatterjee happens to be the richest Bengali in the world, one of the ten richest overall—I mentioned him in B. Comm. Honors, but I never expected his son would be sitting in my rooms taking my picture—he speeded up the way computer networks communicate. The world is small, but Gauripur is huge: remember that. Every cell phone uses CHATTY technology. Some day that boy who took your picture will be even richer. And I don't imagine he told you any of that."

"He said his father owns a telephone company, and his mother writes books about India for American ladies." Why would he lie to her? Sleeping in buses and servants' hotels was the least impressive thing she could imagine. She didn't understand this American behavior. Impressive people looked and acted prosperous and confident, or else what's the use? "Maybe he's looking for a wife?"

"I'd be *very* surprised. But we talked about you. He said you have a quality."

"And what did you say to that?"

"I told him there was a struggle going on for your soul. He said he took a picture of that." She started to smile, but he was serious. "If you get married here, you'll be lost to me."

"If I get married, you won't lose money sending me to Bangalore," she said.

"It's never about money. You'd be surprised how many women in Gauripur were girls I once taught. Girls with good grades and good minds, with curiosity about life outside of this town. Ambitious girls, not just daydreamers. And we talked then just as you and I are talking now, and that was before India took off, before there were real opportunities in this country and you didn't have to fill your head with nonsense dreams of England or America. And I see those women in Gauripur today, in the market with their husbands and children, and when we cross paths, they bow their head, afraid I'll call them by name. They never left; they never got a proper education. These are girls who wanted to be doctors and teachers, not flight attendants. Their fathers pulled them out of school as soon as they got their high school certificates and had them married off within the month." Peter changed to a mocking, local Hindi: "What if I end up with an unmarriageable daughter, what if she becomes too smart for any local boy? What if some eligible boy will say 'Don't you think I can support her? You think I am sending my wife off to work?'" And then in English: "The money isn't my investment *in* you. My investment *is* you, Anjali Bose."

After a pause, he added, "I don't even blame the fathers or the mothers or the girls or their husbands. We talked about all of this in class. Companies fail when they keep making the same product in the same way, even when the customer base is changing. Well, the base—that's India today—is changing and the old ways are dead ways. This marriage portrait is a wasted effort. Hoping there's someone out there who'll answer your dreams in an ad, that's death. I don't want to lecture you because I don't think you, above all, need it. Don't prove me wrong."

But he *was* lecturing her. He wasn't *talking* to her as he did to students in the classroom. He was telling her in the plainest terms that both the bride-to-be-Anjali of the studio portrait and the gutsy-rebel-Angie who had ridden on the back seat of his scooter were frauds. He had become a dangerous mentor, sowing longings and at the same time planting self-doubt.

"Carpe diem," he said, almost to himself.

"Carpey what?" What did carp have to do with her situation?

"I can't make you take the big step. All I can do is cushion the footfall." He took a couple of deep, wheezy breaths, and asked Ali to please bring him a glass of water. Ali delivered the water on a tarnished silver tray, and with it, a small pill. Peter Champion gulped them both down before tearing two sheets off a notebook he carried in his kurta pocket.

Malaria pill? Aspirin because she'd given him a major headache? Hypertension? Cholesterol? Was he dying? Feeling a new urgency, she watched him scribble a name and address on each of the two sheets.

"Minnie Bagehot will put you up in Bangalore if I ask her to." He handed both sheets to her. "And Usha Desai can help you work on your job skills. I'm cashing in these chips because I want to be proved right. About you."

So, if she married, she'd be lost to Peter. If she didn't marry, she'd be dead to her father. How very odd it was, taking tea in her teacher's room, as she had on so many occasions over the years, and now watching Peter and Ali from the corner of her eye, the way Rabi's picture had captured them: Peter up close, Ali in the background, then Peter walking over and placing his hand on Ali's bare shoulder and whispering something, which caused Ali to smile. *He's treating me like an adult,* she thought. *He's forcing adulthood on me. This is what the adult world is like; this is how adults interact. I'm seeing it, but I shouldn't react to it in any way. It seems odd, but also familiar. Was that a little kiss on his ear? I've passed through an invisible wall and I can't go back. Maybe I'm a ghost.*

And for the first time, she was able to articulate it, at least to herself: *Maybe I'm not here. Maybe I'm not seeing any of this. Maybe "Anjali" is seeing it. "Angie" is somewhere else.* Splitting herself in two was a comfort.

• • •

Angie was crushed that Peter hated the picture, but Anjali was drifting above it with a smile, trying to show her the way. As she walked the familiar path home, LBS Road past Vasco da Gama High School and College and Pinky Mahal to MG Road, along the fence of Jawaharlal Nehru Park, she noticed a light on in the Vasco Common Room.

The college was officially not in session. It was mid-June. School was closed until the monsoon broke and cooled things off, ending the days of crippling heat and the nightly reign of mosquitoes. But the peak hour had passed. It was the quiet time when windows were shut and everyone tried to sleep before bathing—if there was water—and then went out to shop for the evening meal. Once the rains started, the fruits and vegetables would begin to rot, and the open markets would close.

In the Common Room someone had pulled the shades: premature darkness in the late afternoon of an Indian summer day. Without turning on a light, Anjali made her way to the computer room and stood at the door. From deep inside she heard the clacking of computer keys. As her eyes adjusted, she could make out a single illuminated monitor and a shape in front of it, the bulky form and reflective glasses of that harmless neighborhood boy, the computer genius Nirmal Gupta.

Her mother would have called it auspicious. She had her photo. She was alone with Nirmal. And Peter Champion had just crushed Angie's confidence. But Anjali had plans.

Sure-Bet-IIT Gupta had the keys to the Common Room; he ran the computer center, all six units. He was one of the few boys in the college she could talk to, largely because she didn't consider him an eligible bridegroom candidate. And it was easy to guess what might have brought a lonely, computer-savvy boy to the computer room on a dormant campus: the marriage sites, and the hundreds of photos of hopeful girls just like her.

"Don't mind me," she said. "I saw a light."

But he did mind. He'd practically tipped over the computer, trying to hide the pictures of eligible girls. She'd wanted to say, "That's all right. Bengaliweddings.com?" But she asked, "See anyone interesting?"

"The screen . . ." He started babbling; the screen was already blank. He tried to excuse himself. Someone else, some other Bengali, must have been using it.

"I didn't know you were looking for someone," she said. "I thought you were going off to an IIT."

He looked up at her with big moist eyes, like a beaten dog.

"Please, big sister, don't tell anyone. I did not receive admittance," he said.

What else could a bright boy in science do but go to a technical college? "It's all crooked," she said, repeating what she'd heard from her father and others. But she had a favor to ask, and if a bit of sympathy helped, what did it cost her? And so she asked, "Where will you be next year?"—a bold question, but he'd been straightforward himself.

"I have no prospects," he said.

"You'll find something, I'm sure. You're the best science student. Maybe not IIT, but there are so many others." Actually, she couldn't name any.

He thanked her. She smiled and asked, "Would you do me a favor?"

"Of course," he answered, a mite too quickly. "Anything you ask."

That's when she suspected he had special feelings for her, not that she could have predicted how far he would take it. It might have been love, but at the time it was merely a chit she could cash in. "If I gave you a new photo, could you take the old one off and put this one on the Internet?"

"What kind of photo?"

She showed him Shaky's portrait, the plump and dimpled Anjali at an alpine resort. "Can you put it on Bengaliweddings.com?"

All he said was "If you want me to." He took the picture, remarking only that "The portrait is very beautiful, is it of you?" And when she admitted that it was, just maybe a little deceptive, he said, "No, no. No deception. It does you justice," and within a day it was plastered across five continents.

As often happens to those who dither, waiting for that moment when all doubt and indecision would be suddenly resolved, that moment arrived in an unexpected way. The English-language ads had marginally improved the candidate pool; so had the original posting on the Internet. Fifty candidates had been rejected.

More to the point, Anjali had begun to educate herself in the secret ways of the heart. After the new Internet posting, she began receiving flattering inquiries from desirable countries on every continent. There were intriguing dimensions beyond her experience, and the movies she'd watched, and they were all open to her. There were men like Peter, without his complications. There were boys like Rabi and his hijras and prostitutes and gay bars. If she could hold out for a few more months, and if she could learn to value herself above what her untraditional looks and humble economic standing warranted, she might win the marriage lottery. In those months, while conforming to the predictable behavior of a bridal candidate and submitting to all the indignities of daughterhood, she clung to an indefensible belief in her own exceptionality.

THE FINAL EVENT followed the posting of her picture. Two weeks after Nirmal Gupta had put her formal portrait on the web, he'd gone to his bedroom with her picture and drunk a canister of bug spray. He began writing a long declaration of his lifelong devotion to a goddess he'd been too shy to approach, but he'd started the letter after drinking the spray and wasn't able to finish it.

The Gupta parents set their son's framed photo on an altar surrounded by flowers and brass deities. "He was always going to those cinema halls," his mother cried. "He was in love with a screen goddess."

They didn't recognize the portrait as Anjali's.

"The boy lost perspective," his father said. "These boys today, what to say, what to do?"

Buzley, buzlum. Anjali wondered, *Did he even tell his parents he'd failed his entrance exams to an IIT?*

SHE TOLD HERSELF, *I owe it to poor Nirmal Gupta. I owe it to Baba and Sonali. I'll give them one last chance.* She agreed to meet the next acceptable boy: number seventy-five. He turned out to be Subodh Mitra, the first boy to be brought to the house for inspection. His letter alluded to a distant connection to Angie's mother's sister-in-law in Asansol, a grimy steel-making center on the western edge of Bengal. "Yes, I remember the Mitras," her mother exclaimed. "Very respectable. Very well connected!" He was twenty-four years old, tall enough for a girl like Angie, clean-shaven and handsome enough to charm mothers and turn any girl's head. He held an undistinguished engineering degree from a prestigious school, but, according to his posted résumé, he had also earned a First-Class MBA degree from a business college in Kolkata. He'd worked a year in Bangalore at a call center ("customer-support agent," it read), but now he'd returned from the South, ready to marry and settle down. With family power behind him and connections in government, he would never be unemployed. If everything checked out, he would be a catch.

Even Angie could not manufacture serious objections. She'd exhausted every possible reason, both objective and whimsical, for rejecting a boy. Probably her most heartfelt one, in the case of Mr. Mitra, could not even be voiced in the family: she simply could not imagine carrying on civilized discourse with anyone from Asansol. But in the Bose family—just look at her parents—failure to engage in civilized discourse was not grounds for marital disbarment. She remembered Asansol quite well. When the train passed through it, she'd had to secure the coach windows against the coke ovens' soot and sulfur fumes, but the toxic stench still drifted through. Men would breathe through moistened handkerchiefs; women pulled their saris across their nose. Asansol was a place even Gauripur could look down on. Subodh Mitra's place of origin was his only prominent demerit.

Her father tried to read between the lines of Subodh Mitra's CV. "The boy did engineering to please his father, but his heart wasn't in it. When he got a chance to study business, he shone like the sun!"

Anjali had never heard of his Kolkata business school. Probably hundreds of "business schools" and "colleges" were run out of the back rooms of hot little apartments, all advertising First-Class MBA degrees the equivalent of those from Delhi, LSE, and Wharton. She was tempted to argue but kept her silence.

"This is a golden boy." Her father persisted. "His parents are very reasonable. They want this marriage as much as we do. I have counter-offered more than they asked."

Subodh Mitra, the intended, the all-but-fiancé, arrived from Asansol in a red Suzuki, an eight-hour drive on the clogged, narrow national highway, in the first week of the monsoon rains. A red Suzuki! Mr. Bose still negotiated the streets of Gauripur by scooter, just as he had in college—another humiliation for which Anjali and her mother and sister were somehow to blame.

The young man swept into their apartment, bearing flowers and sweets. The photo hadn't lied: he was tall, athletic, and handsome, with real dimples. He was attentive to both parents and showed the proper deference to Mr. Bose. He barely looked at Anjali, fulfilling the etiquette demands of the marriage market.

"Oh, and this must be your daughter, the lovely Anjali. I was enjoying our conversation so much, I nearly forgot . . ." Anjali then allowed herself to be pushed into the conversation.

He complimented her on her white cotton dhoni-khali sari, with its yellow and green stripes: "A very nice selection for the occasion." He went on. "I must compliment the feminine sensibility of the Bose household. Unexpectedly simple, not a showy tangail or fussy kanjeevaram."

She was impressed; a man who knows his sari styles is refined indeed.

He must have been through many such interviews, Angie thought. She had worn her lone kanjeevaram for the day in Shaky's studio. She would wear a red brocaded Benarasi for the actual wedding.

"Anjali is very artistic," said Mr. Bose.

"I can see that. Taste is a rare quality these days. Taste in such matters speaks well of her parents' example."

"Our daughter has graduated from Vasco da Gama, with honors . . ."

The "boy" had to feign surprise and interest, as if he hadn't known all along, and Anjali had to deny, modestly, any great intelligence or motivation. He declared himself passionately devoted to his parents in Asansol, but his ambition was to move to Kolkata and convince his parents to settle nearby. Even Gauripur was preferable to Asansol, Subodh readily admitted. He spoke in elegant Sanskritized Bangla, the pinnacle of decorum. "Mr. Bose, I am myself looking for a post in international communications, hopefully in Kolkata, but failing that, I look with favor on Lucknow or Allahabad."

Lucknow? Angie thought, with horror. *Allahabad?* What modern girl would chain herself to a dreary place like that?

Her parents were impressed by his chaste, mellifluous Bangla, with no infiltration of Hindi, and they strained to meet its standard. This offered Angie the perfect out. She stumbled so badly in the language, half deliberately, that the unruffled, indulgent Subodh continually asked her to please repeat her questions. Then the young couple were allowed an afternoon alone to get to know each other, with the unstated assumption that to know Anjali, despite shortcomings, was to fall madly in love with her.

Once out of parental range, as he drove down LBS Road past the major intersection of MG Road and Pinky Mahal, past the cheap hotels, where Rabi must have stayed, and the Vasco campus and the apartment block where Peter and Ali lived—a light was on in their window—he finally burst out in English, "What a strain! But that was a very good show you put on back there. Very convincing. Very funny, actually." It was his first lapse from his flowery Bangla. His English was no match for hers.

She'd expected that he would park the car and they would stroll down MG Road to Alps Palace or maybe to the hotel restaurant. She wondered if she should take his arm. She wouldn't mind being seen in public with him. She would tell him Allahabad—no way! She didn't know what young people in the early stage of prenuptial negotiation were supposed to talk about. The photo sessions and letters, the gold and sari shopping, the piles of rejected suitors, had happened in a vacuum. But he acted confident and she was good at picking up cues, and anyway, it was happening to an imaginary girl named Anjali while the real person, Angie, could sit back and watch. Hobbies? Thank God for her minimal talent with the harmonium. Favorite foods? How should she pose—sophisticated and international, pizza perhaps—or sweetly, coyly desi, just an unassuming Bengali girl raised on fish curry and rice?

Subodh had no intention of walking or of stopping for coffee and ice cream. They were out of Gauripur in just a few minutes, across the main highway to Patna, five hours to the west, into the monsoon-lush countryside. It was a sunny afternoon between bouts of rain. Rabi had been out here too, on a bus; she recognized scenes from his photos: the now-glistening, once-dusty vegetation, the red soil, the woven patterns of the thatched roofs, the returning long-legged wading birds in the now-flooded fields, the bright saris of women walking along the side of the road. India was beautiful. The countryside was peaceful.

And she felt comfortable, secure, in Subodh's company. This is how she'd imagined it, driving through the countryside in a red car with a handsome, confident husband. It could work. She felt certain that her mother and her sister had never known such a moment. Mr. Mitra's English might impress in Asansol, or Bangalore, and especially in her parents' house, but she held the upper hand.

"A very good show? What are you implying, Mr. Mitra?"

"You are a total fraud. No one with the name of Anjali Bose could possibly speak Bangla as poorly as you!"

"And is this customary praise for all your lady friends, Mr. Mitra?"

"I am an honest man. I speak my mind. I take what's mine."

At least he didn't deny having lady friends.

"Honesty is a poor substitute for decent manners, Mr. Mitra. My honesty makes me ask what in the hell is Lucknow all about? What modern girl is going to settle in Lucknow or Allahabad?"

"My uncle in Lucknow is Civil Judge, Junior Division. In Allahabad my oldest uncle is manager of the State Bank of India." A few minutes later, he added, "For your information, I have no intention of going to either place."

"I have no interest in Kolkata," she said.

"Good for you. Kolkata is dead and buried. And you'd have to learn the language."

To which, of course, she smiled broadly. She decided he was not really a bad catch. A different Angie might have looked him over and said "He's honest, he's funny, he's certainly handsome, he's shrewd. I could do worse." In English she could be as saucy and seductive as any Bollywood heroine. She turned on him with that smile and asked, ever so sweetly, "So all that business about settling your parents in Kolkata was what . . . a lie?" Not that it mattered. A certain amount of mutual inflation was built into the marriage negotiation. She was not above the deployment of subterfuge on nearly any level.

"You've got a big mouth, you know," he said.

He turned off the highway. A muddy trail led through a partially cleared forest to a construction site. The place was desolate. Workers' huts lay strewn about, but the various buildings seemed abandoned. Concrete had been poured for the shell of an apartment block, abandoned because of the monsoons or a sudden withdrawal of funding. Rusted iron rods protruded from the stark slabs. Anjali remembered the word: *rebars.* He stopped the car in a dark grove. This place too was familiar. Rabi had been here; she'd seen the picture. Black and white, to bring out the shadows, he'd said. He'd made it seem a dark and brooding place, ghostly in its abandonment. She opened the car door, prepared to get out and inspect it more closely, to enter the picture, as it were.

"We won't be bothered here," he said.

She turned and asked, "How do you know?"

"I drove in this morning." He'd reverted to Bengali, a language that robbed her of power and nuance. "I had time to find a place."

"A place for what?"

He snorted. "Our marital negotiations."

"What sort of negotiations would that be, Mr. Mitra?"

"Get back inside and close the door," he ordered. "What do you think? You're going to be my wife."

He put his hands over her breasts on the bright green choli under the dhoni-kali sari. "Everyone knows the kind of girl you are."

"Take me home, immediately," she cried.

He smiled that dimpled smile, then laughed. His fingers pulled the end of her sari down. "I don't want to rip your fancy cotton choli," he said. "Unhook it now." She refused, and he popped open the row of hooks, exposing her bra. It was her push-up bra, forced on her for this occasion by her mother. She pulled the loose end of her sari over it. He slapped her hand down and kept it there, on her lap.

"I am within my rights to see what I'm getting," he said. "Just like your American."

Rabi? she thought. *I have done nothing with any American—or any Indian, for that matter.* This couldn't be happening, not while she was wearing her tasteful sari. Isn't that how he had described her sari in the living room? In a Bollywood movie a savior would arise, the ghost of Nirmal Gupta perhaps, whom she'd laughed at with his goo-goo eyes every time they passed on the street. Just like the movies: the good, faithful, passed-over boy comes to the rescue of the virtuous but slightly too proud and headstrong girl, who allows herself to be compromised, but not fatally. Maybe this was her punishment for not taking Nirmal Gupta seriously enough, for underestimating that little letter he'd tried to write before the poison took over. She would say a prayer, *"Ram, Ram,"* and Ram in one of his many forms would rescue her. She turned away and stared briefly at the dead slabs of concrete, but Subodh Mitra's hand on her chin pulled her back, hard.

"Look at me when I'm talking!" he commanded. "I asked around. I know about you and your so-called professor."

"You're crazy. Take me home immediately, Mr. Mitra."

"I did my research. We still have ninety minutes, and we've got some negotiating to do first."

"Don't even think—"

She started to speak, but with a flick of his hand, he slapped her. Not hard, but not an idle tap, either. He unhooked the bra and assessed her breasts. She tried again to cover herself, but he pulled her arms down. "Not much there," he said.

She began to cry, but tears wouldn't come. She knew his hands were on her breasts, pulling hard, then weighing them, like small guavas, and she thought of all the girls she'd envied, the mango-breasted, the melon-breasted, and suddenly the stench of decaying mango penetrated the closed windows, and she could see the husks of fallen mangoes all about the abandoned huts and around the car.

A voice that seemed to issue from deep in the forest commanded, "Do me!" and when she came back to her senses, there was Mr. Mitra with his trousers unzipped, and a pale, tapered thing standing up like a candle in his hand, a thing she knew of but had never seen, a long, tan, vaguely reptilian creature with a tiny mouth where its head should be. In her panic she felt a brief wave of compassion for him; this couldn't be the real Mr. Mitra, but the result of some unfortunate invasion; he'd been possessed by a demon—but before she could study it further, Mr. Mitra's spare hand brought her head crashing down upon it, and she could hear him command, "Open that big mouth of yours . . ." He pulled her head up when she gagged, then down by the hair, pumping her head until she was able to do it herself, and his voice died out into a hum and she had to catch her breath, had to find a way to stop the gagging and the roaring in her ears. When his hand loosened from the back of her head, she was able to roll off and to see what she had done, the mess that was spewing over his pants and her sari, and he grabbed a handful of her sari to wipe himself and the steering wheel, even the window, cursing her all the time for leaving him at just the instant, humiliating him in such a way, ruining his suit, his borrowed car, even her sari. "You bitch, you bitch," he said, along with Bangla words she didn't know.

She stared down at the bra and sari pooled in her lap and tried to cover her breasts. She asked, almost in a whisper, as though to ask was to plant the notion, "Are you going to kill me?" He was still using the ends of her sari to clean himself. She remembered a hugely advertised Hindi movie from years back, *Jism,* and when she'd asked some boys in class what the word meant—she, the top girl in English, and they the simpleton sons of clerks and shopkeepers—they said they'd be happy to demonstrate.

"Don't be stupid. I'm going to marry you," he said. "Your father almost begged me."

If there had been any way of cleaning her mouth, she would have done it. If she'd had a can of bug spray, she would have swallowed it. When she conjured the image of what she'd done, all she could do was vomit, and she did so in her lap.

"Now," he said. "You know what you have to do." Wordlessly, looking through the steamed-up window at the twisted metal spikes, he pulled her panties down.

BACK AT THE house she had to run from the car, through the parlor, directly to the bathroom.

She could hear Subodh in the front room. "It must have been something we ate at the coffee shop. It came over her suddenly."

Her father said, "Please don't worry. She is a healthy girl. We're not hiding any medical history."

Her mother added quickly, "On both sides of the family, extreme good health. No sick leave, ever. As for Anjali, except for the usual jaundice, measles, and typhoid, she is in the pink of health."

Anjali returned, in T-shirt and jeans, her gesture of defiance, but she kept her head bowed. She wouldn't look at the monster or at her parents. She would not collaborate.

Mr. and Mrs. Bose begged him to stay for dinner. Even in remote Bihar, where the big river carp were harder to come by, Bengalis knew how to cook the traditional fish curry. Mrs. Bose had gone to the Bengali market especially for fat, fresh rui, and Mr. Bose had ranged beyond the usual sweet shops featuring ersatz rasmalai for something authentically Bengali.

Still looking down at her lap, Anjali said, "Mr. Mitra said he has to get back to Asansol tonight. Eight hours—he should be making his move."

"Your daughter is correct, as usual," he said. "I should be going. You'll be hearing from my father, I'm sure."

Anjali's parents didn't know how to interpret her interjection. Was it tender concern for the boy's feelings? A desire to get rid of him? She admitted to more stomach distress and a need to sleep in the dark in the back room, and left the parting formalities to her parents.

5

From the back room she could overhear the front-room language of marital negotiation: "Of course, it is all subject to your father's approval . . . But you and she got along beautifully, anyone can see that . . ." And her mother breaking in: "Poor girl, you got her so excited she can't keep her food down . . ." And the laughter, between her father and Subodh—whose very voice brought out murderous thoughts—joking over dowry claims: "My father's a really sharp businessman, so don't let him demand too much. I want this marriage to go through smoothly," met with laughter. "We do too!" her father said. He suggested that maybe a Japanese watch and a computer would close the deal. "Yeah, maybe he'll go for the gold watch—Swiss, not Japanese—a set of matched golf clubs and an American computer and an imported laptop for me—a PC, Toshiba or Dell—and a selection of games and movies," and her father laughed. "We'll have to see about that."

Lying in the dark after Subodh had left, staring at the slowly revolving ceiling fan, timing her inhale and exhale to the *thumpa-thumpa* of its wobbling orbit around the oily, dust-webbed post, she remembered the echoes of an earlier melodrama. *"I will call*— thumpa—*astrologer. I will call*— thumpa—*printer. I will write*— thumpa—*boy's father."* And in this room five years earlier, behind this door, in this very bed, she remembered Sonali's screaming, "Just give me the knife!" until she'd submitted, then apologized.

Her mother slept in the same room, on the same bed. Anjali, eyes closed, feigning sleep or exhaustion, waited for an opportunity to break the silence. She would have spilled the beans on Mr. Mitra, but her mother had simply collapsed on her bed and fallen asleep. Apparently, there was nothing of interest to discuss, not even a giddy welcome to the world of soon-to-be-married women—no "Hello, Mrs. Mitra! He's so handsome! You'll be so happy!" In the front room, just minutes after closing the door on Mr. Mitra and wishing him (if she heard correctly) "Godspeed" back to Asansol, her father dropped his trousers and began rattling the shutters with his snores. Just as though the world had not stopped.

She had expected to be assaulted by dreams. Alone in the bedroom, she'd been afraid to close her eyes until her mother came to bed, but when the rustling of the dress-sari and sleeping-sari was over, and the snoring began, she opened her eyes again. In her childhood, she'd felt the presence of ghosts. She'd often felt their weight on her bed. She and Sonali, lying side by side, had imagined ghostly faces beyond the lone high, unopened bedroom window. They'd filled the long nights with made-up names and the reasons for their reappearance. Any deceased relative could pop up unexpectedly. Family ghosts were always on a mission of vengeance. Their grievances—and she knew all of them, all the stories of rivalry and cheating, the bitterness and unkept promises, the favoritism, the thievery, the poverty, all the infidelities, the dead babies, the deserted wives, the cruel mothers-in-law—could transcend a single lifetime. Fifty years was too brief to avenge all of the indignities of a lifetime. They had to keep coming back. That was her father's excuse: his fate was cursed. A fortuneteller had once warned him he had a jealous uncle, long-long dead, who had blocked every male Bose's path to wealth and happiness. That was her mother's excuse: I must have the same name as a distant auntie; I must be paying for her misdeeds.

And now she knew the old stories were true. There were monsters, and innocent children were their victims, and no one, especially not her parents, could save her from them.

She slipped off the bed and walked through the house, staring down at her parents in their oblivious helplessness. She wandered like a ghost. She dropped her stained sari in a corner of the bathroom. Let her mother discover the traces of her glorious jamai. Nothing had changed in her house, but the world was different. She took Sonali's old red Samsonite from the cupboard and threw her two best saris and all her T-shirts and jeans into it. She stuffed her backpack with underwear and toiletries. She could have turned on the lights, banged shut the lid of the suitcase, dragged it across the stone floor, and neither of her snoring, dreaming parents would have noticed.

She took out her old Vasco da Gama exercise book, flipped through the dozens of pages of perfect schoolgirl handwriting, the meticulous notes she'd taken—*all useless, useless!*—and tore out two clean pages. On her last day in Gauripur, she went to the little table on the cramped balcony where she'd always done her assignments and read her books, and began writing. By the wan streetlight she composed a note and left it in her mother's "just in case" lentils jar.

Dearest Ma and Baba:

I will not marry any boy selected by anyone but myself, especially not this one. If this leads to a barren life, so be it. As you should plainly see, the boy you selected has dishonored me. He should be sent straightway to jail.

I am leaving this morning for Patna to see my sister, whose name you are reluctant to utter.

When I am settled again, I will write. The process may take many months. I am ready to take my place in the world. I beg you not to try to find me.

Your loving daughter, A.

She was Anjali. She could look down and see poor little Angie whimpering on her bed.

The dark alleys of Gauripur by night were unknown to her. The night air was even warmer than the stillness of the bedroom, and filled with groans and coughs and sharp words and the occasional horn—but many sounds were simply unplaceable, maybe the wings of bats, maybe just the creaking of the earth resting from the day's abuse, the brushing of thick leaves against one another, the urgent business in the bushes of dogs and men, rats and mongooses, the endless grinding of a million small claws and the hot breezes against tree limbs and rocks and movie posters nailed to every lamppost, and she thought then, as she often did, that ghosts explained it all, just as the stars at night or the face on the moon had told stories to our ancestors. Men sleeping on the broken footpath, a cast of nighttime characters invisible by day, playing cards under the streetlamp and making animal noises, calling to her to come for a drink (the last thing they expected to see, a determined young lady pulling a noisy suitcase over the paving stones down the middle of the street). The distance between her house and Nehru Park had never seemed so vast, and the park never so dark and full of trees and tall grass, the town itself never so small, disheveled, and evil smelling.

It was five o'clock, an hour and a half before dawn, as she reckoned it. A few lights were already on, servants perhaps, starting their masters' day. Her mother would rise at dawn and perhaps not even notice the empty bed until she returned a few minutes later, with tea. Then she would see the sari. She would pick it up and hold it to her face, and she would sense what had happened. She would do all this before waking her husband. Maybe she'd even find the letter before waking him. Would she be screaming, or crying, or would she coldly accuse her husband—"You see what you've done? No jamais, and now no daughters!" What would her mother do, what would she say? Anjali couldn't predict.

She stood on the footpath outside Peter's apartment. Five-fifteen. Five-twenty. Along LBS Road, the early risers were on the march: clusters of young men laughing and jostling; a troop of haughty langurs after a night of garden plunder, their tails high and curled, sauntering back to the safety of Nehru Park and a day of mugging for photos and begging for ground nuts; older men in khaki uniforms, on bicycles, pulling carts of empty, rattling milk pails; bedraggled rag-and-paper pickers bent under enormous burlap bundles; and men lifting a corner of their dhoti or setting down a briefcase and unbuttoning their suit pants to relieve themselves against the public walls. Municipal workers dumped cartloads of trash along the gutters, swarmed by dogs and pigs and curious cows and a row of squawking crows perched atop the public walls: the predawn stretching and coughing and nostril clearing of a small Indian city.

In an hour—the hour at which she was normally awake to begin her school day—the roadways would be jammed with all manner of vehicles, the noise level so high she'd abandon all hope of conversation, the sun already high and hot. She, who'd aroused such unwelcome interest an hour earlier, was invisible to everyone now. At five-thirty the lights went on in Peter's apartment. She waited another five minutes; then, leaving her Samsonite on the bottom stair, she picked her way to the landing between new rows of terra-cotta flowerpots. She rapped twice on the blue door.

When Ali opened it, she greeted him with a smile and by name, not as a servant but as just another boy of nearly her own age. "I have to see Peter," she said. *Peter,* not *your master,* not *Mr. Champion.* He let her in and then went down the stairs to retrieve her bag.

Peter was standing by the two-burner gas stove, sipping his morning tea. He wore pajama bottoms, and a knotted shawl covered his chest. For just an instant he stared, and she wanted to say "It's me, Angie. I know it's early, I know this is shocking," but he refocused his eyes and smiled. He took a step toward her, arms out, and she took a step forward, then another, and found herself in his arms—he, who'd barely ever touched her, had never even shaken her hand.

Ali came back with the red suitcase. For a moment he seemed confused, then scampered to the almirah and took out an ironed shirt. He lifted Peter's shawl, folded it, then helped Peter into the shirt. He buttoned it. The action was, to Anjali, tender, even erotic. Ali's fingernails were long and red. Then he took down a mug and poured tea for her.

"Ginger cookie?" Peter asked, and Ali lifted a cloth off a platter. "Please," he said. "Things must have taken a bad turn."

"Very bad," she said. "I should have seen it coming."

"As I remember your last visit, we didn't part on the best of terms. There was that question of a marriage portrait. After you left, I thought to write you an apology—"

"I was so confused. I went straightway to the college and asked poor Nirmal Gupta to post that portrait on the biggest wedding site he could find. You said that picture would only cause trouble, but I thought that it would change everything. And just look what it did. I still don't know anything except that I was vain, and I caused that boy's death, and for a while, I thought maybe mine too. The boy my parents want me to marry attacked me. I had to leave."

Peter signaled to Ali and pointed to the almirah. Ali came back with a round cookie tin. Inside were stapled stacks of hundred-rupee notes. He began counting them; each stack a hundred notes, ten thousand rupees. Twenty, thirty, forty, fifty thousand rupees, half a lakh, more money than she'd ever seen, ever handled.

"This may seem like a lot of money," Peter said, "and for a girl in Gauripur, it may be. But you can make this in a couple of months in Bangalore." He slipped the entire tin into her backpack.

"You have the two names and addresses I gave you?"

"Yes," she said. She pointed to the Samsonite. "Everything I have is in that." She sipped her tea and nibbled on a proffered ginger cookie. "Two saris, two salwar-kameezes, three pairs of jeans, and my T-shirts." She patted the closing flap of her backpack. "And addresses of your two friends in Bangalore."

"Don't lose those addresses, Angie. I'll write them so they expect you.

And guard the money just short of your life. The train to Bangalore leaves at nine o' clock. Ali will walk you to the station."

"I didn't reserve," she said. "How could I reserve a train ticket with my father sitting in the railway office? He would have heard of it." She had imagined his furor over and over again: *"Bose-babu, quick, quick! Daughter is buying one-way ticket to Bangalore!"*

"Anyway, I thought there'd be a wedding."

"Or you counted on a magic solution?"

"I want to go to Patna and visit my sister there. Then she can buy a train ticket for me."

"Then the intercity bus is your only option." Peter seemed to be contemplating a gargantuan task. "Lord," he sighed. "I did it thirty years ago. We had to close the windows against dacoits and tribals with bows and arrows. The price you pay for procrastinating."

She recognized the word but had never used it.

"Putting things off—you've got to work on that."

"I will."

"When? Tomorrow?" But he asked the questions with a smile, gathered up the remaining cookies in the cloth, and knotted the ends. "Who knows when you'll get to eat next?"

"Thank you for the ginger biscuits," she murmured to Ali.

Ali went to the pantry and came back with a bottle of water and two bruised apples. In elaborate Urdu she could barely follow, he asked Peter for directions to the bus station. Peter instructed Ali to take enough money with him to buy the bus ticket to Patna for her, so she wouldn't have to take out her cookie tin in the crowded station.

IN HER PERSONAL dire-straits scenario, she'd always planned on escaping to Bangalore by train. She'd never anticipated taking the intercity bus. Buses were for laborers and farmers, the very poor. Intrastate buses ran every few hours, daily, west to Patna. From Patna, she could continue to Varanasi and Allahabad. Given the elasticity of space on the roof and floor, there was always room for last-minute boarders to squeeze in. People who ride by bus are humble, she'd been told, and respectful to their economic betters. Space could always be cleared for a young college girl in a T-shirt and jeans.

But going all the way across India by local buses—anything beyond Varanasi—was like voluntarily entering a black hole, especially the black hole of central India called Madhya Pradesh, with its jungles and tribals, and hoping to come out the other end somehow intact. A distant relative of her mother's, the family's lone adventurer, had once made it all the way to Jabalpur, the equivalent of the place where ancient mariners assumed they would fall off the edge of the world. Central Madhya Pradesh still had places where even the police were afraid to go. And Jabalpur was not even a third of the way to Bangalore.

On the four-hour trip to Patna, she could still smell the mud and the decayed mangoes, the taste and rubbery feel of something terrible in her mouth, the searing pain, and even more, the transformation of a handsome boy, dimples and all, into a monster. Walking out of her house as a confident, desirable bride-to-be in a flashy sari, in a red Suzuki, wondering, *Coffee or a sandwich?* And running back sick, her sari wet with blood and men's stuff she never knew about. Jism. On the bus, an old man who boarded late and could have sat anywhere took the aisle seat next to her and almost immediately put his hand over her breast, as though he owned it, as though it was something he'd bought along with his ticket and paan, even as the outskirts of Gauripur were passing by. He was looking straight ahead, and she stared at his unshaven white stubble, his dirty white kurta, and his jaws working mightily on his betel leaf. Then she stared down until he removed his hand. He got up and chose another seat.

SONALI'S TWO ROOMS were not far from the bus station. S. DAS, the buzzer panel read.

"I couldn't call, Sonali-di," Anjali apologized as soon as Sonali unlocked her front door. They spoke in Hindi, as was their custom. "It was all so sudden."

"Do they know you're here?" Sonali asked that with a smile. "Anyway, come in." She eased the knapsack off Anjali's shoulder and carried it indoors. "It isn't much, but we aren't complaining."

Sonali and her little girl slept in the back room, much in the way Anjali and her mother shared a bed in Gauripur. Sonali had gained ten kilos since the divorce. At twenty-four she looked more like a younger aunt than an older sister.

It wasn't late, barely past seven o'clock, but little Piyali was already asleep on the chowki in the bedroom, a bony leg nestling a bolster and an elbow shading her eyes from the ceiling light. In a way, Piyali was lucky. Her father had dropped out of her life. No visits, no checks, no harassments, no disappointments. Anjali reached out and stroked the child's hair.

In the tiny kitchen alcove, Sonali put the kettle on the gas stove and spread salty crackers on a chipped plate. "So, what now, Anjali?"

"I had to, didi," Anjali said, "I had to leave." Anjali longed to talk woman-to-woman, for the first time in her life. As Sonali slurped down tea, Anjali recounted the assault by Subodh Mitra. "He was so charming," she cried. "And they were going to marry me off to him." *The brute, the monster.* She thought—but couldn't say, of course—*it would have been just like your marriage, except that he showed his true nature even before the ceremony.* She expected sympathy and finally support from her sister, but something was holding Sonali back. *If I can't confide in Sonali-di, who's been through it all, whom can I talk to?* Sonali-di had to understand; she wouldn't tolerate Baba making the same mistake again.

"So I ran away, when they were asleep. What else could I do, Sonali-di? I *had* to."

"You want to know what you could have done? With your Vasco degree and your wonderful English? You could have made Ma and Baba happy and married him. And if it didn't work out, you'd still get a better job than me."

Marry him? My sister hates me!

Sonali opened the steel trunk that had once contained her dowry of saris, bedding, and kitchen utensils. It was nearly empty. Like their mother, she preferred neem leaves to mothballs. Sonali handed a small pillow to Anjali. It reeked more of mildew than neem. "You can stay the night," she said.

"Thank you," Anjali mumbled, shocked. "I intend to be gone in the morning." Not exactly her initial plan, but now her only choice.

"In fact I'm glad you stopped by," said Sonali. And before Anjali could smile, she added, "I have to go out a little later. I don't expect Piyali to wake up, but if she does, you'll be here."

"Go out where?" Anjali asked, but from the look on her sister's face, she knew.

"Just an hour. Maybe less, maybe more," she said.

"What are you doing, Sonali-di? Seeing a man, isn't it?"

"You think a secretary is just a secretary?" Sonali asked. "You're such a child still." She gave the pillow a whack with her palm before slipping a pillowcase over it. "Men are men, they're all the same. You don't have to lead them on, it's in their nature." Piyali whimpered in her sleep, and Sonali immediately lowered her voice. "Look at us," she muttered, "take a good look at Piyali and me, do you really think I'm better off being divorced? Do you have any idea what the word *divorced* means to any man? It means 'Take it, it's free.' Wouldn't I be better off married, no matter what?"

"You had no choice, Sonali-di! He practically moved those women into your flat!"

"What do you know? Nothing, you know nothing, and you come to my house and lecture me? This handsome Mr. Mitra of yours thought —no, he was positive—that he was Baba's choice of jamai. What he does to you *before* the wedding or *after,* does it matter that much? Does it matter enough to ruin other people's lives? Four lives, in my case. Baba's and Ma's, Piyali's and mine?"

And so the great divide was not just the thirty years that separated Anjali from her parents—that wasn't a divide, it was a chasm—but the five years between her and her sister. Five years ago, Sonali had capitulated to her parents' demands. Five years ago, it would have been impossible for Sonali to have resisted, and fled. A wife might conceivably leave her properly arranged husband and move back in with her parents, even divorce him for cruelty or drunkenness, but never for the laughable motive of personal happiness.

"But you sent me money, didi," Angie said. "You're the one who told me not to cripple myself." Every few months, Sonali had sent her small money orders and inland air-letters, care of an unmarried, club-footed girlfriend she had gone to Hindi medium school with.

"That was for clothes and whatnot," she said. "It wasn't meant to heap more shame on the family."

That night, lying with her niece on the chowki while her sister "stepped out," Anjali thought about how the world had gone mad. Sonali was jealous of her sister's still-open future, Anjali decided, because she could do what Sonali hadn't. In just a day, India had gone from something green and lush and beautiful to something barren and hideous. Her sister had deserted her, and her parents were prepared to marry her off to a monster whose father demanded a set of golf clubs.

THERE ARE WAYS of crossing India by overnight buses, short-haul trains, even by flagging down truck drivers, but very few that single young women would ever try. The discomfort, especially at night, as cold air and rain blasted through the open windows and men relieved themselves anywhere, then crawled about, feigning sleep in order to grope the sari-bundled women: intolerable. If she spoke to no one and answered no questions and requested no favors—posed, in fact, as a tourist on the model of an Indo-American like Rabi—she prayed no one would dare bother her.

At a crossroads village south of Nagpur in eastern Maharashtra, near the Andhra Pradesh border—really just a cluster of tea stalls and a petrol pump called Nizambagh—prostitutes and their children, and maybe just desperate women fleeing their villages for work in cities, swarmed the parked row of long-haul trucks. The women were lined up, holding their babies, and the drivers lifted their lungis and the women climbed onto the running boards and performed their services. It was not a view of India from behind a limousine window. Anjali walked like a ghost past the trucks; nothing shocked her, nothing disgusted her. She could see herself armed with a knife or a gun, walking down the row of trucks parked at night and executing every single driver and his helper. If hell and all the citizens of damnation had an Indian address, it was here. If she ever saw Rabi again, she'd have something to tell him. Had he been here? Had he caught this picture?

Somewhere down south in Bangalore, drawing closer every hour, a luxurious neighborhood called Kew Gardens and an old lady named Minnie Bagehot waited with a room for her, she prayed, and an Usha Desai to give her a job bigger than her father's.

On a hand-painted signboard, she saw the arrows: west for Mumbai and south for Hyderabad, which she knew to be in the direction of Bangalore. It was a crossroads for her as well, two possible fates, different buses. She went to the ladies' toilet, the very center of hell, the foulest few square inches in the universe, and changed into her last clean T-shirt, her favorite, Panzer Delight. She was nearer to Mumbai than Bangalore, just a day and a half away to the west, just the Ghats and a desert and a second range of mountains to cross, but no one could tell her when the Mumbai bus would arrive, and she couldn't bear the thought of another minute of the lingering stench. The Hyderabad bus was ready to leave. She couldn't wait; she couldn't stand to watch the women and children and the truck drivers with their insolent faces, and the knowledge that she was just a little luckier, but fundamentally no different.

The numb certitudes of her life: *I have no family. The only money in my pocket comes from a man whose world is alien to mine and whom I'll never see again. I have no job, no skills. School teaches little.*

It was noon in Hyderabad, a legendary city she never thought she'd visit. At least she had been dropped at its bus depot early in the morning and been able to sit on a bench for two hours and sip hot tea before heading to the line for the last bus, the final leg. "Bangaluru? Bangaluru?" she kept asking, having learned Bangalore's southern name, though she could not read the southern script. By following vague hand gestures and leaving her perch two hours before the scheduled departure, she'd managed to stand near the head of the line. At boarding time, however, passengers lugging heavy burlap sacks and taped-together cardboard boxes had rushed from behind and shoved her aside. But nonetheless she was now on the bus to Bangalore. Five hundred and sixty more kilometers to go. Two thousand kilometers behind her. Assuming no breakdowns, there'd be another hot day and a cold all-nighter on the bus. Bangalore by morning.

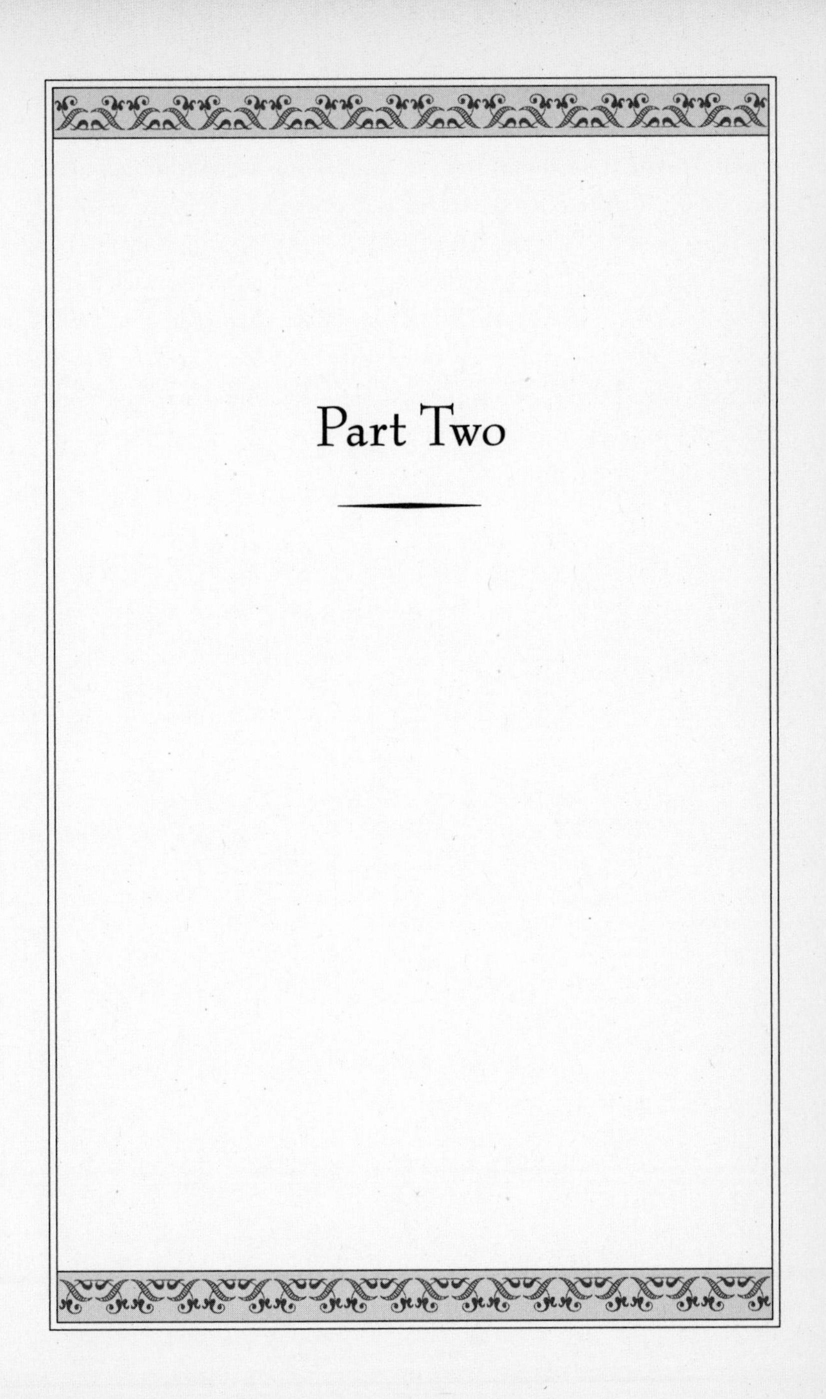

Part Two

1

A dozen times in the night, the bus from Hyderabad passed through cities many times the size of Gauripur, and Angie thought, *This must be Bangalore.* Six million, seven million, Peter had said, sixty, seventy lakhs, how could she imagine such numbers? But the bus would merely stop under a streetlamp to let off or take on a passenger or two, then ease back into the black of the night. She couldn't read the strange scripts of southern languages, and they seemed impossible to speak, all thudding consonants linked with breathless spurts. She, so proud of her Hindi and English and even, if pushed, her Bangla, had been struck deaf and dumb.

Gradually the stops grew more frequent, the towns more closely connected, and the streets busier, even in the dark. Then, a few minutes after sunrise, they joined a long line of buses and pulled into Majestic, the open-air, bowl-shaped Bangalore bus depot.

She hadn't expected to start her new life half-frozen, exhausted, and starving. On the crowded intercity buses, she'd fought sleep all night, every night, guarding her precious cookie tin, which she held with both hands on her numbed lap. All she'd eaten during the week since leaving Patna were greasy samosas and scalding tea, which hawkers passed through the bus windows. Most passengers had either brought home-cooked food in tiffin carriers or gotten off the bus for hearty meals at roadside stalls. The spicy smells had tormented Angie, but she hadn't dared leave her suitcase unprotected in the luggage rack. The hard-sided Samsonite was too heavy to carry on and off the bus for food breaks. Now, as passengers elbowed her aside to lift their baggage out of over-head racks and stepped on her painted toes in their scramble to get off, the arrival in Bangalore seemed like the beginning of another ordeal.

Even from the side of the bus, at seven in the morning, she could see building cranes swivel, scoop up giant vats of concrete and tons of bricks, and reach into the dawn-bright heavens. Mechanical cranes controlled by a single man, not the long lines of women and children tipping their small bowls of concrete. The roads around the depot were already clogged with traffic. This was energy, something palpable that she'd never experienced, and it left her frightened and indecisive. She'd never witnessed "progress" or placed herself in its path.

Angie was finally standing and stretching but she felt unrefreshed; the dull ache of an early morning sun after a cold, wakeful night, the throbbing diesel clouds off a metallic ocean of dented bus roofs, the hundreds of vendors and laborers shouldering their bags and boxes, all with a purpose and a destination, drained her confidence. Unlike Gauripur, Bangalore had built its fancy bus depot far from the city center. This was the first morning of her new life, but it felt like death. Barely seven in the morning, and even villagers were loading their burlap sacks of fruits and vegetables and heading up the roads feeding into the city. All she had was an address on a torn piece of paper: Bagehot House, Kew Gardens.

She'd assumed South India (when she'd considered it at all) to be at least as backward as Gauripur. But Gauripur, and Bihar state in general, were exceptions to the industrious, prosperous north. South Indians were smart in math but too frail and pious to show much initiative. She remembered her Indian literature class, taught by a Keralan priest, in which she'd tried to read a novel by a southern writer named Narayan, set in a village—Malgudi, the writer called it—probably not too far from Bangalore. Father (Dr.) Thomas pronounced its characters the authentic voice of South India, as comforting to him (not even a Hindu) as sweetened rice, as healthy as fruit and yogurt, and as stimulating as thick, rich, steaming traditional coffee. The book offered nothing to her except the revelation that traditional Hinduism, one of the pillars of her parents' lives, was totally irrelevant to the life she wanted to live.

So, who was responsible for something as roaringly capitalistic as Bangalore? Certainly not diminutive vegetarians reciting the Vedas under a banyan tree. While still on the intercity bus, glancing out the window, she'd seen more crosses than she'd ever imagined in India. Christians, then? Certainly not South Indian Christians like Father "Elephant Fart" Thomas. Who supplied the energy, the go-for-broke, rule-bending, forget-about-yesterday, and let's-blow-it-all confidence for this transformation? Foreigners like Peter Champion? Internal migrants, displaced northerners like her? Peter had once talked of accident and propinquity in the rise of capital; if Bombay is oversubscribed, overpriced, where can new capital go? It went farther south. If she ever ran into Rabi Chatterjee again, she'd ask him to take a picture of the Bangalore bus depot and send it back to Father (Dr.) Thomas. Where's your tiny, tranquil Malgudi now? He'd die!

Everyone but Angie Bose was on the move. She sat on her red Samsonite at the curb, dazed, hungry and confused. In her nearly twenty years, until meeting up with Subodh Mitra, she'd never felt overmatched. She'd made a joke of any challenge. But in less than a week she'd moved from the passive duties of childhood, waiting for marriage and adult life to begin, into something not quite like womanhood, without instruction. The immense journey and the enormous implications of her impetuousness remained. *What-have-I-done? What-was-I-thinking?* Nothing in her earlier life could guide her. Nothing was relevant.

Here and there, middle-class youths much like her—although most had alighted from express trains and had not sat cramped and half-starved all night in a freezing bus, crossing deserts or steaming jungles—presentable young men in business suits and attractive young women with soft hands and letters of introduction and hearts set on making it in Silicon City, wheeled their bags directly to the taxi stands, around the burlap-covered mounds of produce and the jumble of cars and cycles, and through the crack-of-dawn mayhem caused by rural India assaulting the city.

Still sitting on her suitcase by the curb, Angie picked up a tattered English-language Bangalore newspaper and started reading. From the scowls and mutters of porters and passengers, she assumed she was being cursed for being in the way, but since they were speaking in Kannada or Tamil, she chose to ignore them.

She scanned the stories, none of them particularly relevant to her but all of them interesting and frightening, and she settled on an op-ed column by the paper's resident wit, "Dynamo." He declared that it was wrong to think of Bangalore as all "heartless materialism, lacking a proper respect for history." Dynamo claimed there was more passion—even knife play and gangs of hired thugs—behind every deed transfer in Bangalore than in *Chinatown* or *The Godfather;* more twisted connections between families than Faulkner ever dreamed of; more convolutions and memorable characters than in a Dickens novel. If Hindus buried their dead instead of cremating them, there'd be more crushed bones under the latest skyscraper than under the Great Wall of China. In fact, it could be said that history is proving to be Bangalore's most profitable industry. Every true Bangalorean is becoming an Arnold Toynbee. Every day in every municipal office, Bangaloreans are lining up to inform themselves of their ancestral stake in every deed transfer of the past two hundred years and how they might profit from it.

She did not relate to Dynamo's allusions to films or literature, but she was stirred by the evocation of reckless, even violent energy. If so many thousands—so many lakhs—had made the same decision she had, to come to Bangalore and start life over, and if she could regain her self-confidence and retain her stamina, then she had nothing to fear. She had good English and a quick smile. She had Peter Champion's two friends to count on. He had promised to write to them about her. From her curbside Samsonite perch, she could see scooters, auto-rickshaws, and bright new cars clogging every roadway, many of them driven by girls her age or younger.

What she knew was simple but profound. Energy and confidence create links between bright new cars, a rising ring of skyscrapers, and busy people clutching shopping bags with fancy logos. She wanted to be one of the people being waited on in upscale shops. She saw girls her age wearing crash helmets and maneuvering their motorcycles between stalled cars and around bullock carts, and she was determined to be one of them. She had nothing to lose, no good name to tarnish. No one knew her parents, and her parents had no idea where she was.

All of this and more she learned during her first half-hour in Bangalore from a single newspaper left folded on a bench. Kids fresh out of college were the new managers. She noted their names, from every region of India. Boys still in their twenties were building apartment blocks. Girls in their twenties were opening lifestyle shops. Hadn't Peter Champion let drop that she could be earning a monthly salary bigger than her father's, and for what—just for exercising her only talents, conversational English proficiency and a pleasing phone voice?

"Need taxi, big sister? I carry your luggage to taxi, no problem, and make sure meter is working."

Angie clutched her backpack even tighter. Her parents had warned her to be wary of Good Samaritans offering help in public places. In her parents' paranoid vision of the world, Good Samaritans were pickpockets working in teams of two. In Gauripur she had rebelled against this crippling cynicism, but not here in this bus depot. The young touts badgering her had been fellow riders on her bus, country boys, but they'd hit the ground running. They kept circling her, inching closer and closer. Then suddenly they melted away into the crowd of embarking and disembarking passengers.

A gang of older youths now menaced her. "Need hotel, big sister?

Clean room. Close by bus and train. Concession rate. Bherry, bherry respectable."

She needed to sit tight and look composed while thinking through her immediate questions: How far is Kew Gardens and Minnie Bagehot's house from the bus depot, and could she afford an auto-rickshaw? She'd never been on her own in a real city. In Gauripur she'd always walked between school and home, and except for emergency trips to Dr. Triple-Chin Gupte's storefront clinic in Pinky Mahal (most recently for an excruciating ingrown toenail and before that for a hilsa fishbone stuck in the soft tissue of her throat), where else had she needed to go?

"Mind over matter" was one of her father's favorite adages. "Where there's a will, there's a way." So long as she didn't put all her eggs in one basket and remembered to look before she leaped, she'd be fine. Better than fine. She was not desperate; okay, she'd felt abandoned when the bus that had brought her to Bangalore pulled away from the curb, and, okay, okay, she'd panicked when the vendors and hostel touts had swarmed around her, but she hadn't felt despair. What she felt now . . . was guilt. Why had she had to hurt her parents to realize they cared for her, cared too much? Mind over matter, Baba. Silently she begged his forgiveness.

FINALLY A POLICEMAN approached and spoke to her in Kannada. The language sounded so alien, the tone so ambiguous, that she wasn't sure whether he was offering help or ordering her to move on. "Kew Gardens?" she asked.

The policeman shrugged. He tapped her suitcase with his lathi.

"Kew Gardens?" she repeated.

Again he shrugged. He looked her up and down and tapped the side of the suitcase. After a pause, he said, "Majestic." Then he made a sweeping gesture with his baton. "Bus stand, Majestic." He pointed his baton at the line of auto-rickshaws a few yards away. Then he lost interest in her and sauntered toward a knot of boys selling toys from trays suspended around their necks.

Angie slid off the suitcase and pulled it to the auto-rickshaw at the head of the stand. "Kew Gardens," she announced, as though it was the only street in town.

The driver turned his head from side to side and helped her load the big red bag on to the narrow seat beside her. He took off, bobbing and weaving on a thoroughfare that would have been generously wide anywhere in India but here was too narrow for the variety of vehicles. Motorcycles darted in and out of traffic lanes, almost brushing her elbow. Hyundais and Skodas were twice the size of anything she'd seen in Gauripur. Mercedes-Benzes, liveried chauffeurs at the wheel, sped past. Huge American cars, many with women drivers, snaked around her auto-rickshaw. To avoid panicking, she concentrated her gaze in the direction of the footpath that had to run alongside the road, but the footpaths—*Sidewalk,* she told herself, *think American*—had been torn up to make way for new sewers. She shut her eyes and kept them shut for a long time. When she opened them again, the road was wider, the trees shadier, the older buildings statelier, and the newer buildings taller and fancier. Towers of blue glass reflected the perfect blue sky. Bangalore had been built by a race of giants.

"How much farther?" she asked the driver in Hindi.

Without turning his head, he answered at length in one of the South Indian languages, extending his arm in an all-encompassing sweep. The only words she understood were "soon-soon" and "MG Road." Another MG Road. Peter Champion once said, "Every American town has its Main, Oak, and Elm, just like India has its Gandhi-Nehru-Shastri." But Bangalore retained British place names too, like Kew Gardens and Cubbon Park.

"Hindi?" she asked. "Don't you understand Hindi?" The auto-rickshaw was moving erratically through fast-moving traffic on a wide artery flanked by office buildings, government offices, and shops.

Finally the rickshaw lurched to a stop by a muddy puddle a couple of feet from the curb. All the buildings on that block were office towers, with street-level showrooms and fancy shops. It was barely eight in the morning and the shops were still shuttered. High-rise office buildings in Bangalore indexed their tenants' names on signboards visible from the street. The tall building immediately in front of the rickshaw boasted corporate logos of companies from twenty different countries, marked by their flags.

"This isn't Kew Gardens," Angie snapped. "I'm looking for a house, a private home. Bagehot House."

"MG Road," said the driver, smiling shyly.

He got out of his vehicle and gave the back tires vicious kicks. It was clear that the rickshaw had died. He held out his hand for the fare. "One hundred rupees," he said, this time in Hindi. She stayed put. He checked the rate card against his meter and asked again for one hundred rupees. It wasn't fair that he was demanding to be paid for dumping her who knew how far from Kew Gardens. A hundred rupees would pay for a month's to-ing and fro-ing in Gauripur. But before she could decide whether to complain or haggle, she got out on the street side, and the driver grabbed her suitcase with both hands and dropped it with a thud into the puddle in the gutter.

She flung a ten-rupee note at him. "Go to hell!" she screamed in English, startling herself for saying something she would never have said in the old days. The driver's actual competence in Hindi, expressed in fouler words than any movie villain's, came pouring out, but he was quick to scoop the ten-rupee note out of the puddle and dry it on his shirt.

Angie rolled her suitcase past three buildings, wondering if Kew Gardens was anywhere within walking distance. It was not quite eight-thirty in the morning; the sidewalks were still relatively empty. No one to ask for the right way to Kew Gardens. No one who looked English- or even Hindi-speaking. She'd seen only one major road in the center of old Bangalore, and she began to imagine the sheer extent of the city in every direction.

From the sidewalk she could make out an outdoor coffee bar with patio umbrellas on an elevated plaza between two skyscrapers. A gaggle of voices floated down to her, tinkly voices of hyperconfident breakfasters, chattering in American English. Finally, a language with familiar cadences! She climbed the stairs to the plaza and found herself in a crowded coffee shop. Not just any coffee shop, not another Alps Palace with mold blooming on water-stained walls: this was a Barista. Most of the small round tables were occupied by large groups of noisy patrons her age, dressed, like her, in jeans and T-shirts. Many of the girls were smoking, gesturing wildly, and giggling like schoolgirls. Except for vamps in movies, Angie had never seen women smoke in Gauripur. At the outer fringes of the plaza, young men and women were plugging away, doing work on laptops.

In Bollywood films, the coolest stars casually meet in a Barista. Angie felt cool as she trundled her suitcase to the counter indoors. She would splurge on a tall iced coffee with a scoop of ice cream. In fan magazines, actresses were photographed while seductively licking strawberry-pink or saffron-yellow ice cream off a long-handled spoon. Hadn't she just saved maybe ninety rupees on the auto-rickshaw ride to nowhere? But when it was her turn to place her order, she asked for the cheapest, smallest hot coffee listed on the board above the counter. She blamed her Bose family training in frugality for the failure to splurge.

Really, why shouldn't she buy into the self-indulgence on display all around her? She knew her worth, and she had money—okay, borrowed, in a cookie tin in her tote bag. She'd shaken off the dust of Bihar and the mud and jungles in between, and now she was in Bangalore, where the towers are made of blue glass, but they could just as easily be gold. She'd done it entirely on her own. Next time in a Barista, she promised herself, she would order the most expensive coffee on the board.

"New in town?" asked a cappuccino drinker at an adjacent table, glancing down at Angie's Samsonite. She wore an I ❤ MUMBAI T-shirt.

"Just got off the train," Angie confessed, flashing her biggest smile. "I got in from Kolkata an hour ago." It's a new life, who's to know?

"Cool," said Mumbai Girl.

Angie put her coffee down on Mumbai Girl's cluttered table. A young man in a black muscle shirt that showcased his biceps gave up his chair for her. "Fresh Off the Train. F-O-T. Cool," he said.

"Now I've got to find Kew Gardens," Angie confided. "Do you know where it is?"

Mumbai Girl shouted over to the next table, "Any of you guys rooming in Kew Gardens?" Her English was perfect, better than Angie's. And the responses from the other tables were also in English: "Hell of a commute!" "Try Kent Town instead." "Isn't your ex looking for a roomie?" "Don't sign a long lease straightaway. Landlords are crooks." "And all landladies are bitches."

"Chill, F-O-T," Mumbai Girl counseled. She got on her cell phone. "Moni," she said, "Lalita here. Barista's, where do you think? Really? She agreed? I'm surprised. No, I'm shocked. Look, there's a new Bangla babe here." She looked up at Angie with a big smile, then winked. "Moni, you'd better get here fast. She's a real cutie. Hot and going fast. You want her in BanglaBazaar before those MeetMate guys snag her."

Cutie? Angie thought. Cute was something small and soft and dimpled. She was too tall and skinny for cute.

Mumbai Girl put her hand over the phone and whispered, "His name is Monish Lahiri—we call him the Bengali Svengali. Movie handsome, but kind of short. Not short-short, but shortish. He romances all the girls, so he's too busy to concentrate on just one. Anyway, he's minting money on his Facebook ripoff. He has us recruiting all the F-O-T Bangla babes and studs for his directory."

Angie tried to follow it all and came up . . . short. *What's a Svengali?* she wondered.

Lifting her hand off the phone, Mumbai Girl said, "I don't know—pretty tall, hundred and seventy-five, hundred and eighty, maybe. Wear your shoe lifts."

"Tell him a hundred and sixty," Angie said.

Lalita continued. "Cool, Moni. Oh, she says a hundred and sixty." She turned to Angie. "Moni started the trend. Now every group in Bangalore, the Gujaratis, the Tamils, the Konkans, the Punjabis—everybody's getting into these Bangalore directories."

Angie's head was spinning, faces popped up like flashbulbs, voices twittered, coming from nowhere, or everywhere, and she couldn't understand a word they were saying. Maybe she'd strained something, hauling her Samsonite up from the sidewalk.

The smart-looking boys working on their laptops made her occasional Gauripur heartthrobs look like cow herders. Her clothes might be sour, and she hadn't been able to comb her hair, and she was pulling a muddy suitcase, but she still had her smile. She was in a Barista on MG Road in Bangalore, the new center of the universe. Her smile was more valuable than any amulet or mantra. But damn, her voice seemed slow and muffled and everyone else's loud and fast.

"Way cool—did I hear the magic words 'new girl in town'?" a bearded, mustached man in Ray-Bans called out. Angie assessed and dismissed: too short and dark, too loud and outgoing, too much laughing and joking, the mustache too full and hairy, and the double strand of gold chains definitely unnecessary. Probably a local boy, she thought, trying to ingratiate himself with cooler, big-city types, pushing too hard. If he'd been in a Bollywood movie, he'd be the hero's comic sidekick, too itchy and impetuous, cracking too many jokes in a too-high-pitched voice, too eager to please, getting the turndown from every girl he meets. He slung his arm around a tubular girl with spiky hair in a very tight T-shirt from which she threatened to spill at any minute.

"Do you have a room yet?" *Javaroomyet?* "Say no, we can squeeze you in." He said his name was Mike and his English was easy and a little coarse. He introduced the others: Millie and Darren. The tubular girl was Suzie. Darren was a handsome boy in a T-shirt and jean jacket, more her type, Punjabi-tall and fair, with none of Mike's strained flash and swagger. Millie was the classic "tall, slim and wheat-complexioned" girl of the marriage ads, with highlighted hair, twirling her cigarette with practiced ease.

"Can't smoke in the residence. Can't smoke on the job. Gotta get my fix when I can," she said, lighting another.

"I'm Darren. This week, anyway." Darren sniggered. "I think I'm going to kill him off. I fancy myself a Brad."

"You're not cool enough for Brad, lover boy," said Suzie. "He broke up with Jen last year."

"He's a has-been," laughed one of the girls. "He's with Angelina now. She'll spit him out her backside!" The girl looked like a servant; you'd never think she knew a word of English, let alone loud, aggressive American English. She called herself Cindy.

"So let me lay it out for you," Cindy continued. "If you say you're Brad, they'll say where's Angelina? Then what'll you say? Quick, quick, Old Bitch'll be listening in, hears anguished attempt of expendable agent to extricate himself from the deep shit he's gotten himself into . . . and you're out on your ass, wasting company time just 'cause you wanted to be Brad Pitt. Not cool, dude."

"I was Jen a few weeks ago," said Millie. "That's all I ever got. 'Where's Brad?' I said, 'Brad? Brad's *so* last week, man. Now what-say we cure your printer blues.'"

"Yeah, well, HP's a little loosey-goosey," said Darren.

"Motorola's a little uptight," said Mike.

"Mine'd shit bricks," said Cindy. "Play by the rules, that's all we ever get. You got a name—stick with it."

"Dudes, dudes, what is this, a bitch session? What'll our new friend think?" said Darren.

What could she think? She was numb with confusion. Brick-shitting was a new one on her. *Shit, piss, fuck, asshole:* so much to learn. And *cool, cool, cool:* everything cool or not cool, but never warm. These must be call-center agents, her competition and would-be colleagues. Her neck hurt from keeping up with the repartee. She felt the way she had on a family visit to Kolkata so many years before, recognizing the Bangla words but missing the meaning. She should know all this, it should all be second nature, this was the currency of her deliverance from Gauripur—but she truly didn't understand 90 percent of it. These people seemed better than she was, even though their vocabulary was minimal and they looked like servants or movie prostitutes, except maybe Darren, who was now pouting because he couldn't play Brad.

"Gotta keep it fresh," said Mike. "Russell Crowe's still good, but there's the bloody accent. Nicole's great. Bill and Hillary. George and Laura, but when you use those names, they might hang up on you. Lots of names out there. What's yours, honey?"

When she said Angie, Millie and Suzie admitted to having been Angies too, on different days. Suzie said, "I stopped being Angie when one American guy said, 'Yeah, you're Angie like I'm Mother Teresa.' They're catching on. Gotta be careful."

"They got 'tudes," said Darren.

"Yeah, but we got game," Mike responded. They high-fived. Angie wanted to cry, so she smiled, and Mike turned to her. "Bitchin' name, Angie. Real cool. Great smile. Love it." Still too enthusiastic, *not cool,* she decided. How could a bitchin' name, if she heard right, be cool? She remembered a favorite Championism: *used-car-salesman friendly.* She felt better.

Angie or Suzie or whatever, leaning across the table with her breasts all but pouring out, and one of them, she saw, with a butterfly tattoo fluttering up from the dark interior, would have caused a riot in Gauripur. And the tall girl with highlighted hair, calling herself Angie on Tuesday and Saturday and Millie on Monday, Wednesday and Friday, who had to smoke on breaks and at the coffee shop, said she was looking for a new roomie at two thousand a month with kitchen privileges. Angie said she hoped she had a room through a relative in Kew Gardens, a statement that caused no dropped silverware, no raised eyes. Two more boys from a neighboring table, a Steve and a Charlie, offered her a ride on their bikes, which, too late, she realized meant motorcycles. They were with girls, a ponytailed one named Gloria and a green-haired one named Roxie, "from Chicago," she said. "Where else?"

Ah, but did they teach you a Chicago accent? she wondered, remembering Peter. *That'll be five dallers.*

"Mukesh Sharma called again last night," Cindy said, "poor fucking loser, I almost feel sorry for him. He calls himself Mickey now, but it's the same old Mukky."

"You can block him," said Mike. "A guy calls support three, four times a week—they'll deal with him. You can say whatever you want to him, even the Old Bitch'll back you."

"Mukesh Sharma is a real Hannibal Lecter. He creeps me out from twelve thousand miles away," said Suzie. "I don't know why they let those guys into the States. University of Illinois used to have some class. I keep hoping I get him—he won't have the balls to call back again."

Mike started singing, "I get no kick from Champagne." He had a surprising voice: deep, American. "Mukky Sharma lives in Champaign."

"Well, no wonder he's crazy," Angie said, "living in Champagne!" Everyone laughed, and she didn't know why what she said was so funny. The sun was so bright, pouring directly into her eyes and boring into her skull. How does a person even manage to live in Champagne? They drink it like crazy in Bollywood movies. What's the word—*flutes*? An actual Indian name like Mukesh Sharma sounded strangely comforting in this ersatz America, with all its Mikes and Steves and Charlies.

"Indian guys in the States," Millie explained. "They're the sickest perverts. They spend all day in the lab, then they spend all night on the Indian marriage sites. They're so fucking horny, they invent computer problems just so they can be patched through to Bangalore and talk to an Indian girl. They don't know we have their name and credit history and previous calls on our screens as soon as they call in."

Cindy was playing to an attentive circle. "He goes, 'Hi, my name is Mickey. What is your good name please?'" She did a good imitation of a certain kind of Indian accent—Angie's father's, for example. "I say, 'Angie.' He goes, 'Am-I-detecting-an-Anjali-under-that-Angie-disguise, Miss Angie?' I nearly said, 'No, but am I detecting some kind of sick shit under Mickey?' What he really wants to know is, what's the weather like in Bangalore today? What's playing at the Galaxy? Do we still hang out at Forum? What about Styx or Pub World? What's your real name and where do you come from and are you married and how old are you and 'Please, Miss Angie, your height in centimeters . . .' Gawd, I hate this job!"

Darren raised his arms. "Silence, please. Kolkata Cutie needs to hear our tribute to Mukky Sharma." Everyone looked at Angie, raising their coffee cups in her direction, and began singing in what seemed to her nonsense syllables:

I get no kick from Champagne,
Urbana too is a kind of a zoo,
But I know now what has to be true—
There's something sick coming off of you.

"Lyrics by Girish Gujral," said Bombay Girl. "He'll come over soon enough."

Angie knew the meaning of the words *fuck, shit, asshole,* though she'd never used them. Where do young Indians learn to use such language? What frightened her was the simple truth that if a boy from an American college, even a psychopath, had sent in his marital résumé, her father would have lunged at it. Any Indian going to any American school was, by definition, a catch.

"There's always the phone-sex line," Mike said. "You'd be way cool. They actually favor exotic names and Indian accents."

"A girl in our dorm went over to phone sex," said Suzie. "The money's good, but you have to find weird ways of keeping those guys talking."

"Not that you couldn't," said Mike.

"Oh, just shut up," said Suzie. She waited for silence. "You have something more you want to say . . . Mahendra? Oh, sorry, Mike."

My God, how a simple name change changes everything!

"Three hundred bucks a night weird, I hear," said Darren. *Who was he in his pre-Bangalore life,* Angie wondered. *Dinesh? Dharmendra?* "Pretty cool."

"One step up from the streets," snorted Roxie. *And you, Roxie: Rupa? Rukhsana?*

The women didn't seem jealous or possessive. Most of them were plump and the men already getting stout, like her father. Their friendships didn't seem like lead-ins to marriage. The young people in Bangalore had no parents, no nearby families to appease. No gossip or scandal could compromise them. They had come from all over India to get away from gossip.

It was exciting just to be part of such a flow, even for one morning, and to be carried along like a twig in a flood. She'd been accepted, no questions asked, even if she didn't understand most of what she'd been hearing. It was English, but . . . From her perch on the Barista's plaza, she could see the tops of skyscrapers flashing their international names in blue and red neon. She knew those companies: IBM, Canon, Siemens, Daihatsu. None of them existed in Gauripur. A Pizza Hut in Gauripur would automatically become the luxury hangout, the Place to Be Seen, and would draw longer lines than a cinema hall. In Gauripur there was only Alps Palace, a Welcome Group hotel with a vegetarian restaurant and innumerable tea stalls, where men sat or stood, sipping and spitting. For Gauripur's alcoholics there were two back-street liquor stores where bottles were wrapped in straw and newspaper and smuggled out in used plastic sacks with sari shop logos.

High on the side of one building she could read hand-painted placards: ENGLISH LESSENS. CALL-CENTRE PLACEMENT. FRESHERS TAKE NOTE. FOREGIN LANGUAGES TAUGHT; FRANCIAS, ESPAGNOL, ITALINO. She found it reassuring, as though they'd known she was coming and might need a brush-up course, even if Bangalore spelled words differently.

She would like to stay. Barista was comfortable, with a touch of conspicuous luxury and a hint of intrigue. The young people were just like her, open and friendly, and probably held the kind of job she was hoping to get. She'd heard that ten thousand agents a month were hired, and six or seven thousand quit or were let go. What could a girl buy, with fifteen thousand rupees coming in? For one thing, she could stop in a Barista and order cold coffee with ice cream and not think twice. For Angie, a lakh — 100,000 rupees — represented a lifetime of scrimping and saving. In Bangalore, she could be earning a lakh, or even two lakhs, every month.

She was swept up in visions of stuffed clothing closets, a scooter, and an apartment of her own. Big-city ambitions; small-town desires. Her poor sister worked her fingers to the bone — fingers and more — for two thousand a month, if that. From a few tables away, a pleasant male voice spoke up. "Kew Gardens is on my way," but Angie was still lost in her future. In a few months, after promotions, before she turned twenty, she'd be earning more than her father, far more than her father.

Those pleasant words from a distant table had been meant for her. Suddenly there he was, in blue jeans, white shirt, and blue blazer, belt buckle at her eye level, dangling his car keys. He seemed slightly older than the others but still young, plump, and round-faced, with glasses: a harmless, even friendly face. "My name is Girish Gujral," he said. "They call me GG. I hear you need a ride to Kew Gardens. My Daewoo is at your service. Don't worry, it's on my way."

He kept on talking, but she couldn't make out the words. His lips were moving, but nothing got through to her. She thought she should stand, get closer, and shake his hand, but as she tried to rise, her legs went numb, then her head filled with light, her knees buckled, and she was falling against him. He threw his arms around her, keeping her half-standing, then let her down to the ground, easily. She saw faces, all the girls and some of the boys she'd been watching, arranged in a semicircle around her. Mr. GG cradled her head in his hand and shouted to the others, "Get toast and juice." Then, to her, he almost whispered, "When did you last eat?"

"This morning," she lied.

"Not to pry, but are you by any chance diabetic?" he asked. She was offended; diabetes was for old people.

"Of course not."

"So it's just my manly charm?"

"Pardon me?"

She didn't know where she was. Lights kept spinning behind Mr. GG's head. Her head was a big, hollow, swaying balloon; her legs and arms were numb. Then she was drinking the juice and tearing off mouthfuls of toast.

A minute later, she was back in her chair. The world had stopped spinning, and Mr. GG was buttering another stack of toast. He said, "You're looking much better." He pushed the platter closer to her. "You seem to have fallen in my lap. What am I to do with you?"

Just like that, she made the lightning calculation: She who hesitates is lost. She who worries over the future or her reputation or skimps on comforts and counts only the rupees in her pocketbook and not the dreams inside her Samsonite, she who dwells on can-it-get-any-worse, and not pie-in-the-sky, cannot compete.

"My name is Angie Bose," she said, introducing herself to him formally. "Thank you for the offer of the ride."

A COURTLY STRANGER had offered her a free ride to Kew Gardens, wherever that was, and she'd been in Bangalore not much more than an hour. In Gauripur the only answer would be a polite "Thank you, no." But in Bangalore? "Why not?" was the smart answer.

Besides, she didn't have to own up to anyone at Barista that she had spent all her life in Gauripur. She didn't even have to be Angie Bose; she could invent a flashy Bollywoodish first name, like Dimple or Twinkle or Sprinkle. Why not? No one in Bangalore seemed to be stuck with a discernible identity. She could kill off Angie Bose, and who would know, or care? She could be anything she wanted, a Hindi-speaking girl from Varanasi or a Brahmin from Kolkata. Who do you want to be?

Bangalore doesn't care. Bangalore will accommodate any story line. She could eliminate her parents and her sister. No, she couldn't bring herself to do that, but she could make them more solidly, more powerfully middle-class.

The man who'd called himself GG led the way out of Barista to a sleek Daewoo sedan parked at the curb. Let the story line of her life write itself! Like a typical Bollywood heroine—the eternal innocent, the trusting small-town girl placing herself at the mercy of a confident, benevolent older man—she climbed into the stranger's car. She'd seen this movie a hundred times.

2

Anjali Bose decided she'd already encountered at least one version of every likely male she would ever meet. Not every man was as befuddled as Nirmal Sen, or a bully like her father, or a rapist like Subodh Mitra, or a lying cheat like Sonali's ex-husband, or an exploiter like Sonali's current boss, or a brutish john like the truck drivers of Nizambagh. Some were kind but twisted, like Peter Champion. All the fifty-odd matrimonial candidates she'd rejected had to belong in one of those categories. Any young man she had recently met, or might in the future, would fit into one of them—everyone except maybe Rabi Chatterjee. It would be interesting to see where Mr. GG and his big silver Daewoo fit in. In broad daylight in a big city she felt she had nothing to fear.

He started off predictably. "Did I hear you were from Kolkata?" Uh-oh. She rummaged through family memories, arranging a few street names and neighborhoods, just in case. Where should she come from? Ballygunj, Tollygunj, north Kolkata? They were just names to her; if anyone asked about addresses, she'd be exposed. Salt Lakes? Too new. Dhakuria Lakes? No longer trendy. Bowbazar? Sealdah? Too poor, crowded, too dingy. *Don't say a thing*. Mr. GG continued. "I've never lived in Bengal myself. People say they're all-talk and airy-fairy, but—"

She cut in. "We have our share of dolts, Mr. Gujral."

"Please call me Girish. Or GG."

He didn't press her to reciprocate. As they passed a five-star hotel, he said, "Three years ago, all this was an old apartment block. They got rid of five hundred families and replaced them with two thousand tourists." He pointed out a new shopping center: "Big black-money operation there. Dubai money." He seemed to know the inside story about every new building they passed. "First mixed-use high-rise in Bangalore. Ground-floor boutiques, middle floors for offices, and top five floors, luxury condos." For the condo owners there were two indoor swimming pools, a spa, a spectacular roof garden, and of course full-time maid service. If you had been lucky enough to get your bid in before construction had begun, you'd bought your condo for two crores. A steal. That was three years ago. "Now you could sell it for eight crore plus."

"I'll have to keep that in mind," she said.

Mr. GG laughed.

She read aloud the passing signboards: AID'S LATEST PROJECT! ACT NOW! LIVE IN 10-CRORE LUXURY AT ONLY 5-CRORE PRICE! Mr. GG seemed proud of Indian achievement, and the wealth was breathtaking, yet he also seemed somehow ashamed of it. She understood, in a way: Bangalore excited her, but it left her depressed. All the money made people go slightly crazy. And what was this about AIDS? She'd heard about it, a big problem, but in Bangalore they advertise it? "Isn't AIDS . . . ?"

"AID is All-India Development. People used to joke that you can take medicine for AIDS, but it's AID that will get you in the end."

The morning's "Bang Galore" column, which she had read while sitting on her suitcase at the bus depot, was still fresh in her mind. Dynamo had written, "In Bang Galore, crores are the new lakhs," and now she understood. In her experience, crores were like light-years, signifying numbers too large to comprehend. Crores were reserved for serious occasions with mystical gravity, such as government budgets and projects ("1000-Cr. Barrage Planned for Upper Jumna . . .") or whole populations ("with India having crossed the hundred-crore threshold and Mumbai's masses now pressing three crore . . ."). A lakh was a hundred thousand. A crore was a hundred lakhs.

Crores were mentioned everywhere. In that same discarded paper, she'd read of a hundred-crore land deal, converting rice paddies into a gated colony (subscribe now!) with schools and a golf course cum health club and a shopping mall with international designer boutiques inside the compound (no crowds!). She'd read charges that an underlying 4.5-crore bribe paid for the land. But no poor farmer was ever going to profit from it. Farmers were as welcome as their bullocks inside those gates. Someone had already found an ancient title to the farmland, or invented it and paid off a judge. If crores were the new lakhs, was everyone automatically a hundred times bigger and stronger just for being here? Did it also mean that if you failed here, you failed a hundred times faster and fell into a hole a hundred times deeper?

Mr. GG drove her past her first Pizza Hut, and then a Radio Shack, and a Starbucks — no, wait, StarLucks, but with almost the familiar logo she had studied in her Corporate Management course back at da Gama. At the end of the course, Peter Champion had told her, only half-joking, "Congratulations. You know more about Starbucks than any eighteen-year-old girl in Bihar. And I bet Starbucks is eyeing the market in India. I smell coffee in your future." Seeing the wondrous logos was as miraculous as watching a family of white tigers crossing the road.

Mr. GG had gone to an IIT for civil engineering, then to architecture school in the United States, and after returning to India he had picked up an additional MBA from an IIM. He'd had a job in a place called Pasadena, but his older brother had died in a traffic accident, and Mr. GG had to return home to look after his parents, his widowed sister-in-law, and two nephews. His wife had refused to leave the States. "Was she an American girl?" Angie asked.

And he replied, "She was American by birth and Punjabi by name and background, and her parents were very proud Punjabis, but she was raised over there. I find American-raised Indian girls too independent. They lack true family feeling."

She couldn't let that one pass. "There are many Indian girls who've never left India who lack what you call true family feeling, Mr. GG." Maybe she was American after all. "My sister ran out on my parents. She waited for the middle of the night and left a note saying she would not marry the boy they found for her, and when she was ready she would write them again. We haven't heard from her in the past five years!"

How liberating it felt, creating characters, obliterating oneself, being a composite.

"Well, then, she's probably dead," he said. "Five years is a long time for an Indian girl to be gone. A girl on her own, bad things can happen. My wife had a job. A small job, mind you, office manager in a branch bank, one step up from teller. She could have done much better here."

But Angie was already calculating the benefits of staying behind: why would any self-respecting modern girl come to India when she already had a job in the States? Being an office manager sounded like a worthy goal. Why would any childless wife give up America, safely removed from a nagging mother-in-law? But Mr. GG hadn't gone back to Delhi either. He'd taken off for Bangalore because making it here meant making it anywhere in the world.

"And what did you do in the States, Mr. GG?"

"I inspected buildings."

"Then all this new construction must keep you very busy." And very rich, she supposed. It was common knowledge that inspectors made more money than the builders and the architects because of bribes and kickbacks.

"Putting on a hardhat and pawing through pipes is extremely boring," he said. "It's much nicer staying inside my air-conditioned office, drinking pots of tea. Last night I inspected an enormous project in Djakarta that isn't even built yet. We live in a virtual city, Miss Angie, inside a virtual world."

She couldn't tell if he was serious or just playing with her. The long story came to this: "Forget all the clutter you see—Bangalore is the most advanced city on the planet. Let's say a Danish-Dutch consortium puts up a shopping center and apartment block in Djakarta, designed by a Brazilian architect. Dazzling plans, prize-winning stuff. It's going to be the biggest shopping center in Asia, bigger than anything in Japan or China. But none of those world-class thinkers really, intimately, knows the Indonesian building codes or the reliability of the supply chain or the union rules or a million other little things like plumbing and electrical systems and subsoil drainage. Are you with me so far, Miss Bose?"

She wasn't. She hadn't the foggiest.

"Of course."

"Those are things known only in Bangalore. We have the building codes for every city in the world. We have ecological surveys and subsoil analyses for every square centimeter on the planet. So our back-office architects and engineers sit around their computers, modeling the buildings on special software, scan the blueprints, correct the budget forecasts and the deadlines, and then our financial guys run the numbers and we come up with a tighter figure. We can save our clients up to twenty percent. We don't budget for bribes and kickbacks. We're cleaning up the world, one shopping center at a time."

His architectural consulting company, a Swiss-Canadian collaboration, 50 percent locally financed, was three years old. It had started with five architects who returned from the United States and five engineers, and now it employed three hundred people.

So he inspects buildings that aren't there, in cities he's never been to.

"Every business in the world is outsourcing. Without us, the world would collapse. Maybe in a couple of years some version of a Bish Chatterjee will come along and buy us out and we'll sit down and figure out the next big thing."

Idly, she said, "I know Bish Chatterjee's son, Rabi. Wouldn't we collapse without them, Mr. GG?"

"Hold on a second. You just said you know the son of Bish Chatterjee? I'm still processing that. How many Chatterjees are there in Bengal? A guess."

"Crores," she said.

"How many of them might be named Bishwapriya Chatterjee?"

"Lakhs," she said.

"And how many Rabi Chatterjees and how many Anjali Boses, would you say?"

"Crores of Anjali Boses." *But maybe only one Rabi Chatterjee,* she thought. She flashed a smile.

"Ah-hah! Very cool." He smiled back. "So technically speaking, some cognomen of yours has met the cognomen son of some cognomen Bishwapriya Chatterjee. Maybe you should be a lawyer. To answer your other question: yes, we would collapse without international collaborators. For a while, at least. Then they'd collapse without us."

"You're very sure of yourself, Mr. GG," she said, and thought, but was afraid to ask, *What's a cognomen?*

"I'm beginning to think I'm not nearly as brazen as you. That's a compliment, by the way."

Bangalore was endless! Just when the tall new buildings began to fade, a new center opened up, a new satellite city with even more office towers, car dealerships, dug-up sidewalks, and cranes, with never a letup in traffic. If Mr. GG intended any funny business with her, it would have to be in front of thousands of people. But she couldn't imagine him even trying. He seemed a round-faced jolly sort, not like Subodh Mitra, whose profile reminded her of a long-snouted street dog.

"Have you seen *Chinatown*?" he asked, and she thought immediately, *So* that's *his little game! That's where he's taking me. Back alleys, and men in pigtails.* She'd read about evil Chinatowns, with their opium dens and concubines.

"I like sweet and sour," she said. Gauripur once had a Chinese restaurant, run by a refugee family from Kolkata's Chinatown. Her parents took her there once and declared the food inedible, although she'd liked it, but it soon went out of business. "Premature sophistication, misreading of the commercial environment," Peter would say. Mr. GG was laughing. Apparently she'd said something funny, or else he was making fun of her.

"I was referring to an American movie. It's about how L.A. really got built. It's about power and deals and corruption and a lot of buried bodies. You can rent it some night."

She remembered the newspaper article from that distant time a few hours ago, at the Bangalore bus station. "Why should I?"

"Because you said you wanted to know what Bangalore is like. Well, it's a lot like L.A., but it took L.A. a century. They had a movie industry, and we've got hi-tech. We're both virtual and we've both got buried bodies, but we'll be a much bigger city in maybe five years."

She really didn't understand. She'd used a computer in the da Gama Common Room, but only for games. *Virtual* was one of those frightening words. "I have a question. What is an L.A.?" she finally asked.

"Oh, my God—and you say you're from Kolkata? It's Los Angeles. California. U.S.A. Hollywood, the poor man's Bombay."

In front of pokey little shops where pariah dogs still languished in the sun, rows of posters proclaimed: AID PRESENTS: SITE OF FUTURE FIVE-STAR LUXURY HOTEL and FUTURE HEADQUARTERS OF (fill in the name) MULTINATIONAL CORPORATION, ending in the parenthetical (INDIA, LTD.). Painted signboards featured luxury flats underscored with prompts: SUBSCRIBE NOW! ONLY TWO REMAINING! Artist's renderings of strolling couples in a landscaped garden, flowers and fountains, and flashy cars pulling up—all in a place where nothing had yet been demolished or erected and no trees were standing. Future, future, future! And enough of the future hotels and headquarters had already been built and filled to lend credence to any claim. Every company in the world had to have a Bangalore address, and every modern mogul from India, Korea, Japan and the Middle East had to have a Bangalore condo or mansion.

"Who do you know in Kent Town?" Mr. GG asked. He acted as

though she had no right even to know any resident of Kent Town. "That's old money. The money's so old, it's moldy. It's so old, they still calculate in annas, not rupees."

She hadn't realized that Kew Gardens was a street in Kent Town. "I don't know anyone. I have a letter of introduction from my old professor to Mrs. Minnie Bagehot."

This too amused him. "A letter from an old professor who knows Minnie Bagehot. So, you've got powerful connections. You want to be a Bagehot Girl, then?"

For the first time, he sounded slightly interested in something she'd said. "I didn't know there was such a thing. What does it mean—a 'Bagehot Girl'?"

"It means a very proper, upstanding girl from a very good family. Or it can mean someone who does a good imitation of being a proper, upstanding girl from a very good family."

"And am I special enough to be a Bagehot Girl, Mr. GG?"

"I detect possibilities."

"You have software for that too? Detecting possibilities?"

"You have a certain style. Even without software I predict that you'll do fine. You'll get a job, no problem."

"Why do you say that? You don't know a thing about me. Maybe I'm a total fraud. Maybe I'm a dolt and I'll flub my interviews." Of course, she was fishing for compliments—you're fresh air, you're radiant, and your English is perfect.

"Your English is decent and you've got a pulse. In Bangalore that means you'll find a job. And if you feel your highest calling is to know the difference between NH and NC or MS and MD or maybe even AK and AR, you'll do fine."

She had no idea. Strange monsters dwelt in the linguistic interstices of the English language. All things were possible. Morays could paint French cathedrals, but at least she already knew the difference between medical doctors and multiple sclerosis, thank you very much.

And then for some reason, perhaps to clear the air of her misrepresentations, she confessed, "Back at that Barista, everyone was friendly, but I didn't understand a word of what they were saying."

"It's just Bangalore babble," he said. "It's not meant to mean anything. Just that they're here and have jobs and with it comes the freedom to talk nonsense. They're like locusts—in six weeks they'll be moving on. Chennai and Hyderabad beckon."

"Will I be moving on?"

"I don't think so. I think you'll stick in Bangalore. I hope so, at least."

Chennai or Hyderabad would be unacceptable. She saw herself as a high-quality individual, destined for the best job in the top place, and according to what she'd heard and what she could see, that was Bangalore. If she needed a job, why not start at the top? Why not use her only "contact," as the business world put it? She pulled out some old questions from Peter Champion's class. "What is your corporate culture, Mr. GG? Are you hiring?"

"My 'corporate culture'?" He seemed amused. "I've never been asked a question like that. Offhand I'd say it's making the most money with the fewest people in the shortest time. And yes, absolutely, we're hiring. If you have an architect's or engineer's license from an IIT or an overseas equivalent."

"Now you're being mean. You must be needing someone to answer your telephones. I have a high school–leaving cert and two years of college, B. Comm. with English proficiency, first class."

"Very nice," he said. "Now let me tell you something. Three years ago they called us a 'scrappy little startup.' Now we're 'worldwide leaders of a new industry.' You're just like Bangalore, Miss Bose. Today you're a scrappy, starving little startup. So what's *your* corporate culture? What's your plan? If you play it right, in three or four years you'll have your own corner office. And by the way, we don't use telephones."

They were finally in a proper residential suburb. Many of the houses were old Anglo-Indian-style one-story bungalows, crumbling and partly demolished, hidden behind towering trees and overgrown vegetation. They had names, and she read some of them aloud: THE HEATHER, SNOW-DROP LODGE, PRIMROSE PALACE, and HYACINTH GLORY. Names right out of British poetry, she remarked. His explanation was that the original builders and later occupiers had refused to believe—or perhaps had known only too well—that they would never see England again. The street names had undergone orthographic decolonization: CHARLESS WRIHGT ROAD and KENT TOWN, or KENTT or KHENNTAON; words changed their spellings block by block.

She'd been noticing the impatient march of gleaming new mansions, built on tiny plots, and three- and four-story luxury apartment buildings with doctors' clinics and fabric shops on the ground floor, wedging their way between the remaining bungalows. Every old mansion that died had given birth to half a dozen offspring.

Every block seemed to contain a small church, an old house converted to that purpose, with a signboard announcing its name and denomination and times of services. Farther on, an immense white mosque occupied an entire block. On the streets around the mosque, on the back seats of scooters and motorcycles, clinging to their husbands and holding their children, were Muslim women clad head to toe in black and looking at the world through thin eye slits. Where had all the Hindus gone?

"This little area is called Bagehot camp," Mr. GG announced. "We're coming up on Bagehot Alley and Kew Gardens Road." The street sign read BHAJOT.

"And there . . ." He paused for effect. "There in all its glory stands—well, leans—Bagehot House. Every architect in Bangalore has dreamed of getting his hands on that property. There's even a book about it."

Of course, had Angie Bose been intellectually curious (or had Peter Champion bragged even a little about his accomplishments in those months before she'd left), or had she even thought to ask GG, "Oh, who wrote that book on Bagehot House?"—and if the answer had come back, "Some American guy, Champion's his name, if that means anything," Angie's resulting gasp might have forced GG to slam on the brakes. Had she known to drop the name of her benefactor, GG might have corrected his tone of mild condescension and begun treating her as a fellow sophisticate. He might have asked, "*You* know Peter Champion, that gypsy-scholar who wrote *Classic Indian Architecture: Public and Private*?" Or "Peter Champion? Don't tell me he's still alive!" But of course she was not intellectually curious, at least not about the realm of books.

In a neighborhood of old mansions, Bagehot House was the largest. It was dark and sprawling, its grounds untended. The outer wall, topped with glass shards, had lost most of its stucco; the old bricks were crumbling, and parts of the wall were worn down to shoulder level. Even from the car she could see holes in the roofs of the larger outbuildings. Other houses at least maintained a pretense of serviceability, with uniformed chowkidars seated outside the gates and pots of flowers lining the driveway. Bagehot House looked abandoned.

"Well, you wanted Bagehot House, and now you've got it." He pulled to a stop around the corner and across the street, facing what had once been the front gates and lawn. "The old biddy is sure to be inside, but it'll take a while for her to hobble to the door. Every developer in Bangalore is praying for her to pop off."

Anjali visualized the developers as vultures circling a dying cow.

No room for sentimentality in this city, she realized.

The house was daunting enough, but she wondered what she owed Mr. GG or what he might try to extract from her. He was the first real man, the first settled, unattached professional man she'd ever met. He'd traveled, been married, and he'd taken an interest in her. In just one morning, three hours into her new life, she'd been lifted from Gauripur into a new city, into a new century and a new currency, where crores were the new lakhs, lakhs the new rupees. She would have gone anywhere with Mr. GG, done anything he asked. Next to Mr. GG, Peter Champion seemed flimsy and Rabi Chatterjee a mere child. All that remained was making a first move, a sign of interest or intent, and she didn't know if she should make it, or even if he would recognize it. And so she just waited.

"You're wondering what comes next, isn't it, Miss Bose?"

He could read her mind. "I am a little frightened," she admitted. "I haven't slept in a bed or eaten a meal since I left." Oops, that was getting too close to the truth. *And I haven't bathed and my clothes are filthy and I can still smell the privies and see women and girls climbing into trucks while drivers lifted their lungis . . .* Mr. GG's concerned face drew a little closer, and he took out a handkerchief and daubed her eyes.

"If things get really bad, you can always go back to Kolkata."

How to tell him she'd been to Kolkata three times in her life, and she couldn't even go back to Bihar? Banned from Bihar: that had to be the pits. Bangalore was it, the beginning and the end. What was it that Rabi Chatterjee had told her? She repeated it. "It's all a matter of light and angles, isn't that so?" she said.

That seemed to stun him. "I suppose you could say so." He studied her face; she flashed him a full-wattage smile. He relaxed.

"A girl like you won't be lonely for long."

A girl like me? What did it mean, and who or what, exactly, am I like? Why does he hope I'll stay? And so she voiced the question. "A girl like me, Mr. GG?" He seemed to know her better, or thought he did, than she knew herself. He did reach out for her hand and gave it a squeeze and she drew closer, expecting at least to give or to receive a hug or maybe a kiss, but Mr. GG was the perfect gentleman, which left her even more confused.

"What I meant is a girl like you is full of surprises. Next time we meet, I might not even recognize you. But I'm sure we'll meet again," he said.

She replied, "I'd like that."

"Unassailably genteel, but no mod cons." He thrust a hand out the driver's window and gestured toward the derelict mansion that was to be her new home. "You must be wondering why I haven't directed you to more modern lodgings. Or at least offered you temporary hospitality in my house." It hadn't crossed her mind. "With my parents and my sister-in-law and her children visiting, spontaneity is a burden."

Why is he telling me these things? she wondered.

He squirmed a bit in the driver's seat, and she prepared herself for whatever was to come, but he only released his seat belt, got out, and took her muddy, battered Samsonite from the trunk. Then he opened her door and took her hand to help her to the curb. He handed her his business card. "You're wondering how you can thank me, aren't you, Miss Bose? Not to worry, let's just forget it for today." He scribbled a cell-phone number on the card. "That's for when Mad Minnie makes life inside hell."

With a mock salute, he strode back to the Daewoo. Angie tried to reconcile Peter Champion's Mrs. Bagehot with Mr. GG's Mad Minnie. She was glad, she decided, that she had his private phone number. No shame in accepting help from people willing, even eager, to assist her. A job is the key to happiness, she calculated. A job brings respect and power. Money brings transformation. Stagnation creates doubt and tyranny. Money transforms a girl from Gauripur into a woman from Bangalore.

3

Anjali waited by the curb until twelve o'clock. No one had entered or departed the property. Two goats wandered through the untended gate and soon lost themselves in the undergrowth. Finally, she followed the goats, dragging her bag behind her. The carved iron door knocker, surely an original relic, had lost its matching plate. A single horn of the brass ram's head thumped into the door's soft, bare wood like a woodsman's ax into a rotting stump.

A stooped old man with stubbly cheeks and chin opened the door. He wore a frayed service jacket like a railroad porter's, but with the name BAGEHOT stitched over an unmended pocket. The elbows were torn and the jacket was not clean.

"I would like to give this to Madam Bagehot," she said in Hindi. The old man, whose first name she later learned was Asoke, silently accepted the torn-off sheet on which Peter Champion had handwritten Minnie Bagehot's name and address and then signed it. He shuffled back inside, leaving the front door slightly open. She took this as permission to enter but then wondered if she should stand and wait on the threshold or take a seat on the long teak bench in the foyer. She stood stiffly by a round hall table with a cracked marble top, keeping her backpack and mud-streaked suitcase close to her for some minutes; then she tiptoed to the bench so she could peek into the hallways and rooms that led off the foyer. The corridors were cluttered with bulky armoires, chests and tall-backed chairs and seemed to stretch endlessly in every direction. She made out a main sitting room and a formal dining room with chandelier. The light was dim and filtered through sun-bleached velvet curtains. A broad stairwell descended from upper floors.

From what she could determine from the foyer, Bagehot House was a storage barn, more a warehouse for unusable possessions than an active residence. In the sitting room a hundred years of carved wood furniture and worn upholstery lay piled in a jumble. The walls were filled with portraits of women in ball gowns and bearded men in belted and braided military uniforms, shoulder pads with tassels and pointed helmets topped with what appeared at a distance to be upside-down banana peels. All available horizontal surfaces had been taken over by silver trays piled with dishes and ivory-handled cutlery. Everything seemed secondhand, even the air. Yet she sensed that every object had once held immense value. For some reason she was suddenly reminded of Peter Champion's words: *every note a symphony.*

She was hesitant to wander too far indoors. There were probably house rules against curiosity, and she didn't want to ruin her chances even before getting started. After twenty minutes, however, she wondered if she was not being tested, if Minnie Bagehot was not watching from behind a crack in the door just to see how many liberties she would take if she thought herself unobserved.

At twelve-thirty she heard voices from the second floor. She stood at the bottom of the stairs and smiled broadly. Three girls her own age, two of them dressed more or less as she was, in T-shirts and jeans, the other in a green salwar-kameez, were chattering in English as they came down the stairs. Anjali heard a breathless "I told him no way!" and a passionate rejoinder, "They should fire him on the spot!" They were nearly upon her before she was noticed.

"Well, hi," said the first girl down, the *no way* girl. She had spiked, highlighted hair and was much shorter than Anjali. "I'm Tookie D'Mello—Teresa, formally speaking. So you're the new boarder?" She held out her hand. Her scoop-neck T-shirt revealed deep cleavage and featured the three monkeys named see-no, hear-no, and speak-no, which were circled in red, with red lines struck through them. Where are the stores that sell cheeky T-shirts like the ones Anjali had seen today, cut so deep? Even if she borrowed one, Anjali doubted that she could produce even a shadow of a cleft.

"I was promised a room, sort of promised—I hope I have a place." Her story—the Gauripur teacher knowing Bagehot House's proprietor and orally guaranteeing that she would be accepted as a boarder—seemed too convoluted an explanation.

"Don't worry, there's always a place," said the second, she of the pale green salwar-kameez. She introduced herself as Husseina Shiraz, from Hyderabad. Her voice was warm and low, a good phone voice and, from what Anjali could tell, a perfect American accent. A Muslim girl from fabled Hyderabad, but no black sack and eye slits for her. She was as tall as Anjali and as fair, with the same green eyes. Anjali repressed her first impulse, which was to say *Did you say Hyderabad? I changed buses there yesterday!* And then she censored a second thought: *We could almost pass for sisters, more than my own sister and I could.* Husseina also seemed to notice that likeness, staring almost to the point of remarking on it, then turned her head. *Sisters,* Anjali thought again, *only if I dressed up in expensive silks.*

"Or space will open up," said the third, much shorter and darker, with glasses, dressed in what looked like an old school uniform of gray tunic and white shirt. "Sunita Sampath," she said. She described herself as "a local girl" and named a small town halfway between Mysore and Bangalore. *Whom did she know, to make it into Bagehot House?* Anjali wondered.

"Sunita even speaks this wretched language," Tookie joked.

"I can give you lessons," Sunita offered.

When Anjali gave them her full name, with its unmistakable Bangla identifier, Tookie rattled off the names of half a dozen Bengali women she worked with. Refugees from marital wars, Anjali wondered, or well-heeled adventurers from progressive families, pursuing the perfect match? Tookie was obviously Goan, neutralizing Anjali's sour memory of Fathers Lobo and Pinto, dull teacher-priests back at da Gama. Tookie sounded friendly but flaky as she ran down her list of ethnic stereotypes: Goans are party beasts, Tamils dorky number-crunchers, Pathans burly hotheads, Bengalis flabby eggheads. Then she added, "Maybe not all the Bengali guys I know. There's one exception. One genuine Romeo." Anjali was about to interject *Not the famous Monish Lahiri?* But she was smart. She caught herself in time.

Instead she asked, "Where are you girls off to?"

"Smokes and caffeine," said Husseina. "Then it's hi-ho, hi-ho. Back by midnight."

"After more smokes and booze," said Tookie.

"Actually *I* don't drink," said Husseina. "My fiancé would not approve."

"Nor do I," added Sunita. "Or smoke."

And I never have, thought Anjali. *But I had a fiancé.* For an hour, at least. It was a frightening word.

Bangalore worked off the American clock. Everything about Bangalore—even its time—was virtual. Call centers ran 24/7; shifts were constantly starting or ending nine to twelve hours ahead of American time. Peter had said some of the girls even kept Los Angeles or New York time on their watches, calibrated to a mythical home base so they wouldn't be trapped in complicated calculations if asked the time. No "Good morning!" when someone was calling at midnight in America. Some white callers liked to play games, she'd heard, "exposing the Indian." And of course there were the lonely Indians in America, like Mukesh Sharma, trying to tease out phone intimacy from call-center girls.

Then she became aware that all three girls seemed to be looking over their shoulder at the front door. Husseina broke away from the group. "Oh-oh, got to go," she whispered. "Ciao, ladies." She pulled open the heavy front door before Asoke could shuffle to it. The other two tittered. Angie spotted a taxi waiting at the curb. She was about to ask Tookie where Husseina was off to when suddenly a black-sheathed wisp of a woman, with close-cropped white hair, moved like fog into the hallway.

Sunita and Tookie mumbled, "G'day, madam," and sidled out of the hallway, leaving Anjali alone with Minnie Bagehot.

"Cat got your tongue?" the woman snapped. "No greeting? Where are your manners, young lady?" Ten seconds into Anjali's new life at Bagehot House and—from fear or fatigue—she had committed some fatal mistake in etiquette. The old woman turned her back on Anjali and led the way to the dining room. Very straight posture, Anjali noted; Mrs. Bagehot glided rather than walked, the only sound being the clicking of her glasses, suspended on a silver chain, against her strand of pearls. She gripped the carved armrests of a chair at one end of a long, formal dining table and carefully lowered herself into it. She wore white lace gloves without fingertips. Anjali tried not to stare at the bluish tint of the exposed finger pads as they gathered up thin sheets of a handwritten letter. Angie recognized Peter Champion's spidery scrawl.

"G'day, madam," Anjali mumbled. *Should I stand? Should I sit in the chair next to her or across the table from her? My clothes must smell, best not to get too close.*

"I can't hear you. Did you wish me good day? Rather late in the day for that. Come closer." It was a command. The old woman indicated that Anjali should seat herself in the chair to her left by rapping the tabletop in front of that chair with the knuckles of both hands.

Seen from inches away, Mrs. Bagehot's forehead, cheeks, and throat were deeply wrinkled, and the wrinkles were spackled with pinkish face powder and orangy rouge. Her eyes were large and brown, her lips so thin they couldn't quite hide stained dentures.

Minnie Bagehot waved a gloved hand at the clutter on the dining table: stacks of floral-patterned, gilt-rimmed china dinner plates, salad plates, soup bowls, soup tureens, platters, tea cups and saucers, cake stands, butter dishes, red glass goblets furry with dust, a couple of tarnished silver trays, and a few pieces of crockery Anjali couldn't identify. "What do you think?"

Anjali was being interviewed by an imperious octogenarian whose good opinion she needed. She didn't have to like Minnie, but she did have to humor her if she wanted a cheap, safe roof over her dazed head.

"I am truly speechless, madam."

"This is a historically important residence, as your former teacher has doubtless informed you. In this very room, on these very plates, a very long time ago, His Majesty Edward VII dined, as well as innumerable minor royalty."

And they haven't been washed since, she thought.

Minnie's voice was deep, almost masculine, and her accent, so far as Anjali could determine, perfectly British. Unlike earlier generations of Indians, Anjali was too young to have heard a pure English accent or to have experienced the icy rectitude of the British character. Mrs. Bagehot's questions left her defenseless. "May I ask why you have come to Bangalore?"

No problem; she'd already rehearsed it. "My father just died, madam. I have to support myself." *May my lies be forgiven. I am dead to my father; therefore he is dead to me.*

Minnie's painted face registered no response. "Will you shame the memory of such company?"

She answered, "I shall never be worthy of royalty, madam."

"But your teacher says you are quite the best English student he has ever had! Is he lying? I must admit I am most fond of that boy. He doubtless told you of our friendship."

"Of course, madam." She lied.

"He wrote his book right here, staying in these rooms, interviewing me and tracking down old pictures. He even made a complete inventory of all the furnishings—their origin, style, provenance, and date of manufacture. It's still somewhere on the premises."

His book? Had the old lady confused Peter with some famous scholar? He didn't just tape village music—he actually wrote a book? She almost laughed out loud: *For a minute, I thought you said he'd written a book!* She knew Peter as a man who read books, but she never imagined knowing a person who'd actually written one. If anything, that knowledge was more wondrous than taking the gift of his money and knowing his sexual secrets. Then she connected the dots: the mysterious American who had written the very special book that Mr. GG had been praising was her own Peter Champion.

She wondered whether she should lower the expectations concerning her English proficiency or add to this praise of Peter Champion. Mrs. Bagehot arched an eyebrow. "My English was judged very good in my school, madam. But . . . that was in Bihar." Anjali said it as though she'd uttered a confession. "I've only been in Bangalore a few hours and I've already heard much better English than I'm capable of." *Of which I'm capable?* Minnie frowned, and Angie scrambled for a save. "Better American English, at least."

Minnie briefly smiled, or twitched her lips. "If you can call that English." She seemed to be taking in everything Anjali had said and for some reason was finding it amusing or not quite relevant. "This residence has ten bedrooms, but only four are kept open. We had a retinue of over one hundred, including drivers, gardeners, cooks, butlers, khidmugars, chaprasis, bearers, durwans, and jamadars. Now only Asoke is left, and he has worked here for over seventy years. The garage in the back housed twenty motor cars—when I say motor cars, I am referring to Bentleys and Duesenbergs, not the rattletraps Indian people drive. My late husband staged durbars for five hundred guests, nizams and maharajas and the viceroy. For entertainment we knocked croquet balls into the hedges and played badminton under torchlight, and the guests arrived on fabulous elephants decked out in silk brocade, with gold caps on their tusks and wondrously decorated howdahs, making their way in a procession down Oxford Street, which I hope you've noticed is now Bagehot Alley, turning in at Kew Gardens Corner, then up to the porte-cochère. There, each dignitary would disembark down decorated ladders, still stored somewhere on the premises. If you doubt me, there are photographs to prove it."

"I know it is true, madam," she said.

"How so?"

Anjali's talent for spontaneous dissembling never failed her. "I've seen Mr. Champion's book," she said. "Then a photographer named Rabi Chatterjee showed me more pictures. He said there are many wonders in Bangalore, but that Bagehot House is the most important."

"Perhaps you've also seen pictures of my late husband?"

"I don't believe so, no, madam."

She lifted her arm, and Asoke shuffled to her side. "Asoke, album lao," she commanded. Page after page of blurred and faded photos of Raj-era life in Bagehot House had to be admired, awe expressed, weak tea in chipped cups sipped, stale ginger cookies nibbled, and finally Anjali passed the landlady's interview and was admitted as a paying guest with probationary status.

"Unfortunately, no bedrooms are open at the moment," said Minnie, and Anjali must have flinched. *But Mr. Champion promised! Where am I to go, then?*

"I quite understand, madam," she managed to say.

"No proper bedroom, that is." Anjali detected a softening of tone, and leaned forward. "You might even hesitate—"

Was she being tested? A British game of some sort? A test of her dignity, of her self-respect? Her desperation? Should she grovel?

"I have a shuttered porch, humble but livable, cot, chair, and dresser, two hundred a week, bed tea and one tiffin included."

"That would be most satisfactory, madam." A thousand a month, she calculated, with food, in Bangalore. I can live for months on Peter's gift!

"In England after the war, we would have considered this a very desirable bed-sitter for a single working girl." After assessing Anjali's reaction, she added, "I understand that some ladies in Kent Town are asking for more, with no food," she said, but left the corollary unstated—I am doing a great favor, but if you break house rules, you'll be out on your ear.

Anjali didn't know what the house rules were because Minnie deployed them according to her whim. The only rule she spelled out, in a cross-stitched sampler that hung above the bookcase containing her collection of hardcover romance novels was

ALL GLORY TO THE BAGEHOT NAME
MAY IT NEVER BE DARKENED BY SHAME

Fortunately Tookie D'Mello knew everything and loved to share it.

On Anjali's second day in Bagehot House, Tookie said, "We'll have to go out to Glitzworld some night. I know the bartender. That's my advice to all freshers in Bangalore. Get to know the bartenders."

Everything in the old days had a white version and a black one. It was understood, by Tookie at least, that Minnie could afford the low rents and the weekly arrival of fresh mutton and brandy because of a secret agreement with certain local interests. Rolling off Tookie's tongue, "interests" took on a sinister sibilance. These interests paid a monthly stipend (as long as Minnie lived and not a second beyond) in return for exclusive rights to the deed to the entire Bagehot compound, including the main house. The interests were patient; they apparently had many irons in many fires.

"The thing to keep in mind," said Tookie, "is that Bagehot House is a madhouse. The old lady is crazy. The rules make no sense. The grounds are haunted. The girls who live here aren't what they seem."

Angie could go along with Tookie's cynical theories. In a country that runs on rumor, every event has its own powerful, unofficial motivation. Nothing is as it seems. Everything is run by dark forces. Back in

Gauripur, Peter Champion "had to be" a CIA agent. Always, a search was going on for a "larger explanation," but no matter how grand the invention, it was never large enough to explain the failures and disappointments. What else explained Peter's thirty years holed up in Bihar? Who knew what those same voices, the they-saids, "knew" about her? Subodh Mitra had thought he "knew" about her and "her American." Her parents lived in that world, the other side of the great divide.

But in Bagehot House, generations of otherwise discreet and well-mannered girls had constructed an alternative history to explain Minnie Bagehot and passed it on, with new refinements, down the generations. Minnie had poisoned Maxie in order to take over the house and grounds. No, said others, it wasn't poison. It was a stabbing, made to look like the dacoits' doing. It was well known, at least at the time—nearly sixty years ago—that young Minnie and even younger Asoke were having a torrid affair, stumbled into, or over, by the gin-dazed Maxie. Asoke even now only played at being a servant.

Barring mishap, Minnie might go on forever. She'd been a widow for nearly sixty years. Her mind was sharp, but seriously off track, dwelling only on defunct virtues like Shame, Honor, Duty, and Loyalty. ("God," said Tookie, "sounds like something out of the catechism!") Has she told you about the stable of elephants? The Prince of Wales and the rajahs and the nawabs and whatnot? And Rolls-Royces, and dancing guests plucking champagne flutes off gold trays? Just ignore them. The old girl wasn't there. Ever.

Minnie was eighty-two, give or take. She dropped the impression that she and her unnamed first husband, a colonel, had "come out" to India from Dorset when the officer corps of the Indian army was still a recognizable offshoot of Sandhurst, all pukka sahibs in piths and puttees. She suggested he'd died during the Partition riots, protecting British wives and children. In reality, according to the alternative history compiled by decades of Bagehot House Girls, Minnie had entered Maxie Bagehot's life as a twenty-six-year-old divorcee, abandoned by the colonel after Independence and the turnover of the cantonment to the new Indian army. Maybe there had never been an official registry marriage with either man. Minnie was vague and forgetful about the documentary side of her early years.

Minnie and Maxie Bagehot: aka Mini and Maxi, a private joke among generations of Bagehot Girls.

In the Bagehot Girls' snide recitation of their landlady's handed-down life story, Minnie had never been to Dorset or anywhere in England. Minnie Bagehot was the product of the old cantonment culture, the untraceable interaction between an anonymous soldier and a local woman, decades or centuries ago. Minnie was Anglo-Indian, her mother a nanny, her father a stationmaster, and she'd set herself up as a domestic organizer (whatever that meant, but easily guessed, Tookie giggled) for British widowers and bachelors who'd decided to stay on. She'd known her way around the old Bangalore and she showed the proper firmness toward natives and deference to authorities. She knew how things were done and, more important, how to get things done.

She'd made herself indispensable to Maxfield Bagehot and eventually she'd made herself sufficiently irresistible to ensure her proper survival. He'd married her—or at least solidified an arrangement of some sort—sometime in the early 1950s, when he was in his seventies, with not many years or months left on his clock, and she in her late twenties. The champagne days of durbars and decorated elephants, foreign and domestic royalty, were long in the past, long before Minnie, old as she is, had arrived on the scene. At best, she might have sipped tea with the new Indian officer corps. Tookie could do a fair imitation of Minnie. "Sikhs and Mohammedans, the martial races, loyal as mastiffs, not to forget those nearly white chaps, the Parsis and the Anglo-Indians."

The old Brits like Maxie Bagehot knew that so long as their former underlings and aides-de-camp, the proud remnants of a once mighty army, were in charge, they'd be shielded from the rabid majority. Throw in a Gurkha or two and you'd have a functioning country. Everyone knew that India needed the bracing authority and esprit de corps of a military dictatorship, with some democracy around the edges. And just look at what we've been left with today. People *dare* to call it progress.

When Minnie moved into Maxie's house, he had been a widower with no reason to return to England. His grown children had decamped to Rhodesia and Australia, never to write or visit. A fine house, a loyal and underpaid staff like the adolescent Asoke, a coven of old friends like himself, early tee times, and a British army pension went a long way in those days. So long as the imported whiskey holds out, they used to joke. And Bangalore? Well, Bangalore was a splendid place, so long as the natives kept their filthy hands off it. Bangalore's weather, a year-round seventy-five degrees, with no bloody monsoon and no mosquitoes, was the clincher. No finer place in the Empire, they agreed, not that an empire in the expansive sense of the word still existed.

And so, as a Bagehot-Girl-in-training, Anjali took to heart her first set of instructions: nothing is quite as it seems. There are unbendable rules, but no one really knows what they are. "Bringing shame" can mean anything the Old Dame wants it to mean at any given time. In fact, Anjali's little alcove room had been let to a girl from Mangalore named Mira, a "fun girl" (Tookie's highest compliment) who got "dumped" (the Bagehot House word for sudden eviction) for having come back from work at two in the morning. Nothing strange about that—but her mode of approach sealed her fate: she was on a motorcycle, clinging to a boy.

"My question to you is," said Tookie, "who's watching at two in the morning? Is the Old Dame an insomniac who sits by the window in the dark to catch rule breakers? Or does she force poor, overworked old Asoke to spy on us all night? Even the walls have ears here, so play it cool and close to the vest."

4

In her first three days in Bangalore, Anjali calculated that half of her mission had already been accomplished. Maybe even more than half: she'd escaped Gauripur, crossed India, gotten to Bangalore, met a "boy," as her father would label Mr. GG, and secured a desirable room. Well, maybe more like a miserable half-room in a moldering but fabled residence. But when she wrote her first letter to Sonali, she didn't want to frighten her sister with tales of what she had witnessed in interstate bus stops on the long odyssey or sound superior about having a room to herself in a mansion and being served by a servant in livery, or having smitten Mr. GG, so she wrote instead that she had arrived safely; that Mr. Champion's friend, who owned a huge house, had rented a prettily furnished room to her; that she expected to meet Mr. Champion's other friend, who ran a job-training school, soon; that, once she had found her way around Bangalore, she would send little Piyali a typically Karnatakan toy. Then she added, as a P.S., the questions that burdened her most: "Have Baba and Ma forgiven me? Have they asked about me?"

She could take time to get settled, rest, fatten up. *I was starving! I could have died!* Winning a place in Usha Desai's training center and then finding a job seemed a snap-of-the-finger inevitability (she ran through the list of acceptable synonyms: *a walk on the beach, a cinch, a piece of cake, a picnic,* just to convince herself she wasn't losing it). If she could pass stuck-in-the-Raj Minnie Bagehot's crackpot tests, she would ace very-new-millennium Usha Desai's. So long as Peter's rupees held out, she could tell herself that she deserved some downtime to escape the tyrannical gentility of Minnie's boarding house and explore the city, window-shop in the newest mall where Tookie bought her designer T-shirts, find her way back to the Barista on MG Road and this time order iced coffee with a scoop of ice cream, try Continental cuisine or sushi in a restaurant inside a five-star hotel. She wouldn't be procrastinating; she would be developing the composure and confidence that make for professional success. Her goal was to *be* relaxed, not just appear relaxed, when she presented herself to Mr. Champion's job-training contact.

Contact: noun. She remembered *contact* and *mentor* as loaded words in the most popular of the da Gama first-year B. Comm. courses. An adjunct professor, a recent graduate of the Indian Institute of Management in Ahmedabad, had taught the popular course. He wore white three-piece suits and drove an imported Prius. According to his business card, which he distributed to his students on the first day of classes, he was the CEO *and* the CFO of CommunicationsFutures, Inc., which had headquarters in Gauripur and branch offices in Bradford, U.K., and Hoboken, U.S.A., but he described himself as an iconoclast. "Break your feudal habit of revering masters and elders," he harangued his spellbound students.

Early in the academic year, he'd brought Peter Champion in to guest-lecture on developing contacts and networking. "Don't even think of tackling the job market until you have contacts with connections": that had been Peter's mantra. As a diligent student she had memorized the lecture's bulleted points, but until now she hadn't worried about whether they made sense. She hadn't needed to, because she was never going to be in the job market, Baba having already shunted her into the arranged-marriage market. Now she would have to put Peter's business counsel to a sink-or-swim test.

In the curtained privacy of her alcove, she lounged in a silk kimono that Mrs. Bagehot had lent her until she had time to go shopping, and she scribbled *contact, mentor, neutral acquaintance,* and *personal friend* as column headings in a new notebook she had bought at a variety store on the corner of Kew Gardens. Ms. Desai and Mrs. Bagehot were contacts. The Bagehot Girls were acquaintances for the moment, but they—at least Tookie and Husseina—might slither into other categories. She invented another classification: *informal mentor.* Rabi Chatterjee was a reach for any column in her book, since she hoped, but couldn't be sure, that their paths would converge again. She had known him for only a few hours, but she felt close to him, closer than she did to Sonali-di, because he had talked to her as though she was his equal in intelligence and experience. He had opened her eyes to the color and light shimmering under Gauripur's grit. She entered him in both the *informal mentor* and the *personal friend* columns.

She kept Mr. GG as her final entry. She savored going over and over again their chance meeting in the MG Road Barista, his offer of a ride to Kew Gardens, the long trip, and every word he had spoken during it... Was he nothing more than a transient acquaintance doing his impersonal Good Samaritan deed of the day? Could she get away with entering him as a contact with international business connections? In the best of all possible scenarios, he was a well-connected, deep-pocketed suitor. Why not? She created a skinny new column: *suitor.*

Peter would be appalled if he could see how she had expanded on his networking theory. His provocative critiques of Indian business models would have been hard for any student to ignore or forget. Peter didn't pull punches: historically, Indian society wasn't structured around networking and contacts, but rather around family and community. In backward places like Bihar, allegiance to family and hometown and religion and language group and even caste counts more than competence. Peter's lesson of a year and a half ago became a fresh revelation. He could have been talking about Baba. Even in Bihar, Baba's only friends were Bihar-born Bengalis. Everyone else was deemed slightly, or grossly, untrustworthy. Baba couldn't escape the community that he, and the three generations of Gauripur-born Boses, had known. But with his two daughters, even in Bihar, he'd failed.

So that was the secret of Mumbai's and Bangalore's great success. You work at KFC or StarLucks or Barista, and the person working next to you, and your boss, and the people you serve have absolutely no interest in your community or where you came from.

Like at Bagehot House. Before Tookie, Anjali had never been friends with a Goan. In fact, not with a Christian either. Her impression of Goans had been based on the teacher-priests at Vasco da Gama—dull, pious rule enforcers or rule followers, afraid of their shadows. And what of that mysterious group she'd always called "the minority community"? Some of the workers in her father's office were Muslim. Back stabbers, her father called them—traitors and terrorists. Her father complained of their laziness, their four wives and twenty children. "They don't work on our holy holidays. They don't work on their holy holidays. Next they'll demand time off for Christmas and Easter."

Now she was sharing a bathroom with a Muslim *and* a Christian.

At their first lunch, Tookie had advised Angie to keep two boyfriends: one for the workplace, offering convenient rides and innocent companionship, and a fun-time boyfriend. Tookie's job-site-and-Barista beau was named Reynaldo da Costa, a goody-goody Goan who wanted to marry her before sleeping with her ("What a bore, no?"). Her fun-time guy was Rajoo, a local bartender ("A badass, but what a trip, man").

"How about you, Husseina?" Angie had asked.

"Oh, I have a fiancé, in London."

"Muslim girls—what to say?" Tookie teased. "How do you know this fiancé of yours isn't raising a big English family with a fat blond floozy?"

"I don't." Husseina said that with a smile.

Buzley, buzlum.

• • •

Usha Desai, Mr. Champion's friend, was Anjali's only reliable "contact," but Anjali held off calling her because . . . she was ashamed to admit it even to herself . . . she hoped Mr. GG would call and suggest a more exciting career option or spring her from the dull boarding house and fly her off to a foreign city for a surprise vacation: all that was possible in the Bollywood version of her life. She didn't call Mr. GG, of course—what sort of young woman, except a Tookie, initiates contact?—but she found the thought of calling him and flirtatiously playing the damsel in distress very pleasing. She knew she should be grateful that Peter had sent a letter of introduction to Usha Desai, which meant she was assured admission into this woman's prestigious career-training academy and, on completion of the training, a job that paid better than Baba's or Sonali's. But calling Peter's contact and setting that process in motion meant banging the door shut on all that could be, all that *might happen if given a chance.* Network, or trust intuition?

Anjali promised herself that she would call Usha Desai soon but procrastinated, her excuse being that she wasn't yet savvy about big-city office etiquette. She needed Tookie's and Husseina's mentoring before she made the call. She needed more time in Bangalore. She needed to study Tookie and Husseina closely so that she could pick up their ways of sounding self-confident, or at least professionally competent. She had made a little bit of progress, but not enough.

In Gauripur, she'd slept between Sonali-di and Ma, and after Sonali-di's wedding, just with Ma. In Bangalore, the dark, musty mansion was empty most nights, but for Mad Minnie and arthritic Asoke, because the resident girls were at work; sleeping here, surrounded by noises coming from the untended, overgrown grounds, terrified Anjali. Ghosts and monsters circled her. An angry Baba and a tearful Ma clawed the thin cotton quilt she pulled over her head. She needed time to overcome her fears.

Gauripur memories collided with Bagehot House nightmares. Smothering memories: the same neighborhood noises at the same time, day and night. Chopping the same vegetables from the same vendor at the same market, spicing them and frying them in precisely the same manner, eating at the same hour after her father's nightly three pegs, then piling the dirty cooking pots in the sink for the part-time maid to clean the next morning, putting away the leftovers, and going to bed by ten o'clock at her father's command of "Lights out!" You could run away from home, but not from the rituals of family.

Some sleepless nights she looked down through the shutters at the grounds, now a jungle, but once the setting for croquet hoops and badminton nets. In modern Bangalore terms, it embraced just one city block, a few crores of value, but somehow it engaged the whole soul of India. Anjali heard the nighttime coughing and throat clearing of rural India inside the Bagehot compound. She saw cooking fires in the second floor of the broken-roofed garage that had stored Maxie's fancy cars; the building's windows were long gone. Old Asoke, recognizable because of his white livery jacket, flitted ghostlike in and out of patchy moonlight, carrying trays of food to the shadowy villagers who inhabited this dilapidated realm. Perhaps Minnie's retinue—their children and grandchildren—had never left, though they now bore no connection or obligation to the owner of the main house. More likely, they were invaders from the countryside; like her, they were both refugees and squatters. Staring down at that night world of Indian survival, of rural life in the middle of a thriving city, Anjali asked herself, *What makes me more special? Why would Usha Desai accept me as a trainee and help place me in some American company that pays salaries as fat as Tookie's and Husseina's?*

A girl of fifteen or so, backlit by a cooking fire, straddled the ledge of a window frame, combing out her hair. *Oh, Rabi,* Angie thought, *if you were here now, you'd make a picture of this. Every minute in Bagehot House, day or night, is a portrait in contrasts, lights and angles, old and new, and this strange, indescribable present moment in history. I could be your scout. You might have gone to all those terrible places, the whorehouses and gay haunts, but I can find you scenes you haven't dreamed of! I could carry your cameras and lenses and lights. I'm smart, I notice things, I can learn.*

For a week Anjali put off calling Usha Desai. Bagehot House had only one phone, an old-fashioned, heavy black instrument with a short frayed cord. Minnie kept it, together with a bound logbook for recording all incoming and outgoing calls and a wind-up clock, on a card table in the foyer. The rules and rates for its use by boarders were listed in red ink on a piece of cardboard taped to the wall above the table. Only Minnie and Asoke were permitted to pick up the receiver when the phone rang. Boarders were charged for receiving calls as well as for making them; they paid an additional surcharge for calls that lasted more than five minutes. Since Tookie, Husseina, and even Sunita had their cell phones, Anjali was the only one affected by Minnie's rules. She thought the rates unfairly steep. Fortunately, except for Usha Desai and Mr. GG, she knew no one to call in Bangalore, and she invented new excuses hourly for delaying that career-building call.

On the eighth day into her new life, worried that Peter would get wind of her procrastination and write her off as a bad investment, she steeled herself to dial the number for Usha Desai. To use the phone free, which meant without Minnie's and Asoke's knowledge, she had to loiter in the foyer until Minnie retired to her bedroom for her midafternoon nap and Asoke slipped off to the "village" on the Bagehot compound. After two rings a taped message came on, informing callers that they had reached the Contemporary Communications Institute, the location of the institute, and the instruction to leave name, phone number, and a brief message after the beep. Anjali had never spoken to a tape. By the time she started to say her name, the dial tone came on, and she hung up, flustered. Such a bumpkin!

She would be prepared for the answering machine the next time she dialed the Contemporary Communications Institute. She knew she should mention Peter's name with her first breath—that would set her call apart from other supplicants—but should she refer to him as Mr. Champion or as Peter, and should she mimic a regional American accent ("Five dallars!") to show off her aptitude?

At lunch the next day, with Tookie pub-hopping with friends and

Sunita away at her job, Anjali took advantage of being alone with Husseina, Queen of Cool. She asked, "If you closed your eyes and heard me for the first time, would you guess I'm Indian?"

Without a second's hesitation, Husseina answered, "Of course. How else could you sound?"

Was Husseina assuring her that an Indian accent wasn't necessarily a demerit for a future call-center agent? Anjali decided Husseina intended her remark as a pat on the head, a well-grounded opinion that a non-desi English accent was seriously overrated. She pursued the point: "How did you come to sound so American?"

Husseina stripped forkfuls of mashed potato off the top of the wedge of shepherd's pie on her plate. "If you really want to know," she said finally, "I had no choice. My parents sent me to the American School in Dubai."

What was the point in Anjali's even trying to compete with the rich, cosmopolitan Husseinas of Bangalore? She didn't stand a chance of getting a job here. Why had she bothered to run away from Gauripur, and run away so melodramatically at that? It was unfair that the Husseinas led charmed lives. Her hands curled in rage around her napkin ring. All of those call-center workers at Barista, who had so dazzled her during her first hour in Bangalore—were they also graduates of expensive foreign schools, getting reacquainted with their parents' homeland?

Asoke shuffled around the dining table, removing plates and the cruet stand. Husseina gulped down a full glass of water. "If I'd had a say in the matter, I'd never have left India." It seemed a startling confession, coming from Her Serene Highness, the never-ruffled Husseina Shiraz. "The American School was a very great mistake. My parents were clueless! Not that anything can be corrected now." Her words were bitter but delivered lightly, and with a smile. "Spilled milk, water under the bridge, sleeping dogs, et cetera, et cetera."

Anjali was dying to ask Husseina about growing up in glamorous Dubai and, if she dared, what Husseina meant by "mistake." She waited until Asoke finished serving dessert, which as always, except on Sundays, was a gelatinous blob that Minnie called blancmange. "I wish we could talk some more."

"We shall," Husseina said.

"I have a favor to ask." Anjali ignored Husseina's frown. "I have a contact in town, a lady who runs a job-training academy of some sort. If I phoned her, do you think she would reject . . . is my accent, you know . . ."

"Miss Husseina, Miss Anjali, Nescafé?" Asoke interrupted them. Minnie charged extra for after-dessert instant coffee. Asoke removed the matching sugar bowl and creamer and their coffee spoons without waiting for them to answer. "Sweet course finished, miss?" He clearly meant to hurry them out of the dining room so that he could lock up the dining-kitchen-pantry area and disappear into the village of squatters for the rest of the early afternoon.

Husseina waved him away with an imperious hand. Her blancmange remained untouched in its glass dish. "Let's do a little rehearsal," she said, turning to Anjali. "Pretend I'm that contact. Say what comes into your head when I ask questions. You've just rung me, the contact lady. I'm picking up the phone. What's the contact's name?"

"Usha. Usha Desai." She heard Asoke pace the hallway.

"All right, I've picked up the receiver after four rings," Husseina said. "Usha Desai here." She modulated her voice, making it sound middle-aged and slightly stuffy. "To whom am I speaking? Please state your name and business clearly."

"Hullo, madam . . ."

"No, no. Never *madam.* Unless it's a crone like our Mad Minnie."

"Hullo, Mrs. Desai. My name is Anjali Bose . . ."

"No. No, and again no. How do you know she's married?"

How could she not be, Anjali thought. *The woman is middle-aged and she's prosperous.* "I don't," she admitted.

"Make *mizz* your default for her. Okay, give it another go. Usha Desai here. Who is speaking?"

"Good morning, Mizz Desai. My name is Anjali Bose, and I am, I mean I was a student of Mr. Peter Champion in Gauripur, Bihar. He has recommended I enter your training facility."

"That's very thoughtful of your teacher. Have you applied for admission? What are your qualifications for admission?"

Anjali dropped her imaginary telephone. Bumpkin, bumpkin, bumpkin!

"Who is this teacher?" Husseina continued the role-play. "He sounds like a foreigner."

"Mizz Desai will know him," Anjali protested. "Mr. Champion said she knows him. Everybody knows him."

Husseina lifted a skeptical eyebrow. "All right, feedback time. Your greeting to her is fine. Introducing the teacher's name and place are also fine. Say what you need to say simply and precisely: Good morning, et cetera, et cetera. My name is et cetera, et cetera. I was a student of et cetera, et cetera, in whatever town, and wait for the contact's reaction. She might go, 'Oh, dear old et cetera, et cetera. How is he?' And then you come back with 'He's hale and hearty, he sends his et ceteras." Is there a wife? If so, don't forget to mention her, so there's no hint of hanky-panky. Go on to 'My teacher said I must call you when I reached Bangalore to see if you could find a place for me in your training school.' After that, you play it by ear. Those classes can be shockingly expensive. Just so you know what expenses you're committing to."

Husseina's casual aside on fees was the most chilling information yet; Anjali hadn't counted on having to peel off rupees—thousands of them—from Peter's stash for the CCI course.

Anjali didn't waste her energy cultivating short, bespectacled Sunita Sampath. Sunita had nothing to teach her. She was too familiar a type; a middle-class Hindu girl from a nearby small town, the eldest of five sisters and a brother, with a Second Class Bachelor of Arts degree in English literature. Her brother was in Bangalore, but out of work and estranged from the family. She was working to help her family until her father found her a caste-appropriate bridegroom. "I am not a demanding person," Sunita confessed to the Bagehot Girls, "but I'll nix any candidate who expects a dowry."

Poor Sunita, thought Angie; as though being short and myopic was not bad enough, she also underplayed the marriage market. What kind of desirable boy thinks so little of himself that he doesn't demand a dowry? And are you of such little value in the eyes of your father or even yourself that any boy with minimal qualifications and no self-assurance can just grab you? *Even my father thought I was worth a matched set of golf clubs.* And then she thought, almost ashamed to admit it, *Yes, Sunita, you are of little value.*

Of the Bagehot Girls, Husseina was the one who could help her most, Anjali decided. But though she tried to corral Husseina in the foyer whenever the other boarders were not around, she couldn't get close to the sophisticated Hyderabadi. Anjali pried, but Husseina Shiraz disclosed next to nothing of her family or her hopes and wants. She deflected Anjali with a wink and a clever phrase: "What happens in Hyderabad stays in Hyderabad." As for her family's fortune, she had a two-word explanation: "Daddy dabbles." Her English was perfect and her voice so low, so appealing, and ultimately so authoritative that Angie conjured her own picture of the Shiraz family: an armada plying between India and Hong Kong, Singapore and the Gulf. Tookie, on the other hand, was compulsively friendly. Instead of "Hullo," she always greeted Anjali with a hearty "Hey, got yourself a guy friend yet? If not, I can set you up."

Tookie was inscrutable. Maybe all Christians were inscrutable. One of Tookie's sisters was a nun in Mozambique, one brother a priest in Massachusetts, but she declared herself a devotee of guiltless gratification. "I have a thing, you see" she'd explained to Anjali, "for boys, booze, and cash. Lots of cash." She had three sisters and five brothers, with whom she communicated only at Christmas. Her stories about her family were amusing but nasty. Her father hadn't worked in fifteen years, since a bus accident left him unable to sit long hours — except on a stool at a pheni bar. Her mother, who didn't believe in divorce, had chosen instead to go crazy and was living in an asylum.

Tookie's tales of her dysfunctional family fascinated Anjali. How could a daughter spill shameful secrets about her parents? She herself had been raised to hide unpleasant family failings from nosy outsiders. Tookie could make violent incidents sound hilarious. She had funny nicknames for her brothers who hadn't entered a religious vocation — Brother Sloth, Brother Gluttony, Brother Envy, and Brother Lust — four of the seven deadly sins. If Husseina was an invaluable mentor, Tookie was a pretty good coach for loosening up.

And today Goan Tookie was greeting Anjali with something more than her usual offer to set her up with a "guy friend." Today she was offering "a Bengali guy hunk."

Men's names came swimming up from Anjali's first morning in Bangalore, at the Barista. Mumbai Girl and her work buddies. All those high-fiving, caffeine-fired call agents with made-up American names: Darren, Will, Mike, Brad, Tom, Fred, Hank, Paul, Josh, Jeff. And Mukesh/Mickey Sharma, the sicko caller from Champagne. She said to Tookie, "Who would that be . . . Monish Lahiri?"

Tookie dropped her spoon. "What! Tell me again how long you've been in Bangalore?"

She would have to learn to keep her silence. "Actually . . ." She groped for other Bengali men's names. "I could come up with other possibilities." No need to mention Mr. GG since he was a Punjabi.

"Only one important thing to remember, Anjali." Tookie paused to retrieve the spoon from the floor and flick dust mites off it with her napkin. "Check out the date's income. The body parts are interchangeable."

Anjali couldn't believe that she was seriously considering being set up by Tookie, let alone enjoying Tookie's salacious references to men's body parts. "Girl talk" is how the prim Sunita referred to Tookie's chatter about sex, as in "I have no time for your girl talk and you wouldn't either if you had to send money home."

"How's your brother doing?" asked Tookie.

"He's found work," Sunita answered. That wasn't what Tookie was asking.

The boarders confided in one another mostly over their early lunch. Tookie and Husseina worked all-night shifts—Tookie handled claims for an automobile insurance company, Husseina spelled out mortgage and home-loan options for Citibank customers, and Sunita had a day job, meaning a middle-of-the-night American job, for a home security company called SecurTrix. "You wouldn't believe the number of home break-ins there are in America! Every night I get these 'Help me!' calls, and I have to alert local police to get out to some address I've never seen in some American city . . . all this from India!"

Over lunch, which invariably consisted of rice-clogged mulligatawny soup, a main course of insipid mutton stew, or goat-meat shepherd's pie, and a dessert—Asoke's culinary skills having been honed as an adolescent in that very house and not been challenged since—Anjali did her best to glean information on work-site etiquette at call centers. For instance, Husseina and Tookie lost their temper if anyone addressed them as call-center agents. They were "customer-support service specialists," and don't you dare forget it. She also squirreled away information on the American mentality and economy. From Tookie's insurance perspective, every car on the American road must be a dented wreck and all drivers were the walking wounded. In an exaggerated American accent Tookie would exclaim, "My job's a bitch! I'm burned out, man!" To Husseina, all Americans were heedless borrowers mired in debt, their home ownership hanging by a thread. From a distance, Husseina said, America might seem enticing, but viewed up close it was a scary place to live. Somehow Tookie always managed to steer the dining-table chatter back to nasty gossip about their landlady.

"You can't trust anything these Anglo-Indians say. If Minnie's precious viceroy was ever in this house, you know Maxie would have locked her away in the servants' shed." Tookie, like Minnie, was not one to disguise her prejudices, except when she thought Minnie was eavesdropping. Anjali drew a deft lesson from Tookie's version of Mrs. Bagehot's life: obstacles are steppingstones. The unsentimental stay smart. They trade up.

For her part, Anjali offered up morsels of a mythical Gauripur cast in a lurid, Bollywoodish light. Ali the gay servant was a big hit with Tookie. In Anjali's telling, she passed her old saris along to him. The comedy of Hindu marriage arrangements—she was careful to omit her horrible car ride with Subodh Mitra—was a winner. Rabi Chatterjee was transformed into an old school friend, maybe the suitor she was destined to marry. She fabricated all this in English because English was the only language the Bagehot House boarders had in common. Besides, English was the language of fantasy. Hindi and Bangla brought only dreary reality.

For the time being at least, Anjali's obstacles were manageable money troubles. She had depleted her stash from Peter Champion (which she now told herself was a merit scholarship and not a loan). To save on expenses, Anjali began to dip into other tenants' bottles of shampoo, squeeze swirls of their toothpaste onto her old brush, scoop dollops of their expensive face creams from squat little jars, and squirt imported cologne from frosted-glass flasks. Gauripur's Anjali had been too timid to experiment with expensive toiletries, and Gauripur's Angie too proud to stoop to stealing. Bangalore's Anjali, a creature of fantasy, considered herself a wily survivor, leveling an uneven playing field.

Besides, Anjali rationalized, Tookie and Husseina could afford to be stolen from. Not that they bragged about their salaries, but they huddled over which make of motorized scooter they should buy, which area of the city made the most sense for investing in a condo, and which banks were courting them most aggressively with offers of low-interest mortgages and loans. They spoke often of "the bottom line," and "long-term interests." Tookie's paycheck had to be astronomical, since she was a "team leader" in charge of ten or twelve "freshers." What must a constant cash flow be like? She vowed to get it together enough to call Usha Desai's number again. Tomorrow, or the day after.

• • •

One afternoon, with all three of her fellow boarders gone to work, Minnie asleep after lunch, and Asoke off to visit the outbuilding squatters, Anjali did some incautious snooping around in the closed but unlocked ballroom, billiards room, conservatory, reception hall, smoking room, and the three ground-floor bedroom suites with attached bathrooms and dressing rooms. The ballroom floor tilted at such an upward angle that she had to catch her breath to simply walk across it. The dressing rooms were twice the size of the room in which she and her mother used to sleep. Two sets of curtains, one thick and one sheer, hung from a velvet-covered pelmet above each window. Sparrows had nested in the sconces and chandeliers, and no one had removed the twigs and twine. Rats had chewed through the brocade upholstery of settees and gnawed on the heavy wooden chaises longues. Geckos darted up and down cracked statues of cherubs.

She was about to sneak out of the ballroom when a row of photographs along the far wall drew her attention. Unlike the usual commissioned portraits of vanished officers with their banana-skin helmets, these were wide, black-and-white landscapes, seemingly military scenes, framed in pewter. As she drew closer, she began to feel sick. Sari-clad bodies lay strewn along a riverbank. The faces were young, no older than she was. Bodies of Sikhs—you could identify them by their turbans—lay stacked like firewood, and walking among the bodies were uniformed British soldiers, grinning broadly. One had his foot on the head of a dead Sikh, striking the pose of the Great White Hunter. Maybe he was the young Maxfield Bagehot. She hoped he was. If so, all actions and opinions of Maxie and Minnie were unforgivable and all transgressions by Bagehot House boarders heroic. Another painting featured a distant row of hanged men, Sikhs with their hair chopped off, hanging by their turbans, silhouetted against the setting sun. Bagehot House was a museum of horrors.

She felt herself swelling with rage, then venom. There had to be a reckoning. She wondered if other Bagehot Girls over the years had taken the same secret tour, and how many "dumps" resulted from their quiet acts of deliberate spite. She missed Peter Champion—he could have explained these photos. Maybe she was the first since Peter to invade this warehouse, to touch the objects and feel the blunt insult of history.

She was tall, and icy. Nothing could touch her. If Minnie had been standing at the door, about to invoke Bagehot House rules, Anjali would have pushed her down and walked over her bones. She slipped a silver goblet under her sweater. In school, she'd never really warmed to the history-book chapters devoted to India's "heroic freedom fighters," and the exalted statues of "martyrs" to Indian independence had left her cold. There were families in Gauripur even today living off the glory of their great-grandparents' arrests and jailings. Now three old pictures had driven home an appreciation she'd never felt.

I am Indian, she thought. *I'm Indian in ways no one else in this house is Indian, except maybe poor little Sunita Sampath. I have no roots anywhere but in India. My ancestors were hated and persecuted by everyone but themselves. I understand Sonali-di, even Baba.* Finally, she had a test for authenticity: *Which side of this picture are you on? Is your foot on my head, are you a hanged fighter, or were you laughing at the sight of men dangling by their turbans and women's bodies clogging the riverbanks? Everyone in my life has tried to change me, make me want something alien, and make me ashamed that I might not be good enough. Why should I want to change my name and my accent, why should I plead for a chance to be allowed to take calls from people who've spent too much money or driven their cars into a ditch?*

She sauntered back to her bare cubicle in a better mood. At least now she knew she didn't have to be cowering and grateful. Minnie wasn't just the past—she was that thing the newspaper column had described; she was *Chinatown,* she was the bones under the building boom. Bagehot House was considered a respectable address, a first stop for young working girls. Bagehot House carried its own recommendation. Minnie was admired for running a no-nonsense boarding house that was good training for the corporate world, but there was nothing admirable about it. Anjali, who'd looked on the British period as a long comic opera, felt a sudden connection to all the Indian dead, and the indignities they suffered. She saw her parents still cowering and still recovering from the scars of colonialism and the dazzling new Bangalore as a city of total amnesia. And it was all a lie. House rules did not apply, not when dispensed from a Minnie Bagehot to a young woman like Anjali Bose. She wrapped the silver goblet in a T-shirt and stuffed it inside her Samsonite.

The second time Anjali tried the Contemporary Communications Institute, she again got the answering machine. But this time the voice on the tape informed callers that the institute's office was closed until the start of the next session, for which there were no vacancies. The answering machine did not accept messages. Anjali wasn't fazed. Usha Desai must have received Peter's letter about her. No way could the "no vacancy" message apply to Peter's best student. In fact, she'd be disappointed in Peter's networking skills if Usha Desai didn't get in touch with her at Bagehot House instead of waiting for a call from her. Just in case the tape allowed it, she launched into an unpremeditated message: "This is Anjali Bose, a student of Peter Champion in Gauripur. He sends his regards and told me to contact you as soon as I got to Bangalore. I am now at Bagehot House. The phone number is—"

But there was a click, and the dial tone came on.

Three weeks into her stay, Anjali discovered that she was being charged the same rent for her closed-in porch as the other three boarders, even though those three had huge rooms, each with a high ceiling, an overhead fan, and a door that could be bolted and padlocked for extra security. So what if Sunita's sofa smelled of cat pee, or that the gilt-edged mirror in Husseina's room had a crack right down the center, or that bedbugs drove Tookie crazy?

She asked the others if she should confront the landlady.

"Confrontation is never the way," Husseina advised. "Never tip your hand. A dab of honey is always the answer."

Tookie jumped in. "Definitely, go with the honey. First few days, you're on probation. The old girl wants to make sure you meet her standards."

"What standards?"

"Only the old girl knows. I think it's a low threshold of pain. My first week here a paying guest got kicked out because she picked up her soup bowl and slurped it instead of using the soup spoon. The old girl's a stickler for idiot table manners."

"But there are dozens of rooms just on this wing. Why can't she open up another one for me?"

"Get real! Who knows what you'd find? I can't imagine what's behind any door. Snoop around for yourself. But if the old girl catches you, it's a dump for sure."

"Have you snooped?" she asked.

Sunita looked up from checking her text messages. "Wouldn't dare!" she exclaimed. "The public rooms are strictly out of bounds. *Verboten!*" She was learning German from language tapes in hopes of getting an early promotion at her security company, which had just been taken over by a German conglomerate.

Tookie laughed. "Why risk everything? As far as I'm concerned, the bottom line's all that counts. We may be inmates in a madhouse, but we're paying bargain rates because the old girl's stuck in a time warp. She thinks the rupee is still five to the dollar. In a newer boarding house, we'd be forking out twenty times more cash for pokey rooms shared with three other girls."

"Actually, I *have* copped a look," said Husseina. She cast a glance down the long, dark hallway. "We might not be the only roomers in Bagehot House. We're Minnie's only paying guests, yes, but . . . I'll let you figure out what I'm getting at."

"I took a tour," Anjali admitted. "You can't imagine the trash she's got down there."

"I wouldn't call it trash, exactly," the regal Husseina snapped. "Unsorted, maybe. Like a museum without a curator."

A museum of unsorted, uncurated horrors, Anjali thought.

They left the decision to Anjali with this final reminder: taking the risk of confronting Minnie might mean getting dumped, which was bad for the pocketbook, temporarily at least. But expulsion from the airless Bagehot House, with its cloistered secrets and ornate rules, promised a release into Bangalore's special freedoms—love and adventure. Minnie provided clean rooms cheap *and* a touch of the Old Bangalore prestige, but at a cost to one's self-image as a modern, quick-on-her-feet, fun-loving Indian girl.

5

Shh—she's talking to Maxie's ghost!"

The Bagehot House Girls had gathered at the top of the stairs at twelve noon, waiting for Asoke to sound the gong announcing tiffin, which was Minnie's term for the lunch-hour meal that she had Asoke serve them in an alcove off the padlocked formal dining room. But Minnie was in the foyer, speaking on the telephone. Her back was arched forward as she cupped the heavy receiver with both hands against her left cheek; her voice was louder than usual and sounded giggly-girlish.

"She has a gentleman caller!" Sunita gasped.

Regal Husseina gave an unregal wink. "Tookie, you put one of your guy friends up to this trick, didn't you? Just look at Mad Minnie, she's blushing under all that thick makeup!"

"And *you,*" Minnie simpered. "It's been ever so long! And I'm not getting any younger, but I'm still good for a waltz or two. Or three."

Tookie crossed her heart. *I'm above reproach,* her look said, as she led the other three down the staircase. Sunita coughed to warn the landlady that she had company in the foyer.

"Oh, splendid! Well, ta-ta, for now." But Minnie didn't hang up. She turned to face her boarders. "For you," she announced, holding out the receiver. None of the young women reached for it. The earpiece was caked with beige face powder. "What's the matter? I'm not charging you for receiving this call, Anjali."

"Me, madam?" The only person who knew where to reach her was Mr. GG. She hoped her excitement wasn't too obvious to Husseina and Tookie. "Anjali Bose here," she mumbled as Minnie pushed the receiver into her face.

And from a vast distance she heard a familiar voice: "Angie, it's me, Peter."

His voice was *so* American, *so* not like the Americanized banter of the Willies and Mickeys and Hanks at Barista.

"Peter! I was just talking about you!" It wasn't a lie, not really. She had mentioned his name when Husseina played the role of Usha Desai, to prep for the call she had not yet made. "Where are you, Peter?" *Oh, please, please,* she prayed, *let him be far away from Bangalore.*

"It's Peter" were the words she'd most feared. She imagined what he'd ask: *Why haven't you called Usha Desai? How much money have you squandered?* She hadn't prepared her defense. *I tried to call Mizz Desai, but the lines were occupied, I mean, the line was busy.* Or a bold lie: *I called but she didn't recognize my name.* Except that Minnie would then find out she had made a freebie outgoing call and definitely dump her. Or *I just came down to the hall to call her. It's mental telepathy!* How could she admit the humiliating truth that she had been scared away by Usha Desai's answering machine?

"Well, I'm glad you made it to Bagehot House. You couldn't be in safer hands than dear Minnie's. Now about CCI . . ."

Minnie, Tookie, Husseina, and Sunita huddled around her, listening in. Even Asoke, waiting at the door to the dining room to serve the soup course, showed interest in Anjali's one and only telephone call in over three weeks. This was one time she didn't savor being the center of attention.

"CCI?" Anjali asked. She felt the idioms and accents she had practiced assiduously in Peter Champion's conversational skills classes desert her.

"Usha's outfit. Contemporary Communications Institute. She said she hadn't heard from you."

"Oh, CCI," she mumbled. So her Gauripur benefactor was tracking her lack of progress. *Mumble a noncommittal response; don't admit to procrastination.* "I agree . . ."

"Pardon? You're breaking up, Angie. Bad connection."

"Monday next I am planning . . ."

"Can't stay over till Monday, but at least I can make sure you have an interview set up with Usha. Listen, I'm flying in for the weekend."

"Here? You are coming?"

"Getting in Friday afternoon."

Tookie mimed a lover's swoon, collapsing into Husseina's arms. "Romeo, Romeo, wherefore art thou"—she mouthed the words.

"This Friday you are coming?"

"Minnie's readying a room for me."

"In Bagehot House you are staying?"

Minnie snorted. "Where else would I put the adorable boy?"

"I thought it best to deliver Gauripur news in person, Angie."

An "Omigod!" slipped out before she could stop it. Why couldn't Peter accept that she had scoured Gauripur out of her life as roughly as her father scooped corns and calluses off his feet with a used razor? She tried to recover by asking after Ali.

"We have a lot to talk over, Angie."

"Does that mean . . ."

Minnie rapped her lace-gloved fingers on Anjali's back. "Long-distance call," she said sternly. Anjali got the hint and kept her goodbye brief.

"The dawning of a new durbar." Tookie giggled as she grabbed Anjali by the waist and fox-trotted her away from the landlady. "Would you believe the old cow is jealous?"

Asoke ushered them into the eating alcove without sounding the tiffin gong. Their places were set as usual on a wiped-clean plastic tablecloth. As they took their seats, Minnie launched into a soliloquy on the difficulty of hosting a Bagehot House gala, a true durbar, without the help of Maxie, God rest his soul in peace. The number of guests other than the guest of honor had to be limited to eight, because only ten diners could be accommodated at the table in the formal dining room. In her excitement, she'd taken out her hearing aid. "Let's see now, dear Opal Philpott absolutely cannot *not* be invited. You've all heard me talk of the poor, dear brigadier general's untimely death."

Sunita murmured a dutiful "Yes, madam."

"Dropped dead playing polo," Minnie informed Anjali.

Tookie nudged Anjali's foot with hers. "Last time she told the story, the late, lamented codger took an accidental bullet in the head during a tiger shoot," she whispered.

Asoke shuffled around the table, serving the soup course. Thick cream of cauliflower, Anjali noted happily, instead of the usual tasteless mulligatawny. She was about to dip her spoon into the soup when she caught sight of wiggly, white bugs among the florets. Her mother always soaked raw cauliflower bits in salted water for half an hour to tease bugs out *before* she started currying them. How was her mother coping? Had her own scandalous running away brought Sonali-di and Baba closer?

"Asoke could hand-deliver an invitation to Ruby. Ruby Thistlethwaite never made it to New Zealand as she'd hoped." Minnie took a dainty spoonful of soup and blotted her lips with her linen napkin, leaving a scarlet lipstick smear. "No. Dear Opal would never forgive me if I invited Ruby, not after Ruby insulted the brigadier general at the Gymkhana after too many gin fizzes."

"Widow Opal's the only living friend she has," Tookie muttered. "And she's barely alive."

By the time Asoke cleared the dessert plates, the landlady had come up with no additional names. She discovered, and casually reinserted, her hearing device. She asked Anjali—almost begged her—if she knew of Bangalore friends of her former teacher who should be invited. Anjali was absolutely sure she didn't want to meet Usha Desai yet, not on Minnie's terms, but what a fluke opportunity to impress Mr. GG with that fact that she knew the American expert on Bagehot House history well enough to get him invited to the dinner party. "Actually there *is* someone," Anjali offered. "Mr. Gujral is a fan of Mr. Champion's book on your home."

Minnie beamed. "Perfect! Make the call today at your convenience, no charge. Asoke, smelling salts. Oh dear, I'm in such a tizzy about the gala, my head is spinning like a top!"

Asoke pushed the landlady's chair away from the dining table and helped her stand. Then he pulled a small green bottle out of a pocket of his soup-stained livery jacket, unscrewed the cap, and held the bottle to her nostrils. She took a shallow sniff. "You girls are also invited," she said as she allowed Asoke to help her out of the room for her usual afternoon nap.

"How can the old cow stand that smell?" Tookie shuddered.

"More important, where does one buy smelling salts in this day and age?" Husseina said. She turned to Anjali and winked. "Smooth move. Getting former and future suitors acquainted!"

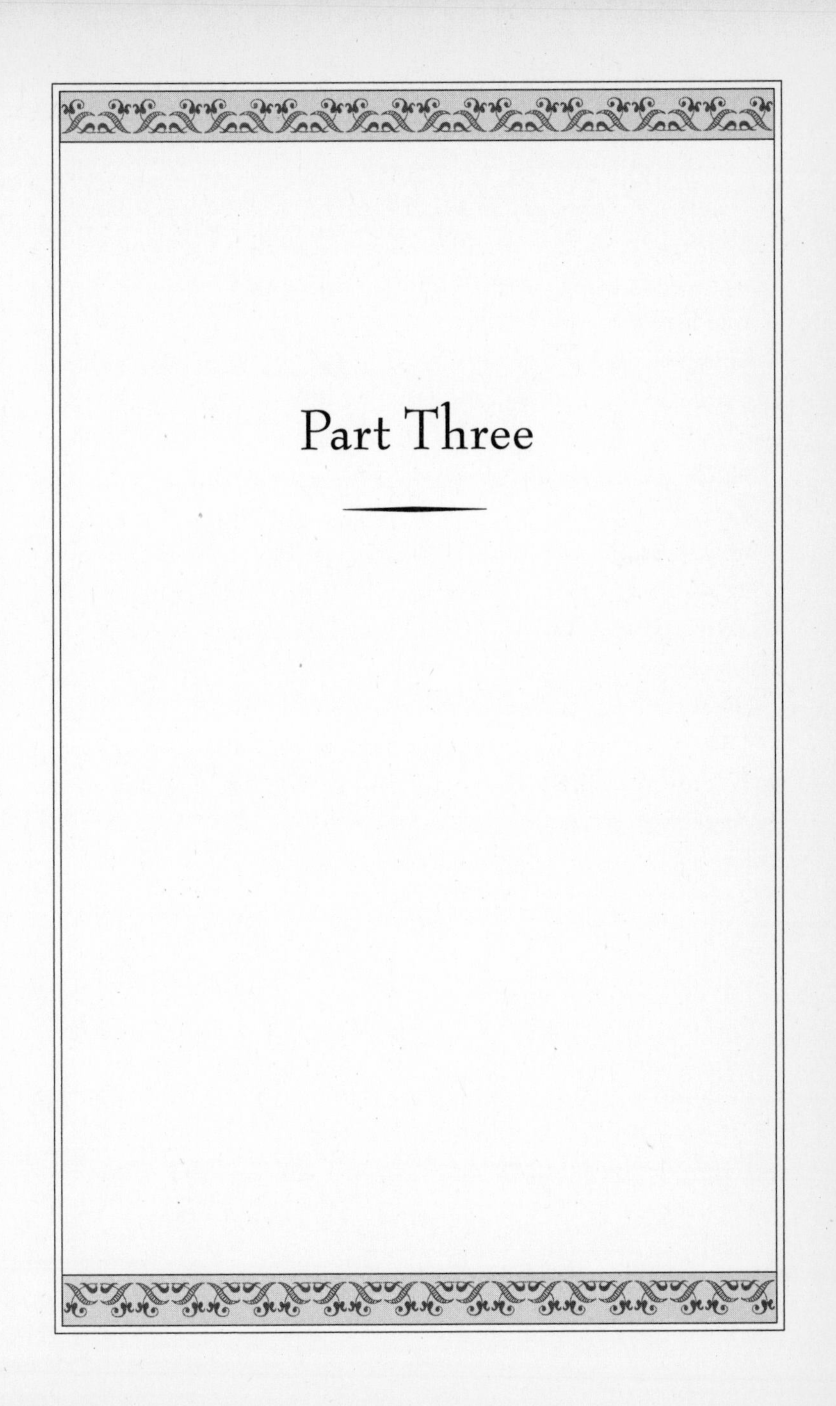

Part Three

1

Bagehot House was staging its first durbar in sixty years.

By late afternoon of the day that Peter Champion called from Gauripur, a Wednesday, Asoke had recruited a small army of the compound's squatters to haul musty Raj-era furniture, mildewed velvet drapes, and a rat-gnawed Oriental rug out of a downstairs bedroom, scrub the cracked mosaic floor and water-stained walls with disinfectant, sweep cobwebs from the blades of the ceiling fan, and refurnish the room with lighter furniture from Minnie's private suite: a twin platform bed with a thick slab of foam instead of box spring and lumpy mattress, a dressing table with an oval mirror and upholstered stool, a three-drawer chest, a coat tree, a compact writing desk with hinged lid, and a chintz-covered overstuffed loveseat.

All—well, many—of Minnie's claims about Bagehot House's Raj-era opulence were true. There actually were stacks of silver trays and silver tea services, wooden chests of heavy silver cutlery, cut-glass decanters and goblets, gilt-edged champagne flutes, fine bone china bearing the Bagehot family crest, silver-capped elephant tusks and tiger-skin throw rugs stored on the premises in locations known only to Asoke.

Live caparisoned elephants were beyond his powers. But he had the power to—and did—conscript scores of the squatters on the Bagehot compound to do the work that must have been done by liveried butlers, bearers, cooks, and sweepers in the heyday of durbars.

But who was paying for the delivery of live chickens and ducks and fresh-killed mutton, Anjali wondered. Baskets kept arriving: fruits, vegetables, sweets, a cake. And finally a case of French champagne. Champagne? Who could afford such gifts? None of her fellow boarders, not even nosy Tookie, offered a convincing guess. Minnie had mysterious purveyors.

On Friday morning Asoke had a half-dozen teenage boys chop down boughs from flowering trees, which he then stuck in umbrella stands made out of hollowed elephant feet. Minnie herself supervised as two garage-dwelling mother-and-daughter teams rinsed and dried stacks of dinner plates, soup plates, water goblets, punch bowls, and lemonade pitchers. Asoke trained a squatter girl, the one Anjali had seen straddling a window frame and combing her hair in the firelight, in the correct way to wait on tables, then sent her into the snake-infested jungle behind the main house to gather flowers. The girl must have been fearless; she sashayed barefoot into the dense vegetation and came back with two bucketfuls, which Husseina and Anjali had to arrange and rearrange in improvised vases—mainly lemonade pitchers, punch bowls, and old chamber pots—until the arrangements won Minnie's approval. Anjali remembered Peter's little joke: "I have a way with older women." The preparation for his visit was indeed monumental, an overturning of history itself. Out with the pewter-framed portraits of colonels with apoplectic pink complexions; in with brass-topped Indian tables and wall hangings of blue-skinned Krishna, the God of Love, at play with ivory-pale almond-eyed milkmaids. Watching as Minnie, giddy as an infatuated schoolgirl, fussed over plans to make Peter welcome, Anjali felt an odd sense of power. Minnie knew nothing of Ali; Anjali held that secret.

• • •

EARLY ON FRIDAY evening, as Anjali paced the cluttered floor of her alcove, trying to decide which of two tops to wear with her slinkiest pair of black cotton pants, Husseina poked her head in. "Which do you think?" Anjali asked. "I don't have a decent mirror in this rat hole. Minnie has some nerve charging me the rent she does!"

Husseina took the tops from Anjali. "I was wondering if you would like to borrow one of my gharara sets. Minnie thinks of tonight as a dress-up night." She managed a theatrical shudder. "Who knows what sumptuous moldy gown she'll deck herself out in."

Anjali thrilled at the chance of greeting Mr. GG in one of Husseina's elegant formal outfits. The one and only time they had met, they'd *clicked.* And what had she been wearing that first day of her new life in Bangalore? The sweaty, rumpled jeans and T-shirt in which she had finished her odyssey all the way from Gauripur. She coveted Husseina's look of effortless stylishness. But on her, Anjali was convinced, Husseina's expensive clothes would look seductive as well as sophisticated. How could Mr. GG not be overwhelmed?

Husseina's room was huge. Anjali envied the massive four-poster bed, the rosewood chests of drawers and cupboards with lion's-head brass pulls, the sun-bleached velvet curtains and the elaborately framed paintings: golden-haired little girls in frocks with frills and bows, kittens playing with balls of wool.

"Borrow what you like," Husseina urged Anjali, as she unlocked the door to a ceiling-to-floor almirah. "Sunita's ironing the salwar-kameez I'll be wearing tonight. That girl's so selfless, it's almost annoying." The interior of Husseina's almirah glowed with a pastel rainbow of silk. "Key lime, lemon chiffon, apricot, mango, raspberry sorbet. My just desserts, I call them. Go on, take your pick. I'll be in blueberry."

"I couldn't," Anjali said, without meaning it. She fingered the silks, georgettes and organzas.

"Don't you like them?" Husseina sounded hurt.

"They're beautiful."

Husseina pulled two pistachio-green gharara sets out of the almirah. One was decorated with crystal beads, the other with sequins. "Swarovski," she said. "That's what I wore on my first real date with my fiancé after we were engaged. We had ice cream sundaes." She shut the mirrored door of the almirah and pointed to their reflections. "Pistachio matches your eyes." She pulled Anjali closer to her, pressing her body hard against Anjali as if trying to fuse their flesh. "The same greenish eyes, would you believe?"

Husseina's sudden intensity frightened Anjali, but she didn't want to risk losing the chance to borrow an expensive gharara that might inflame Mr. GG.

"We could be sisters," Husseina continued. "If we dressed alike, I bet we could pass for twins." She laughed as she handed the crystal-speckled outfit to Anjali. "I want you to have this. And not just for tonight."

"Oh, I couldn't . . ." Anjali said, but she grabbed the top. Rich and mysterious Husseina could afford to be magnanimous, so why insult her by refusing her exquisite gift? As Tookie often remarked, there was no point in worrying about Husseina's motives: "She's so rich, she lives on a different planet."

Husseina draped the shimmery top over Anjali's navy stretch T-shirt. "You're going to look very beautiful for your young man."

My young man? She decided Husseina was referring to Peter Champion, not Mr. GG. "He's not *my* young man." She could take Husseina into partial confidence. "Peter isn't young. You'll see tonight."

"But you call your teacher by his first name?"

"It's an American thing. Actually, he's more like my father's age."

Husseina arched a finely plucked eyebrow. "What's twenty, twenty-five years in the giant scheme of things?"

"He may be older than my father . . . and he's got someone else."

"Ah, the fatal hesitancy. That fatal someone else."

Anjali couldn't tell if Husseina was consoling her or teasing her. "I think Americans like to say, 'He has a partner.'"

Husseina laid a maternal hand on Anjali's shoulder. "It's all a business arrangement. You'll get used to it."

"In the giant scheme of things." Anjali repeated Husseina's phrase. It was a comforting notion. "It's all a matter of light and angles, isn't it?"

2

Mr. GG, carrying a huge bouquet of flowers and a copy of Peter Champion's book, was the first to arrive. In the old days, according to Minnie, guests in ball gowns and tails were greeted by a long receiving line that ended with Maxie, Minnie, and the guests of honor. Gout and poverty had forced Minnie to dispense with such Bagehot House traditions. Asoke, instructed to meet guests in the portico with a welcoming salaam, ushered Mr. GG to the threshold of the formal drawing room, then hobbled back to his post. Minnie, majestic in a brocade caftan, had installed herself in a wing chair in the center of the room and Anjali on an ottoman right next to her a full hour before. The other three boarders hovered behind her like ladies in waiting, offering her appetizers of meat-filled pastries and refilling her glass of rum punch.

"That gentleman with charming manners, is he the fan who wants to meet our Peter?" Minnie asked Anjali in a tipsy whisper. "He cuts a dashing figure."

Anjali couldn't get over how dashing! She had remembered Mr. GG as a lithe man with a slight paunch, but here he was, tall and princely in black silk sherwani and white ruched churidar, gliding toward the hostess.

"Where are your manners, child? Go on, get up, introduce him to me."

"Mr. Gujral!" Anjali couldn't hide her excitement. She rose from the low ottoman in such a hurry that the stiletto heel of one shoe got caught in the threadbare weave of the rug, and if limber Mr. GG hadn't managed to tuck Peter's heavy tome under one arm and rush with the bouquet to steady her, she would have taken an unromantic fall instead of merely bruising a few flowers.

"I keep having this effect on you," he joked. Then he turned his full attention to Minnie. "Ah, finally I have the fortune of meeting the chatelaine of this gem of a manse that I have long admired." With a gallant flourish, he presented the dented bouquet to her. "How do you do, madam? Girish, please. Not even my clients call me Mister Gujral."

Minnie accepted the bouquet with a tinkly giggle and handed it to Sunita to place in a vase. "Girish, it is. How do you do, Girish. Thank you for making time to dine with a recluse in a mausoleum."

"Gem," Mr. GG said, air-kissing the gloved fingertips she offered him, "not mausoleum. And speaking of gems"—he returned his attention to Anjali—"has it been a week or a month since . . . Barista? It *feels* like twenty-four hours." Anjali glowed, flattered by his courtly come-on. "What a transformation, and you're not even wearing glass slippers!"

Glass slippers? She hadn't the foggiest. Her slingbacks were python skin, yesterday's impulsive splurge at a just-opened boutique on VM Road.

Husseina broke away from Tookie and Sunita, and introduced herself to Mr. GG. "Punch? No, you're more champagne than punch." She clapped her hands and called out to someone in the pantry. A rough-looking boy in a sweatsuit appeared with a tray of champagne flutes. "Please." She urged Mr. GG to accept one.

Mr. GG plucked two champagne flutes off the tray and offered Anjali one and Husseina the other.

"Oh, I don't imbibe, GG," Husseina explained. "Excuse me. I have to check on the kitchen staff. They're new." She walked away.

Anjali who had already taken a sip of her first-ever glass of champagne, worried that Mr. GG would consider her a lush. Why couldn't she have taken her cue from Husseina?

The noisy appearance of another guest provided Anjali with a convenient distraction. Two stout youths from the squatters' settlement in the "back garden" deposited Opal Philpott, in her pre-war wheelchair, next to Minnie. Tookie, looking uncharacteristically frumpy in a red velvet dress, fetched a glass of punch for Opal and another gin fizz for Minnie. Sunita made a face at Tookie. "Don't ply her with more," she pleaded as they joined Anjali and Mr. GG. "She needs food. Where is this American anyway?"

Tookie laughed. "Tipsy is the only way I can take the old cow."

"Where *is* the guest of honor?" Mr. GG pursued the point.

She hadn't the foggiest. He had not been in touch since the call from Gauripur. Flight delays? For all she knew, he had changed his mind about deserting Ali for a whole weekend. In any case, she was enjoying the princely GG's undivided attention.

"Patience, GG," Husseina said.

Anjali envied Husseina's easy grace. "Patience," she repeated. "Peter never breaks his promise."

And Peter Champion, toting a large khaki duffel bag and a cloth book bag, entered the drawing room as though on cue. He wasn't alone. He was flanked by two Indian women in their midforties.

"My dear, dear Minnie." He greeted Minnie with an affectionate kiss on each powdered cheek. "You don't look a day older than you were the last time I saw you!" He handed her a bottle of imported brandy.

"Rubbish, transparent rubbish! But gratefully accepted." Minnie rang a small bell hanging by a silk cord from an arm of her chair, to summon Asoke. "Asoke is becoming a dunderhead! How come he hasn't relieved our guest of his baggage?"

Anjali hung back with Mr. GG in a corner of the drawing room. The Mr. Champion she had known in Gauripur was tall and balding and often wore his thinning hair drawn back in a limp ponytail. The Gauripur Peter rode an ancient scooter, wore a kurta and blue jeans, and shunned the company of women. The Bangalore Peter was shorter than she remembered, wore a dark suit, white shirt, and red tie, and acted chummy with the two beautiful women, one in a tailored silk pantsuit and the other in an embroidered silk sari.

Peter introduced the two women to the hostess as his friends Miss Usha Desai and Mrs. Parvati Banerji. "Where's my brightest-ever student?" he asked, looking around the room. When he spotted the glamorous young woman in a pistachio gharara and realized that she was Angie, he bounded up to her, swept her up in a movie-like hug, complimented her on her big-city transformation, then whispered in her ear, "We have some serious business to discuss tomorrow. Tonight, though, is Minnie's night." Then he introduced her to pantsuited Usha Desai and sari-wrapped Parvati Banerji, adding that Parvati Banerji was Rabi Chatterjee's maternal aunt. He had gone directly from the airport to CCI, he explained, because he had business to discuss with the CCI board.

"Parvati and Usha are partners," he added.

It made sense, coming from Peter, but she would never have guessed.

Usha must have noted her confusion. She smiled and said, "I think Peter means a partnership. Parvati and I are CCI's cofounders." She promised to call Anjali on Monday to set up an admissions interview.

At least Usha Desai spoke English with a slight Indian accent. That made her less threatening. Anjali turned to Rabi's aunt. "I love listening to Rabi," she gushed. "He's so brilliant."

"Around Rabi all you can do is listen." Parvati laughed. Perfect American accent. California, Anjali decided. "He's my only nephew, his mother's the youngest of us three sisters and lives in San Francisco. Tara—that's my sister—was expecting him home for his dad's fifty-fifth birthday, but you know Rabi! He's gallivanting all over India, places I've never been to."

"Will he be visiting you?"

There was no mistaking the pleasure Parvati took in Anjali's admiration of her nephew. "Right now Rabi's somewhere in Kerala on a nature photography kick." She gave Anjali's cheek an affectionate pat. "I feel I know you a little bit. Do you mind my saying that? I don't mean *know* you, other than from a photo of you in Gauripur. Rabi left it with us before he rushed south. He was into portrait photography when you met him. We—that's my husband and me—loved his Cartier-Bresson phase, but he's over that."

"If he comes back . . ." Anjali stopped herself, embarrassed. How could she be so forward as to beg for an invitation? She knew what drew her to Rabi, but to his aunt? The spontaneity of her offer of friendship to a stranger about whose background she knew nothing? She envied Parvati's capacity for trust.

"Oh, Rabi will be back. He's in no hurry to return to America."

Mr. GG sidled toward Anjali's group, bearing a plate of savories and a freshened flute of champagne. Anjali had never handled social niceties like introductions. Was it man to woman? Younger to older? How much biography was appropriate? She let Mr. GG hover at the edges of the group to find his own conversational opening.

The CCI partners eased the awkwardness by taking the lead. Hands thrust out, firm shakes, their names. They seemed to recognize Mr. GG's name when he introduced himself. So Mr. GG had to be a celebrity of some sort in Bangalore. Anjali found her voice. "And Girish, I'd like you to meet my teacher, Peter Champion. Peter, Girish Gujral."

The four guests drifted into esoteric conversation about virtual construction and the projects under development by Girish Gujral's firm, Vistronics. Opal Philpott and Minnie Bagehot, stuck in their chairs, were engaged in a loud debate about what precise incident at the Gymkhana had led to the ferocious enmity between Ruby Thistlethwaite and Opal. Husseina was either still in the kitchen, supervising the squatter women's cooking and plating, or was on the empty front porch talking to her fiancé in London on her cell phone.

With the hostess and guests temporarily occupied, Tookie and Sunita huddled with Anjali.

"Isn't he too old for you?" Sunita sounded worried.

Tookie asked, "So have you fixed a date yet? And where have you been hiding this Girish guy? Girl, you've got more secrets and more angles than a Delhi politician. When you're finished with him, can you set me up?"

Not in that red dress, Anjali thought. Some girls are just made for blue jeans and T-shirts with scooped necks, and some of us can wear expensive silk.

Opal and Minnie were about to come to blows with their hand fans over which man was the guiltier party, "that silly goose" or "that cad, that bounder," when Husseina finally reappeared in the drawing room and announced that Asoke was ready for the party to move to the dining room.

FROM HER PLACE at the head of the table, Minnie tapped her water goblet for attention, and then with some gallant help from Girish Gujral, she heaved herself to her feet. In a deep, firm voice she delivered what sounded like a well-rehearsed speech of welcome to all guests: new visitors, old friends, and residents.

"When I inherited Bagehot House and everything you see tonight and much that you do not, I was still a young, innocent, and impressionable woman. Little more than a girl, actually. When my late husband introduced it to me, I confess I was overwhelmed. So overwhelmed that I felt unworthy of it. I trusted its maintenance to my just and brave husband and his loyal staff. Somehow or other, I was led to believe that the newly independent country of India would honor its responsibility to maintain and even enhance its inherited splendors. Many of your country's founding generation—I need not recite their names—have been entertained at this very table. But my years as a memsahib were tragically cut short. They lasted three years, to be precise. And over the next sixty years, I have learned that she who owns Bagehot House owns a sacred trust. And she owns it alone. She must fight for every drop of paint, every pane of glass, every broken tile. Our honored guest tonight has made that case: Bagehot House ranks with the great estates of Europe, with finest extant architecture of the Portuguese or the Mughals or even the British. I include the vaunted Taj Mahal. For over fifty years, I have provided native girls from good families a sense of the lost India. They have learned from this architecture and from these furnishings, and, I hope, from my personal example, that India was once the home of confident serenity. There was poverty then, of course, there has always been squalor in India, and unspeakable suffering . . . when in the history of India has there not been ignorance and superstition and poverty? But the poverty of sixty years ago was borne with the quiet dignity of their race . . ."

Anjali felt the sting of Minnie's words: *your* country, *your* leaders. She could have crushed Minnie's water glass into Minnie's fist. She remembered the row of hanged Sikhs, the smiling white soldiers with their boots on the corpses, the old photos that had been carried out of Peter's temporary bedroom.

Peter rose, surprising Minnie in midsentence. He dipped his head in Minnie's direction, smiled, and thanked her for her hospitality, cutting off the rest of her speech on the deliberate mutilation of the glories of the Raj. He then launched into a dinner-table speech of his own. "That is a reading of history I think we recognize. It is very remote from my own experience, but not alien to generations of visitors and respected authorities.

"I've been thinking back to my first visit to Bangalore some thirty years ago, and to this very house. Bangalore was then a neat and tidy city. Its people were, as always, courteous and helpful. I would go to the hall of records and state my request in writing. Then I would be handed a heavy brass medallion inscribed, as I remember, with a number rubbed so smooth it was nearly invisible. Centuries of petitioners had held it. I would take a seat with other petitioners on a long bench. Patience. The patience of India, that's what struck me most. Hours would pass. Perhaps it is another aspect of the dignity that our dear Minnie spoke of. And that smooth brass medallion felt like an egg entrusted to me for hatching."

He turned to Asoke, who was serving the soup course, and asked him in Hindi, "Where are they now, I wonder? Do they simply vanish? I hope some museum is hoarding them. Perhaps our gracious hostess has stored one or two on the premises."

Asoke put his tray of soup plates on the sideboard and limped toward the pantry.

"In any event, after a few minutes, or a few hours, a gentleman would emerge from the inner sanctum, call my number, and usher me into his chamber. Tea would be ordered. And there, rolled up on his desk, would be the original specifications for any residence or official building that I wished to study. And, strange to report, those elderly officers took an interest in my research. They added suggestions. They were extraordinary public servants. They wrote poetry. They were passionate patriots.

"Of course, such access today is impossible. Original documents confer legal advantage, and modern Bangalore is all about lawyers fighting for advantage."

"Hear, hear!" Girish Gujral interjected.

Asoke returned from the pantry, bearing a brass medallion on a small silver platter, placed the platter on the sideboard, and resumed serving the soup course.

"Well, I'd expect nothing less," Peter said. "An echo of times when both Asoke and I had dark hair on our heads."

Where was Peter going with this nostalgic prelude? Anjali wondered anxiously.

Peter paused for a long sip of water, then, his eyes on Girish Gujral, he continued. "But I'm also a child from overseas, and it was in India that I found my soul. My first Indian home was a village in the hills of

Uttar Pradesh. I had been given training in basic Hindi—Bollywood Hindi, I called it—but in my village they spoke a tribal language that had never been recorded. So I was supposed to start teaching public hygiene, but before I could teach anything I had to learn the language my students spoke. I count that as a blessing. If those villagers were to learn anything from me, I first of all had to learn from them. Those two years set me on a course. It set the stage for what I've been doing all my life.

"When I was a young man, I traveled all over India in search of something that was missing. I guess we called it purpose. It even brought me to Bangalore and to this house."

At Peter's mention of her house, Minnie perked up. Opal was preoccupied with gumming some vegetable slivers from her soup.

"I was able to take measurements and inventories and go through city documents. The book I wrote could not be written today. I would not be allowed official access. And for me, this is the most worrisome aspect of modern India—the disappearance of trust. I look at modern Bangalore, and at Delhi and Bombay, and I wonder, what are we creating? Not in our private sector, but in the public? Can we keep that old patience—dignity, as our hostess calls it—and the passion? Have we lost our sense of civic morality forever? The newfound prosperity in this city is breathtaking, and I don't mean to disparage it. Prosperity is a good thing. But I'm not so sure of the wealth that comes from outsourcing. I wish the prosperity was rooted to something. I wish it built something beyond glass monuments. It seems as flimsy as a kite or a balloon. What comes drifting in with the winds might just as easily drift away."

Husseina signaled Asoke with her eyes: it was time to bring in the next course.

"Fortunately, we have experts with us tonight. I've come back to Bangalore to learn, not to teach. I hope my suspicions and my doubts can be laid to rest. Usha I've known since her doctoral studies in Delhi. If anyone can persuade me that outsourcing is healthy, it is Usha Desai. I met Parvati for the first time this afternoon in the CCI office, but I know her nephew, and of course, the world is familiar with achievements of her brother-in-law, Bishwapriya Chatterjee."

Girish Gujral glanced at Anjali with new awe. So, it was *that* Bishwapriya Chatterjee, the legend. Anjali could almost hear the wheels turning: how is it possible for one innocent teenage girl from small-town Bihar to know the legend's family, and to know Peter Champion? She tried to keep a blank expression on her face.

Peter moved on to acknowledging his long acquaintance with this young lady from Gauripur, Anjali Bose, as her teacher, and his desire to get to know Girish, the force behind Vistronics.

From the pantry, Asoke sent in the teenage girl with the long hair combed by firelight to remove the soup plates and spoons. Her long black hair was tamed into a lustrous braid and decorated with fragrant gardenias. She had a saucy walk, which, Anjali jealously noted, also seemed to catch Mr. GG's attention.

"The defense of an entire industry has fallen on me." Usha sighed.

"Not at all, Usha," Peter protested.

"Peter, if training young Indians to sound convincingly like young Americans is all we do, or even a fraction of what we do, I'd agree that we'd be performing a disservice to our country. But it's not what we do."

The discussion continued through the fish course, for which Minnie had put out special fish knives. Anjali looked to Husseina for cues as to the appropriate cutlery for each course. She was dexterous with her fingers but clumsy with a fish knife. She had never sat at a dining table laid with formal china, silverware, and glassware. Nor had she ever heard serious arguments delivered with genteel humility. At home, she and her parents ate with their fingers and treated dinnertime as the nightly occasion for the venting of grievances. The same grievances, night after night.

She sensed that Peter was mildly rebuking Mad Minnie and challenging Usha. But hadn't he been the one who had lured Anjali to Bangalore, boosting it as the city of India's future and talking Usha up as the deliverer of liberty and prosperity to ambitious small-town women like her? She glanced at her fellow boarders for some kind of confirmation. But Tookie looked desperate to escape for a cigarette, Sunita seemed bored, and Husseina was distracted.

"I'm saying it could be ephemeral," said Peter. "We're tied to American prosperity. If America goes under, we'll drown."

But isn't that what Peter had been teaching her at Vasco da Gama and in his private classes? American corporate models? Starbucks? Regional U.S. accents? Get out of Gauripur before you stagnate? Maybe Usha Desai and Parvati Banerji caught certain important nuances, but she didn't. Under her glamorous outfit, she was still a sad, stupid bumpkin.

Girish disagreed with Peter. "If you dismiss it as outsourcing, then you're simplifying a complicated reality. Vistronics is a kind of outsourcing—we've drawn on a variety of resources—but no one else in the world is doing what we do. We might have started as an appendage technology, but we've evolved. Now we're outsourcing to Kenya and Bangladesh. And do you know what? I see us, in maybe three years, outsourcing our technology to the United States."

Right then and there Anjali fell in love with Mr. GG. He was so right. And so handsome and rich. Not that Peter was wrong, at least not entirely. But Mr. GG cut through Minnie's veils of nonsensical nostalgia and poor Mr. Champion's middle-aged missionary zeal, and he presented a future she longed to live in.

The discussion became more acrimonious through the meat courses. Husseina hustled Asoke and his helpers through the serving of roast duck, chicken fricassee, and mutton stew because she and Tookie soon had to catch their company vans for the all-night shift at the call centers. But Anjali didn't want the meal to end; she didn't want Mr. GG to leave.

Peter's friend Mizz Desai, Anjali noted, seemed to be on Mr. GG's side. She was saying, "When Parvati and I started CCI, our American corporate clients were adamant that our graduates sound American, think American, and fool American callers into believing their customer-service complaints and queries were being resolved by American workers in American cities. That was just four years ago. Our training program had students studying DVDs of American sitcoms, sporting events—"

"And U.S. politics." Parvati broke in. "State capitals, interstate highway numbers, pop stars, rock stars. We had the students study *Star* magazine. Pathetic, except that it's pretty funny."

"India was déclassé, and Indian-accented English laughed at," Usha continued. "So what does that do to a well-prepared, intelligent, motivated young agent who's mocked as soon as she opens her mouth? That's what we told our corporate clients. Do you want a human answering tape, or do you want a proactive, efficient employee?"

"Some of them came around," Parvati said. "They said just make sure our customers can understand the English that the agents speak." Her own accent was eerily perfect American. She spoke of having trained young women from mofussil towns and villages to handle complicated questions on insurance claims. Women who might have remained illiterate and dependent were now earning decent paychecks. "The point Usha and I have made is that the Indian accent is a sign of competence."

They were the experts, with their professional degrees and their years of experience with comparative business models and communications systems, but they just didn't get it: to a Gauripur runaway like her, Bangalore wasn't about global economics. It was an emotional and moral tsunami; it washed away old beliefs and traditions, the comforting ones together with the crippling, and if you survived, you knew you had the spunk and the grit to rebuild. "Excuse me, madam," Anjali interjected, and she suddenly found herself standing, the focus of everyone's attention. "It's more."

If Usha Desai was irritated at being interrupted, she didn't show it. "Please, Miss Bose, continue," she said, smiling; then she sat down.

Anjali had meant just to listen, just to absorb ideas, but now she was on her feet. And there was Mr. GG, also on his feet, raising his goblet of water in a toast.

Everyone at the table turned to Mr. GG, though none of them lifted their glasses. "Let's hear from the young women themselves," he urged, but his eyes were fastened on unemployed Anjali.

"Go on," Tookie urged Anjali. "You start."

The debaters stared at Anjali. She had their full attention. There was no backing away now.

"Hear, hear!" Mr. GG beamed at her. "Speech, please. We're all ears."

Let words tumble off my tongue, she prayed. "I have been in Bangalore only three weeks. I have no job, no paycheck, and no family here. But I have seen more and learned more in Bangalore than I have from twenty years in Gauripur. Here I *feel* I can do anything. I feel I can change my life if that's what *I* want!"

"Brava!" Tookie applauded.

Even shy Sunita dared to speak. "And I *do* change lives. It's not glamorous work, my life hasn't changed, but every day I save lives of people I'll never see. I work for a company that reports break-ins and medical emergencies of older people living alone, people who can't get up when they fall down. If I wasn't in my cubicle answering calls, American houses would be vandalized and senior citizens would starve to death on the bedroom floor."

Peter looked amused, and Minnie pained. But Anjali was inspired. "The word is . . . *revolution,*" Anjali said. "That's it. We're soldiers in a social revolution."

"A bloodless revolution, we hope," Usha said.

Mr. GG chortled. "Oh, there will be blood." No one laughed. "That's the title of an American movie," he explained.

Husseina ignored Girish Gujral's attempt to lighten the conversation. "My friend, my sister Anjali is quite correct. You don't have to be a villager to recognize there's a revolution going on."

Minnie rang her bell to disrupt the talk of revolution. But Husseina was not to be stopped. "History tells us you cannot have a revolution without winners and victims. Most of you here are winners."

Most of you? Not most of us? To Anjali, Husseina sounded as removed from the Bangalore scene as Mad Minnie was. What had she unearthed, with her intuitive correction of the intelligent, worldly CCI women? There was a long, awkward silence.

Finally Peter responded to Husseina. "This same conversation is being repeated millions of times tonight, all over India. We know we are in the middle of a revolution, but is that a good thing? Where will it end? Are we riding a tiger, have we started something we can't control?"

"Anything is better than what we had," Tookie snapped at him.

Minnie rapped her fan against the armrest of Opal's wheelchair. Opal had fallen asleep. "Talk of revolution is poppycock! In a country like India, any mention of revolution is dangerous. Pure poppycock!" She gave Opal's wheelchair another vicious rap, but Opal stayed asleep. "Those of us who have lived through a real revolution know how bloody it is. How dare you turn it into a joking matter? We will not sit around *my* table and laud the virtue of revolution. What you Indians need to do is clean up your refuse and keep your mouths shut."

And with that she broke up the dinner party before Asoke had a chance to serve the dessert course, trifle.

3

Peter was already at the plastic cloth–covered table in the eating alcove, sipping tea and reading *Voice of the South,* the local paper, when Anjali came down on Sunday morning, a little before seven. She was glad to see him back in his familiar uniform of kurta and blue jeans. Asoke hovered about him, offering him coddled eggs and fresh batches of toast. Peter had asked her to join him over a very early breakfast both because he had a morning flight to catch and because he wanted to talk to her without the other boarders listening in. She took the facing seat, prepared to be lectured on the many ways she had disappointed him. Okay, she had . . . what was the damning word Peter had used? She had procrastinated. She was the Ultimate Procrastinator. If only one of the other Bagehot Girls would come down earlier than usual for chota hazari, which was what Minnie still called the day's first meal, and oblige Peter to dull the full force of his vocabulary! Okay, okay, her benefactor should not have had to incur the expense of traveling personally to Bangalore to introduce her to his local contacts. She was sorry; immensely sorry, really.

Peter looked at her over the top of his paper and wished her a subdued good morning, but he didn't put the paper down. It was a brief glance, but Anjali didn't miss its reflection of private despair. How could her failure to follow through pain him so deeply? If she had had Tookie's genius for flippant small talk, she could have eased the tension. She did her modest best. "Your friend, Usha Desai, is so different from the way I'd pictured her." There, she'd brought up the subject of CCI, her reason for running to Bangalore; get Peter's harangue over with. He would keep it short; he had a plane to catch. "I thought she would sound more American."

He folded the newspaper and pushed it toward her. "I don't think she's ever been out of India. Do you read *Voice of the South*?"

"Only when I find a discarded copy," she said. She didn't add that she had done so only once, and that was at the bus depot.

"Except for Dynamo's column, it's a rag. But you should get it just to read Dynamo. Very up to the minute."

"I try not to waste money on buying anything I don't absolutely need." She lied.

"Well, splurge on *Voice.* Dynamo has his finger on the pulse." He asked Asoke to remove his plate of uneaten toast. When Asoke was out of the room, he said, "Last night he couldn't take his eyes off you. I had no idea he was a friend of Minnie. She doesn't leave the house, but she stays wired."

He? Who couldn't take his eyes off me? Asoke? And then it all fell in place, click-click-click: *he* was Dynamo, and Dynamo was Mr. GG, and Mr. GG was madly in love with her. Before she could say a word, Peter continued. "I always said you have a kind of magic, Angie. Somehow or other, you manage to be in the middle of things. Who can explain it?" But she didn't let on to Peter that it was she, not Minnie, who'd invited Mr. GG. *Dynamo couldn't take his eyes off of you.* She squirreled that away to savor later.

"Well, shame on Dynamo! I thought well-mannered people didn't stare. Good thing I didn't notice. If I had, I'd have told him to stick his eyes back in his head." She glowed with pleasure at having ravished smooth Mr. GG into callow worshipfulness.

"He had his driver leave off today's *Voice* so I wouldn't miss his column." Peter drained his cup of tea and poured himself another. "He's gung-ho on this outsourcing revolution. Maybe I'm just getting old and cranky." And then a shadow passed over his face, as though the sun itself had been eclipsed. *Here it comes,* she thought. *Prepare yourself.*

"Angie, have you been in touch with anyone in Gauripur?"

She wondered which way to go. Maybe with the truth. "No," she admitted. "I've been so busy here." She was about to ask if Mr. GG had been in the back seat of the car when the driver dropped off the paper. He must have been hoping for a glimpse of her. She bet he was the kind who planned "accidental" sightings. Maybe he had gotten a thrill just from being driven down her street. She felt sexy thinking of him.

"Angie, I can't put this off any longer . . ." Peter's voice sounded anxious and gravelly, but he stopped short because Asoke was back from the kitchen, this time balancing a platter of browning banana slices and golden papaya wedges on one palm and a tray of clean cups and water glasses on the other. Anjali eyed the papaya. Minnie had never served fresh fruit since Anjali had moved in. She had Peter to thank for better breakfast fare as well as romance and free career training.

Asoke removed the folded *Voice* from the table to make room for the fruit platter; then he took out small fruit plates and fruit knives from a credenza. There was pride in his movements. "Finger bowl coming," he assured them.

Peter thanked Asoke and plucked a wedge of papaya off the platter. "Don't tell Asoke I am used to licking my fingers clean," he stage-whispered to Anjali. "And make sure he doesn't throw out the paper before you've read it." He separated the papaya flesh from its green skin with his fork instead of dirtying the fruit knife, with its mother-of-pearl handle. "Whether you like it or not, you'll find out if Dynamo's faith in the Bangalore experiment is justified. You're the guinea pig."

"Guinea pig? Is your American friend calling us guinea pigs?" Husseina entered suddenly. She was wearing her black silk dressing gown over black silk pajamas as she usually did for breakfast, but this morning she had hidden her long, lustrous hair with a black scarf. Some pre-shampoo hot-oil treatment, Anjali assumed. Muslim women from rich families inherited effective beauty secrets. Husseina slid into the chair next to Peter. He acknowledged Husseina's presence with a nod instead of a good morning.

Anjali sensed tension and tried immediately to defuse it. Guinea pigs were not pigs, but maybe Peter had offended the Muslim Husseina by likening call-center agents to them. "Oh, Peter was just chitchatting. How do you Americans say it, Peter? Shooting the breeze, no?"

"No." Peter objected sharply. "I wasn't joking. Bangalore is a lab where a clutch of scientists run bold experiments. You're the specimen. You are *not* the scientist."

Anjali intervened. "Husseina, pour you a cup?"

"Nor are you the owner of the laboratory." Peter finished his statement.

"Is it ignorance? Or with you guys, is it genetic arrogance?" Husseina stabbed two curls of butter in the butter dish with Peter's unused fruit knife. It was a vicious gesture, and Anjali saw Asoke, who was still hovering solicitously behind Peter's chair, cringe. Some days Asoke served butter shaped as hearts, diamonds, cloves, and aces. Curls, pats, and balls of butter meant either Asoke had been in a hurry or that he was ill. "What makes you think I am *not* the scientist? What makes you so sure that I am the sacrificial specimen instead?" She smeared butter on a triangle of cold toast, added a dab of marmalade, and handed it to Anjali. Asoke's homemade marmalade was too bitter, but Anjali didn't dare refuse Husseina's demand for solidarity. A sisterhood of guinea pigs. She wished that this morning Husseina had asked Asoke to leave her breakfast outside her room, as she often did, instead of coming down and ending Anjali's attempts to extract from Peter additional flattering information about the lovesick Mr. GG.

Fortunately Peter backed off. "I am happy to be corrected." He glanced at his watch, which prompted Asoke to ask, "Taxi, sahib?" On the rare occasion that a Bagehot House boarder required a taxi, Asoke had a squatter flag one down from an intersection three blocks away. It meant a tip for the squatter, and probably a cut of that tip for Asoke.

"Auto-rickshaw. I'll tell you when." Peter rose from the table. "Asoke, two teas in my room. Do you mind, Angie?"

Asoke was aghast. "This papaya not tasty, sahib?"

"Sahib?" Elegant Husseina let out a scornful snort. "Did this pathetic old man really use that word?"

"Lost my appetite, that's all." Peter helped Anjali out of her chair.

Eager to hear more about Mr. GG, Anjali scrambled out of the dining room ahead of Peter.

"Do you write regularly to your sister?"

It was the first thing Peter said after Asoke had served them tea and left them alone in the cavernous, underfurnished guest bedroom, pulling the heavy door closed behind him. Just banal chatter to put himself at ease, Anjali decided. They sat, Anjali in the only armchair and Peter on the bed, with a low, wide table between them. Peter had stripped the mattress of sheets as though cleaning up was his job and not Asoke's. No need to bristle at him for asking after Sonali-di and accidentally reviving the raw pain of her final night in Patna. She would guide Peter back to the subject of Mr. GG. She needed to make efficient use of the fifteen or twenty minutes Peter had reserved to say goodbye to her in private. "I used to," she said. "I visited her the day I left," she said, turning on her practiced smile. "We are back-ing and forth-ing quite a bit by letter."

"Angie, Angie, don't lie to me."

What was the point of exchanging letters if the sisters couldn't get beyond polite, perfunctory formalities? "All right. If you want to know the truth, she thinks I'm selfish. She doesn't approve of my having left home."

Peter's packed duffel bag and bulging book tote lay on the floor just inside the door, ready for him to carry out to the auto-rickshaw. His multipocketed, handloom cotton vest, convenient for stowing airline tickets and wallet, was laid out at the foot of the bare mattress. She wouldn't allow flashbacks of her quarrel with Sonali-di to beat back fantasies of her future with Mr. GG. She wanted to gush to Peter about love, not family. "How is Ali?" He would want to talk about Ali just as much as she wanted to speak of Mr. GG. She checked his face for an automatic softening. But he stared at her as though she had punched him. She lowered her gaze to his lips, which pursed and parted a couple of times. He seemed on the verge of a profound confession or a disturbing confidence.

"I have very sad, very important news for you," he said. He reached for his vest, extracted a newspaper clipping from the breastpocket sewn into the lining to safeguard cash, and held it out to her. "This is the reason I came."

She recognized a smudged face in the tiny photo in the clipping from *The Gauripur Standard:* Baba's studio matrimonial portrait. A beady-eyed, mustached young man doing his best to project confidence and purpose. She had seen the original in the family album, which was stored, swaddled in a woolen shawl, in Ma's dowry trunk. Ma was proud of that photo. Anjali and Sonali had caught her taking the album out of the trunk and surreptitiously flipping it open to Baba's studio portrait on several Sunday afternoons while Baba slept off the heavy Sunday lunch of mutton curry. Ma, Anjali realized, was in love with the man she had conjured from that photo, but not with the obsequious Indian Railways bureaucrat her parents had forced her to marry. Ma had nagged Baba constantly. In Gauripur, Anjali had dismissed that nagging as white noise and paid no attention to Ma's words. The Ma who had brought her up must have been a bitter woman. Anjali tried to visualize Ma as a dreamy teenage bride-to-be, swooning over the youthful face in Baba's posed studio portrait. That girl must have prayed hard that she would be selected over rival candidates. Shaky Sengupta was an illusionist, and Anjali now better understood how the art of all the Shaky Senguptas was supposed to work: incite fantasies of permanent prosperity and protection. When disillusionment strikes, get out of range of the victim's vengeful feelings.

And then, *click-click*. That picture, in that paper. It could mean only one thing. Sonali-di must have selected that photo to send to the *Standard*. Baba was dead. He must have been cremated within twenty-four hours of his passing. Peter had hurried her away from acid-tongued Husseina so he could deliver his shocking message in private. She turned away from the clipping, which Peter was still holding out to her. She pushed his hand away. As long as she didn't read the obituary, she could pretend he was alive. Baba and Ma could live on, squabbling continuously, which was their version of conjugal togetherness. Peter held out his handkerchief to dry the tears she didn't know she'd shed.

"I can understand your wanting to be with your family at a time like this." Peter sneaked a look at his watch. "I'll take care of your travel arrangements as soon as I get back. If you want to come back here, I can arrange it with Minnie. The Patna-Bangalore return ticket can be left open."

"Patna?"

"Your mother has moved in with your sister. Would you rather I read this," he tapped the clipping, "out loud?"

"No. Just give it to me."

The whole time I've been here, Baba's been dead. I had these dreams, I had moments of forgiveness and moments I wanted to be forgiven. He'd been in my dreams, and now he was a ghost.

She heard a voice, in Bangla: "You killed him." Was it her mother? "You were too good for that boy. You had to make more money than your father. You had to be your own boss. You never thought what Baba went through at the office. All of Gauripur laughed behind his back, 'There goes Bose-babu, two daughters, one divorced, the other a . . . a runaway. Went to Mumbai, became a prostitute.' He couldn't take it any longer. He ended his life."

> BOSE, PRAFULLA KUMAR. 48, suddenly at his residence in Gauripur. Asst. sub-inspector (Goods), Indian Railways (north Bihar). Third-Generation Gauripur native. Like his father (Dipendu Kumar) and his grandfather (Neelkontho Kumar), Prafulla Kumar joined railway service straightway after obtaining B. Comm. Man of unyielding faith and steadfast integrity, elected Vice-President of the Gauripur Durga Puja Committee for seven consecutive years and was holding that office at his untimely demise. His patrilineal survivors include six brothers, who migrated permanently to Kolkata. He is mourned by his widow Archana Debi, his married daughter Sonali (Das) and granddaughter residing in Patna. He was predeceased by his second daughter. His ashes join cosmic unity. His loss to the Bengali community of Gauripur is immeasurable. We, members of the Durga Puja Committee, mourn his absence with inconsolable hearts and crestfallen minds. *Nagendra Nath Bhattacharya, President, Durga Puja Committee.*

She had to puzzle out the word *predeceased.* It was a new English word for her to absorb. *You are dead to me! Predeceased* suggested a less violent end; her family had pressed the DELETE button and she had vanished into the ether. No corpse, no cremation. They had morphed her into a ghost. Baba was dead, but so was she. She felt dizzy. Her teacher was talking at her, tossing words as if they were life jackets and she was drowning.

"This isn't the time for self-blame," she heard him say. That had to mean that Peter, somehow, blamed her. But she wasn't the one who had done the killing; *they* had—her father, her mother, her sister. Her father was—had been—"fit as a fiddle" according to the railway doctor, who was also a Bengali and the treasurer of the Durga Puja Committee. The doctor, stethoscope around his neck, would drop by the Bose flat two or three evenings a month, enjoy a whiskey and her mother's deep-fried savories, listen to her father's heart, and pronounce him "fit as a fiddle."

"If you're wondering, it wasn't from a heart attack," said Peter. "But that's the story they're putting out."

What was he saying?

He died "suddenly"; that can only mean a heart attack, a stroke, something to do with high blood pressure. All Indian men suffered from high blood pressure. Salty food, smoking—it was a known flaw.

"I am taking up too much of your time. You'll be late for your flight," she said. For all his empathy for Gauripur students, Peter didn't understand their family problems, especially not hers. She'd grown up with chaos masquerading as coherence. Fear, not steadfastness, had kept her father in dead-end Gauripur. Fear had forced him to follow his father's and his grandfather's footsteps into the railway office of Gauripur. She was an ungrateful, unworthy daughter; she accepted that. She was selfish and recklessly impatient. In fact, she embraced her flaws. Confessing unworthiness delivered a newfound freedom.

Her family had orphaned her. She had not even any pretense of a home back in Gauripur. The Bose flat would already be occupied by another tenant. Ma must have been taken in by Sonali-di. A month ago Sonali-di had been the disgraced, divorced daughter; now Sonali-di was the good, dependable one. She pictured her mother in Sonali-di's drab apartment, fussing over her granddaughter, cooking, cleaning, and faking middle-class respectability while Sonali-di did for her boss whatever he demanded so she wouldn't lose her job. "You have more to go back to in Gauripur than I do." She rose from the armchair, not sure if a goodbye hug was appropriate.

"I don't have Ali to go back to, if that's what you mean." He slumped on the mattress, cupping his face with his hands.

She heard the sobs. "Oh, Peter!" Anjali rushed to her teacher and sat cross-legged beside him on the mattress. Peter's love story emerged in halting phrases. Ali had run off to Lucknow for back-alley surgery. She heard the phrases "instant gratification" and "black-market butcher" over and over again. Peter had counseled, cajoled, finally begged Ali to please be patient while he researched and ranked safe big-city clinics and experienced surgeons. But Ali had acted on a grapevine lead in Lucknow from one of his secretive acquaintances. "Instant gratification" had compelled Ali to risk death or maiming.

"He wanted to be a woman. He thought that's what would make me happy."

Awful as it seemed, as terrible as the judgment, she felt greater pity, greater pain, for Peter than she did for herself. Now Baba was dead, but he had first killed her off. She sat with Peter until Asoke knocked on the door and announced that he had taken it upon himself to flag an auto-rickshaw, which was now in the portico, its meter running.

4

At exactly nine on Monday morning, just as she had been promised, Anjali received a call from Usha Desai to set up an interview. "I can see you at eleven A.M. on Thursday. The only other possibility this week would be three P.M. on Friday." Though Peter's friend's voice was as soothing as it had been at Minnie's gala, her manner was more businesslike. "I have to be out of town Tuesday and Parvati is busy all day Wednesday."

"Friday, please. Friday is suiting me better," she stammered, to give herself time to prepare for the interview.

"Do you know where we are located?"

A wilier student applicant would have done her research and found out not only the CCI street address but how best to get there by bus. Anjali was relieved to hear Usha Desai reel off the information in a nonjudgmental voice before Anjali could mumble no. "Apartment 3B, Reach for the Galaxy Building, Reach Colony, Ninth Cross, Indira Nagar, Stage I. If you say 'Reach Colony' to the driver, he'll know. Three P.M. on the dot, please."

"Thank you, Ms. Desai. I'm much obliged."

"Much obliged? You couldn't have learned that phrase in Peter's class."

"No, madam. I mean, Ms. Desai."

Usha Desai's manner softened. "Peter broods over you like a mother hen, you know," she confided before saying goodbye and hanging up.

Asoke appeared in the foyer just as Anjali was slipping out. He tapped the telephone logbook with the ballpoint pen attached to it by a red-and-blue crocheted cord. "Incoming call. Please to sign."

Reluctantly Anjali scrawled her initials, the time, and the date on the line Asoke indicated. Minnie might make an exception for calls to and from her "darling boy," but obviously not for calls to Anjali from the darling boy's business contacts. Anjali had reverted overnight from being Peter's special friend to just another Bagehot House boarder on permanent probation. But Anjali was no longer the impulsive, naive runaway whom Mr. GG had deposited at Bagehot House's rusty gates. Her father was dead. Dead of shame and heartache. Dead, cremated, ashes scattered in some muddy stream or more likely some ditch, since the ghats of the holy Ganges were too far away. She had murdered her father. She felt grief. Grief for her mother, for Peter, but also for herself. The source of true pity is self-pity. She'd read that. Her father had mistaken ambition for restlessness. Why was it wrong for a daughter to want more than what her father could give her? Why couldn't Baba have let her go instead of forcing her to run away?

Not owning a Bajaj Chetak like Tookie's to zip around town and get to know distances between neighborhoods, Anjali miscalculated the time an auto-rickshaw would need to ferry her from Bagehot House to Indira Nagar. She arrived at the Reach Colony complex of buildings twenty minutes late for her three o'clock interview. At least she was looking head-turning chic, she consoled herself, in the designer shirt-and-slacks outfit she had borrowed without permission from Tookie's closet.

Reach for the Galaxy, a four-story building with aspirations to luxury, stood between two identical blocks, Reach for the Stars and Reach for the Universe. So that explained the colony's name. The apartment façades were painted with black-rimmed rectangles of bold colors: red, yellow, blue, and white. The top floors of all three were still under construction, bristling with bamboo lifters and half-walls of raw brick pocked by window cutouts, with outer walls waiting for their final coats of plaster and paint. The boxy balconies of the lower floors were littered with children's toys and draped with drying laundry. A team of uniformed malis watered a still-scruffy cricket pitch, while a construction crew worked to complete the second floor of a supermarket for the convenience of Reach Colony residents. The billboard map indicated a yet-to-be-built shopping center and Montessori school: the Bangalore dream, a self-contained, self-sufficient city for the affluent.

Usha Desai lived in one of the four apartments that took up the third floor. Galaxy had an elevator shaft, but the elevator had not yet been installed. Even the air was tinged with the smell of wet concrete. Anjali had a flash memory of crumbling Pinky Mahal: she had spent her life amid empty promises and the expectation of decay and dissolution. What must watching glass skyscrapers and shopping malls rise intact from hacked earth and churned rice paddies do to a child? At that strange dinner party of Minnie's, she had *intuited* the Bangalore spirit and blurted out her longing for it. But now, as she stood before the front door of apartment 3B, she wondered if she had the brashness to gut her Gauripur past. Except that she had already lost it. Peter had flown in just to inform her of that loss. Her father was dead. Her mother and sister had chosen to be dead to her. Moving forward was now her only option. The wooden nameplate on the door bore two names: DESAI DATA SYSTEMS and CONTEMPORARY COMMUNICATIONS INSTITUTE. She rang the bell and was let into the apartment by a maid who was about her own age.

"I hope you didn't have trouble finding the place," Usha Desai said. Her voice was creamy-smooth, betraying no annoyance at Anjali's lateness. "I should have told you that I live in a building that looks like a Mondrian."

Anjali wasn't going to let on that she didn't know what a Mondrian was. She was here for one specific purpose: admission to CCI. *Stay focused.* "It's almost like a painting," Anjali offered.

Usha was wearing a gray salwar-kameez set this time, not an imported couture pantsuit, as she had at the Bagehot House party. A fifty-year-old with a teenager's body: Anjali marveled. She wore her graying hair in a bob and her reading glasses on a silver chain around her neck. Diet, exercise, authority, composure: she radiated self-discipline. And speed: she covered the long, narrow hallway to the parlor as though her legs were motorized. Anjali's mother and maternal aunts were plump, slow-moving women younger than Usha, quick only in perceiving slights.

Usha led Anjali through the parlor into a sunny, spacious room she called her office. It was furnished with a squat glass-topped desk, swivel chairs, filing cabinets, and a colorful Sankhera sofa and armchair set. Lined up, facing the windows, were two large exercise machines, which Anjali had seen advertised in lifestyle magazines that Tookie passed around, and a stationary bicycle. The windows looked out on a part of the Reach Colony that she hadn't noticed from her auto-rickshaw: a partly bulldozed strip of forest, and beyond that, an intact small village. Perhaps the villagers provided the colony's labor; or equally plausible, perhaps they ignored the encroaching urbanization altogether.

Anjali was about to invent excuses for her tardiness—a motorbike had bumped her auto-rickshaw?—but Usha cut her short. "Let's not waste more time. I have a meeting in Electronic City later this afternoon."

Parvati Banerji was seated at the desk, a stack of dossiers before her and more stashed in a leather tote bag, on which the letters PB were stamped in gold paint. Two large dogs lounged at her feet. They looked like groomed, pampered versions of pariah dogs. The larger of the two growled at Anjali. "Chill," Parvati commanded. She calmed the dog by stroking it behind the ears; then she shot Anjali an amused look. "You aren't afraid of dogs, are you?"

"No," she lied, but she didn't approach the desk. Anjali hadn't known anyone in Gauripur who kept dogs as pets. There were packs of stray pariah dogs, which lived off scavenged garbage, and fierce, unleashed German Shepherds owned by rich men to scare burglars off their property.

"How's Mrs. Bagehot?" Usha asked. She checked the large dial of the men's watch she wore on the inside of her wrist, and frowned.

"That was an odd evening, wasn't it?" Parvati added. "The poor dear hasn't been out of her house in forty years." She pulled a slim folder from the stack on the desk. Anjali assumed it contained information on her, though she hadn't formally applied to CCI. Probably the letter of introduction Peter had promised to send. Could Desai Data Systems have pieced together her bio?

"We don't want to rush you," Usha said. "But traffic's bound to be atrocious."

Parvati tossed a treat to each of her dogs. "Mind you, we're not biting the hand that feeds us," she explained.

Usha checked her cell phone. "We're all profiting from the boom in Bangalore, but we wish the city fathers would widen the roads!"

"Well, shall we get started?"

Usha flipped shut the lid of her cell phone. "Hold on a sec. I have to make sure Mother takes her new pills. She's hidden them again, but I think I know where." She darted back into the hallway.

Anjali was grateful for the delay. The thought of being interviewed by two women powerful enough to open doors flustered her. She was confident that she could charm or tease favors from men in positions to help her once she figured out their vanities and weaknesses, but she had honed no strategy for getting what she needed from women.

Parvati swiveled in her chair, pointed to the sofa and chair, and asked Anjali to please sit down. "Make yourself at home. Usha won't be long. She knows all her mother's hiding places." Then she went back to reading dossiers and making notes. Anjali sank into the low-footed Sankhera chair, which turned out to be an uncomfortable choice for a long-legged candidate with frazzled nerves. Newspapers in English, Hindi, and Gujarati lay in a basket on the floor within easy reach, and glossy business weeklies were displayed on the matching Sankhera coffee table. What would more impress Parvati: pretend to be engrossed in a periodical or pretend to be lost in rich inner resources?

"Usha's a saint," Parvati sighed. She wheeled her desk chair closer to Anjali. "When Urmila-behn—that's her mother—took ill, Usha resigned her job. She'd headed HR—that's the human resources office—at a huge textile company, so building up CCI *and* being a dutiful daughter was a breeze for her. Her sister and brother had no time for their mother. The brother said flat out that he wasn't about to relocate from Australia. The sister flew in from Canada for two weeks, then flew right back, saying that her husband and children needed her more than her mother did."

Dutiful daughter. Anjali squirmed in shame. How was she to respond when she herself had chosen personal fulfillment over her parents' welfare? "Why is it that Indian women become so selfish when they leave India?" Parvati continued. Anjali's face felt hot. She inferred that her forehead was probably visibly perspiring when Parvati called out to the maid to bring a glass of chilled water for the guest.

"Mr. Champion speaks very highly of her too," Anjali managed to say, but *very* came out as "wery."

"Of course we have to face the same kind of ethical crisis within India. My parents spent their last years in Rishikesh while I was in Bombay with my husband and sons. We have to go where the jobs are."

The maid carried in three glasses of water on a tray and a plate of cookies. She was wearing a pretty purple salwar-kameez with a bead-fringed dupatta. In Bangalore, you couldn't tell who was a student and who a servant.

"In my own case, I left home for the possibility of securing employment that I could be good at," Anjali mumbled in self-defense. *At which*

I can be good? Avoid complicated constructions. Keep your mouth shut until the formal interview starts.

PARVATI WAS STILL going through the pile of dossiers and Anjali still unfolding her legs, crossing them alternatively at the knees and at the ankles, when Usha reappeared. "Well, at least you two have had a chance to get acquainted. Would you like a cup of tea, Anjali? Coffee is doable too. Kamini doesn't have to get to her computer classes for another couple of hours."

In Bangalore, even servants took computer lessons! In Bangalore, even servants were in competition! Soon Bangaloreans would be importing their domestic staff from Gauripur! Anjali declined the offer of tea or coffee.

"Maybe we could start by having you tell us a bit about your background," Usha suggested.

Don't get rattled. Live up to the image you cut in Husseina's and Tookie's clothes. Fake coolness under pressure. "P'hine, madam!" *She saw right away how her saying "P'hine" had jolted both interviewers.* "My name is Angie Bose." She rattled off her rehearsed self-introduction. "We're Bengalis, but my family settled in Bihar long ago. My Hindi is better than my Bangla, and my English is better than both—"

Parvati interrupted her. "So we should call you Angie?" She checked off something on one of the forms in front of her. "Angie, not Anjali. Fine. The last name's still Bose?"

"Did you catch the difference, Angie?" Usha asked. "*Fine,* not *p'hine.* Efff. *Flower, frost, forest, fever, full, fool, fluff, fish, fat, fell, fast, five, fair, far, farther, further* . . . for want of one right consonant sound, et cetera?"

She had failed the interview even before it had begun! For want of the correct *fff* sound, her future might be lost. Peter's gift of money wouldn't last forever.

"Excuse my nervousness. *Fine.*"

Parvati consulted the form again. "Angie, what are your career goals?"

"You are asking for my job goals, madam?" She had prepared for this question. "My ambition is to be a call-center agent. It is my vocation."

"Call-center agent!" Usha snapped. "Please. Customer-support specialist. U.S. companies are very uncomfortable with any term that smacks of outsourcing."

Parvati intervened in a soothing voice. "We're interested in you as a person. We want to know what makes you tick, what makes you leave family and hometown, what sports you play or follow, that sort of thing."

"You want I should recite my job qualifications? Highest marks in first-year B. Comm. course in statistics, certificate in advanced conversational English, diploma in American English . . ." She let her voice trail off because Usha was playing impatiently with a tiny bronze trophy in the shape of a woman golfer on the neat desk. *Move on to sports and hobbies.* "Forward on the da Gama women's field hockey team . . ." Should she brag about having been a mean ball flicker? Ma and Baba had been ashamed of her unwomanly stick-wielding skill. "Silver cup in inter-missionary-schools girls' Ping-Pong tournament . . ."

Usha Desai held up her hand, signaling Anjali to stop.

You want I should? Ping-Pong? You loser! But Parvati was trying to be kind. "Would you describe yourself as a people person? Or are you a loner who likes to be by herself and read a book?"

Okay, she had an ally in Rabi Chatterjee's aunt. Good cop, bad cop?

Parvati's roller-ball pen hovered over boxes to be checked off on the form. "Do you consider yourself a logical thinker or a go-with-the-flow, roll-with-the-punches type?"

She hadn't read a single novel since graduating from high school. "People person," she admitted. Not that she wasn't a reader, but what she pored over were fanzines about Bollywood hunks. She was a movie groupie, not a bookworm. *Ask me about Shah Rukh Khan or Akshay Kumar, go on,* she silently challenged the two middle-aged women.

"How about logic versus intuition?" Usha asked.

"I'm a very logical person." Anjali craned her neck to read the upside-down words listed on Parvati's form: *perfectionist; pliant; cautious; argumentative; compromiser; team worker; leader; secretive; loyal; competitive; manipulative; tough negotiator; diplomatic; impulsive; stubborn; plodder; methodical; serious; solemn; critical; fun loving; fun to be with.*

She had wants, she had longings and terrifying yearnings, oh, she had so, so many passions and obsessions, but none was named on Parvati Banerji's official interview form! *You're failing!* Suddenly a dam gave way inside her. "Do you want an honest answer? You want to know why I left Gauripur?"

"I'm told it's the best policy," Usha said evenly.

Instead of the pithy, sanitized answers she had prepared for likely questions, she heard herself offering these composed and cosmopolitan career women crazy fragments of Gauripur life, which made up the story of her own half-formed life. She unburdened on them Sonali's bitter compromises, Nirmal's fatal humiliations, Peter's hazardous generosity to her and his pained love for a young man (*oh, my God, I've exposed him*), her father's fatal despair, the criminal selected for her to marry: the injustice, the indignity, the powerlessness. Her happiest memory was walking in Gauripur with Rabi.

"What can you know of people like Sonali and me and Nirmal? I had to get out before I died like Nirmal. You ask me what motivated me to come to Bangalore. I didn't have a life in Gauripur, like Peter has. I had to go. I am here to dictate the terms of my happiness."

"Well, I'm glad Peter is dictating his," Usha remarked. She handed Anjali a tissue from a packet in the pocket of her kameez.

It was only then that Anjali felt tears welling. She panicked. "I didn't mean to expose him." There was no taking back the confidences she had unleashed. Then, defensively, she explained, "I'm not the only one who knows. Rabi took some pictures. He described Ali as the most beautiful woman in Gauripur."

"We don't find anything wrong with it." Parvati put Anjali's dossier back in the pile. "Are you feeling better after that emotional detour?"

"My advice, whether you want it or not, is this: don't launch into a self-indulgent screed during an interview." Usha extracted a sheet from a loose-leaf binder.

Screed: the day's new word. "I'm terribly sorry," Anjali said. "I don't know why all that gushed out of me. It just happened. I don't mean to make excuses for doing badly."

Usha handed the sheet to her. It was a photocopy of the poem "The Raven." "Do you know what the title refers to, Angie?"

What a relief! "A ray-venn?" she asked. "A large black bird with a big white beak? Like a kite, or a crow?" She was back in Peter's apartment, the pencil in Peter's hand punctuating each word. *Again, again, no, again.* Without being asked, she began to read the sheet. The "weak and weary," the "quoth the raven," the "never-more" all presented themselves fully formed, natural, without a pause.

"Peter prepared you very well."

Did that mean she was too advanced for the CCI program? "I still need training, madam."

"Well, thank you for coming in this afternoon." Parvati signaled that the interview was at an end.

"We'll call you. And please convey our good wishes to Mrs. Bagehot."

On cue Kamini came out of the kitchen to show Anjali out. In the hallway, Anjali thought she overheard a soft laugh and something like the words "Well, definitely not your cookie-cutter . . ."

5

On the auto-rickshaw ride back from Indira Nagar to Kew Gardens, Anjali went over and over the questions the CCI partners had put to her, how stupidly she had answered them, and how she *should* have responded. Husseina's prepping hadn't seen her through the actual interview. She was anxious to describe her experience to Tookie and get her feedback before Tookie left for her pre-work-shift bar-hopping ritual.

When she got back to Bagehot House, she changed into her own clothes before knocking on the barely open door to Tookie's room. All three of her fellow boarders were there, giggling and whooping about a column in *Voice of the South,* which was spread out on Tookie's bed. Sunita had found the paper on the top of the credenza in the breakfast alcove.

"Hey, girlfriend!" Tookie high-fived her. "Take an eyeful of this! That Dynamo dude's got it right! Totally nailed us!"

Even Sunita managed an air-high-five and made room for Anjali on the bed so she could read Dynamo's column.

THE NEW MISS INDIA

By Dynamo

Dynamo this week is smitten. Congratulations to the New Miss India, Aziza Habib, selected last week in Goa by a panel of Bollywood heavyweights and at least one befuddled Hollywood B-lister, as the next Aishwarya Rai, self-evidently the most beautiful woman in the world. (By national consensus, any Miss India automatically doubles as the world Number One). Once again, the time-tested standard of Indian beauty has been upheld: simpering, doe-eyed, classically trained dancers in traditional attire (until they strip down to Western evening gowns and spike heels) in front of dozens of slobbering producers with checkbooks and film scripts at the ready.

My question: Which of these lovely ladies is more in touch with the soul of modern India?

Every week, Bang-a-lot (or maybe I should call it Bang-amour) receives (not "welcomes") several thousand young women from every part of this great country. They arrive by plane, by train, even by intercity bus. They come from the great cities and the mofussil towns. From Lucknow and Varodara; from Gauripur and Dhanbad. They represent all religions, all languages. They come bearing school-leaving certificates, letters of reference from old teachers, but most important, bearing hope and energy that is infectious. They don't simper, they don't dance (don't ask them!), and they don't wear saris or evening gowns. They stride in comfortable salwars or in blue jeans, and Bang-amour had better get used to it and be grateful for them. Our torpid institutions—like Bollywood standards of compliance—will try to beat them down, but that train has already left the station.

While the moguls of Mumbai thrust their retro beauties in our faces, these call-center hopefuls manage to attract a smaller but more discriminating cadre of admirers. Bollywood has no use for India's women, apart from ornamentation. Far from Bollywood being India's international calling card, it cynically holds its "heroines" and their vast male audiences in a stage of infantilism that should cause us great international shame.

Anjali read it through twice before Husseina grabbed the paper from her. Mr. GG had sneaked Gauripur into his column because he had fallen head over heels for her. Husseina said, "This guy must be dating a customer-service agent."

"You mean he's having sex with one?" Tookie grinned.

Anjali wasn't ready to let them in on Dynamo's identity—it was her special secret. She snatched the paper back from Husseina and read the column out loud, enunciating each syllable as self-consciously as she used to in dialogue drills in Peter Champion's advanced conversational skills class. How could her friends miss the obvious fact that Dynamo, aka Mr. GG, had penned a love letter to her, and to her alone? "He says he is smitten," she protested. "Smitten, that's how he describes what he is feeling. *Smitten*'s a chivalrous word!"

"He sounds more like an anthropologist to me," Husseina countered. "We didn't exist until he discovered us and talked us up. We're *his* newest tribe."

Sunita missed Husseina's irony. "Hip-hip, Dynamo! I'm very okay with being a new breed of working girl."

"Please, career women." Tookie corrected her. "Dynamo's smitten with a harem full of career women." She refreshed her lipstick and blush. "Well, got to hit the Brigades so I can get through my shift. Anyone coming along?"

Husseina and Sunita declined, but Anjali eagerly accepted and hopped on behind Tookie on her Chetak. She was in the mood to celebrate Mr. GG's public homage to her. On the night of Minnie's dinner party she had been certain he would call her the next morning. No, she had expected him to surprise her by showing up at the front door of Bagehot House with a bigger bouquet than the one he had brought Minnie. What a sly suitor!

One of Tookie's co-workers bought the first round in the first pub; strangers bought the next several. A secret admirer (of Tookie or of Anjali—it wasn't clear which) bought them second drinks at the second pub; a leering man in a Ralph Lauren shirt bought the next; a plump middle-aged man wearing Ray-Ban sunglasses indoors bought a few more. By this time Tookie began to repeat what she was saying, and

Anjali felt more like an Angie. After the third pub, Angie lost count of who paid for what at which club. This was only the second night she had tasted liquor. In Gauripur the fast boys in Peter's American English conversation group went out for beers after class maybe once a month, but they'd never asked her to join them, and if they had, she'd have been genuinely shocked. Women from respectable middle-class Gauripur families didn't drink, period. Her father drank local whiskey in private, as other neighborhood men who could afford to probably did. The really rich—and there were only four or five such families—guzzled, it was said, imported scotch and brandy in the back rooms of the Gauripur Gymkhana; menial laborers soaked up cheap country liquor in remote shacks on the fringes of town and apparently dropped dead on their way home. She'd read in the papers about illicit liquor distillers being jailed.

By eleven-thirty, when the bars were required to stop serving drinks, Angie was throwing up on the sidewalk. She couldn't remember any Bajaj Chetak ride back to Kew Gardens, let alone negotiating the steps from the front door to her room. At the lunch table the next day, Tookie gave her a big vitamin B-50 capsule and a lecture. There were two kinds of call-center boozers: big-city, upper-class practiced hedonists who could hold their liquor, and American-wannabe village bumpkins who got so puking drunk that they missed work. Angie prayed that Mr. GG hadn't witnessed her pub-crawling escapade the night before.

6

It was Parvati Banerji who called Anjali with the news that she had been admitted to CCI's two-week cram course and that she was expected at eight o'clock in the morning of the following Monday for the first class, which would be held in Reach for the Galaxy 3A, the apartment adjoining Usha's residence.

"Usha usually runs the accelerated program, but I'm pinch-hitting for her this session." Parvati went on to explain that Usha's elderly mother had undergone complicated surgery to repair a heart valve, and had suffered a post-op stroke. "Severe deficit, I'm afraid." There was no predicting when Usha would return full-time to CCI.

"Pinch-hitting?" *Was that a form of Eve-teasing?*

Parvati laughed. "Don't sweat it. Our course includes an intensive culture-familiarization unit." She made arrangements for the CCI minivan, which ferried students to and from the institute, to pick Anjali up in front of Bagehot House at 5 A.M. on Monday. "The gate's still standing, isn't it? Or have hoodlums carried it away to sell as scrap iron?"

"Not to worry, please. I'll be ready for shuttle bus by five minutes to five."

So her life, her real life, would begin (again) in six more days.

She was determined not be overwhelmed by fellow students at CCI as she had been by call-center employees at Barista her first morning in Bangalore. To give herself an edge, Anjali went to bed early that night. She needed rest; she needed not just sleep but *dream-free* sleep. Banish the ghosts and night monsters. But she couldn't keep Baba away. He stormed into the room, screaming, "You're dead to me!" She scrunched her eyes shut and whispered, "You're dead to me too. Go haunt the 'Perfect Jamai Candidate' instead. He killed us both and got away." Baba melted into Subodh Mitra, and Subodh Mitra pulled her to a sitting position on the bed and, morphing into Ali, dirty-danced around her, to a Bollywood soundtrack.

Sometime that night Husseina rattled the beaded curtain to Anjali's makeshift room, startling her out of bed. She'd been deep in an anxiety dream, and she wasn't certain she was actually awake. Husseina pressed a painted fingernail to her full lips and motioned for Anjali to follow her down the hall to her room, which, according to Tookie, had been the bridal chamber in which Minnie the blushing bride had yielded to the dashing, retired army officer Maxie.

A half-packed overnight case lay open on the four-poster bed. "I believe in traveling light," Husseina announced, smiling. "I'm leaving tonight. I'm so outta here, I'm already gone."

I'm awake, Anjali thought. *This is happening.* A dump? But that was unthinkable; Queen Husseina was not subject to the fate of commoners like Mira of Mangalore or Anjali of Gauripur. "Going home? Why?"

Husseina took in Anjali's look of shock and broke into a laugh that ended in a coughing fit. "Home to Hyderabad? What exactly is my home?" She flung open the doors of her almirah and pulled out the dresser drawers. Opulence! *What was it like to be so rich?* Anjali wondered, coveting Husseina's clothes, shoes, jewelry, stacks of wispy lingerie. She felt Husseina's arm slip around her shoulder and smelled Husseina's brand of sandalwood soap. She gave a squeeze, then let go. "They'll look even better on you, Anjali."

Of all the questions she had, Anjali could only ask, "Why?" Meaning, why are you torturing me with this display of all the stuff you own?

"Why am I leaving, or why am I giving all of this to you?" She tugged a slinky silk kameez off its hanger. "It's just a little trade, Anjali. My clothes for your clothes. It's a very good deal for you. It's something girlfriends do all the time, isn't it? Your jeans and T-shirts for all this. I'll throw in some underwear too." She scrunched the kameez into a ball and lobbed it into the open suitcase.

"But my things aren't even clean." *Why are you doing this?* But as in a dream, the words wouldn't come out.

"So? Bobby wants me to wear jeans tonight. Did I ever tell you about Bobby?"

"You're engaged to a cousin in London," said Anjali. "At least that's what you keep saying."

"Bobby is my fiancé."

"He's in Bangalore?"

"Actually he's not my fiancé. We've been married for seven years. He flew in from Bradford last week. He's so British, I barely understand him."

Bradford dimmed the luster of Husseina the Mysterious. *Married seven years? But she's my age!* This was dream logic.

Husseina flopped on the bed beside the suitcase. "I haven't been entirely honest with everybody. Actually, I've never been partially honest with anybody. But an air of mystery can be useful in a town like Bangalore, can't it? The truth is always more shocking than lies, isn't it?"

Now who was babbling? But Husseina was talking into a vacuum, not expecting answers. "I've noticed," she continued, "you have a touch of mystery about you."

Guile, yes; mystery, absolutely not. "I wouldn't know the first thing about acting mysterious," Anjali mumbled, to which Husseina merely cocked her head and retorted, "Perfect! Appearing innocent is the first step."

Anjali flashed on something Peter had said. Innocence and blindness, something about them, but she couldn't keep them straight.

Husseina finished packing a toiletry kit and threw it into the suitcase. Then she lifted a Gucci purse off the topmost shelf of the almirah and fanned out a fistful of passports. "My father does favors," she said. "People give him things, like free identities. What should I be tonight? American? No, too risky. Canadian? Too cold. Qatari, Aussie, Kiwi, Pakistani, Indian . . . what-oh-what does poor little Husseina want to be? Where do I want to go? I've got all the damned fucking choices in the world. I've got a million of them." She gestured at Minnie's posters of bland British children playing with pets. "I'm like those fucking little girls up there on the wall. Instead of kittens, I've got passports. That's all I've got."

Tookie, not Husseina, was known for foul language and cursing. Anjali rushed down the hall to her room, plucked her jeans from the clothes tree and her T-shirts and underwear from the hamper, and then hurried back. Husseina had already stripped down to her bra and panties. "Thanks," she said, "just leave them on the bed. You can pick up your loot tomorrow."

Dream logic or not, she was beginning to put things together. Husseina had acted strange the night of the gala. She'd been out on the porch, with her cell phone. And she'd been angry, difficult at breakfast. Husseina's careful façade was chipping.

"Did you give Minnie a month's notice?"

"Fuck the bitch! End of one chapter."

"What should I tell Tookie and Sunita?"

"Tell Tookie anything you want. Be careful with Sunita—she's not as innocent as she seems." Then Husseina launched into a monologue. "I'll go out as an Indian tonight. Maybe I'll be an American tomorrow—that might be fun. Fake identities are very easy when your whole life's been one big fucking fake." She read through the list of Panzer Delight cities before slipping the T-shirt on. "Been there, done that, except maybe Bratislava. Good to know there's still something worth living for." She was shapelier than Anjali. Then the jeans; there too, tighter and less boyish. She tucked her hair under Anjali's most colorful scarf, talking all the while.

"You want to hear something funny? I never told anyone this. When I was in the ninth grade at the American School in Dubai, I got a phone call from my father to go to the airport, pick up a ticket, and fly back to Hyderabad right away. I thought someone had died! When I landed, he showed me a picture and said, 'This is my auntie's grandson. They call him Bobby. He is a good boy, with a scholarship to London. What do you think of him?' As if anyone cared a fig! His next words were 'You will be marrying him tomorrow.' I was only thirteen, and I had a paper due on Hawthorne and I wondered if getting married could be an excuse to pass in the paper late. Of course I couldn't mention it, but no one would believe it anyway. Truth is always more shocking than lies, isn't it? The next morning my new husband left for England and I went back to the ninth grade and no one knew I was married. My husband didn't write to me at school. He didn't write me, period."

None of this made any sense to Anjali. Even Husseina's tone confused her. She was like a spinning top. There was an edge to every word she spat out, as though the next one might come out in a scream.

The mysteries of Hyderabad, explained but not comprehended. Panzer Delight, with all its umlauts, would be out the door and heading back to Europe. And she, Anjali Bose, ghost of Gauripur, would inherit a closet full of expensive silks. No one had ever confided in her, except maybe Peter and Ali. She owed Husseina something heartfelt, or profound, but she was a girl with a bright smile and nothing else. She dredged up Peter's words again, hoping she'd got them right. "Innocence is attractive in a girl," Anjali said. "But I suppose blindness isn't."

Husseina stared. At last she said, "I almost misjudged you. You're not a vulgar little bore like Tookie. Or a cunning little mouse like Sunita. You see through things, don't you? And you keep quiet. It's important to keep quiet."

"I'm just repeating nonsense. Forget anything I say." She didn't like the way Husseina had stared. She didn't like Husseina's tone, the nakedness of her disregard for their fellow Bagehot Girls. Anjali had tried to act smarter than she was, remembering phrases from smarter people, and Husseina had caught on and given her credit and now she knew some kind of uncomfortable secret about Husseina that she shouldn't.

When Husseina spoke again, it was woman to woman, her hand on Anjali's shoulder, her face up close. "Frankly, I don't know where I'm going. Bobby said, 'Trust me and don't tell anyone you're leaving,' but he doesn't trust me. He's sending a car and driver, that's all I know. Life is very strange, isn't it?"

"Nothing is the way it seems," Anjali replied. "It's all light and angles."

"Yes, light and angles. May I quote you?" asked Husseina.

And I must remember truth is more shocking than lies, Anjali counseled herself as she went back to her alcove. That was the only lesson she could extract from Husseina's unforced revelation. She left the door curtains parted slightly and sat cross-legged on her cot in the dark until Husseina —sexy in her T-shirt and jeans, tiptoeing with a suitcase, unlit cigarette in her lips—slipped past.

She couldn't wait for morning to usurp Queen Husseina's room and role in Bagehot House. As soon as she was certain that Husseina had fled, and even imagined a car slowing down and a car door's muffled slamming—one of Minnie Bagehot's fantasy Duesenbergs pulling up to the curb with the lights dimmed—she went into the master bedroom, trying on one luxurious silk kameez after another and admiring her new silk-enhanced curves in the cracked full-length mirror. And then she stretched out, for the first night in her life, alone on a full-size mattress. Husseina's room was dark, private, and silent.

It was accidental that she awoke early, at six A.M., in that unfamiliar room. Perhaps Tookie had come back late from work and brushed against the door. Or dogs had barked, crows had cawed, or it was something internal, a sense that something was wrong. Maybe Husseina had never left, no driver had turned up, she was lying, or she was crazy. Women didn't give up a closet of silk for a handful of unwashed cotton. She didn't need an alien rainbow of expensive silks in exchange for her faithful Gauripur T-shirts and well-worn jeans. She would miss the umlauts of Panzer Delight. The umlauts, not a handful of passports, were the true sign of a wider world.

And so she got up, straightened the bed cover, grabbed a white salwar and kameez — the closest thing in the closet to a sleeping suit — and went back to her old room for one last nap. Her old room might be loud and dusty, but at least she'd earned it. Husseina might still come back. It might all have been a dream. She again fell asleep, but almost immediately, it seemed, there came a light shaking of her curtain, and then it opened. Minnie Bagehot invited herself in. It was seven o'clock.

"What are you doing here?" Minnie demanded. "I watched you leave."

"I would certainly have given you proper notice, madam."

"But I distinctly saw you sneak out of the house with bag and baggage in the middle of the night. And smoking a cigarette, no less. Smoking on the public street!"

So, it's true: Minnie never sleeps and never forgets. She marks little demerits on a piece of paper, adding up to a dump. "Madam, I have never smoked a cigarette in my life. It must have been Husseina."

Minnie grabbed Anjali by the shoulders. "You have the audacity to lie to me? You think I'm a blind and cuckoo-in-the head old lady you can cheat? I recognized your clothes. Husseina would never dress like you or that Goanese." She let go of Anjali and shoved her down hard on the cot. "It's a matter of breeding, simple breeding. You are the sad outcome."

Anjali's first impulse was to throttle Mad Minnie and stuff her Raj-era vocabulary back down her gullet. Her fingers itched to circle the scrawny throat, its papery wrinkles caked with pink foundation. Anjali's father died because she had brought dishonor to the family. Guilt reheated itself into rage against everything that Bagehot House stood for.

"Breeding?" She could feel her voice rising. "You want to talk about breeding? You stupid old cow! You are not God. You are not even British—ha! You are one of us, and you are living on Indian goodwill!"

Minnie backed away, perhaps startled by the sudden increase in volume. She lived inside a bubble and had selective hearing. She didn't respond to words, to insult, or to anger. "I haven't the slightest idea of what that little outburst was about. What are you trying to tell me? A rich Mohammedan stole your clothes and ran off without paying her bill?"

Anjali could hear the unspoken implication: *stole from the likes of you?* "I haven't the p'oggiest notion why, but she wanted to trade clothes."

"Preposterous!" But for the first time, Minnie looked perplexed. She shuffled toward the door curtain. "I'm sure there's a simple explanation."

"Things like that are never simple. It is just a mystery." *Let it go at that, for now.*

Minnie dismissed complications with a wave of her hand, like a spoiled child. Or like self-appointed royalty with severe memory loss. Her self-confidence bounced back. "Perhaps I misidentified the culprit."

"Culprit, madam? What is the crime? She left without saying goodbye? We pay you a month's rent in advance."

Minnie's voice dropped to a soft, conspiratorial mumble. "Just yesterday, I came to a very difficult decision. It's that prostie, that Goanese. I should never have let her in. I'm sure she's conspiring with dark forces. She has to go." Then Minnie explained that since Anjali was the protégée of that dear boy Peter, she was willing to hold off on collecting rent until she'd found a suitable position. ("I do hope you're looking. There was a time when I could call on governors and ministers for favors, but they've all . . .") Anjali could pay all that was owed from her first paycheck.

That fabled first paycheck already bore unrealistic burdens, so why not add a few more?

Strange negotiations first with Husseina, next with Mad Minnie, but in both cases Anjali was coming through the winner.

"You don't have to thank me," the landlady continued. "I too was once a young woman of modest means on my own in an unfamiliar town. I too have been the beneficiary of kindness." It was her Christian duty to repay the grace she'd once received.

"Christian duty" was a concept alien to Anjali. Duty meant dharma and a host of caste and social restrictions she'd never seriously observed. Squatting in a cracked, dingy bathtub used by generations of Christians and Muslims, then submitting to Subodh Mitra and not resisting with her life, had wiped the slate clean of any remaining dharmic duties.

"Bangalore's become an evil place. Remember the way it used to be when Maxie and Bunty were in charge?"

Bunty—wasn't that the widow Philpott's husband? Mad Minnie really had lost her marbles. Or was retreating into the past another one of her tricks of survival? "Gone to the dogs," Anjali snickered, in the best All-India Radio news-anchor Britishy accent she could manage. "My Bunty would go bonkers if he were still around."

"There are goondahs resident on the property," Minnie fumed. "I'm a prisoner in my own house. I don't dare shut my eyes in my own bed." From inside the soiled lace glove on her left hand, she extracted a sheer white handkerchief embroidered with a pink B inside a lilac floral ring, and blotted her anxious, watery eyes. "Forces are gathering," she warned. "It's no use, Opal. We're doomed."

Cut the melodrama, Minnie. All you are is a cobweb about to be swept away! One good housecleaning and you're gone!

But Minnie babbled on. "You've seen what the vermin have done to my rose garden. It's a jungle! And to think that the Prince of Wales himself brought me cuttings from England! The vermin have taken over the compound. I see their lights from my window. I call the police, but they do nothing. They won't, or can't, who knows? No good Christian deed goes unpunished. A long time ago Asoke begged me to let some of his village brothers rest up for a night or two. Those peasants were making their way on foot to Madras, walking, can you believe, with their women and children and bundles and body lice and oozy sores. Now they think they own my compound. The Bagehot name doesn't strike terror anymore. Maxie would have had them flogged. They mock me when I catch them with loot. I'm missing a silver goblet, but who cares? What they don't cart off and sell, they destroy. I keep my eyes peeled, what else can I do?"

So, it was true after all that Minnie sat by her window all night and kept watch! What the Bagehot Girls had got wrong was why and whom she was watching. "Vermin!" Minnie repeated. "They're keeping a death watch." So, her clinging to nasty imperial prejudices was another trick of survival. Minnie knew just how powerless she was in Bang-a-Buck Bangalore. Anjali held out a conciliatory hand. "I think I understand, madam," she said, meaning it. She too hailed from the heartland of suspiciousness; she'd spent a lifetime publicly agreeing with, and privately dismissing, the not-dissimilar prejudices of her parents concerning the threat posed by anyone not of their blood. But to understand was not to approve.

The old lady grasped Anjali's hand in both of hers. "You'll be my eyes and ears. I must write your benefactor and thank him for sending you to me all the way from the mofussils. The dear Lord works in mysterious ways."

Minnie inhabited an impenetrable, Minnie-centric universe. Why take offense? Better for Anjali to press her momentary advantage. "I wonder, madam, if I might ask for one more favor?" The old lady seemed receptive. "I wonder . . . when Husseina left, she said I could take over her room. Would that be possible?"

Minnie's eyes were closed behind her thick glasses—her way of quelling dissent or reaching a decision in her own sweet time. "I don't see why not."

I'm undumpable! It was a high-five moment, with no one to share it. So she could keep a luxury room and have it for next to nothing, so long as Minnie trusted her to spy on the squatters.

End of supplication. End of begging. She was ready to take her place. And not just in Bagehot House.

• • •

SHE AWOKE AGAIN at ten o'clock in Husseina's bed, with the feeling that the night before and the early-morning intervention had been dreams of a future, and that *today's the day!* This day would be different from any other in her nineteen years. She indulged herself with Husseina's imported shampoo and conditioner, lipstick and mascara. She slipped on Husseina's wispy bikini briefs and lifted and separated her breasts with Husseina's expensive black bra. From the full-length mirror, a tall, languid lingerie model smiled back at her. The mirror-woman was definitely Angie, not Anjali. Anjali was an insecure, dump-wary tenant; Angie was an entitled squatter and scavenger.

She suddenly realized why the teenage girl seated in the shed's window frame in firelight had stirred a visceral kinship. From a silver tray on the dressing table, she picked up Husseina's comb and smoothed the tangles from her long, wavy hair. In Gauripur her mother used to massage syrupy red hibiscus-scented hair oil into her scalp every single morning, a pre-bath mother-daughter ritual. A full head of thick, black hair is a woman's wealth, her mother insisted, as she concocted home remedies for all kinds of hair damage: yogurt-rub to cure dandruff, pastes made from oily berries to add luster to frizzy hair, seed-soaked potions to reverse hair loss. At bedtime, her mother had forced her to wrap her braids with thick cotton tape to prevent split ends.

What if the bitter wife and nagging mother had actually been a contented, creative woman? Angie stood at the window in newly acquired underwear and dragged Husseina's comb harshly through her hair. She wouldn't let Gauripur memories ruin this day. Comb vigorously; comb until your scalp hurts; comb all knots of guilt out of your selfish head and prideful hair.

When the comb broke in two in her hands, she moved away from the window. From the magic closet, she selected a slinky pink salwar-kameez set and tried it on. She hadn't looked so good in months — maybe never. Looking great was the shortest cut to feeling great. Add a pair of purple, high-heeled slingbacks and a Chanel purse. Arrogance bled into self-confidence. She was starting her life over. She was starring in the Bollywood version of her breakout from Gauripur. *Bangalore! Bangalore!* A chorus of sweaty, spangled dancers circled her. *Today's the day! Today's the day!* They sang and shimmied. She felt male dancers lift her from the dreary world of Sunita Sampath. She floated free, the spirit of Mr. GG's Bangalore. Mr. GG, the love interest played by Shah Rukh Khan, awaited her in the next scene. She flashed on Ali swaying to a Bollywood soundtrack in Peter Champion's flat. She loved Ali. She loved Peter. She loved her sugar daddy, GG. Most of all, she loved the lithe, saucy, dance-crazy new Angie!

TOOKIE ACCOSTED HER on the stairs late that afternoon as she made her way down to take a stroll in the neighborhood; better still, she wanted to drop in on the super-cool Darrens and Roxies at Barista. It wasn't enough to be seen by squatters and street vendors. She wanted to be envied by total strangers.

"Honey, you look *hot!*" Tookie exclaimed. "Join me for a cappuccino? I'm meeting Reynaldo in a few." Then, with a wink, she added, "Just don't try to steal him from me."

Anjali, channeling Angie, took a couple of strides back and forth and executed a half-twirl. "Foxy?"

"Talking of stealing, isn't that Husseina's kameez?"

Poor Tookie had no clue that she was about to be dumped. So why take offense at her question. "We traded."

"Well, aren't you the sharp trader!" The working woman checked her imported imitation-ostrich pocketbook to make sure she had her company ID, cigarettes, and credit cards. "Our High and Mighty Miss H must be cracking up! Either that or she's up to hanky-panky with some boy other than that fabled fiancé stuck in London. I heard her go out last night, but I didn't hear her come back in. She's risking a dump."

"I don't think she cares," Anjali said.

"How do you know? Anyway, where has she gone?"

Now it was Anjali's turn to play mysterious. "She said, 'Anywhere.'"

"I'll find out from Rajoo. Nothing happens in town without Rajoo making it happen. I call him the Minister of the Night."

"Your nighttime bad boy Rajoo?"

"If a cappuccino sounds pretty good right now, let's get going. Reynaldo's a punctuality freak."

Reynaldo, short, tubby, and hairy (except for a tawny balding spot on the crown), was on his second iced coffee when the two women arrived at Barista. The tip of the plastic straw was chewed flat, Anjali noticed. He was the fidgety anxious kind of date. No wonder Tookie kept Rajoo on the side. Since Mad Minnie's house rules did not permit partying on the premises, coffee houses and bars were where Tookie met her two men friends. Tookie had her work-and-fun routine down right: get on a shift from ten P.M. to six A.M., and you have plenty of time for hitting the pubs before being picked up at the Bagehot House front gate by the company minivan.

In the restroom, Tookie confided that the best thing about Reynaldo was that he was undemandingly dull. Mister Moderation, she'd nicknamed him. Rajoo was Mister Too-Much. "I have this yin-and-yang thing going with them. How about you? What turns you on?"

"I'm dying to find out." Anjali laughed.

Reynaldo left soon after the women returned from the restroom. The oldest of his seven brothers, a pharmacist in Ontario, was sponsoring his application for "landed immigrant" status in Canada, and he had a mountain of documents to put together.

Tookie waved him off with a cheery "Ciao!" Her voice dropped to the low register of girlish intimacy. "I know what you're thinking. What do I see in Reynaldo?"

"It never occurred to me to think that," Anjali lied. She sucked the last noisy sip of her iced coffee through her straw, then with her fingers she fished brownish ice chips one by one out of the glass and laid them on her tongue. Deal with that breach of table manners, Minnie!

"If his visa comes through, I'll marry him and go to Canada. If it doesn't . . ." She put her helmet on. "Don't turn judgmental on me, girlfriend," she warned, leading the way back to her Bajaj Chetak. "Ready?"

"Ready for what?"

"To find out what turns you on, of course."

They started out at Pubworld, where the big screen featured European videos and sound throbbing to the max. Did Angie see correctly? Was that Panzer Delight? Yes, it was, in a ten-year-old video, confirmed by a little identifier tag at the bottom right. She wanted to scream, "Look at me! I had that T-shirt!" but no one was watching, and no one could hear. Then they went on to Opus, where two crooners took turns singing and where Tookie bid on a bottle of champagne being auctioned off for charity, but was outbid by a glamorous woman with perfect teeth, whom Tookie identified as a TV celebrity. TV? Anjali thought, *I haven't seen TV since I got to Bangalore! Who watches it, and who has the time?* Their last stop of the night was Glitzworld, where Rajoo tended bar. Rajoo was Mister Too-Much all right: too pomaded, too flashy, too imperious, and too indiscriminately lecherous. With Anjali, however, Rajoo chose to act the gallant. He plucked her right hand off her lap when Tookie introduced them and held it up to his lips. She let her fingers rest on Rajoo's plump, moist lips, savoring a new confidence, wondering what did turn her on.

Young men were pounding the bar for more drinks. He ignored them. A scrawny young busboy brought out two trays of still-dripping glasses from the kitchen and arranged them by highball, beer, and wine. "Lalu!" Rajoo snapped his fingers and pointed to heaps of plates and glasses stashed in plastic bins under the bar. "Idiot." He apologized to Anjali. "What to expect? Your friend Sunita's stupid brother."

Before she could respond—the very idea of Rajoo's hiring Sunita's brother and the possibility that Rajoo, from behind a bar on Brigades Road, controlled an empire of hirings and real estate placement sent her spinning—Rajoo leaned forward simply to stare at her face.

"You've got to say this about Tookie," he said. "She has the prettiest friends in Bangalore."

7

Anjali took advantage of Tookie's new, almost fawning, admiration for her to set up a visit to the campus of Trans-Oceanic Services (TOS), Tookie's all-night home. That way, she reasoned, she would experience a day at a call center, gaining a decided edge over other students at CCI. Except for rare trips to her father's railway building in Gauripur to bring him a file or spectacles or acid reflux pills, she had never been inside a business office. And Bangalore office complexes were vaster, glitzier, scarier than the long dusty room with rows of wobbly wooden chairs and file-cluttered wooden desks in which her father had worked. Tookie acted eager to do Anjali a favor. Security was tight in all downtown glass-tower office buildings, but she would get her "badass beau" Rajoo to call the head security officer of TOS. "I'll switch to a day shift for the next couple of weeks, girlfriend." She even offered Anjali a bonus: she would arrange for Moni, "the Bengali Svengali," to bump into her.

It was available, the world that she, Anjali/Angie, aspired to. She *did* aspire to it, didn't she? In any case, it was a challenge, and challenges turned her on. She had no idea of the entrance requirements, or if she had the skills and the stamina to stick it out. She knew only that she was a young woman with a very slight advantage, and she'd better grab Bangalore and whatever it offered, or else she'd end up living her sister's life.

On the morning of the scheduled visit, Rajoo showed up at Bagehot House to pick up Tookie and Anjali—in a chauffeured Jaguar. "You sure make things happen, Rajoo. I owe you one," Tookie said.

He acknowledged Tookie's compliment with a leer worthy of Bollywood cads. "Give and take, take and give. That's what society is about, no?" Anjali hung back as they bantered. To her, Rajoo, in his indigo silk shirt, tight white slacks, and dyed-blue snakeskin boots, looked more Dubai than Bangalore. She couldn't visualize Mr. GG in such a getup. Squatter kids materialized from the green wilderness of the Bagehot compound to check out the fancy automobile. The chauffeur scrambled out from behind the steering wheel to shoo them off.

But Rajoo intervened. "Like these wheels?" he asked, beaming at them. They moved away from the car and clustered around the flashy stranger, who was extracting a wad of rupees from the back pocket of his snug-fitting pants. "It's a matter of giving and taking," he explained to Tookie, who looked pained as he distributed a one-hundred rupee note to each of the kids. "Not baksheesh," he told them. They rewarded him with worshipful stares. "Make it work for you. I'll be back to collect my cut." Since he was speaking in English, the effect must have been meant for Anjali.

Tookie cut it short. "Some of us working stiffs have cards to punch," she snapped at Rajoo as they strode toward the car. Anjali followed.

"I hope you weren't expecting a Rolls, Miss Bose," Rajoo joked, catching up with the women. "Deep down, this capitalist is a Gandhian."

It was Anjali's first-ever ride in a Jaguar, and she sank into the leather seat, savoring its aroma and its chauffeur's imperious honking, his lane-changing maneuvers, and his way of swearing at slow traffic.

When the Jaguar pulled up in front of the guardhouse of the TOS compound, the chauffeur leaped out and held the car door open for his boss instead of the women. Rajoo speed-dialed his contact in the TOS office tower before helping Anjali out of the Jaguar. Tookie was left to clamber out without help from either her nighttime fun-beau or his chauffeur, and get in place in the employees' line at the guardhouse. Intimidated by the elaborate security procedure, and feeling more Anjali than Angie, she stayed close to Rajoo. He sensed her anxiety and personally escorted her through the security post; informed the uniformed guard that she was not carrying cameras or tape recorders on her person; watched her print her name and address, *Anjali Bose, 1 Kew Gardens,* as well as sign into the logbook; took her visitor's badge out of the guard's hand; and clipped it to the shoulder strap of her purse. Since Tookie would be working a full shift, he even offered to send his car and driver back in a couple of hours so that she wouldn't have to take crowded buses back to Bagehot House. *Give and take, take and give:* he was practicing what he preached. He got off on power and gratitude. To show gratitude, she flashed her halogen smile at him, but she declined the ride back. "I'll take a taxi," she said, lying.

The visitor's pass allowed Anjali access only to the roof-floor cafeteria and the landscaped grounds of the TOS campus. Tookie had just enough time to give her a tour of the roof floor before reporting for her shift—this day, working as "Tess" from Lubbock, Texas—in a monitored bay on the third floor of the tower.

The open-air cafeteria-cum-patio roof floor of the glass and steel tower was crammed with benches and refectory tables under broad, tasseled umbrellas. It looked like a luxury resort floating above a modern city, missing only pull-down screens of Goan beachfront hotels. Agents on break huddled over laptops, white buds in their ears, colas within easy reach. But when she walked past, they invariably looked up from the screen to size her up. They had to know that since she wasn't wearing a TOS employee photo ID around her neck, she wasn't one of them.

Without even trying, Anjali slipped into her high-wattage Angie persona. Angie was smart, sexy, and special. Angie's steps had a bouncy lightness, her posture an eye-catching swagger. She took her time crossing the width of the terrace to the railing, from which she could view landscaped lawns ribboned with concrete paths. Early-afternoon shadows cast by neighboring office buildings left dark prison bars on sunlit stretches of pampered grass. Young men and women employees strode the footpaths, chatting, leaning toward one another, but not quite touching. Malis and sweepers manicured the edges. Below her lay the New India: business-efficient, secretively erotic, and servant supported. She felt a rush of sympathy for the high-fiving, head-banging, hard-drinking friends of Tookie she had met on Residency Road and the Brigades. The call-center survivalist inhabits separate yet simultaneous lives. These were the luckiest times to be young, adventurous, and Indian. And the saddest for those like her, who knew she could be anything she wanted to be, but hadn't the foggiest idea of what she wanted.

Over the PA system a self-important voice announced, "Paging Ms. Anjali Bose! Ms. Bose, please meet your party at the espresso machine! Paging Ms. Anjali Bose! Your party is waiting!"

Why was Tookie's team leader allowing her a break this early? Confused, Anjali turned her back on the poster-worthy view of New Millennium India and scanned the employees relaxing around the espresso machine. There were three women, two in color-coordinated salwar-kameezes and one in a snug Versace T-shirt and white capri pants, and two mustached young men in starched shirts and carefully pressed slacks, chatting and sipping, but no Tookie.

"Ms. Anjali Bose, please meet your party!"

A tall, lithe man, likely in his late twenties and definitely handsome, maybe even beautiful, approached the group by the espresso machine. Anjali liked it that he had no mustache. She liked even more the way his shiny black hair flopped over an eyebrow. She started walking to where the PA system was instructing her to "meet her party" and realized that she loved the prominent biceps of the polo-shirted, chino-wearing beautiful man. He was holding a stack of magazines, each as thick as the Gauripur telephone directory, against his chest. The five employees acknowledged his arrival with smiles or nods, but he didn't join their conversation and they didn't make an effort to draw him in. Tookie had told Anjali about "team ethos," and so she assumed that the beautiful man and the chattering five were on different teams of customer-service agents. He stood slightly apart but did not look at all isolated. Anjali guessed that he too was waiting for someone. Why shouldn't that someone be Ms. Anjali Bose? She preened when she caught his body jolt to attention as their eyes met. He immediately headed in her direction. Even with an armful of magazines, he moved like an athlete, a cricketer at the pitch.

"Anjali Bose. Who else could you be but Anjali Bose?"

So this had to be the Bengali Svengali. Tookie D'Mello had set up this meeting, but she hadn't let on what a heartthrob he was. What else hadn't she let on? Not a hint of India in his accent, but he didn't sound American like Rabi Chatterjee or Mr. Champion.

Even before introducing himself, the heartthrob said that finding her was like locating your car in an airport parking lot: the sudden realignment of your steps when you press your smart key and somewhere down a long line of cars the lights go on and the horn beeps.

The analogy of cars in an airport to people meeting in the TOS dining patio—or of her to a car, if that's what he'd meant—sailed over her head. She'd never had a car, Gauripur lacked even a single parking lot, and car keys, in her experience, were far from "smart"; in fact, they were dumb as nails. She took it as more evidence of her unenlightened state and feared asking what he was talking about. And so she flashed a broad smile of recognition. "But you've never seen me," she said.

"The day I can't spot a pretty Bengali face in a crowd is the day I change my name to Singh." He guided her to a small bistro table and dropped the stack of magazines on it. "You're everything Leila said."

"Leila?"

"She called me as soon as she saw you, remember? But I was working and I couldn't run over."

Ah, Leila the I ❤ MUMBAI girl. She'd seen Anjali pass out—did

Moni know how desperate she'd been? No one would recognize her now.

Should she be Anjali for this champion of Bengali culture? She peered at the magazine cover on the top of the pile. A pretty girl, identified as "Bengal's Latest Beauty Export to Bangalore" and posed against a modern city skyline, stared back. But the modern Bengali Beauty, like the ladies in fake antique Mughal miniatures sold in Gauripur bazaars, was holding a lotus blossom in her manicured hand and gazing dreamily at a birdlike speck soaring above the geometric tops of office towers. Anjali picked the magazine off the top of the stack and turned it over. On its back cover, perhaps again in parody, the art director had reprinted a British-era map of historical Bengal—including all of Bangladesh and Indian West Bengal, Upper Burma, much of Orissa as far south as Puri, and north as far as Assam and west all the way to Bihar, even the area around Gauripur, the catchments where Anjali's parents' families had been marooned, and labeled it as "The New Bengal-Bangalore Raj." How grand and powerful Bengal had been in her great-great-grandparents' days!

Moni took out a digital camera and aimed it at her. "Amazing, isn't it?" And before she could ask what, exactly, he gushed, "How big Bengal was! A long, long time ago, my family was in Upper Burma, involved in teak. It's not even on the map. They kept elephants to load the logs, and then they floated the wood downriver; they had family members with sawmills all along the riverbanks and they trained little native boys, Burmese, to walk on the logs with hooks and steer our logs into the mill. Our logs had little flags on them, like branded cattle. Imagine all that!"

"We're from Bihar," she said. Gauripur too was just off the map.

"We were a mighty people." He snapped her picture without asking permission. "Moni Lahiri at your service. But sad to say, no relation of Jhumpa Lahiri, the renowned novelist and Bengali beauty."

She would have responded by saying "We Bengalis are still a mighty people," but she didn't want to be photographed with her lips parted.

Two of her teeth were crooked—gaja danta, or elephant tusks, her father had all too often lamented when he had been bridegroom hunting. He should have paid Canada-returned Dr. Haldar, Gauripur's only orthodontist, to align her teeth if they had bothered him so much. She had to stop thinking about her father; she had to keep bitterness and guilt out of her expression for the Bengali Svengali's camera. Try out the cover model's dreamy look but without corny props like bird and lotus.

Moni took a break from his viewfinder. "See that guy serving food over there? Third one in?"

Anjali looked in the direction that Moni had indicated with his chin, a dimpled chin she found irresistible. Four men wearing hairnets and white aprons were lined up behind the long cafeteria counter. The third waiter was unmistakably Bengali; Anjali could tell from his facial structure. She suddenly wondered if Indians born and raised in America, Rabi Chatterjee, for instance, lost that ability to identify ethnicity just by looking at an Indian face.

"His name's Mohammed Chowdhury, from Bangladesh," Moni Lahiri informed her. "I heard him and a couple of other guys speaking Bangla, and his accent and voice were so pure I asked if maybe he also sang. And does he ever! I featured him in a Rabindra-sangeet, and people were amazed. He showed up in a silk kurta, some of his friends played tabla and harmonium . . . so it was a big Indian bash starring a Muslim from Bangladesh, and he ends up the most perfect Bengali among us. And of course when he was back here serving food the next morning, no one recognized him."

Moni waved in the servers' direction, and Mohammed Chowdhury lifted a hand in response.

"In case you were wondering, my family doesn't consider itself the deep-down, sprung-from-god's-head kind of Brahmins," he said. "The last name might make you think so, but all it means is somewhere along the line we snared a Brahmin male. My father went to Johns Hopkins to study medicine, found work at Mass General in Boston, flew back home for two weeks to get married, settled first in Toronto, moved on to Madison, Wisconsin, and finally to St. Louis, Missouri, where he had two sons and a daughter. One son became an oncologist, the daughter's a biologist. Me, I'm a wastrel wannabe and amateur photographer with an MBA from Wharton. Anyway, if you think I'm babbling, it's to distract you from posing. You have energy. That's what I want to get across on your cover photo. Prettiness I can Photoshop."

The Bengali Svengali was going to put her on the cover of a glossy? That made Anjali self-conscious. She assumed her signature halogen smile but could feel tightness in the muscles around her lips.

"Don't try so hard." He glanced over at the freezer section of the cafeteria line. "Feel like an ice cream? They have sherbets, popsicles, frozen yogurts, everything."

She knew sherbet from Alps Palace in Gauripur. Rabi had photographed her in Alps Palace with his boxy camera. "Sherbet, please," she said.

He brought her two scoops of mango sherbet and a plastic spoon, but nothing for himself. She was relieved to have something to do with her hands and dug the spoon into the orangy-yellow sherbet. It was denser, sweeter than sherbets at the Alps Palace. She hoped Rabi would call her when he returned from his wanderings to his Aunt Parvati's house in Bangalore.

"Do me a favor," Moni Lahiri said, picking up his camera again. "Sit on the table."

She put her dish of sherbet on the chair seat and complied.

"No, no, sit on the table and bring a spoonful of the stuff just to your lips. Desire and promise of gratification. That's it! You'll be Miss Two Scoops. Refreshing as sherbet on a hot day." He handed the dish to her as she rearranged her legs on the tabletop.

"Now raise your left arm halfway up, as though it's around someone's shoulder."

"Whose?" she asked. *Yours?*

"I'm thinking Queen Victoria's. There's a statue of the old girl in Cubbon Park. I can Photoshop you into her lap."

There was that word again. Photoshop had not appeared in Mr. Champion's workbooks.

"Now, face me and keep your left arm up, as though it's resting on a railing; no, it's on my shoulder. Good. We're getting there. Look at me as though I'm the answer to all your prayers."

"Mr. Lahiri, really." She giggled.

"Concentrate. Give me intensity. Great! Love the set of that steely jaw! How about the eyes? You're in love! That's better. We're nearly there. I'll Photoshop you stepping out of a first-class air-conditioned carriage at the railway station. No, next to that big victory obelisk in Cubbon Park. You're taking in Bangalore for the first time. Or would you prefer Electronic City? I've got a hundred Bangalore backdrops."

"So it's all a matter of light and angles? And backdrops?" She was afraid to ask about obelisks.

"It's a Photoshop world," he said.

So this was the famous Monish Lahiri. It wasn't hard to look head-over-heels in love with this handsome man with floppy hair, bulked biceps, and quick hands. She could imagine pouring shampoo on his hair, kneading it over a lavatory sink, and rinsing it off with a pitcher of water. She'd never had such intimate fantasies. She'd never really fantasized touching any part of a man, especially not his hair. And now she found herself imagining other things, and she blushed, avoiding his gaze. Her body was itching, starting from down below. It was embarrassing, a disease perhaps.

"Tookie said you'd be perfect for a cover. She didn't exaggerate." He followed this up with a brief Bangla poem she didn't recognize.

"Isn't it a little early for poetry?" she asked. "Anyway," to discourage further excursions into the thicket of modern literary Bangla, she added, "I'm here to learn better English."

"I can teach you that. St. Louis English anyway. No, make that SoCal-speak, since Santa Monica's my latest home base. Or was." He wriggled his fingers as if to magically conjure up a scene. "Pretend it's nighttime in California," he said. "Actually, it really is. It's about two in the morning. We're on a blanket on a beach in Santa Monica. We have a bottle of nice, light red wine. The moon hides behind a cloud. A slight chill comes off the water. The stars wink in and out. I pour, and we drink. We're watching the planes rising from LAX, or coming in."

She liked this make-believe game about being romanced on a beach with a lilting name by a Bengali-American MBA with a dimpled chin and floppy hair. A chill was an inspired touch. The suitor would offer his jacket, lean close, and drape it over her shoulders.

"*Really,* Mr. Lahiri," she exclaimed as though he really had done so.

He looked amused. "Really," he repeated. "But you don't need lessons. Your English is good enough."

Only good enough? What did that mean, in the Bangalore world? Good enough for what—some dead-end job talking to Mukky Sharma? Or the sex lines—is that where they put Indian girls who were just good enough? Where an accent is advantageous? She envied Moni Lahiri's ease in both Bangla and English. She envied people blessed with two mother tongues. Her English was good, but it would never be a mother tongue.

He seemed unaware of having hurt her feelings. "I've got a confession," he said, his voice soft with guilt. And he did lean close to her, so close that she was afraid she would impulsively touch his shoulder with hers, or worse, run her fingers through his straight, fine hair. "I'm not really a wastrel. I came back to India because this is where the money is, money and opportunity. I didn't want to be just another unhappy American doctor having to toe the HMO line. Like Baba and Dada."

The country was being overrun with repatriates and immigrants. India had become the land of milk and honey for everyone except young people born and raised in Gauripur. It wasn't fair! Moni Lahiri had seduced her with fantasy games of wine and sand, only to betray her.

"C'mon, Miss Bose, you've got the most expressive face in the world—you're angry at me, but I'm not sure why. Why?"

"Everyone here comes from somewhere else."

"In Bangalore, that might be true. That's the reason for *this.*" He pulled a publication from the middle of the stack. "You'll be the star of the next issue."

"*This?*"

"It's my baby. *The Bangla HotBook of Bangalore.*" He handled the booklet tenderly. It was the seventh edition of a directory that listed names, phone numbers, and local addresses, plus hometowns, of the three thousand newly arrived Bengalis in Bangalore. "Only singles, of course. And newly singles. I've put my MBA skills to use."

She'd thought it was a book of pictures, shots of models like the girl on the cover. She flipped through the pages. There were sections announcing Bangla "First Date" mixers, and for the straitlaced, puja celebrations; announcements of who had been promoted, who was looking to date, and which Bangla-friendly companies were hiring, along with ads and discounts at restaurants and discos. Then she studied the list of names: two full pages of Boses, even three other Anjali Boses, along with rows and rows of the usual Bangla names, the Banerjees and Chatterjees, the Dases, Duttas, Ghoses, Guhas, and Sens, skipping ahead to the Roys and Sinhas. Then, suddenly anxious, she flipped back a few pages: Mitra, Subodh. Home address: Asansol. So he hadn't been lying; he'd actually worked in Bangalore. And maybe he was still here.

"Something the matter?" Moni asked.

In her most innocent voice she asked, "Who's this Subodh Mitra?"

"Nice guy, but not the sharpest knife, if you get my drift. You know him?"

The thought of Subodh Mitra slicing his way through Bangalore with a dull knife brought back all the terror: the dark mango grove, the rusting rebars, the blood on her sari. She was no longer under an umbrella in sunny Bangalore. "The name sounded a little familiar."

"Tall guy, a little heavy? He left here a couple of months back, off to Bengal to find a wife, he said. Going through hundreds of bridal pictures finally got to him. One day he ran up to me and said, 'Moni! I found her! Miss Perfection!' You had to be happy for the guy. He was gone the next day."

She tried to hide her disappointment. Any friend of Subodh Mitra was no friend of hers. The itching stopped. For no particular reason, except perhaps to press her bona fides, she said, "I might have been that girl."

He dropped the directory on the stack of magazines. "No way. Subodh's a nice enough guy, but no way cool enough for you."

And how cool am I, Mr. Lahiri? But she didn't ask. They sat there for another few minutes. The tables near them filled up. She waited for him to ask her out. Her father would have considered Moni Lahiri, MBA, with homes in America and India, the "perfect boy," but the perfect boy was slipping through her fingers. Was there something she should do, should say? "I have to get back," he said. He handed her the copy of *The Bangla HotBook*. He didn't ask to see her again. Rabi had given her a phone number, Mr. GG had given her a ride, and Peter Champion had given her money. Moni gave nothing, yet she felt connected somehow.

"Do you have a cell-phone number to list in *The HotBook*?"

She said she didn't. Bagehot House was the most temporary address in Bangalore. A cell phone was an unimaginable luxury.

He scrawled a number on the back cover of the directory. "Anytime," he said.

She watched him stride to the elevator and hop in just as the door was closing. It was his fault that she felt newly abandoned. She visualized the two of them walking, side by side, on the crisp, green spaces of the TOS compound. She felt his body against her, and her arms, her back were itchy. She wanted someone to scratch them. She wanted to hold her arms out to Moni Lahiri, but he was already gone.

Just like that, a Bangalore legend enters my life, and then he's gone. Like the dancers in a Bollywood movie, a flash of skin, a hint of hidden wonders, then in a second they're gone.

8

Today's the day, every day's the day: she felt that rush again.

She wasn't so far from the place where she had made her first grand entrance into Bangalore, her lucky spot, the Barista on MG Road. Things that had confused her just a few weeks earlier were starting to clear up. In her red kameez and cream-colored salwar and expensive makeup, and after weeks of fattening up on Minnie's potatoes and mutton stew, she was steadier on her feet. Tookie said she had that Bagehot House greasy glow. At least she wouldn't pass out.

The scene of her Bangalore Grand Entrance was a cheap rickshaw ride away.

The tables were full but the mood was subdued, lacking the high-spirited silliness and cast of characters she had encountered on her first morning in Bangalore: no Mumbai Girl or overly friendly Mike, no Millie the chain smoker or Suzie with the butterfly breasts. Maybe they were on different shifts; maybe they'd moved on to newer IT call-center hubs that were luring away Bangalore veterans with better pay. Out on the fringes of the coffee sippers she spotted Mr. GG hunched over his computer. She bought a small coffee and moved in his direction.

Mr. GG wasn't as dashing a figure as she remembered from the night of Mad Minnie's gala. In just two weeks it seemed he'd aged and softened into a short, squat man, with hair thinning on top. She remembered looking down on Peter Champion's balding head, the mosquitoes landing but not swatted away. There were no mosquitoes in Bangalore, at least not this month. The buttons of Mr. GG's white shirt strained against his belly. Like her pot-bellied father, she thought, and like the young people in Bangalore, getting fat on snacks as they worked through the night, fat on cafeteria food, fat on beer and savories after work, fat on being free and rich and away from home.

"Still in Djakarta, Mr. GG?" Now she was the one standing, his face at her tummy level, and she could read the shock and surprise on his face. She flashed her famous smile, and he hit SAVE and flipped the lid down.

"Miss Bose! You're looking very fit and happy."

"I am."

"Very pert and glowing."

"It must be Minnie's mutton stew."

He laughed. "I assumed it was because you are in love."

She bantered back. "I *am* in love. With Bangalore."

"Why haven't you called?" he asked.

"I don't have a phone."

"Let's get you a mobile, then. You can't not be within reach by voice or text in this town."

"I don't have the money."

"Maybe not today, but you'll have it tomorrow. But only if you carry a mobile in your handbag."

And so, half an hour later, Anjali Bose of 1 Kew Gardens, Bangalore, had a tiny silver cell phone, paid for by Mr. GG. She could call her sister or her mother or anyone in the world as long as she had the person's number, which she didn't, except for that of Moni Lahiri and Usha Desai and, if she thought about it, Rabi Chatterjee and Peter Champion.

The phone presented more options than she could possibly master. "Is there a master number I can call for jobs?" she joked, and Mr. GG put his telephone number on speed dial for her. There seemed to be no need in the world that the phone could not satisfy. Owning a cell phone wasn't quite as impressive as inspecting virtual buildings in foreign countries, but on that morning, just having one, even a simple model—an unheard-of extravagance, in her family experience—felt nearly as miraculous. For weeks she'd been watching how everyone on the streets of Bangalore used this remarkable device, even the Muslim ladies in their black burqas: clutching their husbands, holding their children, and chatting on their silvery little phones as they rode on the back of a motorbike. Tookie carried hers in her hand, like a second purse; Husseina's had been stashed in a secret pocket sewn into her custom-tailored salwar. Anjali wondered where Husseina was honeymooning with Bobby of Bradford; she was the first-time owner of a phone, with no one to call.

"Any other numbers?" Mr. GG asked.

"Put in my father's," she said, and gave him the familiar Gauripur number. A sudden image of the heavy black phone, on a stool in the living room, its thick, dust-clogged cord gnawed by mice, appeared in her mind's eye. That number and the house must now belong to a stranger.

"And Usha Desai," she said, then recited the number, which she'd memorized. "And this one"; she read the number from Moni's torn-off slip of paper. "Call it ML."

"That's not a lot of numbers for a popular young lady," Mr. GG said.

"Put in Peter," she said, and gave him the number. She wished she had memorized Rabi's California number. That would have impressed Mr. GG.

"And how are things at Bagehot House?" he asked when he had inputted the numbers.

"The building's still standing."

"I meant the old lady. How's she holding up?"

"Surviving. But her mind is failing."

"Appearances can be deceiving," he said, smiling. "I trust in only the durability of the virtual universe."

Her bargain with Mr. GG went unspoken; in exchange for a few smiles and bright comments, she'd get a lift back to Bagehot House. He bowed to her: "Your Daewoo is waiting, Miss Bose."

The starving, bedraggled, overwhelmed Anjali, the one who, weeks ago, almost had to be carried into the Daewoo, had plumped into a "pert and glowing"—Mr. GG's words—cell-phone-owning *HotBook* cover girl.

Once again, she was walking to the Daewoo.

Mr. GG held the door open, always the gentleman. Vacation brochures were scattered on the front seat. "You asked about Djakarta," he said, "but we wrapped that up three days ago. Right now"—he put a brochure into her hands—"I'm working *here,* on a very cool condominium development in Puerto Vallarta."

"A pristine desert lapped by sparkling seas," she read.

"Mexico," he said, obviously amused. Anjali could see that he enjoyed imparting to her his wider knowledge. "Those seas won't be sparkling or lapping for very long without some high-level intervention. The good thing is, we've done oversight in Qatar and Dubai so we know something about heat and sandstorms and what they do to swimming pools and golf courses and yacht basins and how huge the power and sewage and refrigeration problems can be. It's a fun project. It's like building a small country."

A fun project? In her English class, Peter Champion used to warn Anjali about this: "You'll hear *fun* used as an adjective. Resist it. Fun is a noun, not an adjective." Not to be outdone, or overwhelmed by Mr. GG's worldliness or the strange languages and place names he invoked, she said, "One of the girls in Bagehot House went to an American school in the Gulf." The news seemed to silence him.

A moment later, he completed her thought. "I know. The famous Husseina Shiraz. I think she's no longer in residence—am I right?"

How would he know that?

"Some big changes on the way," he said. "All we can do is stay one step ahead." The city traffic was thinner than it had been that morning, when Rajoo's chauffeur had, cursing and honking, dropped her off at the TOS tower; they were moving along well, too well. She didn't want the ride to be over.

Mr. GG must have noted her reluctance. "I want to show you something new," he said.

Cubbon Park, she hoped. Moni had mentioned Cubbon Park. She was a woman with a phone and a glow from being in love with love.

"We'll stop at my place on the way."

"Where is that?" She knew Kent Town and Indira Nagar; she knew of Dollar Colony because Parvati Banerji lived there and Rabi crashed with the Banerjis when in Bangalore. Mr. GG had to live in an upscale area, something like Dollar Colony. She imagined him pulling up with her in front of a gate guarded by two watchmen; she would walk on a graveled driveway that sliced a flowering garden in two; she would beam at his white-haired parents as they greeted her warmly. Did he have living parents? "I'd love to meet your relatives," she heard herself say.

"I said *my* place." He had two addresses, he explained, a family residence beyond Kent Town, where he lived with parents, the widowed sister-in-law, and an older brother and his wife and infant nephew—and a private office, with a kitchen and sleeping accommodations close to Vistronics.

Every day is today! The morning had served her well, and now she was ready for whatever the late afternoon might bring.

THE OFFICE-APARTMENT occupied a corner on the top floor of a modern six-story building overlooking the winding paths and gardens of Cubbon Park. Only a few tall, old trees obstructed the hazy view of the city. Those treetops sprawled beneath Anjali like a wild, tufted lawn.

"Tea?" Mr. GG asked. A small kitchen and pantry lay just off the dining area. The familiar splash of water in a kettle, the snapping on of the gas stove: calming, reassuring Indian sounds. She wasn't sure why he had brought her here. A virtual voyage to Puerto Vallarta? To Djakarta? As long as it wasn't Gauripur, Anjali Bose had no fear of him.

This was, after all, her second time in a man's bedroom. This one, unlike Peter Champion's, was orderly, well-appointed, its walls hung with cartoonlike paintings, architecture magazines spread in an arc, like a lady's fan, on the table. She liked what she saw, liked what she saw very much, and she realized she wasn't safe at all. A pleasant itch coursed up her arms, just as it had when Moni Lahiri had snapped her photo for his *HotBook*. After all, she could tell herself, it's not as though she'd awakened that morning, then coldly decided to visit her personal Barista on MG Road, and then gone over to Mr. GG, rousing him from his work with the intention of seducing him or letting him think he was seducing her. She was incapable of such plotting. Therefore, she was not guilty of planning it or even wishing it.

She could not be held responsible for anything that happened in her life because she was not an initiator of actions. Angie the bold one, the initiator, was beyond blame, or shame. Anjali just watched and let things happen. Things like this: accepting tea from a man standing behind her as she watched the weaving lanes of traffic and the usual mix of strollers and exercisers in the park under the canopy of trees. The man behind her put his hands on her hips, then under her kameez, and began peeling it upward over her bra. She set the teacup on the windowsill and allowed him to continue.

Now he whispered in her ear, nibbling it ever so slightly before he spoke. "What sort of precautions have you taken?"

"What precautions do you mean?" *Heavens,* she thought, *if I took precautions, I wouldn't be here in your apartment, would I?*

"You know, *devices.* The pill?"

She smiled at him shyly. Subodh Mitra hadn't bothered to ask. Things move slowly, like glaciers, until they erupt like tsunamis.

Torn silver foil fluttered through the air. She heard a zipper, and the thud of heavy trousers falling to the floor. Mr. GG's fingers soothed her itch. "I've been thinking of you since we first met," he said.

It seemed that all the strollers in the park and on the footpaths had stopped and were looking up and pointing in her direction. Everyone in Cubbon Park saw the naked girl in the window. The naked girl in the window looked down on Bangalore. She moved from the window, turned, and faced Mr. GG, who was hopping on one foot to free himself from his trousers. His shoes were still on. Coins were dropping from the pockets and rolling across the floor.

"Please to sit down, Mr. GG," she ordered, and he did. For the briefest moment she thought, *If I want to get out, this is the time.* He reached down to unlace his shoes. "I will do that. Please sit back." As she bent forward, he groped for her bra strap.

Not *her* bra strap, exactly. It had been Husseina's black silk lift-and-thrust.

"Please," she insisted, this time louder, and he retreated. She made a lightning calculation: *If I'm to give myself away, it might as well be to a well-established man who saved me and performed favors and kindnesses. A well-connected man who would owe me.* A girl in a fancy black bra and half-discarded salwar, kneeling before a man on a sofa, pulling off his shoes: she's in control.

She remembered a Gauripur ritual, her own father coming home from the office at the same minute every day. Tea would be waiting, he would sit at a chair by the door and hold his feet out, and her mother would kneel and pull his shoes off—dusty or muddy shoes, depending on the season—and Anjali would bring him his indoor chappals and kurta-pajama. He would unbutton his shirt and slip on the kurta, then unbuckle his trousers and cover his shorts with the pajama. Every night of her life she had performed the same little task, as had her mother and her grandmother and probably her sister too. If all those generations could see her now! Except this time, she was on her knees and nearly naked, and the man was, essentially, a stranger. And she remembered the lines of women in Nizambagh crawling over the trucks, ghost women, spidery thin, fighting each other for access to the drivers, and she hated the price of being a woman, and India, and every man she'd ever known.

"Let's see that famous smile," said Mr. GG. And so she smiled.

She got his shoes off, and the socks—such small, soft feet, such hairy toes—then tugged his trousers by the cuffs and draped them over the back of a dining chair. He was a plump, hairy little man in bulging boxer shorts. He probably had not dressed that morning with the thought of being undressed by a lady before lunch. He made himself busy throwing cushions off his sofa, then pulling out a folding bed.

"What are you looking at?" he asked. She flashed a shy smile, which seemed to satisfy his vanity, but in truth she was fascinated by a couch converting into a bed by one pull from a near-naked man with a hairy back. Nor had she ever stood completely naked and alone, even in her own bedroom or bathroom. Back home she had bathed as older women did, in a sari. The important thing was to be able to tell herself that she'd accepted a ride from a friend, thinking she was going to meet his family, and that she'd been abducted and seduced. She'd be able to tell anybody who asked: in Bangalore be careful of friendly men who say they just want to help.

"It happens very quickly, doesn't it?" she said.

"Were you expecting roses?"

She'd meant it as a compliment. She meant how quickly one changes identities. *Half an hour ago, I was just trying to get a ride in your car. I was someone entirely different, and now I'll never be that person again.* Mr. GG was lying on his bed, pulling off his shorts, and his long, tawny whatsit looked just short of menacing. He rolled the condom over it, just like a villager with a banana in a birth-control film. His arms were open. The springy, curly mat on his chest was waiting for her.

She stepped out of her remaining clothes. She remembered swimming instructions: just jump in, it will feel cold, and you'll think you're going to drown, but you'll get used to it. No shilly-shallying. She was about to learn what every other woman knew, what Tookie and Sonali-di knew, and Mr. GG certainly seemed a more accomplished teacher than Subodh Mitra. All caution flew out the window; the years of good counsel about virtue and modesty, flirting but playing hard to get. She'd never questioned her self-image as a modest, well-brought-up, small-town, middle-class probasi Bengali girl. In a place like Bangalore, where no one was rewarded for being good in quite that way, "good" took on a different meaning. She was grateful for Mr. GG's attention. He'd offered an easy way to pay back his favors and maybe even for Anjali to gain the upper hand.

Just as he said, it was over very quickly. She felt she shouldn't compliment him on the quickness. She shouldn't say a thing, but just smile. Somehow, in the twisting and turning, she'd ended up looking down on him, with his eyes closed. Whatever he'd done had stung a little, but at least the itching was gone.

After catching his breath, he said, "I'd call you a very cool customer, Miss Anjali Bose. Continually surprising, but still sweetly innocent."

She'd expected something like a grade for her efforts, a "best ever" or "a smart, fun girl" or at least "cool," but no matter: she'd passed the test, and Mr. GG had fallen back into drowsy silence. And she'd reduced that ropy, menacing, invincible whatsit to a floppy flap of skin under a sagging condom. After a few minutes he mumbled, "Expect some excitement later today. Maybe tonight."

"How much more excitement can a girl take, Mr. GG?"

He reached out for her hair and let it flow between his fingers. "You're a funny young lady, Miss Bose." After a few more minutes he got up and slipped on his boxer shorts and the same white shirt. Maybe all the men in white shirts she passed on the streets had been doing the same thing a few minutes earlier. Maybe the women too. He shuffled into the cooking alcove, put on the tea water, and punched two slices of bread into the toaster. She took it as her cue and got back into her underwear, then the salwar and kameez. He asked, his voice low and casual, "Miss Shiraz, was she your friend?"

"I'd like to think so."

"Ms. Shiraz's picture made the BBC website," he said.

"Husseina's a celebrity?"

"She wasn't named, but I recognized the face."

"A Bagehot Girl!" Anjali was thrilled. "One of us! Girish, you make Bangalore sound like the center of the world."

"All I'm saying is changes are imminent."

"Now you sound like Minnie Bagehot. 'Evil forces are gathering,' that's her new mantra."

"Well, I don't think I need to worry about you, Miss Bose. You're steps ahead of everyone. May I call you, now that you have your own phone?"

On the drive back, Mr. GG told her what he'd been reading on the BBC website when she interrupted him at Barista. A plot to blow up Heathrow had been disrupted. She had to ask, "What is a heath row?"

"An airport," he said. She knew some names, like Netaji Subhas Bose in Kolkata and Indira Gandhi in New Delhi, and there was Sahar in Mumbai, but she'd never been on an airplane or even in an airport.

"London," he said. "People who travel a lot name the airport, not the city."

"What does that have to do with us?" she asked.

"Butterfly effect," he answered. He launched into a long explanation of how anything that happens anywhere in the world affects Bangalore. She didn't follow his theory and stopped listening to his actual words, cocooning herself instead in the pleasure of his desire for her. He kept reaching for her hand. She wished Kew Gardens was far, very far. She wanted him to keep talking, keep driving, keep lusting. She wanted to love even more than to be loved.

Respecting Minnie's house rules, Mr. GG stopped the car two blocks from Bagehot House. She let herself out the passenger door and walked around to the driver's side. He stayed behind the wheel but didn't drive off. He said, "I want to see you again."

She could tell he wanted to say more, and she wanted him to say more, so she lingered on the sidewalk, tracing invisible circles with a fingertip on his door. Mr. GG didn't bring out the sweet, clean wine-and-moonlight flirtiness that Moni Lahiri had, just a couple of hours before. She couldn't make even make-believe love to Moni in Moni's apartment. Did he live in a rented apartment, or did he own a house? He was a magician, who took Anjali and Angie, waved his wand, and made both disappear, then created an ethereal Miss Two Scoops, the stuff of popular dreams. He Photoshopped her: that was it. But Mr. GG saw *through* her, and *into* her. Her attraction to Mr. GG had a rawness and authority that thrilled her.

"Yes?"

He had expected confirmation, not a question. The engine started up. "Take care," he said. The car eased into traffic.

It was three o'clock in the afternoon, a normally quiet time. A light mist was falling, Bangalore's version of the monsoon. Kew Gardens Corner and Bhajot Lane were unusually crowded. Pedestrians—not strollers, but young men running with purpose—had spilled over the sidewalks and into the roadway, throwing traffic into a honking chaos. At three o'clock most houses were usually shuttered and many of the smaller shops were closed.

I'm a woman now, she said to herself. *I'm quite a woman. I'm hot, according to Tookie. Secretive and oh so mysterious, according to Husseina. Sherbet-cool, sherbet-refreshing, according to Moni. And funny and fascinating, if I'm reading Mr. GG correctly.* All in all, it had been quite a day, and it was still the middle of the afternoon.

9

The promised day had arrived! Shortly after daybreak, Anjali and eleven other students piled out of the CCI minivan for the first day of the two-week intensive course, itself a preparation for a new life as a salaried, independent career woman. She was glad, in a way, that she had procrastinated about getting in touch with Peter Champion's contacts. Big carp in a small pond is a minnow in a lake. She wasn't the frightened country bumpkin she had been in her first few weeks in Bangalore. She felt cocky as she watched the other eight women and three men take hesitant leaps out of the minivan. They clustered around the newly installed elevator, which could accommodate only four at a time. She chose to walk up the three flights to the door of CCI and Desai Data Systems, the first arrival, and she was rewarded with a special smile from Parvati Banerji, who had stationed herself on the third-floor landing to welcome her students.

The floor plan of DDS and Usha Desai's home office, in which Anjali had been interviewed, were identical, except that all three bedrooms had been turned into classrooms furnished with desks and chairs and equipped with computers, whiteboards, and floor-to-ceiling panels that depicted American life.

Parvati began lessons by dashing off a list of words on the whiteboard: *please, deliver, development, circuitry, executive, address, growth, management, garbage, opportunity, hearth, addition, thought.* Words that customer-support-service employees would need and would use on every work shift but would very likely mangle.

"Our goal for the intensive sessions," she announced, "is accent enhancement. The regular program offers accent neutralization, not enhancement."

Anjali saw the trembling fingers of the woman at the desk to her left write *study gole = hanssment* in her notebook. She peered at the lined notebook of the male student to her right. He was sketching her profile, and he was pretty good at it.

A woman's voice from behind Anjali interrupted the instructor. "Ma'am, what is *enhancement* meaning exactly?"

The instructor was ready for that question. "The U.S. companies that come to us want you to sound acceptably American. That doesn't mean you have to imitate American television accents—it just means they expect you to communicate without any complications. We'll work this morning on softening consonants and crispening vowels."

She had each of her twelve students pronounce the words she had listed on the whiteboard. *Please* came out as "pliss"; *garbage* and *manage* as "garbayje" and "manayje." All twelve had problems with the buried *v:* "de-well-op," "day-li-wer." Ms. Banerji smiled through the difficulties. "A small problem of muscle memory from your mother tongue," she explained. "Fortunately we have tailor-made solutions for every MTI problem in this room." She must have caught Anjali's blank look, for she quickly added, "Mother-tongue influence problems." She assured her students that after the two-week course, they would be fluent in the language of acronyms. And politics. And sports. And popular culture. Every problem has a solution.

Even problems in personal life? Anjali wondered. Could the teacher include a lesson in optimism enhancement?

Parvati's lesson plan was more formal than Peter's. She dictated which syllable to stress. She instructed the students to press the upper teeth down on the lower lip so that a crisp *v* didn't dissolve into a whooshy *w.* She drilled the trainees hard, but not even Anjali got the *th* in *growth, hearth,* and *thought.* So much easier to catch the staked fence of a *t* and an *h* approaching and settle on a plump, cozy, softened *d.*

The next exercise called for each student to recite a poem from a reader that Parvati and the absent Ms. Desai had put together. Twelve trainees, twelve poems. Anjali was assigned "I Heard a Fly Buzz." This lady poet was no Edgar Allan Poe. How could anyone be inspired by flies? Flies deserved swatters, not rhymes. Flies meant that something dead, sweet, or fecal was nearby. Anjali guessed she'd been deliberately selected for Miss Emily's fly poem because *f* was hard for Bengalis to pronounce. She remembered Peter's admonition: "Foggiest, Angie, not p'oggiest." She owed it to him to get the *f* sound right in this Bangalore classroom. And she did.

At the lunch break, two students quit. "Shattering. I've lost all my confidence," Ms. Vasudev complained. She intended to ask for her money back. Mr. Shah did not slink away during the break as Ms. Vasudev had. He waited for the instructor to resume classes so he could confront her before storming out. "This is humiliating," he berated Ms. Banerji. "I am a citizen of India. I don't give a damn that Mr. Corporate America doesn't like my accent!" To which Parvati rejoined, "Losing two out of twelve isn't bad. That leaves more attention for everyone else. In fact, two is just the beginning." She had them recite "Quitters never win, and winners never quit," and kept them at it until "vinners" and "kvitters" were wrung from their tongues.

"Let me say one thing to the rest of you," Parvati began, after the first two quitters had left. "Am I disheartened? No. We expect dropouts, and we wish them well. Not everyone is cut out for the things we demand. You'll find that English-language skills are only a part of what we expect, and not even the largest part. Language enhancement is largely mechanical—it's your absorptive capacity, your character, your ability to learn and use new ways of thinking and, of course, new facts, that we're interested in. That's why we interviewed and tested you in the first place."

The two-week prep course actually lasted only twelve days because CCI was closed on Sunday, but three more freshers dropped out at the end of the first week. "Gole=hanssment" was gone. So was the sketch artist. The remainders were at least her equals in English: big city, confident, well educated, and slightly older.

In the training manual two sessions were listed under "Getting to Know the American Client" and subdivided into "Topography" and "Culture." According to the manual, knowing a language without knowing the culture was the same as knowing the words of a song but not the music.

Fifteen minutes into the first of these two sessions, Anjali's head was spinning. Wendy's Burger King McDonald's Jack in the Box Little Caesars Papa John's Pizza Hut Round Table Pizza Domino's Popeyes KFC Waffle House IHOP Taco Bell Chili's TGIF Applebee's Red Lobster PIP Kinko's Staples AAMCO AutoZone Speedy Muffler Maaco Midas Muffler Jiffy Lube United American Delta Continental Circuit City Good Guys Best Buy Office Depot OfficeMax Texaco Chevron Amoco Sunoco Arco Mobil Gulf Radio Shack Record Barn Wal-Mart K-Mart Target Costco GE (electronics) GM (cars) GM (mills) Ford Apple IBM Dell Hewlett-Packard, and every one of them with hundreds of outlets and bottom lines, like a medium-size country itself. Food, electronics, transportation, finance, and fashion: all were familiar, but they were shown to exist on a massive scale that rendered them mysterious. Banks, insurance, brokerages . . . if they had warranties, returns, or breakdowns, eventually someone in India would have to deal with it. Normal Americans, apparently, could name all those national companies and dozens more but did not have personal contact with any of them.

Parvati assured the students on the first day of classes that for every problem, CCI had a tailor-made solution. But Anjali couldn't imagine a company taking a chance on her.

She asked, "Why all these Shacks, Huts, Barns, Cabins, and Alleys? What self-respecting company would call itself a hut or a shack? Why not Mahals and Palaces?"

Parvati had an answer for that too. "Large corporations are alienating. Calling them shacks and huts is a cheap way of humanizing them. When U.S. consumers hear of a Palace or a Mahal, they only think of a Chinese or an Indian restaurant."

In the "Culture" session, Parvati showed one episode each from three popular TV sitcoms, so her students would be familiar with them in case customers referred to characters in *Friends* or *Seinfeld* or *Sex and the City*. Recognize the clients' references; show appreciation for their notion of humor. Anjali didn't find any of them funny.

The TV episodes depressed her. All the characters were surrounded by friends. Anjali had no friends; she had fellow tenants, contacts, mentors. She'd never had a friend, no one she really liked and could bring to her home, or missed when she was out of town, or wished she could get together with to share secrets, as Elaine Benes and Carrie Bradshaw did. Her only friend had been Sonali-di, up to the time of Sonali-di's wedding. She hated these characters; she envied them. Bright and bouncy Carrie didn't work as hard at her job as Sonali-di did, but she still had enough money to splurge more on silly, strappy high heels in one afternoon than Sonali-di made in half a year. Life in India was so unfair.

Most weeknights she lay in bed, going over assigned chapters from the CCI reader. The chapter she had most trouble with was titled "Specialized Language of the Football Gridiron, the Basketball Court, and the Baseball Diamond." She memorized alien phrases that promised to unlock deep mysteries of American English and the psyche of the American consumer. It wasn't easy to visualize a "full-court press" or, for heaven's sake, a "blitz." Why was "knocking the cover off the ball" a good thing to do? How did "throwing a curveball" indicate "an unexpected degree of difficulty"? Then there was "knocking it out of the park." That too was a good thing. But "Grab some pine!" was not. "Stealing a base" and "painting the corner" were commendable. "Flooding the zone" had nothing to do with monsoons. "The bottom of the ninth" had something to do with desperation. Somehow, "three and two, bottom of the ninth" didn't make her tingle with expectation. How was "being born on third base and thinking he'd hit a triple" a venomous insult? And what on earth did "Grow a pair!" mean? She'd never seen an American game, and the names of great players were irrelevant mysteries (could they be any greater than the best of the Indian cricketers?).

She didn't know a thing about American politics, movies, songs, television, or sports, or the coded references they inspired. They were the music, if not the words, of the American language; they were 20 percent of American speech. She asked in class one day, "How can I learn to communicate to Americans if I've never been to their country?"

Parvati offered encouragement. "You're a bright girl, Anjali," she'd say. "That's what I meant by your absorptive capacity." Parvati usually called on her first, expecting the proper, or at least a provocative, answer.

THE COURSE ENDED with a unit that called for role-playing. Parvati led her students through charades in which she pretended to be an American client calling customer service at a make-believe call center in Bangalore. To graduate, the students had to sound convincingly American when answering the client. As homework, the students had to fabricate American autobiographies.

Janey Busey of Rock City, Stephenson County, Illinois, rose from the ashes of Anjali Bose of Gauripur, Bihar, India. On the CCI computer she Google-Earthed the Rock City street map and even found "her" house; she memorized the population (only 315, she noted with horror; not even the poorest, most isolated Indian village was that insignificant);

median age—an elderly 33.5—and 99.7 percent non-Hispanic white, whatever that meant. Median family income, twenty-five thousand dollars, just a quarter-lakh; median house value under one lakh dollars.

Insofar as reality can be composed of raw data, Anjali had created Rock City. The rest of her virtual life was inspired by her own unbounded longings. Janey Busey had grown up in a cheerful, wholesome, Midwestern family of five, headed by a veterinarian father and nurtured by a gift-store-owning mother. She replaced sullen Sonali with two good-hearted, extroverted brothers, Fred and Hank. Fred worked in Rock City's only bank and aspired to become a manager. Hank toiled in the office of the town's only insurance firm, though he dreamed of building boats and sailing to Mexico. Puerto Vallarta, to be exact. Vasco da Gama High School and College morphed into Lincoln High, where kids from Rock City had to hold their own against swaggerers from Chicopee and Davis. Then she got swept off her feet by her fantasies and invented sweet summer experiences of working weekdays in the big Wal-Mart in Freeport and flirting with a stock boy named Karl. She brought herself to tears just thinking of poor, slow, inept Karl shipping out to Iraq with hopes of returning with money enough for college.

For the final exam, Parvati arranged for her group of seven surviving students and herself to be transported in the CCI van to Bangalore's Electronic City offices of GlobalSys, an up-and-coming outsourcer for American and Canadian corporations.

Electronic City, Phase 1, Phase 2! The world was pouring euros, dollars, and sterling into Bangalore! Hewlett-Packard! Citibank! Siemens! GE! Timkins! Birla Group/3M India! Tecnic! Bifora Intercomplex! Dalmia Cement! Wipro! Infosys! Solid, spectacular glass temples built on raw, red clay so freshly cleared, it still bled. The CCI van bore down wide, curving lanes to the edge of the built-up area and disgorged its passengers at the front gate of the GlobalSys complex.

Parvati led her CCI test takers through GlobalSys security and ushered them into a "bay," rows of individual cubicles for teams of customer-support-service employees. She introduced them to two CCI graduates, one male and one female, one-time customer-support agents now elevated to the role of monitors. Neither was much older than Anjali. As was her habit, she studied their clothes and appearance. The boy was tall and thin, with dark-framed glasses, but athletic. He wore a dark suit; his hair was spiked and gelled. And she immediately recognized him: Darren, from her first morning in Bangalore. My God, Bangalore was a fluid world.

"Dharmendra and Rishika will play the parts of callers and monitors," Parvati explained. The monitor's job was to correct every stammer, every mispronunciation, and every error in telephone etiquette. "Don't hate the monitor," she instructed her nervous students. "Please don't take the criticism personally." Anjali remembered her first morning in Bangalore, the muttered references to "the Old Bitch," and another lingering mystery was suddenly solved. "When you turn on your computers, you'll see the credit history and the contracts your caller has signed with our client. Your job will be to scan the contracts as you engage the callers. Don't make them feel as though you're reading their credit history. It's just a chat. You're here to help them. You'll have to learn how to integrate a particular complaint with what you're reading on the screen. Some of the callers might be hostile, but you're not to take personal offense. Nothing here is personal."

And then Darren/Dharmendra took over, in perfect English, crisp and authoritative. To the question "Where are you from, sir?" he responded, "I grew up in Delhi."

"You have a good American accent, sir," the student said.

"No, I have the absence of an Indian accent. Among ourselves, we call it a Droid accent."

Before leaving the bay, Parvati posed one final question to her students. "What's the number-one rule of your profession?"

Anjali ventured a guess. "Phone poise?"

"Right. Don't lose your cool no matter what. You lose your cool, the company loses a client, and you lose a job. Best of luck!"

• • •

THE PHONE IN Anjali's cubicle rang even before she had settled into her chair. The caller's name and address popped up on her screen. Thelma Whitehead of Hot Springs, AR. Alaska or Arkansas? An igloo? Cotton fields? And what kind of name was Whitehead? Wa-wa Indian? Thank goodness, the caller was not from an M state, which she'd never have sorted out. MA, ME, MD, MI, MN, MO, MS, MT: that was a nightmare. And no doubt the monitor was listening in.

"Hi, this is Janey. How can I help you, Ms. Whitehead?"

Thelma reeled off her problems, which, if Anjali understood correctly, had to do with not having received her Social Security check, which prevented her from paying her bill on time.

And how exactly, Anjali wondered, *am I expected to solve your Social Security problems?* "Come again, please?" she said.

"What do you mean, *come again*? I ain't never bin there yet!" Thelma cried. "You don't understand the first thing I bin sayin', do you! I bet you don't even speak our language! Where the hell y'all setting at right now? India? I used to be on y'all's side, but when I get off the phone I'm fixing to call my congressman."

"Miss Thelma, please to calm down!" *Stay calm yourself. You're making mistakes because you're too agitated. No job's worth a heart attack!*

Thelma Whitehead hung up after one last, inscrutable imprecation: "This ain't all bin did yet!"—Anjali didn't recognize those words as English. If only she could say "Go to hell!" Her own anger shocked her, as it had that day in Minnie's spare room.

"Well, that didn't go too well, did it?" Rishika the monitor broke in. "Let's see how many gaffes I counted. She's not 'Miss Thelma.' This isn't *Gone with the Wind.* And where did you pull 'Please to calm down' from? I deliberately threw you a curveball with that thick accent, and you didn't respond very well, did you? You were probably seconds away from correcting her. Remember this: when you're running an open telephone line from America, you're going to get every kind of accent and every level of mangled English. You have to interpret it and laugh along with it or respond to it as if it was perfect English from a textbook.

Everyone in America speaks a different English. And then, in Thelma Whitehead's sugary Southern accent, the monitor concluded, "Hon, you bin losing your cool."

The phone calls kept coming. Why was she being picked to deal with the most difficult names? It wasn't fair. Slava from MD. Shun-lien from CA. Tanyssha from TN. Witold from IA. Esmeralda from AZ. Chang-rae from NJ. Aantwaan from LA. Gyorgy from OK. Weren't there any American-sounding names left in America? Why didn't guys like her goofy brothers, Fred and Hank, call from Rock City, Illinois?

She mustered phone-voice cheeriness for Gyorgy. "Hi, this is Angie, I mean Janey."

"Huh?"

She pictured a large man in a fur coat and knit cap with earflaps, fleeing a pack of wolves in snowy Siberia. "How can I help you this morning, Gee-orr-gee?"

The monitor broke in with an angry "It's not morning for your caller!"

"Sorry."

"And forget how the name's spelled. It's pronounced George. Keep the conversation to the point."

Why wasn't the caller doleful Mukky Sharma of IL instead of Geeorrgee/George of OK? She couldn't afford to flunk out of CCI. She needed a job, she needed paychecks. She had to pay for room and board. Minnie hopped on her desk, a vulture sniffing carrion.

George wanted to know if he could renegotiate the terms of his contract. Of course, these were just practice calls, and she was not expected to know what kind of contract he held or the company he held it with. That wasn't the point. The point was to field a difficult problem and make the client go away happy.

"George, have you contacted your local service representative?"

"I keep getting bounced to you guys. Where are you, India?"

"No, I'm right here in Illinois," she answered perkily. "Good old Rock City, Illinois."

"No shit," said George. "You could have fooled me."

"Why not just tell me your problem."

"I subscribed to one magazine—one magazine, one computer mag—and I get about forty every month and I can't cancel them. Wouldn't you say that's a problem?"

"I certainly would."

Then the call was suddenly terminated, and Parvati herself broke in. "Anjali, what have I told you about agreeing with a caller's complaint?"

"Deflect it," she said.

"Precisely. Do you understand the meaning of *deflect*? Under these circumstances, does it mean 'I certainly would'? What would be your proper answer?"

In a panic, she riffled through mental notes. *Don't agree: deflect. But how to deflect?* "I should have said . . ." She started to explain, but her mind was saturated. All day long she'd been absorbing censure from the monitors. Defend our client, sympathetically if you have to, but never agree with the callers. Maybe once in a hundred calls they'll have a legitimate complaint. The caller already has a grievance; don't encourage it.

She had to admit failure. "I don't know, madam. What should I have said?"

"You might have found a way of exchanging one magazine for another. You might even have found a way of reducing the overall number, maybe by five or ten. And between us, forty is certainly an exaggeration, so you might have asked for a full listing. I doubt that he gets more than five or six."

The phone rang again. "Janey," she mumbled in panic. But this time it was her mobile. Against CCI policy, she'd forgotten to turn it off. She'd barely had time to adjust to having it.

"Janey, aka Miss Bose? Having a bad day?"

Mr. GG! "I could use some cheering up, Mr. GG," she said. At least she'd swatted the Minnie vulture off her desk.

"Dinner tonight?"

"Afraid not."

"Come with me to Mexico?"

She was feeling cocky. "I'll think about it." Miss Anjali Bose didn't have to stay Deadbeat Janey. Not forever. She had options.

Parvati's amused voice came through. "That was your best demonstration of phone poise. Now please put away your mobile, and stay focused. It's the bottom of the ninth."

THE CLASS AND monitors and Parvati met at the end of a very long day. She'd been up since four A.M. It was now three-thirty P.M. She had taken thirty-two calls—a fraction of a normal day's workload for a normal call agent—and now she had to listen, in private, to the monitors' assessments.

She knew from Parvati's body language—a term she'd learned from Peter—that her career was over. "Anjali," Parvati said, "we knew from the beginning that you were going to be different from our usual fresher. We just didn't know how different."

She hung her head.

"You seem to lose your composure under pressure. Your language skills deteriorate."

"Yes, madam."

"I've decided this line of work is not for you."

"I understand." And with this understanding came visions of running out of Peter's money, being kicked out of Bagehot House, and having to go back for good to Gauripur.

"Look me in the eye, Anjali. Customer support is a very demanding and very specialized profession. One of the things it demands is the ability to submerge your personality. No one is interested in you, or your feelings. You are here to serve our client, and the client is the corporation, not the caller. I think you have a great deal of difficulty erasing yourself from the call."

"Yes, madam. I agree."

"I think you can take something positive from this." Parvati passed a file across the table with Anjali's name on it. On it was stamped the word SEPARATED. "Being a call agent requires modesty. It requires submission. We teach you to serve. That's not in your makeup, Anjali."

"I can try to change—"

"Don't even try. I have an investment in you. Just not this one. We'll be in touch."

Whatever that means, she thought as she walked out into the cloudy Bangalore afternoon. Mr. GG's Daewoo was not parked outside. She clutched the folder, keeping the word SEPARATED tight against her silk kameez. The wads of rupees Peter had given her, or lent her, were divided by a hundred in Bangalore. From now on she must take public buses rather than auto-rickshaws. The immediate problem was that she didn't even know the bus route back to Kew Gardens.

10

Three long bus rides, and on each ride straphangers pressed their sweaty bodies into hers. Their hands patted her bottom. Until that afternoon, Anjali had inhabited a Bangalore as virtual as Mr. GG's Djakarta, a futuristic village instantaneously connected to all time zones on the globe, but segregated from raw life lived out on real roads. She had no certified job skill to peddle; worse, she had shamed the three people who had believed in her. And worst of all, Mr. GG had taken her response seriously and not called back to confirm a dinner date.

The bellicose symphony of dusk-time Bangalore rang in her ears as she got off at the stop closest to Kew Gardens, which was not close at all. She was immediately sucked into a tidal wave of pedestrians. She was disoriented by the coughing, hawking, and throat clearing of anonymous office workers, the pulsating police sirens, and the imperious honking of chauffeurs driving imported sedans. Bhajot Lane had never seemed so loud, so clogged. On guard against pickpockets, she shunned beggars and tightened her grip on her shameful folder and expensive pocketbook—a fancy Gucci with Husseina's initials etched in gilt on leather. Anjali found it hard to shake off a beggar mother cradling a comatose infant. The woman pursued her, listing in Hindi her woes—widowhood, starvation, homelessness, tuberculosis, malaria—and called on heaven to shower blessings on alms givers. Another northern villager, a transient in a tattered, dirty sari: Anjali's own fate, if she couldn't find a way out? *Don't you know my fancy silks mean nothing?* Getting no response, not even a reprimand, the woman thrust the infant in her face. Anjalie shrank from the touch of its hot, grimy cheek, and, swerving sharply from the contact, stepped in a puddle of half-chewed, vomited food. There was no time to stop and wipe the muck off Husseina's fancy sandals because the throng of pedestrians propelled her forward to the end of the long block, then around the corner into Kew Gardens and through the wide-open gates into the Bagehot compound.

Strangers swarmed the grounds, trampling flowerbeds and flattening wide swaths of the overgrown front lawn. Men hauled Minnie's garden statuary—cracked stone cupids and armless nymphs blackish green with moss—out of the jungle behind the house and piled them into trucks in the carport. Women rolled drums of rice and canisters of flour and sugar down the steps of the porch. Everyone smiled; they were laughing, spirits were high. The massive wooden front door had been pried loose from its frame and flung over the porch railing so that wide pieces of furniture, such as credenzas and armoires, could be dragged undamaged out of the house. Among the looters, she spotted Asoke's "villagers." Squatter youths who had helped out at Minnie's gala were now carrying off Minnie's Hepplewhite chairs, card tables and decorative clocks, Satsuma vases and elephant-leg umbrella stands, balancing them on their heads.

A convoy of brightly painted trucks and a white van, all honking, careened into the semicircular driveway and parked under the carport. ALL-KARNATAKA AUCTION HOUSE announced the logo on the van, and standing by its open rear doors was Tookie's bad boy Rajoo, peeling off hundred-rupee notes from a wad, diverting—or was it bribing?—freelance looters into dumping their goods into his vehicles. Rajoo's crew placed the pried-off front door over the crumbling porch steps to use as a ramp, then directed the looters to ease bulky pieces from Minnie's public rooms—cupboards, sofas, dressers, hutches, a grandfather clock, even the dining table—down the angled door, wrap them in quilts and dhurries, and segregate them in numbered lots. Anjali wouldn't have given Rajoo credit for such organizational skills.

Rajoo's organizational skills! She was witnessing a premeditated, methodical dismantling of her only asylum in Bangalore. This was different from the occasional spontaneous looting of shops and the breaking of car windows with cricket bats by jobless young men that she had watched from her balcony in Gauripur. You could guard yourself against such sporadic eruptions of anger; her mother hoarded staple foods in her "just in case" bins; her father pasted a fake Red Cross decal on his bike. Rajoo was dispassionate, efficient. The moment Anjali acknowledged this, she went into a panic. By the time Rajoo finished stripping and wrecking Minnie Bagehot's property, she would be homeless and rupeeless. The little she possessed was inside the red Samsonite suitcase. She had to get to the suitcase before Rajoo's men found the cash Peter had given her.

Determined to salvage what she could of her own possessions, she clawed her way through the delirious throngs of scavengers. Tookie would be on her pre-shift pub crawl, and in any case she didn't own anything worth stealing. She trusted Sunita to be cool-headed enough to barricade herself in her room and call the police on her cell phone. Minnie would fall apart in a crisis, but where was Asoke? If anyone could negotiate safe passage for Minnie and her tenants, it would be Asoke, since everyone seemed to be related, or obligated, to him.

She found Asoke in the foyer, and he was acting more predator than prey. He had climbed halfway up a rickety ladder and was demonstrating to eager squatter kids how to rip Raj-era sconces off the walls without damaging them, so they could be sold by Mr. R's auction house. Farther inside the foyer, men she didn't recognize were dismantling an oversize dusty chandelier. She'd fantasized this scene of vengeful vandalism the afternoon she had discovered Maxie Bagehot's museum of colonial horrors, but now that she was witnessing the stripping of Bagehot House, it brought her little pleasure. Minnie and Maxie had been cantonment Bangalore's spit-and-polish opportunists. In Asoke and the auction house crew she recognized a twenty-first-century update. And what was she? Where could she go? Her best bet was to slip past Asoke and sneak into her room, stuff what she owned into her red Samsonite suitcase, and wait for the police to rescue her.

Asoke spotted Anjali as he was handing down an etched-glass wall bracket to a helper, lost his footing on the ladder, and yelled an obscenity as the glass shattered. She darted into the kitchen to avoid a confrontation. Women from the compound were emptying pantry shelves into plastic bins, buckets and cloth sacks. The squatter girl with the luxuriant hair invited Anjali to join her as she tossed large cans of ham and small tins of Spam and sardines into baskets held steady by two elderly women. Next, the girl turned her attention to rows of bottled olives, gherkins, capers and mayonnaise. The contents of a tiny jar mystified her. Anjali identified it: Marmite, Minnie's favorite sandwich spread. The women feigned disgust, and the girl put the jar back on the pantry shelf. She moved on to the shelves in which Asoke stored sweet-tooth Minnie's cans of condensed milk and packets of jelly-filled cookies.

Then Anjali stepped forward, dropped the jars of Marmite and four packets of cookies into her roomy pocketbook, and rushed out of the kitchen. Did that make her a looter too? No, no, she was a victim surviving on instinct. She could imagine her room already ransacked: clothes, shoes, toiletries, and costume jewelry heaped into a bed sheet and the four corners tightly knotted like a washer man's bundle, and her suitcase in which she kept what was left of Peter's gift of cash, her da Gama certificates, and the silver goblet wheeled away and hidden in a shed in the squatters' village. She bounded up the steps two at a time.

The home invaders were busting bedroom doors with their shoulders and with hammers, broom handles, and chair legs. Anjali's door bore gouge marks from claw hammers, but the heavy old-fashioned padlock was still intact. Sunita's room was open, but there was no trace of the tenant. Anjali dared not extract the key from her pocketbook to let herself in. Safer to pretend she was one of the mob, caught up in greed or revolutionary fervor. And it became easy to pretend. She was among the whooping marauders when they broke down the door to the tenants' bathroom and discovered Minnie.

Minnie Bagehot lay on the tiled floor between the bathtub and toilet, naked except for the wig and the rhinestone tiara on her head. The rioters fell silent, then drew away.

She must have collapsed while pulling on a corset. The stiff, sweat-stained undergarment lay on the floor by her feet. A wasp-waisted, pearl-studded ball gown hung from the showerhead. *What vanity!* Anjali thought, at first. And then it occurred to her that maybe Minnie had died from some crazy valor, thinking she could appear at the head of the stairs in a mildewed gown from her golden years and wave the rioters away.

Her prophecy about the gathering of evil forces had come to pass. Evil forces were sacking Bagehot House. But now, stung by this vision of its owner, they picked up their hammers and their booty and retreated down the main staircase.

No corpse deserved to be gawked at. Anjali latched the bathroom door and rested her head against it. Too late to call for an ambulance, and even if it had not been too late, she realized with shock that she had no idea what number to dial. In Gauripur, emergencies requiring intervention by police or firemen didn't happen to decent middle-class families. When Mr. GG had surprised her with her very own cell phone and asked her whom she wanted on speed dial, it had not occurred to her to include the police. How naive she had been until now!

What was it that Mr. GG had said about butterfly effects? Minnie's death meant a windfall of profitable antiques for Rajoo of All-Karnataka Auction House, whose crew was still loading Bagehot treasures into trucks. Now Anjali had in effect been dumped, because the house and its owner and everything it stood for had been dumped. She felt more homeless than she had while riding interstate buses from Patna to Bangalore. She punched Mr. GG's number on her cell phone. He didn't pick up, so she left a message: "SOS . . . Girish, need your help . . . desperate. Please, please hurry. Bagehot House is under assault, and I'm in the middle of it."

She waited and waited for the call back. Who else could she count on for rescue? *I'm sitting on the lid of the toilet in a bathroom in my rooming house, with Minnie's body inches from my toes:* she couldn't, she absolutely couldn't spring this on Moni Lahiri. Moni, the beautiful Bengali Svengali, belonged in her life of daydreams and her Photoshopped future. She called Mr. GG again and left another desperate message: "I'm ready for the trip to Mexico. Girish, please, please, come right now!"

Mr. GG would know how to right her upside-down world. He would insist she move into his apartment and his life. What was keeping him from calling her back? To give her hands something to do, she opened the bathroom cabinet and listlessly went through Tookie's and Sunita's toiletries. She dabbed an index finger into a jar of sandalwood face cream and massaged the cool, perfumed goo into her cheeks and forehead. She rubbed gel into her flyaway hair and squirted hairspray to keep every strand in place. She loosened the tiara from Minnie's tangled wig and tried it on. A cartoonish princess frowned back at her from the mirrored medicine cabinet. The tiara looked right on Minnie, so she stuck it back on her head. Minnie may have lived too long to be happy all the time, but she had died maintaining the illusion. Now Minnie was dancing a quadrille in her final durbar while Anjali again sat on the toilet seat, awaiting resolution.

SHE HEARD POLICE sirens, but because the bathroom window looked out on the old Raj-era tennis court, now a desolate stretch of red clay sprouting clumps of weeds, she couldn't see how many cruisers had pulled up under the carport. She hoped the police convoy included a paddy wagon for arrested looters. She heard barked orders and boot soles crunching gravel. Asoke, followed by a tall, paunchy police officer and three constables, strutted into her view. They conferred by the ragged net on the tennis court. Asoke radiated a butler's air of obsequious expertise. From their body language, Anjali guessed that the officer regarded Asoke as a reliable informant and not a vandal.

As wary of the police as her parents and Gauripur neighbors were, she now worried about being discovered alone in the tenants' bathroom with the landlady's naked corpse. She pressed her forehead against the window grille, hoping the cool metal would calm her. Below, police put up barricades to control entrance to the tennis court. Asoke's squatter youths carried a small fussy writing desk, which Minnie had called an escritoire, and a chintz-covered wing chair into the court. Asoke eased the officer into the chair as though the officer was a high-ranking army guest at one of Minnie's cantonment garden parties. He dispatched four of his youths back indoors. They came back with hand fans, a tall glass of limbu-soda, and Minnie's favorite ginger cookies on a plate from Minnie's best china.

Asoke presented the refreshments to the officer before answering, at length and with extravagant hand gestures, the questions the officer snapped at him. Anjali couldn't understand a word of their speech, it being in Kannada. And wasn't that mousy little Sunita Sampath, suddenly resurfaced, helping to serve the food and drinks, talking to the police, and occasionally pointing up to the bathroom? Soon after he had finished interviewing Asoke, the officer sent his three constables back into the house. They returned with a long file of women in their midteens and midtwenties, taken from among the looters and squatters. The girls who had emptied the pantry shelves and sneered at Minnie's hoard of Marmite were at the head of the sullen file. Why weren't the men lined up when their plundering was so spectacularly brazen? "Hi, Girish, it's me again with an SOS!"

The interrogations had gotten well under way before she gave up on Mr. GG, opened the window, and yelled down to the seated officer in English, "Mrs. Bagehot's here! Heart attack!"

“That’s her!” An agitated shout from Asoke, this time in English. He pointed at the window. “That’s the tenant! There she is!” And Sunita stared as well, smiling but not bothering to point.

Before Anjali could duck, an angry woman, the first to be interrogated, scooped up a fistful of pebbles and flung it at the bathroom window. She inspired her friends. Some squatter men joined in, hurling chunks of concrete loosened from the front wall and broken bricks from the edges of wilted flowerbeds. The window grille, originally installed to deter burglars, repelled the large projectiles. Why had they suddenly turned on her? Anjali’s distrust of the police softened into gratitude. Their duty was to protect her; they had no choice. She backed away from the window, crouched on the tiled floor, inches from Minnie’s body, and prayed for rescue. When the officer, with a policewoman and two male constables in tow, finally burst through the bathroom door, that’s how they found her. Asoke sidled in after them. He didn’t shriek or wail at the grotesque sight. Instead, while the policewomen pulled Anjali to her feet and handcuffed her, he covered the naked corpse with the only bath towel, still damp from use, hanging on the towel rack, a servant’s small gesture of gallantry.

“You are paying guest of this lady?” the officer demanded, and pointed his baton at Minnie’s body. He had the sagging, full lower lip of a heavy smoker and sprayed saliva as he spoke. With her hands cuffed, she couldn’t blot; she could only watch patches of spittle land on her silk clothing and spread. Like a Bollywood cop, the man wore oversize, mirrored sunglasses, like a mask, but the accusatory growl in his voice made her feel like a criminal. She’d already been judged. “Please to describe your relationship to the deceased.”

“She was dead when I got here,” Anjali blurted. “I don’t know why all this craziness is happening.”

“Please to make response only to question posed.” The officer ordered a policewoman to confiscate Anjali’s pocketbook, watch and cell phone before continuing his interrogation. “What is nature of connection you are having with deceased aged lady?”

"I had nothing to do with any of this. She must have died of shock. I wasn't here. Goondahs were breaking into her home and stealing all her property."

"You are putting my patience in jeopardy." The officer extracted a pack of cigarettes from one of his many pockets but didn't light up. "I'm asking one more time only. You are residing as tenant in the deceased's lodging, but owing rent money?"

She lowered her gaze from the officer's plump, moist lower lip to his heavy khaki socks and brown ankle boots.

"Yes or no?"

She said nothing. Why would the officer believe that the dead landlady had offered to run a tab for this handcuffed tenant?

"Your good name please?"

"Angie. Anjali Bose." It conferred no identity. She didn't own the name. She could have been anybody.

"Your name is Anjali Bose? Why your purse is saying HS?" He was pointing to the gilt letters on the leather strap.

"I don't know." She lied.

He made a dismissive gesture, a sweeping of his hand, and the two policewomen dragged her down the stairs, across the foyer, down the porch steps cluttered with Bagehot furniture, past the single-minded auction-house representative in the sky-blue suit and the screaming mob and into a police cruiser. Her foot crunched the photo of dead Sikhs, which lay on the ground, stripped of its pewter frame, something new for the trash bin of history. There was no paddy wagon in the police convoy. There was no convoy.

11

So long as she'd been in Bagehot House, Anjali had felt in control. Surely there was someone around to vouch for her, a Tookie to say "Hi, girlfriend." She was a Bagehot Girl, after all, but in the back of the police car, handcuffed to a grille behind the driver's seat, she realized there was no one in the world she could reach who knew who the hell she was.

In an interview room in the Central Bangalore Police Station, as she sat across a table from a square-jawed, sari-clad policewoman, waiting to be interrogated by a senior detective, Anjali Bose finally broke down. On the ride to the station in the police cruiser, she had acted composed, almost cocky, demanding to know the charges against her. But in that small windowless room, guarded by two uniformed women, one of them about her mother's age, she started to cry, and in crying, started great body-shaking heaves. There were no actual charges, hence nothing to defend herself against. She was being accused of who she was, not what she'd done. The policewoman was someone's wife, since she was wearing a mangalsutra wedding necklace, and probably someone's mother. But in her midriff-covering, four-button khaki-cotton regulation blouse and khaki teri-cotton regulation sari secured on the left shoulder with an Indian Police Service metal badge, she looked merely brutal.

The younger policewoman threatened in broken English to shut Anjali up with "tight slaps." She had a thin, mean face, a stout, muscular body squeezed into a khaki shirt and unpleated khaki pants, and huge, wide feet, judging from the size of her Derby brown leather shoes. Anjali feared the woman was itching to carry out her threat, but she couldn't choke back her dry heaves and grunts, not even when she heard the squeaky leather shoes stride across the room toward her. She steeled herself for the blows. What the policewoman did instead was grab her shoulders in a hold painful enough to make her shriek. Pleased, the policewoman relaxed her grip, thrust her fist down the back of Anjali's kameez, and pulled up its designer label. "Dubai," she sneered. Then in Kannada she launched into what sounded like mocking insults.

She recognized what had unleashed their taunts: her expensive silk salwar-kameez. It didn't seem to matter to her guards that her clothes were wrinkled and sweat-stained from day-long stress. In one day, *that* day, she had flunked out of CCI, witnessed mob fury, been accused of murder, and hauled off in handcuffs. She read her guards' minds: How did an unemployed working girl afford such a fancy wardrobe? Drugs? Who but loose women flaunt their bosoms and hips in tight, attention-getting clothes? Whores! She sat as still as she could while the excitable younger policewoman patted her down with palms that felt as large, flat, and hard as Ping-Pong paddles, first up and down the length and width of the back, then over the front. Thick fingers pressed into her collarbone, swatted her breasts, rested on her nipples, and flicked them as though turning light switches off and on and off and on, *flick-flick,* and when they hardened, both policewomen burst into giggles. Without her cell phone, Anjali felt totally cut off. No one knew what was happening to her. Worse, no one would care that she had disappeared. They would assume that she had raced into new adventures. Helpless, hopeless, she prayed for the detective to enter the interview room. He would admit that the police had made a mistake—or a mistake had been made—and let her go. But where could she go when freed? She had no Bagehot House to shelter her, no mother and sister to console her, no lover to embrace her.

The door lock clicked behind her. She knew, from the guards' abrupt halting of their game, that a senior officer had just entered. Finally she felt safe. Her worry that she would just disappear when Bangalore had had its fun with her, that she would be just another anonymous body buried under the building boom, was over. She twisted around in her chair to flash her signature smile at the man come to deliver her. The man was good-looking in a jowly, hirsute way, about the same age as Mr. GG but taller and thinner. He wore a dark suit with a pink shirt and a paisley-patterned silk tie instead of a uniform.

The man took his time approaching the table and taking his seat across from Anjali. He took more time tugging his watch off his wrist and placing it on the table, and still more time lining up two identical ballpoint pens on either side of a notepad and a slim folder. To make room just where he wanted to put his things, he had to push away a cracked plastic tray that held a small glass carafe of stale-looking yellowish water and a plastic glass. When he was finally ready, he announced, "Very-very serious offense, Miss Anjali Bose."

"What offense? I don't know what you're talking about!"

"Very-very serious," he repeated before introducing himself as the detective in charge. She didn't catch his name and dared not ask him to repeat it. Her bright smile had failed her this time. "What are the charges against me?"

"Treason against the Indian state. Terrorism. Abetting mass murder." The detective glanced at the ceiling and turned his head from side to side as if to relieve soreness in his neck. "Murder of Mrs. Minnie Bagehot, autopsy pending," he added.

"Is the charge withholding rent money? We had an arrangement for that."

"Not a joking matter, Miss Bose. Soon you will be weeping."

"What, then?"

He massaged the sides of his neck with his knuckles. "Miss Bose, we are not playing a guessing game." He fingered the knot of his tie. He moved his watch from the right of the notepad to the left, then back again to the right. Finally, without looking at her, he announced, "Let us talk about terrorism, Miss Bose."

"I had no knowledge that goondahs were planning to wreck Bagehot House." The absurdity of his accusation enraged her.

"Truths only, please. Cooperation is a better strategy than prevarication. This is my recommendation to all serious offenders." But he didn't give her time to comprehend, let alone consider, his advice. In a swift, sudden show of anger, he whacked the table so hard with the notebook that she screamed as though he had hit flesh and not wood. "Now," he said, a smile twitching his mustache. "Now please to tell"—he paused to realign the ballpoints that had rolled inches from her case file before he finished his sentence—"current habitation of your friend Miss Husseina Shiraz. I note her initials are on your purse. We can therefore assume you have stolen same. No need to waste time by sending us on wild goose chase to Hyderabad and whatnot."

Husseina? Husseina had been nowhere near Bagehot House. Maybe she'd heard wrong. She could barely understand the detective's southern rhythms, the weird vowels and thudding consonants. In this topsy-turvy world of Bangalore, detectives extracting "truths" from suspects in police stations probably earned less than honey-voiced customer-service agents in sleek call-center offices. She didn't want to risk offending him by asking him to repeat what he had just said. He was playing some kind of interrogation-room version of the cat-and-mouse game. He was poised to trap her in lies.

"What?" This time it was a whispered admission of anxiety, not an exclamation of outrage. One whack of his lathi across her ribs would crush her. One flick of a practiced wrist, directed against her skull, would spill her brains.

"Your good friend Miss Husseina Shiraz. You are being bosom buddies, isn't it? You are exchanging clothes, discussing secrets, and whatnot. Very expensive silk clothes from Gulf." The detective picked at flaking dry skin on his upper lip. Blood beaded where he had gouged rather than picked. The tip of his tongue chased the tawny red beads. "You are being in communication and whatnot with this bosom buddy?"

His questions were baffling. Haughty Husseina would sneer if she heard any of the Bagehot Girls claim her as a bosom buddy. "We roomed and boarded at the same time. We crossed paths in the bathroom, and we chatted at mealtimes. Just small talk, I can't even remember about what." With Minnie dead, it wouldn't be prudent to admit the Bagehot Girls mostly grumbled and gossiped about her.

The detective threw his head back and made loud clucking noises as though he was scratching an itch deep down in his throat. The older policewoman snapped a command, and the younger one poured water from the carafe into the glass. After several noisy gulps of water, the detective returned his attention to Anjali. "Miss Bose, you are committing stupidity. I already have answers to all questions I am asking." He slapped the folder with his right palm. "Commencing again, Miss Bose. What all you are knowing about your good friend's other life?" He flicked the folder open and extracted an Indian passport. "Not informing on terror plot is heinous offense. Conspirator, co-conspirator, abettor, enabler andsoforth. You are understanding that hard-labor category of long jail time is awaiting such criminal acts, no?"

He wet his right index finger, opened the passport to its front page, and shoved it in Anjali's face. She jerked her head back enough to make out a passport headshot of Husseina wearing the Panzer Delight T-shirt she had traded with Husseina. "You are seeing name of holder, isn't it? Your good name but not face?"

How gullible she had been when she had given up her favorite T-shirt! "We could be sisters," Husseina had gushed, and Anjali had been flattered. No wonder Husseina had asked her friendly questions about her birthday and place of birth.

"What place of service she was in when you were her dear friend?"

"I don't know, I can't remember. She talked about house loans. I don't know what you're getting at."

"Your situation is very much compromised. Your stupidity is compounding already compromised situation."

"I think I'm going to throw up, sir. Please, please, I need a bucket."

He totally ignored her. He swatted the top of her head with the open passport. "Why you sell terrorist whore your good name and your clothes? Who is paying you? You will confess everything. Now!"

"Nobody paid me. We *swapped* clothes!"

"No money changing hands? Then how you are living? Bangalore is eks-pensive city, isn't it? Vhayr *you* are vark-hing? Per diem how much you are earning?" The older policewoman cracked a joke in Kannada, which broke up the detective. He lowered his voice to a lewd whisper. "Your hourly wage is being how much?"

"I'm still looking for work."

He caressed the passport photo with a pensive thumb. "Your name, but your friend's face. Very professional forgery. How that is happening? Where you are coming?"

Where do I come from? It was the question she most dreaded. He was really asking if she had parents or relatives or powerful friends in Bangalore who might intervene if she disappeared or if they attacked her. Had she really ever been in bed with a rich young man in his luxury apartment overlooking Cubbon Park? Otherwise, she was just another dog on the street. "Kolkata," she said.

"Why you are concealing true facts? You think senior detectives are dunderheads?" He reconsulted her slim case file. "Place of birth and previous residence. Gauripur, Bihar State. Detainee trying to pull wool on senior rank officer! Admit please, POB is Gauripur."

"Yes," she said.

"Name of father?"

"Prafulla Kumar Bose. Recently deceased."

He shuffled his papers. "No record of Anjali Bose. One daughter only, living in Patna."

Anjali tasted bile. She was stuck in the flypaper of her past. He popped his next question. "Why Bihar girl coming to Bangalore?"

"To find work," she said. It sounded lame even to her.

"You paid by mens? You prostitute?" Now he was leering. "I think yes. I think you prostitute."

There were no correct answers in this harrowing game of riddles. *Of course not!* she wanted to say, but honesty would be a trap. Saying nothing was a trap, as was saying anything. *I will not scream. I will not cry.* She swallowed back the vomit rising in her throat.

It was not happening to her. This is not happening to me; it is happening to Angie. I am a ghost.

Now the ghost had an answer to Angie's first Bangalore question: Yes, if crores are the new lakhs, a girl can fall ten thousand times faster and deeper than she could in Gauripur. In some new, undefined sense, they were right. She was a prostitute; she was living off men, using skills she didn't know she had in order to manipulate them, and she didn't see any other way of getting what she wanted. Marriage equated to servitude, like her mother's and sister's. But if not in marriage, how did a woman in Bangalore live?

If she'd had access to a radio or a television over the past twelve hours, she would have learned that the London-based husband of a Hyderabad-born Bangalore resident was being sought in Holland, Germany and Malta for plotting a grenade attack on the Heathrow ticket counters of Air-India and five other international airlines all serving Indian cities. The Indian press immediately learned his name and address in Bradford and his wife's in Bangalore. Investigative journalists of two Hindi-language papers, a Kannada paper, and *Voice of the South* reported that the Hyderabad residence, though deserted, had yielded significant evidence in the form of an abandoned laptop. The wife's supervisor in Citibank's outsourced mortgage-consolidation department confirmed to reporters that she had been questioned by authorities. The employee being investigated, the supervisor stated, had quit work an hour into her shift, complaining of dizziness, and had not reported since. The whereabouts of the missing employee were not known or had not been divulged by authorities. According to several reliable sources, the woman had not returned to her rented room in her Bangalore residence, historic Bagehot House, Number One, Kew Gardens, to collect her personal belongings.

A small-scale riot had broken out at Bagehot House. Aroused youth, Hindu nationalists, common criminals, sacked the ancient landmark and carried off much of its furnishings. The venerable owner, Minnie Bagehot, died in the encounter.

That evening, after Anjali had been booked and then shoved into a crowded, foul-smelling holding cell, she convinced herself that she was being justly punished. Her crime was that of constant, heedless wanting; wanting too much; *wanting more of everything, especially happiness.* Her greed and restlessness had fatal consequences. Her father had died to protect her.

She dropped to a crouch, back pressed into a wall splotchy with dull red, still-wet stains of paan juice and maybe blood, and hoped she blended into the crowd of drunks and addicts unsteady on their feet. But gaunt-bodied, wily-eyed, bawdy-mouthed women swarmed around her, sizing her up. Several signaled obscene messages to her with their tongues. A half dozen looked so young that they reminded her of the light-fingered boys she had guarded her cash from on interstate buses. A big-boned mannish woman, wearing a gaudy sari hiked halfway up her hairy calves, blew Anjali lewd kisses. Anjali, more terrified in the lockup cell than she had been in the interrogation room, tried to shrink into a tiny ball. Egged on by the large woman with the rubbery lips, others closed around her and poked and prodded her with their grimy sandals. Two of them grabbed her by her armpits and pulled her to her feet. In her new penitential mood, she accepted their slaps and punches.

Only the older detainees who squatted or lay on the grimy floor, some coughing blood, ignored her. This hellhole was where she belonged; the apartment in Gauripur had been a mirage of home. But how had she gotten here? She had been told by the two people she was most eager to believe — Mr. Champion and Rabi Chatterjee — that she was special, and in her mind being special had meant she *deserved* better, deserved *the best.* Ambition had ruined her; worse, it had disgraced her family. At least her father had had the self-respect to commit suicide. His obituary in *The Gauripur Standard* had omitted the cause of death out of respect for him, but Peter had let it slip. Mr. Champion had begged her not to blame herself for her father's death, which meant he blamed her. She had so distanced herself from the innocent hoping and longing of her Gauripur adolescence that she could no longer call him Peter, not even in her thoughts. How had "Railways Bose" taken his own life? She pictured him hanging from the ceiling fan in the front room. She envied the corpse.

To a trust-fund Californian photographer who played at slumming, life in India might be all light and angle, but if you are an overreaching penniless Bihari, the light is murky, the angles knife sharp. Just last night she'd thought herself one of Bangalore's blessed, a Bagehot Girl. Knowledge, even self-knowledge, was cruel. Tookie was a prostie, Husseina a terrorist, and she a felon. She felt herself drifting to sleep, the willful shutting down of where she was and what she had become.

But her father wouldn't let her. He entered the holding cell, stepping over sleeping, moaning bodies as he approached her. He was dressed in the tawny cotton jacket he wore to work every weekday, crusty ridges of dried sweat radiating from the armpits. In place of his only wilted silk tie, he had a bed sheet knotted around his neck. He beamed when he reached her in her corner and, in a ritual gesture of blessing, touched the top of her bowed head.

The touch *felt* real because it *was* real. A policewoman was rapping Anjali's head with her knuckles. "Stir yourself and follow me!"

12

Anjali was escorted out of the lockup cell and into the booking area where, looking conspicuously relaxed among curt constables and manacled prisoners, stood a Hawaiian-shirted Mr. GG. Seated next to Mr. GG on the only bench for visitors and joking with him in what, to Anjali, sounded like Punjabi was the detective who had accused her of "abetting terror." Mr. GG stopped in midlaugh and sprang to his feet as soon as he noticed her shuffling behind her uniformed escort. "Miss Bose, rescuing you is becoming a full-time job!" he exclaimed, his voice upbeat, almost chirpy.

The policewoman shoved her toward the two men, relinquishing her authority to the detective. She peered at the men as though viewing them through dirty glass.

"Miss Bose!" Mr. GG held both his arms out. He would catch her if she fainted, as she had that first time in Barista. "It's all right now. It's over."

But she didn't lean into him. In a low, dry whisper, she said, "Just let me die."

"I have less gloomy plans for your future," Mr. GG bantered, "the most immediate plan being to get you out of the police thana." He patted his briefcase. "Release papers in triplicate."

The detective smiled at Mr. GG. "Gujral-sahib has rendered at length satisfactory explanations," he announced, without looking at her. "Why you are not informing authorities from beginning of your connections and whatnot?"

"Just let me die," she cried.

"I suggest instead that we attend to necessary business at hand." Mr. GG snapped his briefcase open and held it up to her. Her Gucci pocketbook and Movado watch lay on top of a stack of folders, manila envelopes, and forms stamped with official seals.

"Please to verify contents of lady's handbag," the detective urged her. And when she did not do so, he plucked the item from the upheld briefcase and dumped its contents on the visitors' bench. A Shantiniketan leather wallet stamped with a red-and-black paisley pattern; a key ring with a heavy metal key for the padlock on her bedroom door, a small flat key for the safety-deposit drawer in Husseina's almirah, and a smaller, flimsier one for the tiny wooden chest in which she hid what was left of Mr. Champion's cash; a cotton coin-purse; a CCI trainee badge; two Lakmé lipsticks and a tube of "whitening and brightening" face lotion; a comb; a purse-size pack of paper tissues; two ballpoint pens; four safety pins; a strip of aspirin tablets; a couple of green cardamom pods. "Please to report items missing, if any." He flashed a toothy, superior smile to indicate he was daring her to.

Mr. GG scooped the items back into her pocketbook. He snapped the briefcase shut. "We'll just take our leave straightway, sir," he said to the detective, who was still smiling. "No need to waste more of your urgent time chasing this red herring. Thank you very, very much, sir." He hustled Anjali toward the exit, promising to replace any item pilfered or lost.

Her cell phone was missing. *Getting a replacement wasn't the same. A replacement will be a copy. All the names on speed dial will be copies. I am just a copy. In that hellhole I wanted to talk to Baba. I wanted to hear Ma's and Mr. Champion's voices.*

In the parking lot, Mr. GG announced, "I have a surprise for you."

"No more surprises."

"Okay, I won't spoil the surprise." He gripped her right elbow and guided her toward his car. "You know, until this morning, I never noticed how green your eyes are."

"I hate my eyes."

"That's why Husseina targeted you! She must have taken your picture, then she learned your birthday, but it's your light eyes that did you in."

My sister. My generous benefactor. The mysteries of Hyderabad. The mysteries of Bangalore, the mysteries of everywhere and everyone. You think you're moving forward, you think you're beginning to figure things out, and it's all a trap. My parents were right: everyone is corrupt. There are conspiracies everywhere. But she said only, "I hate everything about me."

"You'll get over it. Time heals all wounds."

"The things that happened, happened to me, don't you understand? My father came to my cell with a bed sheet around his neck, my dead father who killed himself because I ran away to Bangalore. I'm in hell."

He jerked her by the elbow to stop her. "Maybe I don't understand. Maybe I can't. But understand this: You're lucky I have connections with the police. You're lucky I'm not off in Mexico right now. Shit happens, but you are very, very lucky, period. You have friends you don't even know, but you can't just float around Bangalore like a kite—someone will cut the string."

Her kite string had already been slashed. She had no phone and no one to call. Not that she cared. What friends? There was no longer a Bagehot House room to go back to. "Where are you taking me?"

"Patience," he counseled. "You'll find out."

She steeled herself for the next favor Mr. GG was about to bestow. He would insist she move in with him in the flat overlooking Cubbon

Park. In the police thana, she had been called a prostitute. What choice did a woman like her, homeless, jobless, skill-less, have? The police were right: she was a prostitute. What other name is there for a young woman without a job or means of support? "All right," she said. "I'm very lucky I know you."

They neared Mr. GG's car. She made out a shape in the back seat. "Don't get ahead of yourself, Miss Bose. You haven't heard me invite you, have you?" He unlocked the trunk of his Daewoo. "Don't take me for granted."

"I'm hallucinating!" she gasped. Her red Samsonite was in the trunk.

The back-seat passenger scrambled out of the car. "Hey! Whazzup?" He grinned. Tall and skinny, his hair grown out and standing on end. He moved the red Samsonite suitcase to make room for the briefcase. Then he gave her a bear hug.

Mr. GG banged the trunk shut. "Let's just say you've completed a reality TV episode."

"And survived the final round," the passenger joked. "Girish activated his local network *and* the vast Peter Champion network. You can't imagine how many thousands of activists are working night and day for you! Parvati-Auntie's sorry she couldn't come to the thana herself, but her driver's wife's in surgery, so she's keeping vigil in the hospital. Anyway, she said to tell you her home is your home."

"But I've let her down."

"She's an incurable do-gooder. A one-time call agent might not interest her, but an unjustly accused prisoner is right up her alley. But as aunties go, she rocks."

Anjali rested her head on the skinny chest of the young photographer she had met—it seemed incarnations ago—and succumbed to tears of shame.

Part Four

1

Aurobindo and Parvati Banerji's three-story home in Dollar Colony — so named for the area's preponderance of foreign-returned executives and entrepreneurs — had four master-bedroom suites of equal size, each with its sitting area, dressing room, spa bath with separate shower, and small private porch. Two of the four suites were located on the ground floor, one occupied by Auro and Parvati, the other kept in move-in condition for long visits by Auro's elderly parents. "It was in-laws on the ground floor with us, or install an elevator," Parvati liked to joke, "and this was the cheaper solution." An efficient live-in staff of six ran the house and adjacent grounds.

The public rooms — formal drawing room, dining room, an office for Auro, a puja room, and a granite-lavished kitchen — were also on the main floor. The other two suites, fully furnished, were on the upper floor and separated by a second sitting room. They were intended for the Banerji sons, Dinesh, a senior at Harvard, and Bhupesh, a junior at MIT, and their future wives and children. That still left two small rooms with a shared bathroom and shower stall on the third floor for summer visits by Dinesh's and Bhupesh's college friends.

Anjali had been given Dinesh's suite. Cricket bats and field hockey sticks were bracketed to the walls. One wall was devoted to cricket posters and shelves for Dinesh's debate and tennis trophies. He was a well-rounded boy, the ideal of upper-class parents. Even in his absence the boy exerted a force she found shaming. He would bring a perfect bride back to this perfect house, and he would have a perfect American degree and a guaranteed lifetime of higher and higher achievement.

She lifted a field hockey stick. Memories of da Gama's girls' field hockey team. Such simple times. Worries that she might catch a stick, or the ball, and scar her face and not be top-class marriageable. The stick felt lighter than ever. All those mutton stews at Bagehot House must have put some muscle on her.

The first few days in Dollar Colony passed in a daze. The Banerjis were generous, laid-back hosts. They made no demands. They treated her like the victim of a quasi-mental wasting disease. Maybe she'd make it back, maybe she wouldn't. She accepted her role of patient in the Banerjis' care. She spoke little, ate less. The one time that words surged out of her mouth, it was to ask Parvati—to demand more than ask—why Parvati had "deselected" her from CCI. A judgment call, Parvati explained at once, as to how best to allocate resources. Anjali obviously had different, if unspecified, talents. She was a mirror talent; strangers could read themselves in her—just not on a telephone. Talent or not, she had no money, so she never left the premises. She slept too many hours during the day and stayed awake too many hours during the night. Evenings she sat mute, unengaged with the family or their friends, who tended to drop by unannounced and usually stayed on for dinner.

Rabi tried to get her to jog with him in the postdawn coolness of the community's private park, but each time she begged off. Parvati and Auro had their leisure obsessions: Parvati gardening, Auro origami. Auro offered to teach Anjali how to make birds and animals from sheets of paper. *Therapy?* she wondered. She watched his large-knuckled fingers birth tiny hummingbirds, storks, and flamingoes, as well as mice, leopards and hippos. He was her father's age. She couldn't imagine her father wasting his time creating a paper menagerie. Hobbies, like stamp collecting, were for young boys, handicraft for young women on the marriage market. Her father dreaded—had dreaded—looking foolish.

Some evenings she let Parvati persuade her to step across the threshold of the front door, stand on the porch steps, and breathe in the fragrance of her prized frangipani and gardenia. Parvati, comical in a floppy hat, mud-smeared apron, and gardening gloves, vigorously weeded, raked, and pruned her teeming empire. Anjali claimed she had no energy to join in. No will to get well, she could have added, no curiosity about her present, no goals for the future. She had no future. She didn't want a future. The past hadn't happened. The present was on hold. The Movado watch on her wrist was a traitor.

Girish Gujral visited four times during the first two weeks of her stay, but more in the role of solicitous rescuer than fevered lover. Auro, Parvati, and Rabi welcomed him as their newest favorite family friend. He talked animated local politics with Auro, brought artfully wrapped gifts of imported ikebana vases and clippers for Parvati, limited-edition CDs of music from Mali and Sierra Leone for Rabi. Mr. GG was a man of magical connections. For Anjali he left off his office copies of *Newsweek* and *Time* and, from *Voice,* Dynamo's most recent column.

She read each *Newsweek* and *Time* from cover to cover, including the lists of names of publishers, managing editors, executive editors, editors, deputy editors, editors-at-large, staff writers, reporters and contributing photographers, but she absorbed no information. She was reading for language skills, not content. She was numb to world events. She nurtured her apathy. Wars, fortunes, reputations were won or lost *out there.* She was a ghost floating over alien terrain, as much a ghost as her father.

The clipping from *Voice* was different, though. Like an animal sensing danger in the air, Anjali sniffed peril in the title of Dynamo's latest column, titled "Tyger! Tyger!" She squirreled the clipping away in her room, face-down in her nearly empty lingerie drawer. She kept opening and closing that drawer, running her fingertips over the newsprint until they were smudgy gray and had to be soaped clean. The Mr. GG who paid social calls on the Banerjis and sipped single malt was a polite pillar of Bangalore society; the Girish Gujral who stalked the city as Dynamo was radar capable of registering the slightest stirring. She felt simultaneously excited and anxious. Could ghosts who had crossed over, cross back? Once again, she tugged open the lingerie drawer. She groped under the bras and panties that Parvati had thoughtfully bought for her the morning after she had moved in. That thoughtfulness was another reason to feel ungrateful and to resent Parvati. Her fingers scraped the rough, cheap newsprint. No, she wasn't ready.

At six-thirty one weekday morning, instead of the younger of the two maids, Rabi knocked on Anjali's bedroom door and carried in the tray of toast and bed tea.

"Something wrong?" she asked, startled.

"It's time," he said.

Rabi set the tray down on the bed. He perched, lotus-position, on the quilt by her feet. "Glowing with health, as you can see. You should give jogging a try, Angie." He poured tea for her and for himself, added two lumps of sugar and hot milk from a pitcher to each cup. "You should give something a try. Anything."

"I'm not Angie," she mumbled, scrambling to a half-sitting position. "I guess I never was." *Tell me my name. Don't ask me, don't ask me anything.*

"Well, Angie wanted to get to Bangalore. I told you you'd get here if you really wanted it. And now you are in Bangalore."

The next-door neighbor was chanting a morning hymn at the top of his voice. "There are mistakes," Anjali mumbled, "but no pardons." She burrowed her head under her pillow.

"At least Mr. Srinivasan has a decent voice. Otherwise, I'd send him a blast of Farka Touré." He shook her hip, which was covered by a blanket. "Hey, Angie, I don't like talking to a pillow."

"Is your auntie worried how much longer I intend to sponge from the family?"

"I told you, she has patience. She can imagine what you've been through. She knows you have issues — repressions, she calls them — and my aunt and uncle want to help. Not only that, they're *able* to help." He sprang off the bed. "Actually, I came up to your room to share, not evict."

"I'm predeceased. I don't even have a name anymore." She could feel his hand on her hip, over the cover.

"Actually, you do. That's what I came up to share. Remember the shot I took of you in the ice cream store, way back when? It's become a gallery sensation. 'Mona Lisa of the Mofussils.' That's you. You've made this photographer famous."

She felt cool fingertips over her warm eyelids. She wanted the moment to last. But Rabi was all energy. Stories about what he called "the Mona Lisa of the Mofussils Phenomenon" tumbled out. When his first set of Indian portraits were exhibited at a chic new gallery in Mumbai, the one that had gathered the most praise was "Small-Town Girl." Reviewers had rhapsodized over the subject's face, a face both beautiful and vulnerable. Why is she sad? Or is she happy? One of the reviewers had christened her 'Mona Lisa of the Mofussils,' and the tag had stuck. An art critic for a Kolkata newspaper had retraced the Indo-American photographer's steps back to Bihar and even tipped a waiter at the Alps Palace to seat him at the table where the Mona Lisa had posed. An emergent class of Indian entrepreneurs had bought out the entire exhibit.

He ended his stories with a plea. "Do me a favor? Join me for a pre-bed-tea run tomorrow? You don't have to run. We can just walk. Please?"

"I don't own running shoes." Her last resort.

He responded, "I guess my next task, then, is to drive you to the mall."

2

Late that night she steeled herself to read the clipping Mr. GG had given her.

TYGER, TYGER
By Dynamo

Over the years, Dynamo has had the privilege—some would describe it as the challenge, and they would not be unjustified—of knowing Mrs. Maxfield Trevor Douglas Bagehot, who is addressed affectionately by her close friends as Minnie and universally referred to by the respectful as "Madam."

"Madam" passed away in her eponymous Kent Town home under tragic circumstances Friday last. In the spirit of full disclosure, Dynamo acknowledges that he has contributed funds for the upkeep of the Bagehot property, which is comprised of the structure of Bagehot House and its extensive compound. Dynamo further concedes that he may even benefit financially, in light of the undeniable fact that lucrative conversions of cantonment-era ruins by conglomerates have become standard. Dynamo withholds comment on the popular speculation that the majority of such lucrative conversions of dilapidated-beyond-repair single-family habitations are given unstoppable velocity by a select number of conglomerates with underworld connections. As the ditty goes, the times, they are changing. And yet . . . Aye, there's the rub for entrepreneurs with conscience.

If Dynamo had his druthers, he would continue his charitable outlays ad infinitum rather than confront the saddest of all urban spectacles: the rape of relics. The ravaging and razing of things unique diminishes us all. And in a city like Bang-a-Buck, where gaudy architecture is spreading like invasive bacteria and choking what little remains of originals, we are losing signposts to our collective past.

Like many who dabble in the alchemic black art of urban architecture in this confused and confusing age of rapturous rupture, Dynamo has long fixed his gaze on Madam's Bagehot House. (Dynamo hastens to clarify to his readers that his interest in Madam's establishment is devoid of popular prurient fascination with the generations of delectable lady-lodgers, those iron-clad frigates known in popular parlance as Bagehot Girls.) It is the academic perfection of the house and its grounds that have merited Dynamo's affectionate admiration (that admiration having been sparked by his reading at an impressionable age of Mr. Peter Champion's *Classic Indian Architecture: Public and Private*).

Dynamo has it on irrefutable authority that at the time of Madam's sudden-but-not-precocious expiration, the board members of the Bagehot Trust, each of whom is a Bang-a-Buck VIP (no, make that a VVIP), were engaged in a bitter feud regarding financial plans for the immediate future of the rapidly deteriorating property. Dynamo's source, a trustee who has requested anonymity, has divulged to Dynamo that the trust was set up for the sole purpose of executing a legal contract with Madam, who had for two decades or more been afflicted with deep penury. Per said contract the board of trustees acquired the property deed from Madam in exchange for allowing her (1) to occupy the main residential structure gratis, and (2) to obtain and retain 100 percent of rents she collected from respectable migrant working ladies. As additional incentive they guaranteed the delivery of monthly gifts of provisions and liquor—Madam was partial to brandies. At the time of transfer of deed, the trustees, applying actuarial tables, had counted on Madam "to kick the bucket" within months, if not weeks, and by unanimous vote had nominated a committee to explore lucrative commercial development of the long-neglected property. Thanks to either the medicinal benefits of potent brandies or to the ironic string-pullings of the Big Puppeteer in the Skies, and much to the aggravation of the trustees, Madam bamboozled the actuaries. The consequence of Madam's stubborn longevity was loss of unanimity among the trustees. According to Dynamo's source, last month a minority faction on the board proposed the Bagehot property be designated a city or national historical heritage site, thus qualifying for not-for-profit status and funds for preservation and restoration.

Madam, by her own admission, was eighty-two years old. Madam's passing, therefore, was not untimely, but, and this is *the but* that beleaguers Dynamo: *Why* did she die Friday last? *What* precipitated the death? *Who* benefited from it?

If the attending physician is to be believed, Madam's "great heart" gave out. Dynamo counters the physician with a resounding "Poppycock!" Madam is known to have suffered from dyspepsia (both gastronomical and temperamental), but not from a dicky ticker. Dynamo demands an investigation of the factors that induced the shock that induced heart failure. Sources have implied (1) that Madam's only servant was in the pay of a trustee and facilitated the fatal shock to his employer's inconveniently sturdy heart; or (2) that the same servant accidentally happened upon Madam's lifeless body and alerted his powerful paymaster, who then instructed his henchmen to wreck the structure and purloin contents under the guise of a spontaneous riot by Bang-a-Buck's underclass.

Madam's death is a sad fact. But the true tragic victim of this incidence of plutocratic greed is the young lady-tenant of Madam, the innocent job-seeking migrant, who was mistakenly ensnared in a London-based terrorist plot—"implicated," in police jargon—and cruelly harassed and humiliated, her spirit scarred permanently. That young lady arrived in Bang-a-Buck to discover, fulfill, and exceed her potential; instead she became collateral damage of countenanced greed. Did "fearful symmetry," which the bard William Blake alerted us to two hundred years ago, require the extraction of such a price?

Dynamo's suspicions are just that: suspicions. By Madam's wishes, which she expressed in writing to the Bagehot Trust, she was to be buried on Bagehot grounds. No resting place is permanent. Her bones will be crushed or bared by developers' crews. But if there's to be a memorial for Madam, let it be this: Bagehot House

> surrendered its ghosts so that one young lady might break the power of our property triads. In an earlier column, I labeled such ladies "the New Miss Indias." They will transform our country. Dynamo is inflamed by the new species of tyger-lamb. If there is any triumph to be gleaned from this experience, it is that this time the costs of symmetry have been borne by ancient bricks and mortar, not by flesh and blood.

Anjali reread Dynamo's column this time as a love letter. She had mistaken Mr. GG's gallantry for indifference. He hadn't lost his desire for her. He had promoted her from a plaything to an ideal worthy of devotion. She read his "Tyger! Tyger!" again and again.

Clarity came to her with each rereading, especially of the closing paragraph. Dynamo was "inflamed" by her. She resolved to cross back to the colony of the living. In the monstrous evening at the police thana, Rabi had joked about the Peter Champion network. The butterfly effect. How lucky she was to have Parvati, Auro and Rabi for temporary family! Luckier still to have Mr. GG drop by so regularly. She wasn't sure what Dynamo meant by "the new species of tyger-lamb" or why he misspelled *tiger,* but he was "inflamed" by her. That word made her blush. She felt sexy and slightly dangerous. On the top left-hand corner of the clipping she doodled an ink sketch of a Royal Bengal tiger. It needed a signature. Mona Lisa, but not of the mofussils. Mona Lisa of Dollar Colony. *Mr. GG, a second chance? Please?*

3

Over the next couple of postdawn walks in the residents-only park and postwalk breakfast of tea, fruits and yogurt in the garden, Rabi entertained Anjali with anecdotal histories of his mother, Tara Chatterjee, and her sisters, Parvati-Auntie and the oldest, the New York–based gadabout Padma. His mother ("A bit of a flake, you'd like her") was the youngest; Parvati-Auntie was "the responsible middle sister, and don't get me started on the oldest."

But he started with the two house dogs, Ahilya the female and her pathetically enamored littermate, Malhar, which had been plucked off the street: pariah pups, raised inside, grown large, strong, and very territorial, very fierce looking, but never at ease, never comfortable. Never knowing where they belonged. Canines, he called them, not really dogs. It would take generations to breed a true dog from India's abundant canines. "That's the kind of woman my Auntie is," he said. "She follows her heart. She believes love is the answer to everything." *Why is he telling me this?* For Anjali, the parallel between her situation and a street dog's was all too obvious.

And then he gave his take on Dollar Colony, where Auro-Uncle had chosen to settle as the CFO of a startup after retiring from the Mumbai branch of a multinational behemoth. "He lived in Hong Kong, Boston, Los Angeles, Mumbai, and he picked Bangalore for building his dream house! What does that say about Bangalore? What does it say about *him?*"

"The only places I know, or maybe I *think* I know, are Gauripur and Rock City, Illinois."

"Not a very high standard, Angie." Rabi scooped out a tiny, slippery black papaya seed the maid had missed when she was preparing the fruit platter.

"Shall I tell you about Rock City?"

"Please, spare me the mysteries of Rock City. I've read the CCI training manual: learn about one little town and you've learned about the whole country. Learn some specialized vocabulary and you'll discover the whole language. Was Rock City all you hoped for?" He flicked the seed at her. "Bottom line, as they like to say, you were right to back out of CCI."

Easy for you to say, she thought. *You're the richest eighteen-year-old Indian in the world.* "I didn't back out. I screwed up. I *failed.*"

"You didn't screw up—you just couldn't take the bullshit. There's something our friend Peter Champion said about you, way back in Gauripur. He said there was a war going on for your soul, or something melodramatic like that. And he was right. Something in your soul wouldn't let you settle for a call center. Something in your soul made me *want* to take that picture of you. You're cut out for something bigger."

She rolled her eyes. He smiled. She smiled. She hadn't interacted with anyone for three weeks. "What's your hometown?"

"A place called Atherton. It's like Dollar Colony, only bigger, with gates. But I'm a nomad. I can't get stuck in one country or one city or even one house. Neither can you."

Anjali whacked his forearm with her napkin. "Even this one?" The napkin was still folded and pleated in a whimsical shape and inserted like a bouquet into a silver-filigree napkin ring. "This is the fanciest, comfiest house I've ever been in!"

He seemed to be looking at his cousin's hockey sticks and cricket paddles. "They expect poor Dinesh to go for a Rhodes scholarship. He's a wicked tennis player. When we were kids, I used to call him 'Dimmest.'"

"What's not to like about it?" she asked.

"That's the point. They've never even thought about what's not to like."

RABI ASSURED ANJALI that she wasn't in any way a burden to Parvati-Auntie and Auro-Uncle. In addition to the two young "kitchen sisters," there was a live-in watchman, a live-in multitasking dog walker, a full-time gardener who always brought along a nephew or a son as assistant, a chauffeur, and a part-time elderly woman who came twice a day to sweep and mop floors, clean bathrooms and do the laundry. The sisters had a large room of their own on the roof and an adjoining bathroom, shared with the rest of the household staff. The sisters' room had a TV, and when not on call, the younger sister and the dog walker/handyman liked to watch shows, sitting side by side on the older sister's bed.

Were they already lovers? she wondered. A year ago, such a question would not have entered her mind. Unthinkable! Even for Parvati and Auro, it was impossible. But she could read body language, she could read a girl's gaze.

Several times, as she collected her bras and panties from the clothesline on the roof, Anjali heard the TV going in the sisters' room and envied the laughing couple on the narrow cot, sitting so close, their thighs touched. Parvati's unspoken expectations of decorum required that the unmarried kitchen sisters keep their door open while watching TV with a male. *As if,* Anjali thought. The sisters' parents had entrusted their care and chastity to Parvati while they looked for suitable sons-in-law.

So had mine, she thought. Anjali fantasized about changing identities with the girl so overtly happy with the chance perks of her job: a room she wouldn't be evicted from, a suitor in the house, and a sister to share her secrets with. The sisters *had* jobs. They had earned their room on the roof. Anjali was a freeloader.

Rabi was her only confidant, but he and she had traveled to Dollar Colony from different planets. He might sneer at the oversize houses in Dollar Colony, but she could admire them as monuments of self-made men to their epic struggle. Auro, she knew from his cocktail-hour chatter, had slogged his way up from the rented apartment of his Kolkata boyhood. Her curiosity was coming alive. She decided to tease out of Auro why he had chosen Dollar Colony for a permanent home.

"You really want to know?" He poured himself the first of his two nightly Johnnie Walker Blues on the rocks. It was rare that only Auro, Parvati, and Anjali were dining at home. Rabi was away on a photo shoot for a travel magazine. The older of the "kitchen sisters" was listening to music on an old-fashioned portable disc player the size of a salad plate; the younger and the dog walker were watching TV; the watchman was on duty in his wooden kiosk at the top of the driveway. The two dogs gnawed lamb bones at Parvati's feet. "My personal reasons? Nobody's ever asked me that." Auro looked both startled and pleased. "You want the long answer or the short answer?"

Parvati looked up from the thick paperback she was reading and smiled indulgently. "How about a medium-long answer that makes its point before dinner is served?"

He helped himself from the hors d'oeuvre platter of mutton keema samosas. "Did Parvati tell you we were among the first batch to build here when it was still forestland? I bet not, since she was dead set against moving out of Bombay."

Parvati slipped a filigreed ivory bookmark to keep her place in a thick American book, a prizewinner called *The Echo Maker,* sent by Tara from California. Every year, her writer-sister sent her the American and British prize-winning novels. Anjali had tried reading it, but it was too complicated. Still, she would not have understood two sentences just six months earlier. She would never even have opened it.

"I still miss Bombay," said Parvati. "Well, I miss the company flat on Nepean Sea Road. I miss looking out on water." She left the room to instruct the older of the kitchen sisters to start frying the prawn cutlets and roll out the dough for roti. She would make the boiled rice herself. No matter how many world cities Auro had lived and worked in, his palate had remained Bengali, which meant that he devoured a heaping serving of boiled white rice at both lunch and dinner and insisted that only his wife could cook rice perfectly. Anjali heard the cook calling up to her sister from the stairwell and then Parvati worrying out loud, "I hope there's no hanky-panky going on. I don't want to have to confiscate the TV."

It wouldn't be the end of the world, Anjali thought.

Anjali couldn't remember being in a room with Auro and no one else before. She had not taken up Auro's offers to teach her origami. Now that she was his sole audience, she was forced to train her attention on him. He was a moon-faced man, sharp-nosed, thin-lipped, with close-shaven cheeks and a brush mustache that crept into his nostrils. He didn't seem to detect her awkwardness. Pouring himself a second Johnnie Walker Blue, he launched into his pioneer's version of the history of Dollar Colony.

"This block was mostly unsold lots when I bought. There was one Mediterranean-style bungalow with a red-tiled roof on the corner lot, long gone now, and a half-finished California-style mansion across from it. Parvati took one look and said, 'Eesh, look at this, why did we ever leave San Diego?' Land was still affordable and available. I blame my beloved Bhattacharjee sisters: they're such snobs. Parvati and Rabi's mother ganged up on me. If I had been smart, I would have gobbled up two or three lots on either side. Now I have to put up with Citibank Srinivasan's all-night snoring and morning ragas to my left and Hewlett-Packard Gupta's tabla-thumping to my right."

When Auro first got in touch with Ideal Retirement Paradise Development Corporation of Bangalore, it was the early 1980s, and he was working in the Hong Kong office of his multinational company. IRPDC brochures didn't list the soon-to-be-constructed housing complex as Dollar Colony but pitched the complex to nonresident Indians, the NRIs, overseas-based Indian nationals amassing hard-currency wealth. Auro guessed that Dollar Colony, the name that stuck, was the genius shorthand of cabbies and auto-rickshaw drivers.

Their generation of investors was made up of nostalgic expatriates planning far, far ahead for retirement. They knew that America, or anywhere other than the homeland, was no place for an elderly Indian. They dreamed of an enclave of fantasy retirement palaces for like-minded cosmopolitans. Their homes and their neighborhood would reflect the best of the West they'd grown rich in and the romanticized best of the country they'd abandoned as ambitious young men. They demanded mansions grander than the houses they could afford in Britain or Canada or America. And they rewarded themselves with all the luxuries they'd missed out on while growing up: the country clubs, the residents-only parks with jogging paths, the tennis courts, the fitness center and spa. High-end architects and contractors happily realized their fantasies in brick, granite, marble, steel and plate glass.

"Parvati sacked two architects before she was satisfied! The Bhattacharjee sisters know what they want, and they don't quit till they get it. What's that American phrase CCI teaches students? Steel magnolia? Well, Parvati and Rabi's mother are titanium lotuses!"

Parvati came back, carrying a bowl of tiny balls of minced fenugreek leaves and shredded coconut, which she had just fried. "Consider yourself lucky, Auro. Without your titanium lotus you would have been stuck with a white elephant. Did you tell Anjali how the NRI repatriates are becoming younger and younger, and Dollar Colony is looking dowdier and dowdier compared to the new communities?"

"Infrastructure," Auro announced, before popping two of the fenugreek balls into his mouth. "That's the buzzword. Infrastructure."

Grease glistened on his mustache. Parvati blotted the grease with a linen cocktail napkin. "Oh dear, I'm not helping you with your cholesterol problem, am I?"

"We have the best doctors in the world in Bangalore, so why worry? American hospitals are outsourcing diagnoses to us, and I have instant access to the Mayo Clinic. Enjoy today, solve tomorrow. Anyway, these repats are cross-breeding brand-new East-West fruits in their gated Edens."

"We oldies had to send Dinesh and Bhupesh to Britishy boarding schools in the hills," Parvati remembered. "Now the new colonies are setting up their own private schools. Learn yoga, recite the Vedas in Sanskrit, *and* prepare to ace the SATs. They have it all."

"As I said, infrastructure. Medical, economic, educational, communication. I could go on."

Honestly, Anjali didn't understand a word, even as she appreciated being included in the discussion.

DOLLAR COLONY MAY have slipped from being the best address to merely something distinguished, but Anjali was still dazzled by the slightest luxuries, like the Instamatic hot water faucet in the Banerjis' kitchen. Even more than the comforts of the Banerji house—and was this a sign that she was coming out of her depression?—what she coveted as she listened to Auro was the Banerji family. Why couldn't she have been allotted Auro and Parvati as parents, Rabi as cousin? How different a person she might have been if . . .

4

Rabi came back from his photo shoot in Bheemswari on the sacred Kaveri River, excited about mahseer fishing. He was full of stories and digital pictures of skimming the water in round buffalo-hide coracles, and, on his second-to-last night in the fishing camp, reeling in ("Okay, the local guide helped," he admitted) a ten-pounder. He scrolled down the shots from his little silver digital camera. *Every note a symphony,* Anjali thought. *Is the most beautiful woman in Gauripur still inside? What about my pictures from Shaky's studio?*

Anjali had never bothered to learn the names of trees and flowers on her street in Gauripur and had never met anyone who fished for pleasure. Her father would never waste good money on something as dangerous as sport fishing. He couldn't swim, and she could not imagine him paddling a boat or standing in running water. She wasn't sure that before Rabi's Bheemswari trip, she'd ever thought of the mythic mahseer as actually existing. That mahseer was a fighting carp, an immense and magnificent river-dweller with shimmery gold sides, red-gold fins, and thick lips tipped with barbels. What was it Peter called it? Carpe diem. God's carp? To land a golden mahseer, the legendary forty-pounders in the Himalayan waters, was to know the challenge of a lifetime.

The only carp she knew, and knew too well, were of modest size and wrapped in newspaper. Her father would drag her to the fish stalls most Sunday mornings, and while she blocked out the fish stench with her handkerchief, he would diligently peer into the gills of a particular specimen to check for freshness before haggling over the price with a fishmonger. Curried carp seven nights a week, except in hilsa season, and bhekti fry for very special occasions. The Boses, like every other Bengali on the block, were staunch fish-and-rice eaters. They bought their fish in a smelly market; they didn't catch them in the bosom of nature. She'd never connected carp with romance. Rabi's enthusiasm so infected her that she even asked what he'd used for bait. "Flies!" he said, which ruined the effect. How lucky the people like Rabi, who could throw themselves so totally into their work! Even if she had passed the CCI exam and found a job, it would have been just that: a job, not a calling.

"Hey, you must be feeling better! A lot better, Anjali!" He didn't make fun of her questions or the sour face she'd made at the talk of flies and worms. "Freshwater crabs and cooked millet dumplings also worked."

THEY WERE IN Parvati's prized garden in the early morning, Rabi setting up a tripod and focusing his Nikon on the showy, sticky heads of fruits and flowers; she sipping fresh watermelon juice with a straw. He smiled up from his equipment. As the sun rose higher, he had to take new readings on his light meter. This was not an assignment for pay. He, a B&W snob, was paying homage in color to Parvati-Auntie, the fanatic gardener. The post-monsoon flowers, the swarms of butterflies and occasional parrots, budgies and sunbirds: everything about her garden was overstated and overlush. Everyone in Dollar Colony was horticulturally competitive. Citibank Srinivasan had imported Siberian fruit trees. Hewlett-Packard Gupta had transplanted a mini Indonesian jungle. Parvati was an Indian chauvinist: wide avenues shaded by rain trees and flame of the forest, blue and purple jacaranda, scarlet gul mohar, champak, jasmine, roses, gladioli, anthurium, gerbera . . . it's never too late to learn, especially if you admire your teacher. Monet. Light and angles.

"At least I got to Bangalore," Anjali said. *I am trying to get over the heavy stuff. Not there yet, but I've made a start, thanks to your aunt.*

"I always knew you would. If that's what you wanted." *Click! Click!* Rabi went back to the hedges to reset his camera.

She'd never felt so comfortable with a boy. *Why can't we get what we most want in the world?* When he came back, she asked, "When we met in Gauripur, did you think I didn't really want Bangalore?"

"Did I sound skeptical? I didn't mean to. You were looking for a way out. Peter convinced you Bangalore was that." *Click! Click! Click!* A chameleon scuttled over the velvety grass.

"I've gotten over wanting life enhancement. A job that pays for basic needs, that's my goal now."

"Don't sell yourself short." He aimed his lens at a stray kitten circling the birdfeeder. "I happen to be one of a large chorus who think Anjali Bose is a child of destiny." He dodged the dripping straw she tossed at him. "Seriously."

"Don't you dare stress me out with the destiny stuff!"

"Sorry. No, I'm not really sorry. Anyway, changing subjects, have you found anybody yet? You can tell me."

"I wouldn't want to make you jealous."

"I'm jealous of anyone in love. Even more jealous of anyone loved back." He seemed about to confide in her.

"If you think there's something going on between . . ."

But Rabi wasn't listening. "Actually I met a guy in Mumbai—Christ, 'A Guy from Mumbai' sounds like a Noel Coward song." He did a fancy two-step. Then glided into a wicker chaise longue near her canvas chair.

"Now *I* am jealous, Rabi."

"Anyway, I met this Rutgers senior. He was visiting his grandparents.

The last thing he expected was finding another Indo-American who . . . what was cool was that we met in the gallery exhibiting my photos."

Gauripur images flooded her, not the dreary small town of her memories, but the Gauripur she had glimpsed through Rabi's restless lens.

"When you create things, like my mother with her books or a lowly photographer like me, or even origami like Auro-Uncle, you still dream of meeting someone who's fallen in love with you for something you've written or painted, something you've created. Well, he fell in love with my photos of Ali and Peter and you, Mona Lisa. That's how I knew we could be . . . serious. Terrible word, *serious,* why can't we say what we mean? Serious is the last thing in the world . . . never mind. Then he had to go back to Rutgers. Dum-diddle-dee, dum-diddle-day, they always go back to school, don't they? That's more Cole Porter than Coward, right?"

Anjali didn't know those names, but she knew he needed her to agree. "Right," she whispered. No matter how brief their conversation, he would always leave her feeling inadequate; not humiliatingly inadequate, but eager for gaps to be filled in.

"This time I'm a nature photographer, Angie," he announced. New mood, new tone of voice, new intensity, snappier delivery. "I'm going down to a nature preserve a week from Saturday. On the Kaveri again, near Mysore. Big crocs, little crocs. Bats, you love bats, right? The funky kind called flying foxes. Bugs by the ton. I'm staying overnight, maybe a couple of nights." He had reserved a cabin. "Want to give Nature a try? You could be my assistant. Hey, if there's someone you want to bring along, you'd have me as chaperone."

"You mean, just call up someone I'd want to . . . I couldn't do that, Rabi."

"Send a message by carrier pigeon?"

"Well, since it's all fantasy talk, there *is* a Bengali guy I wouldn't mind inviting." She still nurtured a crush on the Bengali Svengali. He hadn't called her since that one magical meeting in the rooftop cafeteria of Tookie D'Mello's office building. Without confessing to the crush, she gushed about her Photoshopped picture on the cover of the latest issue of his directory.

"Oh, I can't tell you how much I adore Photoshop!" Rabi snickered. "It's revolutionized my art!" Then, conspiratorially, "We could always arrange his drowning. The crocs know their business."

She leaned down and punched his shoulder lightly. There, in the lush heart of Parvati's garden, they shared their stories. Did Shaky Sengupta's bridal photo work out? Yes, she admitted, I think it did. But in a roundabout way.

5

A "high tea" for Anjali's friends was Parvati's idea. "You should spend more time with people your age," she said. Anjali suspected that Rabi had put the party idea into his aunt's head so that he could reunite Anjali and the Bengali Svengali under respectable chaperonage. Parvati asked Anjali to draw up a guest list. Anjali couldn't come up with any youngish friend's name other than Tookie D'Mello, who had been "dumped" by Minnie before Rajoo had sacked Bagehot House. Tookie wasn't the most appropriate ex–Bagehot Girl to introduce to the Banerjis; still, Anjali tracked her down at her work site. Tookie snapped up the invitation to Dollar Colony. "That 'Gay India' photographer guy will be there? What a hoot! He's a YouTube sensation! Girlfriend, you landed on your feet, all right. Of course, we knew you would. All I can say is that the Bagehot bitch had it coming!" Tookie didn't explain who she meant by "we." It didn't include Reynaldo, since *that* relationship was in deep freeze for the moment. "Can I bring a friend or two?" Anjali shuddered; she didn't want Rajoo inside the Banerjis' home, where she was regaining her balance. But Tookie didn't mention Rajoo by name, not once. She went on and on instead about the two party-beast girlfriends she had started to hang out with.

Parvati helped plump up the list by inviting two Dollar Colony families, and Rabi added two sets of recent acquaintances: the "faux-scruffy" and the "jock dilettante." Parvati translated the terms for Anjali as Rabi's artsy gallery friends and sport-fishing friends. She added Usha Desai's name, with the penciled note "depends on Mrs. Desai's health that P.M." Auro insisted on including Girish Gujral. "Forget the tea part of 'high tea,'" he announced. "Girish and I will hole up with our drinks in my office and talk politics."

"No holing up," Parvati snapped. "We have opinions too."

THE GUESTS DEVOURED platter after platter of hot, cold, tart, sweet-sour, spicy finger foods prepared all day by the kitchen sisters, and they sipped Assam or Darjeeling tea out of bone china cups, but the "high tea" didn't accomplish Parvati's goal of widening Anjali's network of friends.

The idea was that everyone bring their eligible sons and their eligible daughters. Between them, Anjali should bond with one or two.

The two Dollar Colony families arrived in a convoy of a Combi and two Marutis. The Ghoshes were a family of five: Kolkata-born parents in their midfifties, two of three Calgary-born daughters in their twenties, the third in her last year of high school. Mrs. Khanna, the recent widow of a World Bank executive, brought her two sons on break from Georgetown, and the sons' three American friends. Anjali wasn't sure how much of her Bagehot House drama Parvati had disclosed to the Drs. Ghosh and Mrs. Khanna. The Drs. Ghosh asked the usual polite questions about where she had grown up, what company her late father had worked for, where her married sister had settled. Anjali, for once, told the absolute truth, and that ended the potential Ghosh connection. The older Ghosh daughters, who had master of social work degrees from the University of Calgary and who had set up a nonprofit organization that rescued at-risk urban children, didn't hide their contempt for migrants who invaded Bangalore with the dead-end goal of answering phones all night at call centers.

Mrs. Khanna corralled Parvati and Dr. (Mrs.) Ghosh—all three were collectors of contemporary Indian art—to lament how, after Mr. Khanna's death, she dared not squander any savings on the painters she admired. Anjali hovered near them so she wouldn't look and feel a party-pariah. They strolled from painting to painting, praising Parvati's eye and investment smarts. Anjali had lived with the paintings all these weeks but had never looked at them closely, never peered at the artists' signatures. Even now the names meant nothing to her. Anjolie Ela Menon. Arpita Singh. Rini Dhumal. In her old Gauripur bedroom there had been a browning studio portrait of her paternal grandfather, with a dusty sandalwood garland around it. Anjolie? That was a spelling she intended to try out.

"You're such a feminist, Parvati," Dr. (Mrs.) Ghosh pronounced. "No male artists at all?"

"Not only a feminist. Mrs. Banerji is a Bengali chauvinist!" Mrs. Khanna countered.

So Menon, Singh, Dhumal were Bengali women who had married non-Bengalis! Anjolie Gujral? She sidled toward the front door, waiting for Mr. GG to show up. The dog walker was on front-door duty for the night, which meant he stood on the shallow porch step, helped guests heave themselves out of their cars, led them past the foot-high brass statue of Ganesh seated on a fluffy, fragrant bed of petals, held open the heavy, ornately carved wooden front door, and showed them into the marble vestibule. Since the two house dogs were hostile to visitors—"Poor, dear things," Parvati had said—she shut them in the absent Dinesh's suite for the night.

The Khanna sons and their American houseguests had drifted upstairs to Rabi's suite, where the "scruffies" and the "jocks" were listening to Rabi's cache of African and Brazilian music. Anjali could hear their excited voices. "Dude, check this out!" "Hey, my older brother knows the guys at Wesleyan who started the Modiba label!" "*Legends of the Preacher*? No shit!" It wasn't her kind of music. Actually, except for her excruciating exercises on the old harmonium, she had no favorite music. *Can't sing, can't dance, can't cook, that's me.* She stayed put in the vestibule, just inside the doorway, and was almost knocked down when Tookie and her two friends, all three motorcycle-helmeted, shoved the door open with their shoulders before the dog walker could do his job.

"Angie darling!" Tookie shouted at Anjali, as she unfastened the chin strap, "you won't believe what we've just been through!" She pulled off her helmet and lobbed it to the dog walker. Anjali noticed Tookie's changed hair—cropped at the back, skinny bangs dyed indigo and pink—before she took note of the swelling bruise on one side of her face.

"Eesh! I knew those machines were dangerous! Tookie, you could have died!" A word Anjali had recently learned from Auro suddenly floated off her tongue. "Poor infrastructure, that's the problem. We're stuck with Bagehot-era roads and Tookie-era traffic."

Tookie shrugged her leather jacket off her shoulders. The dog walker was just behind her to catch it. "Girlfriend, this kitty still has six lives left." She introduced her two companions as "gal pals" Dalia and Rosie; no last names. They too burdened the dog walker with their jackets. Both were model-tall, their legs encased in white stretch jeans, their bra lines visible under halter tops, bruises tattooing the bared flesh of shoulders and forearms. The dog walker was too entranced to go back to front-door duty.

"What happened to you!" Mrs. Khanna cried. She and Dr. (Mrs.) Ghosh had just finished their tour of Parvati's art collection and were crossing the hallway on their way to the origami display in Auro's office.

Parvati took charge at once. She shouted to the kitchen sisters to bring a bowl of ice cubes to the powder room. "Any broken bones, do you think? Concussion? Our driver is here, he can get you to the hospital for x-rays. Too many bikes, too many accidents. No, don't sit down.

Oh, dear, are you feeling drowsy?" She ordered the dog walker to alert the chauffeur.

"Can you get her to chill?" Tookie mouthed the words to Anjali.

"Ice pack," Dr. (Mrs.) Ghosh said. "Anjali, take them to the bathroom and apply an ice pack to the swellings straightaway."

Once inside the bathroom Tookie asked, "How can you stand to be around these crisis freaks?"

"Mrs. Banerji means well."

"I heard good things about her painting collection. Where is it?"

Boys-and-Booze Tookie, an art lover? "I'll take you," she said, and tried to remember the names of the lady painters. There was an Anjolie. Dalia dumped the bowlful of ice cubes into the sink. She traced the edges of the largest bruise on her forearm with a loving fingertip. "Medal of war. Sidewalks have become war zones."

"Fucking fundamentalists! We're talking Bangalore, IT capital for God's sake, not the fucking Swat Valley!"

Rosie let loose a war cry. "Bring it on, assholes!"

"You didn't crash? You got beat up?"

"Yeah. Boys with chains and cricket bats, looking for girls coming out of bars. Where do you stand? You can't be a civilian anymore."

Dalia unlocked the door and poked her head out. "All clear! What's that thumpy music? What's upstairs? Action central?" She didn't wait for Anjali's answer.

Rosie and Tookie followed Dalia up the stairs to Rabi's suite. Anjali stood behind them as they peered into the crowded room. Rabi's party was in full swing. Large emptied bottles of Indian beer. Low lights and loud beat. Just-met acquaintances forging cosmic connections. Anjali felt like an alien in Rabi's universe.

Tookie didn't hide her disappointment. "Dude, so not-our-scene," she grumbled as she led her posse back down the stairs. "Give us a ring when you need a pub run on Residency. Ciao!"

Tookie had judged Anjali unfit to be one of Tookie's "gal pals." It brought a closure of sorts. Minnie was dead, the Bagehot Girls disbanded, Husseina an international miscreant, Bagehot House wrecked, and the jungle cleared for Jacaranda Estates, advertised by the development company as "a self-sufficient, ultra-luxurious lifestyle complex for the ultra-affluent." The first phase of her Big Bangalore Adventure was over. What next, and where? *The forces of evil had amassed.*

Tookie's apocalyptic vision and Rosie's war slogan didn't inspire the same urgency that Peter's exhortations to get out of Gauripur had. Anjali lingered on the threshold of Rabi's suite, reluctant to crash, unwilling to leave. The older Khanna son, lean, and looking leaner in a black muscle shirt and black jeans, waved at her with his beer bottle. She smiled back. He was on the fringes of a knot of Scandinavians whom Rabi had fished with in Bheemswari. The Khanna brothers, their American college friends, and the Scandinavians seemed so *in the moment.* The past held her in a headlock. She could step over the threshold; she could fake having a blast; why not? Both the Bengali Svengali and Mr. GG had stood her up; so what?

She ventured a tentative toe inside, and suddenly in a far corner of the hot, smoky room she spotted the Bengali Svengali. He must have arrived while she was attending to Tookie, Dalia, and Rosie. There he was, dimpled, floppy-haired, Bollywood-handsome, Hawaiian-shirted, his back pressed against the wall, a wineglass in hand, as teasingly real as water in a mirage. Rabi stood facing him, Rabi's scrawny torso leaning toward him, Rabi's bony arms encircling him without touching, palms flat on the wall. This had to be their first-ever meeting, but she detected a connection between them . . . not just the music . . . trust, ease, unselfconscious confidence. And some other quality . . . a *tenderness,* yes, that was it.

From the landing of the stairs, she could hear Mrs. Khanna, the Drs. Ghosh, and their three daughters saying their drawn-out thank-yous and goodbyes to Auro and Parvati. "Mrs. Banerjee, I applaud your kind heart," Dr. (Mrs.) Ghosh boomed in her judgmental voice, "but . . . you don't want her around when Bhupesh and Dinesh get back." Mrs. Khanna too had a suspicious nature. "These modern working girls flocking to Bangalore, they're full of schemes, I tell you. They trap innocent boys from good families. I don't let my two hang out on the Brigades!"

Anjali stole down a few steps so she could see as well as hear. Parvati dropped Mr. Champion's name—the famous author—to reassure Mrs. Khanna and the Ghoshes, or maybe to reassure herself; Anjali couldn't be sure. She had thought of herself as the victim of gathering evil forces, just like Minnie Bagehot. To the cautious Dollar Colony mothers, evil forces had taken over, and she—schemer, gold digger, opportunist migrant—was the enemy.

You can't be a civilian anymore, Tookie had warned her. But why must there be a duel-to-the-death before Dynamo's new species could emerge?

Down in the front hall, the hugs and farewells continued. The house dogs had somehow escaped their sequestering, but they behaved themselves. "They're charming on the surface, but cunning inside."

"Mrs. Khanna is giving you the unvarnished truth, Parvati." She was using Bangla, and Anjali, after a few weeks in the proudly Bangla-speaking Banerji home, understood it perfectly. "The time for this beating-around-the-bush politeness is past. You decide what you want to do about the noose around your neck. By the way, that gorgeous gold choker you're wearing, did you get it at Tanishq?"

It may have been an unconscious gesture, but with her left hand Parvati protected her throat. Twenty-two-karat gold glimmered between her splayed fingers. Anjali fled upstairs to her room in shame.

6

Early the next morning, a peon from Mr. GG's office arrived in a noisy auto-rickshaw with a letter and a bouquet of tiger lilies for Parvati. When Anjali heard the rickshaw brake to a stop, she assumed the passenger was Parvati's tailor, a bespectacled, professorial-looking Sikh gentleman who could no longer ride his bicycle to his clients' homes because of cataracts in both eyes. He stopped by once a week to drop off orders completed and to pick up lengths of fabric and sketches for new clothes. Auro kept him busy making dark suits for the office, linen leisure suits for dress-down Fridays, and colorful kurtas for evenings and weekends. For Parvati, who wore saris, he sewed choli blouses, cool-weather capes, and caftans for family-only evenings at home. Anjali snapped up Parvati's invitation to let him sew a replacement wardrobe for everything she'd lost in the Bagehot House riot.

The earnest old man with milky irises copied avant-garde slacks, vests, jackets, and peignoir sets from fashion magazines. The frugal era of mall prowling and drooling over designer outfits on mannequins was over, at least for as long as she kept on the good side of Auro and Parvati. She was teaching herself a new two-step of Desire and Fulfillment. The tailor needed work to feed his family; Parvati, a compulsive benefactor, needed feel-good projects. Why couldn't the Dollar Colony matrons see that she was compulsively dispensing happiness?

But there were clouds on the horizon. The warnings from Dr. Ghosh. Parvati might wave them away, in her goodness, but Anjali couldn't. Objective outsiders saw her as something unsavory. Not just a small-town usurper, but someone with bad connections.

When the dog walker ushered Mr. GG's peon into the glassed-in breakfast patio, Anjali and Parvati were finishing their second round of Assam tea. Auro had switched to drinking strong Karnataka coffee since moving to Bangalore, but Parvati remained a tea snob. Anjali would have welcomed a huge caffeine hit that morning. She associated the smell and taste of brewed coffee with her first Barista cup during her first hour in Bangalore.

A heart-to-heart aimed at encouraging her to move out was inevitable, though Parvati, ever gracious, would deliver the "dump" notice obliquely. Anjali was waiting for the subtle questions: Your family must miss you so. Don't you miss your mother and sister? But Parvati procrastinated. She fed scraps of chapati to Ahilya and Malhar, who were sprawled on the dhurrie by her feet.

Ahilya stood, stretched, then laid her muzzle on Anjali's thigh. *Do I pet her, rub her ears? Would she bite if I touched her?* It was Anjali's first doggy moment.

Parvati launched into a monologue that sprinted from topic to topic, including her CCI lesson plans for the day, Usha Desai's mother's improving health, her fear that Dinesh was getting seriously involved with an international student from Norway, and the importance of getting fish oil and magnesium into people's diets, especially that of poor people. Her heavy briefcase was on the floor by the dogs, propped against a chair leg, ready for the driver to carry to the car.

Every few days she fed CCI questions to Anjali. "Keeping you on your toes," she'd say. Somehow, according to Parvati, whatever future she had would be attached to her ease with the English language.

The dogs made low growling noises when the peon, his terrified eyes fixed on them, approached Parvati. The peon backed away and took cover behind the dog walker. Anjali noted the dog walker's smug grin as he took officious custody of the envelope and bouquet, and laid the envelope on the bistro table. Parvati rubbed Malhar's broad bottom until his growl stopped. Anjali boldly scratched Ahilya's ears. "With these brave fellows, who needs an electronic security system?" Parvati joked. With an unused knife, she slit the envelope open and scanned the note inside.

Anjali recognized Mr. GG's handwriting on the discarded envelope: *Mrs. Parvati Banerji,* and under the name, *RSVP per peon.*

"The Bagehot Trust meeting lasted longer than Girish had expected," Parvati summarized. "Incendiary, apparently." She reached down to pull her roller-ball pen out of the briefcase. "He'd like to stop by this evening so he can apologize for missing the party. Not that that's necessary, but you've seen how Auro loves to argue politics with him!"

Mr. GG hadn't meant to stand her up. That buoyed Anjali's spirits. Mr. GG the assiduous networker was cultivating Auro and Parvati, and Dynamo the futurist was courting his muse. She missed Rabi, but he had left at dawn for another travel magazine assignment. With Rabi, she could blurt whatever outrageous thought came to her because he wasn't judgmental. Mr. GG was signaling his desire for her, wasn't he?—but in a respectful way. What they'd both let happen that one time in his apartment had to do with lust, with the quality of light in the bedroom, and, through an uncurtained window, with Cubbon Park's lushness. Her face felt hot. She needed to do something with her hands, pour more tea if the teapot hadn't been drained, or stick the flowers in a vase, something physical to tamp down her excitement.

"I'll get a vase," she said abruptly.

Parvati stared at her, baffled, so she pointed to the tiger lilies dripping greenish stains on the dog walker's shirt front. "Vase?" Parvati repeated. She had scribbled her RSVP at the bottom of Mr. GG's note and was about to slip it back into the original envelope. "Are you all right? Oh, of course, it's Bagehot House, isn't it? How insensitive of me to have let slip that name. I'm so sorry, Anjali, would you rather I disinvite Girish? He has business in Mexico next week, but we can have him for dinner when he gets back."

"Oh no," Anjali protested. "Please don't change your plans for my sake. I've already been enough of a burden. I feel like such a parasite."

"Stop!" Anjali couldn't remember Parvati ever sounding so sharp. "You are not a burden. Let's get you a flower vase. If you are here long enough, I'll make you an ikebana enthusiast."

The dog walker perked up when he heard the English word *vase.* The Banerjis joked that he knew more English than he let on so that he could eavesdrop. "Swati!" He shouted instructions in Kannada, and the younger kitchen sister bounced in with a cut-glass bowl nestled against her chest, a thick braid dancing down her back. A teenager in love, and not hiding it.

So that was her name. Swati. Anjali felt guilty that she hadn't learned the names of even the kitchen sisters, let alone the compound staff: the dog walker, the driver, the watchman. Swati pried the tightly bound bouquet out of the dog walker's bemused grip. Anjali didn't miss the intensity of that covert caress.

Mr. GG's peon dropped the resealed envelope into his bag. The dog walker responded to that stimulus and escorted the peon out to the waiting auto-rickshaw. Then he ran back into the room and handed one internal air-letter to Anjali, which the mailman had just left off in the mailbox nailed to the guardhouse. Anjali took a look at the address—*P. Champion, Gauripur*—and crumpled the letter. When she went back to her bedroom, she stuffed it into the top drawer of her dresser.

7

Girish Gujral texted Parvati: cu @ 7pm dnr raincheck?

By four in the afternoon Anjali had decided on her look for the special evening. (Artfully) simple, (effortlessly) sexy. She mixed and matched every piece of clothing in her made-to-measure Dollar Colony wardrobe, and by six in the evening she'd achieved that look: dusty rose linen capri pants; rosy dawn midriff-baring sleeveless top with daring neckline; silver anklets and high-heeled snakeskin sandals dyed neon pink; tiny rose-quartz ear studs; and as a hair ornament, one of Mr. GG's tiger lilies.

Anjali came down to the living room at six-thirty and installed herself in a corner chaise longue, where she knew the lamplight was pinkish and flattering. Parvati was on the phone with Rabi's mother in San Francisco, sharing kitchen chitchat twelve hours and half a world apart, including tips on shrimp malai curry (go crazy with the garlic; caramelize the diced onion; slow-sauté the spices so they don't taste and smell raw; canned coconut milk is for amateurs; steep, squeeze, discard coconut flakes and use just enough of the liquid so the jhol has thok-thok consistency). Auro was still showering. Anjali tuned out Parvati's voice, now gone on to serious topics with her sister, in Bangla, the hiss and sizzle of the kitchen sisters deep-frying pakoras, the gardener's son and nephew practicing birdcalls just outside the open window. Soon Mr. GG's car tires would scatter gravel on the unpaved road.

Auro slap-slapped noisily into the room in stiff-soled Kohlapuri sandals. He acknowledged Parvati with a shrug and a mumbled, "What's your sister up to *now?*" on his way to the bar trolley. "What an enchanting vision!" he exclaimed to Anjali. He made a camera with his fingers. "Click! Click! Pensive Woman Awaits Nightfall. Why isn't Rabi here to capture this?" Anjali responded with a half-wattage version of her halogen smile. Auro lifted the lid of the ice bucket. "What'll you have, Pensive Woman?" In his modish turquoise cotton kurta and loose white pajama, his bristly wet hair sleeked back, he looked a relaxed host. "The usual?"

She winced when she thought back to the squabbles and tears on the rare Sundays that her mother persuaded her father to have "Munitions" Mitter and "Tobacco" Nyogi and their families over for lunch. "A waste of my sweat-of-brow savings," "Railways Bose" ranted. "What favor have they ever done for us?" The only person he tolerated as a regular visitor was Dr. Fit-as-a-Fiddle Dasgupta, who was smart enough to leave after a double peg, which he earned by dispensing medical tips: hartaki-steeped water for constipation, ajwan water for indigestion, folic acid pills for child-bearing daughters. "Yes, please. The Auro Special." The Auro Special was a fizzy sweet-sour nonalcoholic cocktail that had become Anjali's new signature drink, and Swati brought out freshly blended ginger and mint paste, lime juice and chilled syrup when Auro was ready to play bartender.

"Don't do anything rash, Tara," Parvati begged her sister on the phone, "and promise you'll call me back in a couple of hours?" She flipped her cell phone shut. "Tara's cooking as therapy. She says cooking calms her, and the more elaborate the recipe, the better. She's sick of the same old, same old fight with Bish about where to retire. Bish wants us to look into Bangalore properties. Whitefield, Palm Meadows, for a start."

"Don't get sucked into Tara's problems," Auro admonished his wife. "Gin and lime? I'm serious, never lend money to relatives, and never, never give marriage advice."

"It better be a scotch tonight, Auro."

"That bad?"

"Bish wants to settle here, but she wants to bring up little Kallie in San Francisco."

"In other words, your sister would rather live in California than in Bangalore."

"Once Bish has made up his mind, it seems there's no changing it."

Auro laughed. "Pull of homeland, et cetera. *We* know about that, except you and I were on the same page." He fixed Parvati's drink: a half-peg of single malt.

"Bish'll keep the San Francisco place for Rabi. That's the only concession he's willing to make. Tara's very upset."

"Upset as in furious? Or upset as in depressed?"

Anjali marveled at how openly they were discussing family fights in front of an outsider. Rabi's mother was lucky to have a sister she was so close to. She remembered her last bitter fight with Sonali-di in Patna. She'd been a novice runaway with a heavy suitcase then. She still had that suitcase, and she was still running. Boldly, she asked "Would you be offended if I changed my mind and asked for a glass of the Sula chardonnay instead?"

"As long as you promise not to get tipsy, my dear," Parvati joked. "Auro, did I tell you Bish is thinking of investing in a winery around here?"

"If it was anyone but Money-Spinner Bish, I'd say it was a crazy idea."

Mr. GG parked his car in the Banerjis' driveway at two minutes before seven. Anjali had surreptitiously clocked him on her hand-me-down Movado. She pretended it was the wine, though it was Mr. GG's entrance that gave her a happy buzz. He was still in the dark suit that he wore to the office, but he had undone the top button of his starched white-stripe-on-white shirt and loosened the knot of his pink silk tie. Instead of a briefcase he carried a cellophane-wrapped gift basket of assorted nuts, candies and dried fruits. He presented it formally to Parvati, who showered him with thank-yous—"Oh, Girish, you didn't have to"—and handed it to the dog walker to unwrap.

"Mrs. Banerji," Girish Gujral announced, thick hands folded in namaste, "your home is an oasis for weary wanderers. You see how I'm drawn back again and again."

Anjali, trusting instinct, decoded his flowery compliment to the hostess as his confession of lovesickness for the houseguest. She had dared hope for only a hint of his feelings and was rewarded with a declaration. *She,* not the house, was his oasis. Pleased, she arranged her legs on the chaise as she'd seen models do on the virtual deck chairs on virtual beaches on Mr. GG's Vistronics website. And sure enough, instead of joining Auro at the bar trolley, Mr. GG settled into the chair nearest her. "Miss Bose, you should always wear a tiger lily in your hair," he said, raising his highball glass.

"Then you'll have to make a habit of sending them, Mr. Gujral," she responded.

Why did clueless Auro have to pull up an ottoman close to Mr. GG's chair just then and bombard Mr. GG with prophecies of a Kali Yuga–scale financial meltdown? In this "epoch of cosmic slump" India must "decouple" its economy from that of Western nations. "We Indians hitched our bullock cart to the U.S. wagon, and now we're up to our knees in horseshit and bullock dung." Citing statistics about investment flight, capital lost, and plummeting rates of corporate expansion, he worked himself into cathartic wrath. Mr. GG refuted each of Auro's arguments and dazzled Anjali with his optimistic theory that a belt-tightening time in the United States equaled an outsourcing boom time in India. Debt collection was the newest growth area for call centers. He was part of a consortium scouting belly-up overseas businesses. "Best of all," he rhapsodized, "this is our chance to leapfrog and win the creativity race. We Indians are genius inventors, not just cut-rate mistris!"

Anjali had to concede that the tight-fitting vest, the saucy capri pants, and the bright blossom behind the ear were no competition for Auro's incitement to debate India's financial future. Auro was for decoupling; Mr. GG ardently against it; Anjali resentful of it for having turned Mr. GG from swain to debate champion. Parvati took her husband's side. "How can you be so smug, Girish? Nobody's recession-proof in this skittish economy." Student enrollment was down at CCI, and a competitor had already folded. She pummeled Mr. GG with more anecdotal proof. Two of Dr. Ghosh's nephews had been let go from their software programming jobs in Gurgaon. Dr. (Mrs.) Ghosh's beauty-and-brains niece-in-law ("top of her IIT class") had expected to pick and choose from fat-salaried job offers even before graduating, but months after finishing school she was still temping. Mr. and Mrs. Pandit, with the unmarried, aging twin daughters on the next block in Dollar Colony, had scratched all bridegroom candidates with IIT degrees from their list.

Anjali sulked. "Coupling" or "decoupling" made sense to her only in the context of her personal life. She didn't feel connected to global issues. She boycotted the conversation swirling around her.

Mr. GG surprised her with a question. "May I invite Miss Bose for a dekko of Bagehot House, what's left of it anyway?" He seemed to be asking for Auro's and Parvati's permission to ask her out for an evening ride. The casual seducer of Cubbon Park had evolved into a respectable, permission-seeking suitor.

Trust your impulses. "I'd love to," Anjali quickly answered.

Parvati hesitated. "Do you feel ready to see it? You don't think it's too soon, Anjali?"

"Well, she'll have to find out for herself, won't she?" Auro scolded Parvati. "And under what more reassuring circumstances than with Girish?"

Mr. GG rose from his chair. "If you are ready . . ."

Anjali couldn't get to the front door fast enough. "Tell me, Girish." Auro persisted in continuing the conversation. "The slump must be affecting your redevelopment plans for the Bagehot property? Be honest, bank loans must have become more iffy, even for a consortium of hotshots."

Mr. GG guided Anjali out the front door. "My dear Banerji, I'm constitutionally incapable of anxiety. It's off to Mexico and Hawaii early next week for me, Mrs. Banerji, but if there's any way I can be of service to CCI before or after the trip, please text me."

Anjali walked ahead of him to his Daewoo to cut short the lengthy goodbyes required by Indian etiquette.

THEY DROVE TO Bagehot House in silence. The rusty entrance gate was missing, probably carried off by scrap-metal scavengers. Heavy wrecking equipment was parked in the torn-up driveway. Two watchmen smoked near a small mound of excavated earth.

"Thank you for what you did." The night in the holding cell in the police station felt more immediate than the weeks as a Bagehot Girl with prospects. Gratitude was a higher form of love than lust. "I can't imagine what would have happened to me if you . . ."

He wasn't listening. He undid his seat belt with an angry snap. "I can't believe what I'm seeing." He strode out of the car without closing the door. "They're tearing this down without a permit."

Anjali let herself out but kept her distance from him. Mr. GG was staring past the bulldozers at the side of Mad Minnie's house, with its broken windows and fluttering curtains, its missing front door and torn, trampled-on banquet-night tablecloths on the floor of its foyer. The house, though structurally intact, seemed to have rolled over, like an ocean liner on its side. He might have been crying. It seemed possible; he was folding his handkerchief. "This is . . . tragic." He still hadn't faced her, so he might have been consoling Bagehot ghosts.

In profile, Mr. GG's jaw, flecked with gray, was just a little slack. Still, he was a handsome man, handsomer in profile than straight on.

She thought, *I'm standing here next to a man I've slept with. I'm standing here where I was handcuffed and dragged into a paddy wagon like a dangerous criminal, and I'm not talking about it. I'm acting as though we're two normal people on a romantic date on a starry evening in Bangalore.*

Some of Asoke's squatters must have stayed on in the partially cleared jungle. Anjali heard low whistling and then a pariah dog's howl of pain. Mr. GG shuddered. "Fearful symmetry," he muttered.

To lighten his mood, she made a callow effort at flirting. "I so envy you, Girish. You get to go to fun places like Mexico and call it work." She stroked the tiger lily in her hair. A petal felt wilted.

"I shan't always have a get-out-of-jail-free card, Anjali."

"What makes you think I'll need another one?" She liked the perky sound of her own voice.

"Come with me to Mexico."

What is he saying? I owe him more than I've given?

"And maybe on to Haiti. Depends on the deal coming through."

I'm just another business deal? Is that how life is?

"Can't promise Haiti."

"Pick up and go? Just like that?" *Like rich-kid Rabi? Like terrorist Husseina?*

"Give yourself a vacation. You deserve it."

"Vacation from what? Evil forces? Minnie's dead." She got carried away by self-pity. "So's my family. Dead. You are looking at a penniless orphan, a parasite, a charity project." The horror was that she wasn't lying, just exaggerating. "I don't need a vacation, I need a job."

"If you want a job, I can set up an interview with the head of human resources at RecoverySys. He was an MBA classmate. We'll get you in on the ground floor of the debt-collection industry." Mr. GG faced her squarely. "Now, what's your passport situation? Don't have one, no problem. I can expedite your getting one."

"In other words, you want me to know you are a big shot?"

"No. In other words, I want you with me in Mexico."

She could have screamed. *Yes, I'm flattered, I'm grateful. Drive me to-*

night to Cubbon Park. Have your peon pick up my stuff from Parvati's tomorrow. She would spell her first name as *Anjolie* on her first-ever passport. She said, "Mr. Gujral, I shall consider your offer and make my counteroffer when you get back from your trip."

Mr. GG grinned. "You were born to be a debt collector, Miss Bose."

All the way back to Dollar Colony, he gushed about the sad, stark majesty of Mayan ruins. She imagined herself scrambling up the stony sides of an alien people's monuments. Every death made possible a new beginning. And then she thought, with a suddenness and finality that shocked her, *I don't want a passport. My new beginning is here, but different from Baba's and Ma's generation. They had to fight the British; their big fight was to establish an independent India and create a nonaligned world. Theirs was a struggle—lost, in Baba's case—against communalism and caste-ism and poverty and superstition and too much religion. They were lucky. Their fights weren't easy, but simpler and clearer than mine with Mr. GG. Poverty terrified Baba. But I'm terrified, tempted, and corrupted by the infusion of vast sums of new capital.* Light and angles, that was it. Truth revealed in an imaginary viewfinder. She stepped out of her Photoshopped Bangalore. Aloud, she said, "I get no kick from Champagne. Spend too much time away from India, and it drives you crazy."

In the Banerjis' driveway, she opened the passenger-side door to let herself out. GG grasped her arm and held her back. "I don't want you to go. Let's get you a passport. Visas are no problem. I have contacts. Don't just walk away from me."

She wondered what the night watchman and the dog sitter were making of the scene. The dogs would be curled up in bed with Auro and Parvati. "And what would you expect of me in Mexico?" she asked, swinging her sandaled feet out of the car. Porch light glinted off the silver anklets.

"Be my—"

Then Mr. GG stopped himself. His face was so pleading, so pained, she almost got back inside. "No," he said, "that came out wrong. Be whatever you want to be. If you don't want Mexico, fine. There's Indonesia. There's America. There's the world . . . I want you with me."

What a sad, pathetic thing it is, a man's cry for what? Favors? Companionship? His private little prostitute?

She felt a surge of power. Glad she had the night watchman and the dog walker as witnesses, she kissed Mr. GG on the mouth. "You'll be back," she whispered, stepping out of the Daewoo. She was careful not to slam the door.

8

Sometime late that night, in the hours when Anjali never slept, she was startled by a sudden, piercing whine. One of the advantages of Dollar Colony was the silence of the dark hours: no cars, no rickshaw horns, no bicycle bells, no cowherd flicking a stick on buffalo flanks. She ran to her window, the one that looked out over the narrow lane, but saw no one. Then she realized the watchman wasn't at his post. He must have gone to the servants' bathroom behind the main house. And the dog walker? Of course: he was with Swati. He'd left the house unguarded.

And then she identified the source of the whine. By moonlight and dim streetlamp she could make out the shape of Ahilya lying on her back, her legs straight up. Anjali had never seen a dog in such a posture, and as she watched—and watched—Ahilya didn't move.

A white van prowled the lane at bicycle speed, then parked, blocking the driveway. Two men in dark, hooded sweatshirts descended from the van and silently opened the heavy iron gate just wide enough to squeeze through. In Dollar Colony, no commercial vans circulated at night. No one was on foot at two A.M.

Ahilya was dead.

Anjali's instinct was to lock herself in the bedroom. How could two men break into the house? There were many windows on the ground floor, the living room was a wall of windows looking out to the garden, but shattering them would make a noise. Parvati trusted her dogs to sound the alarm, but one of them was already dead, and Malhar, despite his bulk, teeth, muzzle, and perpetual growling, was innately timid.

She knew it was up to her to take the initiative. Auro and Parvati were asleep in their ground-floor suite. Even if burglars had driven a truck into the living room and begun demolishing the walls with hammers, Auro's snoring would muffle the noise. Anjali and Rabi shared the second floor, separated by a second living room, but she couldn't bring herself to open his door and enter, as he so jauntily did with hers. And what good would he be in a crisis? He'd want to take a picture. She opened her own door and listened with a kind of attention she'd never exercised, because the last thing in the world she expected was a stranger in the house.

And another thing: she knew, almost immediately, that she was to blame. If she had disappeared from everyone's life after the hours in jail, they'd all be safe. If she hadn't come to Bangalore, none of this would have happened. She had brought destruction on her own home, and on Minnie and Husseina and even poor Ahilya, and now the same thing was about to happen to Parvati and Auro.

It was Tookie, of course, and her new friends, and her Rajoo. Bang-a-Buck had got to her.

Anjali could hear the distant, muffled sounds of movement. She could picture the two men somehow cracking open the rear door, or cutting the window and not letting it fall to the floor to waken the house. She could imagine them now in the kitchen, perhaps with flashlights, then moving into the living room and clearing the tables of anything valuable . . . but when she ran a mental inventory of the downstairs tabletops, there were no valuables worth the effort of breaking in. They weren't like Minnie's tables, laden with "priceless" silver trays, "irreplaceable plates," heavy sterling silver that had once graced the mouth of a king, and thinner-than-thin "historical" crystal goblets and champagne flutes.

And then it came to her: the only valuables were the paintings, by the Bengali women artists. She had no sense of their value, but she remembered what Parvati's friends had said: the paintings were nice, of course, but *such* brilliant investments.

In the end it was an easy decision. *I owe my life to Parvati, and my life is worthless anyway.* Anjali lifted Dinesh's hockey stick from its place on the wall. It floated like a feather in her hands. The stairs were just outside her bedroom door, and as she slowly descended, barefoot, the noises, even the male voices, grew more distinct. They were in the downstairs living room. Why didn't Auro wake up? But of course, he snored too loudly. Some nights, she could hear him all the way upstairs.

No lights were on, but moonlight was pouring through the windows. The burglars had lifted two paintings off their brackets and leaned them against the wall, and with their backs to her, they were working on the next. They were laughing and talking loud enough to be understood, had she spoken Kannada, as though they'd been assured the house was empty. She knew the location of every chair and table in the living room; she could negotiate the passage to the far wall with her eyes closed.

The men half-turned, facing each other, in order to lift the painting off its hooks. And that's when one of the men must have seen her from the corner of his eye; he gave a shout and dropped his end of the painting, and their eyes met and she remembered his face, and that's when Anjali aimed for his head and let the hockey stick fly. It caught him between the eyes, across the bridge of the nose, and he screamed as a plume of blood shot straight out; then he staggered and fell. The second goondah dropped his end of the painting, and it flopped toward her, separating her from him as he frantically turned his head in every direction. He was cursing loudly, and she screamed back at him, in Hindi, threatening to kill him as she had his partner. But he kept the painting between them and she couldn't squeeze her way around it and the sofa it had glanced off. *Please, Auro,* she prayed, *wake up, call the police,* but the bedroom door remained partially closed. And so she screamed again, "Thieves! Thieves!" in English, Bangla, and Hindi, and out of nowhere, from the darkened hallway behind him, Malhar leaped upon the man's shoulders, the low growl no longer a warning but a prelude to full attack. The thief fell, hands across the face, and the dog fastened on one wrist and shook it till the man's arm broke.

It was over in seconds. Both men lay in blood, moaning, and the bedroom door opened and Parvati, still tying the sash of her nightdress, cried, "Anjali! What have you done?" Malhar was dragging his trophy by the wrist down to his hiding place at the end of the hall. And then Parvati saw for herself the damage, the paintings, the man at Anjali's feet, and heard the screams of the second goondah as Malhar pulled him into the shadows like a lamb bone to be gnawed over in the dark.

Parvati screamed. Auro shouted, "Wha?" And upstairs Anjali heard a door close.

THEY HAD THEIR breakfast, or at least their tea and granola with yogurt, at four A.M. The medical vans had taken away the burglars. Swati and her sister had swabbed the floors.

Inspector Raja Venkatesh, known socially to Auro and Parvati, was on the scene. By Anjali's standards he was the perfect Bollywood police inspector: an aging heartthrob, efficient, trim, mustached, with epaulettes, graying temples, and perfect English. Even at four in the morning his starched trouser creases were knife-sharp, and his polished shoes reflected the kitchen spotlights.

"These guys are known miscreants," he said. The second thief had been carried away, sobbing and trembling, as Malhar shadowed him to the door. The first goondah was in a coma from a fractured skull and had been carried out on a litter. "No legal jeopardy attaches to your action, sir," he said to Auro. "Warranted self-defense."

With her recent police history, better that Anjali not be a part of it.

"I trust the same immunity extends to my brave watchdog," Auro laughed. He patted Malhar's broad bottom.

"Of course, sir. And my condolences for the other dog. Poisoned, no doubt." He sipped his tea. "I had no idea of your proficiency with a hockey stick, Mr. Banerji. Maybe we should be looking for you on the club tennis court?"

"Hardly." He chuckled. "Schoolboy skills."

"So brave," said Parvati. "But I do hope the poor boy pulls through."

Rabi was slurping his granola and yogurt. "Those poor boys knew what they were looking for, didn't they?" he said.

Inspector Venkatesh nodded. "They apparently were sent here on a mission—who sent them is still to be determined. Have you heard of All-Karnataka Auction House?"

"Nothing at all," said Auro.

"Nor have I," said Parvati.

Fortunately, Inspector Venkatesh didn't look at Anjali. She remembered the van, and Rajoo peeling off his hundred-rupee notes.

"Who's behind this auction house?" asked Rabi.

"We have traced the abandoned van to that company. Those boys could have been employees." He seemed to be mulling over a mountain of additional commentary. "I need not mention to collectors like you that Indian antiquities—and what we might think of as yesterday's rubbish—have become international attractions. The big houses, the London and New York and Tokyo markets, they are involved with local providers who are not always, as we can see, on the up and up."

And then, almost as if compelled to confess under duress, Anjali interjected, "I think I remember that company removing objects during the Bagehot House riot." It was the least, and the most, she could say. She should have shut up.

He wrote it down. "You were a witness to such removals?"

"I saw a van with that name on it."

"Anjali was a tenant there," Parvati explained. The inspector took the news quietly. "Yes, Miss Anjali Bose. I am already knowing," he said.

She didn't say everything she knew: *His name is Lalu. He is the brother of my fellow Bagehot House tenant Sunita Sampath. He looked like a frightened mouse, just like her. He worked at Glitzworld for a man named Rajoo. Everyone knows Rajoo. He sent food and booze to Minnie Bagehot. I ate the mutton stew that Rajoo sent. Read Dynamo's columns. It's all connected.*

"Miss Bose, let me be the first to inform you that yesterday a passport in your name was found in an abandoned purse in Amsterdam. And yesterday, the body of a young Indian lady was discovered in an Amsterdam hotel. We believe it was your Bagehot House co-tenant, Miss Shiraz. She hanged herself by a T-shirt from the shower stall."

He stood, shook hands with Auro, bowed to Parvati, patted Malhar's head, and nodded in Anjali's direction.

WHEN SHE WENT up to her bedroom, she remembered the letter from Peter. Maybe it wasn't a continuation of the argument they'd had at Minnie's.

Peter's handwriting was feathery light.

> My dear Angie, I am ashamed of how I behaved in Bangalore. You have endured aspects of this beloved country that expats and refugees have been spared. I was too categorical and overbearing. Smugly superior, whatever you might call it—I apologize. Your father's passing is very much on my mind. Life is too short, death too sudden to behave with anything but affection and gratitude.
>
> Your father's passing tells a mighty, and a humbling tale. The persistence of colonial castes like "sub-inspectors," the deputies and the assistants that the Indian system inherited and then respawned, and the stubborn dignity of the so-called "little man" makes me weep. (I've been weeping quite copiously these past several days.) There is such a tone of bent-back dignity to his "steadfast" and "unyielding" life (in the words of the obituary notice), of never quite rising to a po-

sition of leadership, and the unending dedication to duty, duty, duty. No mention of joy, fulfillment, or happiness—it's heroic.

I think of the millions of men in India like your father who still bicycle to work or ride the buses and commuter trains each morning, rooted to the town and the vocation of their fathers and grandfathers. They shuffle papers, drink endless cups of tea, stamp documents, then make their same way back home at the same time each working day of their lives. Places have been found for them, in the millions, and should any one of them pass on, the system would not grind to a halt. And yet, as the playwright said, "Attention must be paid." To understand what's noble in India is to understand that their lives coexist with yours and millions like it in a dozen other new-age Bangalores. I hope you read this as I intend it, not as questioning of your father's achievement in life but as the fulfillment of all that his life and his vision offered him.

I have talked on the phone to your sister and have faith that in time your mother will acknowledge, at least to herself, why you had to run away from home. That time has not yet come. Your sister will keep me informed of her physical and emotional health with the understanding that I will relay the information to you.

On a different subject (forgive me if I'm being presumptuous): You were wronged by the man your father selected. Believe me, dear Angie, I had not meant it literally when I said that your formal marriage portrait would only fetch up monsters. Last week I read of a man (his picture accompanied the story) who had been arrested as a criminal imposter. He has been able to swindle dowry gifts from anxious fathers and much else from their daughters. One of the fathers (unnamed) swore out a warrant. It was mentioned that Gauripur was one place he visited. If this is so, your father must have understood the full story behind your leaving. That man is now in jail. He is an embodiment of another aspect of the New and Old India in one criminal soul.

I too have gone through a lifetime's change in the past few days. You remember Ali (how could you not?). Well, he is gone, along with a sizable portion of my savings. It was his dream that he undergo a certain dangerous and expensive surgery. But from street gossip I hear it went badly for him. Now I fear for his very life. The mutilation of so beautiful a creation is a nightmare from which I'll never awake.

So, to honor him, or at least to honor the changes he brought about, I'm trying not to slip back into my old solitary habits. The flowerpots still light up the steps, bright calendars still hang from the walls, and books are neatly lined in cases. Almost in a daze I seem to find flowers to put on the table at night, and somewhere I found a bright bedspread to cover the mattress. If you ever come back to Gauripur for a short visit or resettlement I hope you'll make your first call a visit to your old friend and teacher, Peter.

P.S. You and Ali are the only two people in decades to have pierced my shell. I wanted to be an instrument in your salvation (to put a high gloss on my interventions); with Ali, my interference might prove self-defeating, if not fatal. I pray that your activities in Bangalore will redeem my clumsy but well-intentioned encouragement, as well as Ali's impulsive embrace of his life's dream.

Peter

Suddenly she was back in Gauripur. It was again the day she'd visited Peter Champion to show him her marriage portrait, and Peter had said she was dead to him if she married. "Weak and weary," she kept repeating. "Ray-venn." He called the portrait somehow obscene. Still holding it, she'd started walking back home, fighting tears, but had found herself walking past the da Gama campus. And she was sobbing again. Let Swati eavesdrop on the howls and growls of a woman breaking down. The tears were for Peter, who still cared for his protégée, and for her father, who, in his clumsy way, had cared too much for the rebel daughter.

In the garden next door, Citibank Srinivasan of the booming voice exhorted elephant-headed God Ganesha, son of Goddess Parvati, to liberate all mortals from the tormenting cycle of reincarnation. In the kitchen Swati and her sister cooked lunch and prepped dinner for the Banerjis, drop-in guests, and household staff. And in a Gauripur sparkly with Anjali's tears, "Railways Bose" lounged, whiskey in hand, feet propped on a low morah, enrapturing Mrs. Bose with his harangue on statewide graft and greed, and Angie dreamed up a perfect groom.

And then he picks up the newspaper, left over from the morning.

There is a picture of a boy he remembers, and an article. What? Is he getting married? What? Is he so famous, his exploits merit the front page? But it is a police report, and the accusations against him are enough to rip a father's heart to pieces.

"Oh, Anjali," he cries, "I didn't know. Why didn't you tell me? I would not have been compelled to do what I now must do."

9

Mr. GG delivered on all his promises. Mr. GG's MBA classmate, Mr. K. K. Jagtiani, director of the HR division at RecoverySys, had his personal assistant, Mrs. Melwani, call Anjali on the Banerjis' land line. Would Miss Bose care to have Mrs. Melwani initiate the setting up of "a chat" with Mr. D. K. Jagtiani, the deputy in charge of human resources (a younger brother of Mr. K. K., she assumed, in a Sindhi-owned business, if family names are any indication), to take place after his return from his business trip to California and Michigan? If so, Mrs. Melwani would request Mr. D. K. Jagtiani's personal assistant, Miss Lalwani, to get in touch directly with Miss Bose to squeeze her into his calendar.

In the Bose family hierarchy of Indian groups to avoid all dealings with, Sindhis usually ranked near the top.

Anjali summoned all of her "phone poise." "Certainly, if I am still available then," she said. "And I'd prefer Miss Lalwani to call me on my cell phone. Let me give you that number."

Mrs. Melwani stopped her. "Not to worry; we have it on file. Telephone numbers, current address, résumé."

Résumé? She had no job experience. Mr. GG must have taken liberties with truth when he'd pitched her to his friend. If Miss Lalwani called to set up the meeting with her boss, she would instruct her to spell her first name as Anjolie. A day could start with guilt and grief but end in hope. Let Citibank Srinivasan aim for nirvana; she was happy to be mired in maya.

PARVATI OFFERED TO coach Anjali for the upcoming interview. If the delinquent debtors were like Thelma Whitehead, her fictitious caller from Arkansas, they would probably resent being dunned by an agent with a detectable Indian accent. She sounded excited. "Thanks for alerting CCI to this brand-new outlet. Debt recovery, how exciting." Anjali would be her guinea pig for a training manual for pay-up-or-else phone specialists. For RecoverySys, Anjali's voice would have to project authority. Start with compassionate authority, shift to credit-score damage, then to legal intimidation. Parvati had met K. K. Jagtiani at a couple of fundraisers, she added, but not his son or cousin or brother, D. K. Jagtiani. At the time of their meeting, Mr. K. K. Jagtiani had been exploring an intercontinental cremation-and-ash-scattering service for overseas Indians.

"I guess that Hindu NRI corpse-disposal scheme didn't get off the ground," Auro laughed. He too volunteered to help Anjali get interview-ready. "If you're going to be dealing with Sindhis, how about we watch some episodes of *The Sopranos*?"

After dinner the next night, he sat Anjali and Parvati down on either side of him on the widest sofa in the living room and started playing the first of three seasons of *The Sopranos*. Dozens whacked, or were whacked. Young whacked old, brothers whacked brothers, cousins whacked cousins, bag guys whacked debtors, enforcers whacked snitches.

"Who needs the mafia," Auro joked, "when you've got an Indian extended family?"

"Is that a dig at the Bhattacharjees?" Parvati demanded. "Let me tell you, Anjali, Tony's mother reminds me of Auro's mother."

"That's totally out of bounds!" Auro fumed.

"Okay, okay, mother-in-law jokes are funny only on TV."

Anjali went to bed at dawn and dreamed of ducks bobbing in the swimming pool. It didn't matter that Anjali didn't know how to swim because in her dream she was Meadow Soprano.

RABI CUT SHORT his scouting trip for his next photo assignment by three days. "Orders from Baba, Parvati Auntie," he announced. "Ma, Baba, and Kallie will be here in two weeks, and I'm supposed to line up properties for Baba to view."

Auro faked exasperation. "Oh, oh, you know what that means, Anjali, don't you? Less time for us. Much less time for Carmela and Tony. Once the two sisters start their adda, there's no stopping. I'll need a vacation from them!"

Adda. Bangla talk-talk over endless tea. Or, in Dollar Colony, over white wine.

The comfort zone of make-believe family in the Banerjis' home collapsed suddenly. She wasn't Parvati's and Auro's daughter; she wasn't even their houseguest; she was their rescue project, like a street dog. Parvati's excitement swirled around her. "Rabi, do you think I should put your mother and the baby in Bhupesh's suite?" "Auro, remember to lay in a lot of beer. Bish likes his Kingfisher, but not warm the way we drink it." "I'll get the mali's wife to come in once a day and take care of the extra laundry." "Oh, I can't wait to have a baby in the house. It's a first for your graying auntie!"

Anjali didn't want to share Parvati and Auro. She begrudged Tara and her baby girl the sweet simplicity of Parvati's love for them. Parvati's sister-love had not been dipped in bile. Parvati hadn't killed her father nor predeceased him. Bitterness soured into dread. The brief, impossible friendship she had forged with Rabi in Gauripur was at stake. Monet, moray, light and angle. Restore mountain, please. But there were only a half-dozen pull-down props, and the Banerjis' living room was not among them. She would have to move on, again.

• • •

Parvati settled into a deck chair under a jasmine-covered pergola and waved to Anjali to join her. "Come, sit by me," she insisted when Anjali hesitated. "I need a break from this stuff." She pointed to the screen of her laptop. "Not quite Napa, but Doddaballapur will get there. Farmland to vineyard, thanks to Bish, who loves wine and wine lovers like his wife and sister-in-law." She put her glass of chardonnay on a stack of real estate brochures by her feet.

Anjali squatted on the grass, envying Parvati, envying most of all her trust in strangers. Even when a well-meaning stranger could open the gates to monsters. Money made for that kind of self-confidence. Money was the safety net of women like Parvati and Rabi's mother. Money made possible ayurvedic spa-pampered skin and radiant hair. They had never been homeless, never starved, they'd never stolen, never had to seduce a potential benefactor.

She had left Gauripur believing in the world of Peter Champion. Poverty was virtuous. Knowledge was protection enough. Love, at long last, would come her way. Nothing would change, year after year, except the names of students. And look at what Bangalore had done to her in just a few months. She had dared to reach above her station, she'd reached for happiness, and all she'd done was bring a shelf of bricks down on her head.

"It's selfish of me, but I'm glad Tara will be settling here. She's been through too much. Not like you, of course, but traumatizing nonetheless. Has Rabi told you about their house fire three years ago? A firebombing, not careless cooking. We still don't know why. The police think international gangs, because Bish is so important. He was badly burned; his feet sort of melted away. He used to have a wicked serve in his Saint Xavier's days in Kolkata; now he walks supported by canes. Tara's afraid of coming back, but I keep telling her that living in Palm Meadows is more or less the same as living in Atherton before she divorced Bish. Oh, you didn't know? She's the only one of us three sisters who did what Daddy wanted, which meant she married the boy Daddy selected, and Bish didn't come from big money, but Daddy said he saw a spark of genius in him—that was Daddy's exact phrase—and she arrived in Palo Alto twenty years old, already the bride of a computer science graduate student and pregnant with Rabi. She divorced him ten years later and lived on her own with Rabi. Well, not exactly on her own, as she'll be the first to admit. She wrote her books. Bish and she got together again and remarried just before Kallie was born. But she's had her years as a single mother and even as a scarlet woman. You know the phrase? Red herrings, scarlet women—they're lost phrases now. She thinks she's lost touch with India in the twenty-plus years she's lived in California. Of course, she visited twice a year while Mummy and Daddy were alive. She reads and clips and Googles all she can, but she says that makes her feel even more an outsider. She says she's tired of our generation of aging Kolkata beauties, and I've told her they bore me too, but your generation of women, Anjali, they're unknowable to me even though I teach them. I sometimes feel that I'm shouting at them across a huge canyon, but they can't hear me, or they're not listening. I can't begin to enter your lives. But I'm curious, not frightened like her."

"What do you find so mysterious about me?" Anjali blurted out. *Tell me who I am, please. Tell me because I haven't the foggiest, other than the fact that I seethe with envy and rage.*

Startled, Parvati rubbed a fingertip up and down the cool stem of her wineglass. Condensation left a stain on the glossy brochure. She blotted it with a monogrammed cloth cocktail napkin. "You know what you can get in Palm Meadows that we couldn't get when we bought in Dollar Colony? Vaastu compliance. Forget feng shui. Hot new builders have created a buzz for ancient Hindu rules and orders. Vaastu compliance for spiritual equilibrium and a temperature-controlled wine cellar for gustatory gratification. I know I'm babbling." She picked up her glass and pushed the brochure away. "The short answer is, I don't know, Anjali, I really don't. The best I can come up with is you're like a reflecting pool. You give back wavy clues to what *we* are or what we're going to be."

10

The Kaveri cuts broad and shallow from the ghats down to the sea, but the preserve is nestled on a bend in the river where the gradient falls and the jungle intrudes to the banks, and a few islands break the navigational flow. On the islands, most days, crocodiles sun themselves and the taller trees are black with hanging bats. Rabi, with his commission from *Discovery India,* has been assigned the assistant deputy's lodge, where the staff keeps an eye on him ("So young!" he heard them say), providing food and drinks for the young lady and the other man.

They paddled their own canoe to the island, Anjali in the middle in a sun hat and dark glasses, feeling very Euro-glam and, as Moni said, the subject of both men's attention and their professional lenses. She stayed in the anchored boat as the two men waded ashore on one of the larger islands and set up cameras and remote releases in front of a few dead fish. Then they reanchored themselves in the deeper channel, still close enough to watch and trip the shutter release. It didn't take long for smaller crocs to come out from hiding. *They'd been just a few feet away! Those boys were messing with the smelly fish and the stubby tripods and there were crocodiles watching them from the bushes!*

"My heroes!" she sighed, a line she remembered from *Seinfeld* when the first of the crocs came out. The fish was half the croc's size and it raised itself on its hind legs to get full extension, the full effect of gravity to help slide the fish down its gullet—a great subject for a photograph.

The boys wished something larger would come out of the water, something canoe-long and twice as wide, but what bait would suffice, except maybe Anjali, tied to a stake? She was agreeable; can't cook, doesn't sew, won't row. Bait's good. "A girl's got to pull her weight," she said.

Rabi suggested, "We could let her twist in the sun for a while, and then when we spot the really big one, we deftly remove the rope . . ."

". . . and hope we can reel her back to the boat in time," said Moni.

"It's a plan," said Anjali.

The Deputy Assistant Manager's Assistant ("Sounds like a name from *Catch-22*" said Moni; Anjali drew a blank but kept smiling) swore there were some big fellows in the river, but usually not on the islands. They sunned themselves on the banks but they favored the slower, warmer waters downstream, where the bigger fishes and otters swam. They'll go for birds too. And sometimes the bats—some trees harbor thousands of bats in the afternoon, and some of the younger ones get pushed off their perches and fall in the water. Sometimes they don't even hit the water before a big croc snaps them up.

That would be a picture. "Make it so, Number One," said Rabi.

In the manager's bungalow there were photos from the old British days, showing crocs attacking tigers. Rabi called it, with an eye to Anjali, "Big-time debt recovery. These guys didn't mess around." Tigers and chitals, crocs and boars. No tigers now, maybe some leopards, but no competition with the crocs. Crocs are at the top of the food chain, except maybe below bats. In gross tonnage per annum, one little bat probably out-eats a croc. Nothing tops a bat.

"Who knew?" said Anjali.

Rabi started to reminisce. "When I was a little boy back in San Francisco, I'd spend weekends with my father. We'd go for long walks on Ocean Beach, or sometimes down past Candlestick. The old Italians would be sitting there in folding chairs with five or six poles stuck in the sand, sipping a beer or maybe their homemade wine, eyes half closed, waiting for the bell at the tip of their pole to tinkle. They'd give it a jerk. Like clicking a shutter release. It was magic."

"I know," said Moni. "My parents had a summer place in British Columbia. I used to jig for rock cod on Galiano Island. I'd stretch out on the dock and wrap the line around two fingers and just lower it into the rocks. If I didn't get a fish, I'd get a crab or a lobster. You stare long enough into dancing water and you think you're in there with the fish, like you've sprouted gills."

Rabi's ego was so vast, it encompassed the world. Anjali felt herself a part of it.

"Watch out for Moni," said Rabi. "He'll Photoshop a pair of nesting pterodactyls."

It's a Photoshop world, she thought.

"We've all been Photoshopped," said Moni. "I know I've been."

She had no memories. Her memories were only starting now. Her life was starting now.

The boys drank beer; she had a soda. Three small crocs were exploring the tripods; like kittens or puppies they were trying to climb them and bite the cameras. Rabi kept clicking away.

"Um, Rabi, old man," Moni whispered. "Turn around very, very slowly."

Not five feet off the bow, two eyes and a pair of nostrils floated, unattached, it seemed, to anything underwater. Except that far away downstream the water eddied at the base of an armored tail. And to think, just seconds before, Anjali had been swirling her hands in the water to clean them of fish slime.

Click!

The rest of the day was devoted to birds and bats. Overripe fruit, halved watermelons, spotted mangoes, and guavas were spread at the base of a rookery tree, the tripods set, cameras loaded and guano hoods attached, remotes set. A few flying fox bats dropped down from the trees despite the daylight hour. It was never too bright in the forest. They moved over the moldering fruits like stooped old men in heavy capes. They reminded Anjali of the priests at Vasco da Gama, with their long coats and bent posture. "The weight of the world," Father Thomas used to say. But in the zoom lens their true nature appeared, and their name held true: foxes. Sharp-faced, intelligent dogs, with wings.

Then the three paddled upriver and drifted back down, Anjali consulting the bird guide, pointing "There, there," and Moni and Rabi taking turns paddling and taking pictures till the light began to fail and the foxes lifted off from their trees for a night of pillaging.

THEY SAT IN three slack, ground-grazing sling chairs, just a small step up from hammocks, swirling dal and chapatis with their fingers, sipping beer, looking out over the water. In their sun hats and full sleeves against the mosquitoes, they could have been nineteenth-century British planters surveying God's handiwork, with full satisfaction. *My boys,* Anjali thought. *My brave, funny boys.*

In the last minutes of sunlight, the smooth river was pocked by leaping fish, swooping birds, and drifting logs—floating eyes and nostrils—that weren't logs at all. The clear, peach-colored sky was sooty with funnels of bats lifting off from the trees.

She had a sudden thought: *Nothing bad can come of this.*

I'm down to one iron in the fire. Debt-recovery agent. If anything is to come of this night, or the future, she thought before turning in, *I owe it to bats and crocodiles. How to explain the wonders of this world?*

Epilogue

It was a winter's day when the air was cool and the sunlight was wan and the mosquitoes were out in their post-monsoon exuberance. We were told to expect a visit by a da Gama alumna who had left Gauripur, found a job, and succeeded in ways our teachers always told us we could too. Her name was Anjali Bose, and many of us remembered her as a tall, outgoing girl, one of the Bengalis in the Hindi-speaking heartland of Bihar. She'd gone to fabled Bangalore and worked hard and found a modest position, then risen within it. Our teacher knew her well. He said she had "the spark," and thanks to her and millions like her, India was on fire. Even Gauripur was on fire. He was our fomenter of hope. She didn't bring the fire all by herself, but she was a "collateral beneficiary."

He said she was just one in a billion, but each of us had it in us to be another one in a billion. He said she, and a friend, would come to his corporate management class and give a little talk. If we were ready to listen, and to act, she had lessons to teach us.

What to say about Gauripur since she left? Maybe she'll notice a crane on the horizon, more women and children carrying bowls of cement on their heads, some painters' scaffolding around old buildings, and new apartment blocks being erected. Pinky Mahal's shored-up walls have been repainted sunflower yellow (although we still call it Pinky Mahal), and the flat roof now supports an atrium with a sky-top restaurant, and all five floors are serviced by elevators and even an escalator. Somehow the air conditioning is working, and shops that were dark for months are now well lit and full of shoppers. Alps Palace Coffee and Ice Cream Shop has relocated to the ground floor of Pinky Mahal, installed a dance floor, and hired an emcee.

The biggest change, potentially, concerns the future of Vasco da Gama High School and College. Gauripur is suddenly one of the "it" towns in the Ganges belt, meaning a future IT magnet, as the older, larger centers mature and become too expensive. A mofussil town like Gauripur has been identified as an emerging small city, with cheap land and housing and a cozy population of just under ten lakhs—a million souls about to be launched into space. And so the church authorities are in negotiation with Infosys and others to create a satellite IT campus. Our mayor tells us we are the beneficiaries of the overspill; we're to be the next high-tech mega center. On new maps, we are represented by a star on the riverbank, halfway between Delhi and Kolkata. But the church is also trying to preserve the "educational mission" of the campus and pressuring Delhi to locate a new Indian Institute of Technology or perhaps an Indian Institute of Management, using the existing structures. One way or another, Gauripur will survive another century. The era of South Indian and Goan pedants reciting their lectures is over. "Materialism is outpacing spirituality," the rector told a local reporter. "It is a global phenomenon."

There's now a spirits store on LBS Road. No more back-alley booze. The atrium restaurant serves cocktails, Indian wines, and beer.

Our mayor predicts a promising future for Gauripur, just as placards outside Pinky Mahal once did. When Pizza Hut opened a branch, he announced, "Imprisoned inside every clerk in Gauripur is a painter or musician or poet. No one will ever feel the necessity to leave Gauripur.

We will have schools for music, for art, for science, for medicine. We will have a subway, mark my words! My ambition is to nurture the next Hussein, the next Ravi Shankar, nothing less."

SHE AND PARVATI flew to Ranchi, then hired a car and driver to Gauripur. Anjali had, in effect, been adopted, and Parvati wanted to see it all—the school, the old neighborhood, the studio where Rabi had photographed her—and to meet Peter Champion on his turf, not hers. "Truly," Parvati said, "it must be a magical place, no? How fortunate for you to have been born in such a nurturing town, simmering with potential, just before it took off." Was it the refocusing of eight months' exile or an authentic change? Anjali couldn't tell, but Gauripur wasn't the desert she remembered and had been describing. It was a city; it extended ten kilometers in every direction from Nehru Park. And Nehru Park was refurbished by the Volunteers for Beautification Committee. Children were climbing on slides and pumping their legs on new sets of swings.

She walked the familiar streets with Parvati, but now she saw changes—maybe they'd always been there—a cinema house, the Bihar State Emporium, and apartment blocks rising from razed, abandoned estates. "What a charming town!" Parvati exclaimed, against Anjali's every unstated objection. "This is the Old India!" she said. "I can see what Peter was talking about that night at Minnie's! Poor Minnie."

And so they made their way down LBS Boulevard to Peter's apartment. Evening was falling, and terra-cotta dias lighted the outside stairs. Even before they started to climb, the blue door opened, and there was Peter at the top of the stairs, pushing a much-aged, almost unrecognizable Ali in a wheelchair. "Welcome, welcome," he called. They must have seen behind him, in the well-lit apartment, the crowd of friends and students he'd invited for the talk. Ali smiled and raised his hand in greeting.